PRAISE FO[R]
THE LAST STORY OF MINA LEE

"Painful, joyous... A story that cries out to be told."
—*Los Angeles Times*

"A timely, important novel... Fans of Celeste Ng won't be able
to put down this heartfelt, cross-generational novel about
the powerful bond and fragility of family and what it really
means to strive for the 'American dream.'"
—*PopSugar*

"The book, delicately understated in style, offers lessons
in racism from the viewpoints of both mother and daughter.
But the matter of tracking Mina's killer provides a steady
stream of pure sleuthing that is authentic and persuasive."
—*Toronto Star*

"A sensitive and moving family saga."
—*Mystery Scene Magazine*

"Kim has a gift for page-turning plot."
—*Seattle Times*

"A moving look at what immigrants to America go through
before their journey and what they lose upon arrival, and
how their American children can be caught between worlds."
—Alyssa Cole, *New York Times* bestselling author
of *When No One Is Watching*

"Haunting and heartbreaking, troubled threads between
a mother and daughter blend together in a delicate and
rich weave... With both sadness and beauty, [Kim] describes
grief, regret, loss, and the feeling of being left behind. Fans of
Amy Tan and Kristin Hannah will love Kim's brilliant debut."
—*Booklist*, starred review

NEW YORK TIMES BESTSELLER

Praise for *The Last Story of Mina Lee*

"A magnificent exploration of a mother-daughter bond even when words fail them, when past stories and heartbreaks remain untold."

—*San Diego Union-Tribune*

"Suspenseful and deeply felt, *The Last Story of Mina Lee* begins when Margot Lee discovers her mother's death before reeling back in time to explore the secrets that divided Mina and Margot—as well as those that bound them together. Nancy Jooyoun Kim's debut artfully explores a diverse range of immigrant experiences, the meaning of family and home, and the nature of language—how it can be an ocean that divides, or a bridge that connects. In the process, *The Last Story of Mina Lee* raises questions about the reality of the American dream and illuminates stories that often go untold, in life as well as fiction."

—**Chloe Benjamin,** *New York Times* **bestselling author of** *The Immortalists*

"*The Last Story of Mina Lee* is a fierce, gripping call to love and memory. Nancy Jooyoun Kim has written a beautiful debut novel that is unafraid to delve into the scary, deeply vulnerable places of our hearts. It's a riveting dance between mother and daughter, moving fluidly back and forth through time, documenting the quiet traumas that can divide generations. Tremendously readable, *The Last Story of Mina Lee* is a real page-turner and Nancy Jooyoun Kim is a knockout."

—**Kristen Arnett,** *New York Times* **bestselling author of** *Mostly Dead Things*

"Nancy Jooyoun Kim writes with brilliant exactitude about the anxious topographies of being a mother and a daughter, and the choices that lead to migration. *The Last Story of Mina Lee* is a confident and gripping account of where families bury secrets and what happens when you dig."

—**Ingrid Rojas Contreras, bestselling author of** *Fruit of the Drunken Tree*

"In her stunning debut, Nancy Jooyoun Kim weaves together two poignant story lines: Mina Lee, an immigrant, flees tragedy in Korea for a new start in Southern California. When she mysteriously dies, her American-born daughter, Margot, seeks out the truth of what happened. Gripping and gritty, *The Last Story of Mina Lee* is a story of their yearning, their struggle, and the enduring mystery of family. Unforgettable."

—**Vanessa Hua, bestselling author of** *A River of Stars* **and** *Deceit and Other Possibilities*

"I finished the novel in one sitting (and may or may not have wept through some of it). It's one of those stories that grabs you from the first line and stays with you long after you turned the last page... A vivid examination of immigration and belonging, this moving debut tells two stories in parallel—Margot's present-day discovery of her dead mother in 2014 and Mina Lee's arrival to the United States in 1987. An emotional mother-daughter story wrapped up in a poignant mystery, this book is an unforgettable reading experience."

—Etaf Rum, *New York Times* bestselling author of *A Woman Is No Man*

"A suspenseful and unflinching novel, *The Last Story of Mina Lee* had me glued to the page until its surprising and poignant end."

—Amy Meyerson, bestselling author of *The Bookshop of Yesterdays* and *The Imperfects*

"Nancy Jooyoun Kim's *The Last Story of Mina Lee* reckons with the historical trauma of Korean women and the women of the Korean diaspora. Kim negotiates the boundaries of language, geography, and identity, creating a work that is dynamic and piercing. She uses the language inherited by a deep collective sorrow, or *han*, and makes possible an understanding between mothers and daughters that have crossed the transpacific divide, together and yet alone. Kim confronts the meaning of 'one life in the wreckage' of Korean women's bodies. *The Last Story of Mina Lee* is a glimpse of the Korean American presence, from Seoul to Los Angeles, critical to American history and literature."

—E. J. Koh, author of *The Magical Language of Others* and *A Lesser Love*

"The American nightmare is what the American dream is predicated on but much harder to capture. And yet in *The Last Story of Mina Lee*, Nancy Jooyoun Kim has done it while highlighting all the nuances that could get lost in translation, in particular our ways of creating joy, pleasure, friendship and desire within it. This is a book of mystery, of moments of horror, of gasping surprises, of exquisite compassion and tenderness. Kim captures how hard we try to communicate with each other, how often we fail, but also—but also—the possibility that we might reach something close to connection."

—Corinne Manning, author of *We Had No Rules*

March 2023

THE LAST STORY OF MINA LEE

Thank you for supporting Green Apple Books

NANCY JOOYOUN KIM

PARK ROW BOOKS

PARK
ROW ™
BOOKS ™

Recycling programs
for this product may
not exist in your area.

ISBN-13: 978-0-7783-8803-6

The Last Story of Mina Lee

First published in 2020. This edition published in 2021.
Copyright © 2020 by Nancy Jooyoun Kim

This edition published by arrangement with Harlequin Books S.A.

Park Row Books
22 Adelaide St. West, 41st Floor
Toronto, Ontario M5H 4E3, Canada
ParkRowBooks.com
BookClubbish.com

Printed in Italy by Grafica Veneta

For my mother
어머니께

THE LAST STORY OF MINA LEE

MARGOT

FALL 2014

M argot's final conversation with her mother had seemed so uneventful, so ordinary—another choppy bilingual plod. Half-understandable.

Business was slow again today. Even all the Korean businesses downtown are closing.

What did you eat for dinner?

Everyone is going to Target now, the big stores. It costs the same and it's cleaner.

Margot imagined her brain like a fishing net with the loosest of weaves as she watched the Korean words swim through. She had tried to tighten the net before, but learning another language, especially her mother's tongue, frustrated her. Why didn't her mother learn to speak English?

But that last conversation was two weeks ago. And for the past few days, Margot had only one question on her mind: Why didn't her mother pick up the phone?

★ ★ ★

Since Margot and Miguel had left Portland, the rain had been relentless and wild. Through the windshield wipers and fogged glass, they only caught glimpses of fast food and gas, motels and billboards, premium outlets and "family fun centers." Margot gripped the wheel, hands cramping, damp with fear. The rain had started an hour ago, right after they had made a pit stop in north Portland to see the famous thirty-one-foot-tall Paul Bunyan sculpture with his cartoonish smile, red-and-white checkered shirt on his barrel chest, his hands resting on top of an upright ax.

Earlier that morning in Seattle, Margot had stuffed a backpack and a duffel with a week's worth of clothes, picked up Miguel from his apartment with two large suitcases and three houseplants, and merged onto the freeway, driving Miguel down for his big move to Los Angeles. They'd stop in Daly City to spend the night at Miguel's family's house, which would take about ten hours to get to.

At the start of the drive, Miguel had been lively, singing along to "Don't Stop Believin'" and joking about all the men he would meet in LA. But now, almost four hours into the road trip, Miguel was silent with his forehead in his palm, taking deep breaths as if trying hard not to think about anything at all.

"Everything okay?" Margot asked.

"I'm just thinking about my parents."

"What about your parents?" She lowered her foot on the gas.

"Lying to them," he said.

"About why you're *really* moving down to LA?" Miguel had taken a job offer at an accounting firm in a location more conducive to his dreams of working in theater. For the last two years, they had worked together at a nonprofit for people with disabilities. She was an administrative assistant; he crunched numbers in Finance. She would miss him, but she was happy for him, too. "The theater classes? The plays that you write? The Grindr account?"

"About it all."

"Do you ever think about telling them?"

"All the time." He sighed. "But it's easier this way."

"Do you think they know?"

"Of course they do. But..." He brushed his hand through his hair. "Sometimes, agreeing to the same lie is what makes a family *family*, Margot."

"Ha. Then what do you call people who agree to the same truth?"

"Well, I don't know any of these people personally, but— scientists?"

She laughed, having expected him to say *friends*. Grasping the wheel, she caught the sign for Salem. Her hands were stiff.

"Do you need to use the bathroom?" she asked.

"I'm okay. We're gonna stop in Eugene, right?"

"Yeah, should be another hour or so."

"I'm kinda hungry." Rustling in his pack on the floor of the back seat, he found an apple, which he rubbed clean with the edge of his shirt. "Want a bite?"

"Not now, thanks."

His teeth crunched into the flesh, the scent cracking through the odor of wet floor mats and warm vents.

Margot was struck by the image of her mother's serene face—the downcast eyes above the high cheekbones, the relaxed mouth—as she peeled an apple with a paring knife, conjuring a continuous ribbon of skin. The resulting spiral held the shape of its former life. As a child, Margot would delicately hold this peel like a small animal in the palm of her hand, this proof that her mother could be a kind of magician, an artist who told an origin story through scraps—*this is the skin of a fruit, this is its smell, this is its color.*

"I hope the weather clears up soon," Miguel said, interrupting her memory. "It gets pretty narrow and windy for a while. There's a scary point right at the top of California where the road is just zigzagging while you're looking down cliffs. It's like a test to see if you can stay on the road."

"Oh, God," Margot said. "Let's not talk about it anymore."

As she refocused on the rain-slicked road, the blurred lights, the yellow and white lines like yarn unspooling, Margot thought about her mother who hated driving on the freeway, her mother who no longer answered the phone. Where was her mother?

The windshield wipers squeaked, clearing sheets of rain.

"What about you?" Miguel asked. "Looking forward to seeing your mom?"

Margot's stomach dropped. "Actually, I've been trying to call her for the past few days to let her know, to let her know that we would be coming down." Clenching the wheel, she sighed. "I didn't really want to tell her because I wanted this to be a fun trip, but then I felt bad, so..."

"Is everything okay?"

"She hasn't been answering the phone."

"Hmm." He shifted in his seat. "Maybe her phone battery died?"

"It's a landline. Both landlines—at work and at home."

"Maybe she's on vacation?"

"She never goes on vacation." The windshield fogged, revealing smudges and streaks, past attempts to wipe it clean. She cranked up the air inside.

"Hasn't she ever wanted to go somewhere?"

"Yosemite and the Grand Canyon. I don't know why, but she's always wanted to go there."

"It's a big ol' crack in the ground, Margot. Why wouldn't she want to see it? It's God's crack."

"It's some kind of Korean immigrant rite of passage. National parks, reasons to wear hats and khaki, stuff like that. It's like *America* America."

"I bet she's okay," Miguel said. "When did you see her last?"

"Last Christmas," she said.

"Maybe she's just been busier than usual. We'll be there soon."

"You're probably right. I'll call her again when we stop."

A heaviness expanded inside her chest. She fidgeted with the radio dial but caught only static with an occasional blip of a commercial or radio announcer's voice.

Her mother was fine. They would all be fine.

With Miguel in LA, she'd have more reasons to visit now.

The road lay before them like the peel of a fruit. The windshield wipers hacked away water falling from the sky.

In Redding, California, shrouded by mountains and dense national forests, Margot and Miguel stopped at the first place they could find—a greasy spoon with red vinyl booths, a jukebox, a waitress in white uniform. The hostess, a blond ponytailed college student, led them to a table and handed them plastic menus. An old man in a trucker hat sat at the counter by himself. In a neighboring booth, two girls colored paper place mats while their parents observed.

Being from LA, in particular Koreatown, where Korean food and Mexican joints had been the norm, Margot always thought of the classic diner as "charming" and "novel," a location of unspoken heroism out of a movie or a short story about decent, hardworking white Americans trying to catch a break. Margot remembered when she had moved to Seattle eight years ago and made her first white friends—people who seemed to navigate their identities, their skin tones, their appearances so easily, in such an invisible way, as if the world had been created for them, which, in a sense, it had. Many of them—with their blue eyes and tall noses—appeared intrinsically attractive because even white people who weren't supermodels were at least white.

She didn't want to think that way since, theoretically, it made no sense. *Beauty is a construct, but theory is not the reality we live*, she thought. Theory didn't live in the bones. Theory didn't erase the years of self-scrutiny in a mirror and not seeing anyone at all, not a protagonist or a beauty, only a television sidekick, a speechless creature, who at best was "exotic," desirable but simple and foreign. Growing up, she had often wondered, *If only I had bigger eyes or brown hair instead of black. If only…*

The food arrived, interrupting her thoughts. Margot and Miguel devoured their meals—a cheeseburger and fries, a tuna melt on rye, and tomato soup—like animals. Margot tried to slow down, but everything tasted too good, perfect, American. All she could hear was mutual chewing, sips, and gulps—an orchestra of fulfillment. She wanted to sit here forever, forget about her problems, LA, her mother.

"We should hit the road, no?" Miguel asked. "Wanna switch?"

They paid the bill and went outside, where clouds had cleared out for an evening sky that promised stars. The moon glowed silvery white like a door's empty fisheye. Margot regretted not packing a winter coat, only a windbreaker and a few sweaters for the warmer weather in LA.

About five inches taller than Margot, Miguel adjusted the mirrors, then the seat to give his legs more room. The top of his pomaded hair brushed up against the fabric of the roof.

He merged onto the freeway, driving hard and fast. Whistling around slow-moving cars, he always signaled, never cutting anyone off. Margot had never imagined how quick and nimble her car could be, how such confidence and fearlessness could both impress and terrify her. She had become so used to going at her own, or her mother's, speed.

Her mother never liked the idea of traveling anywhere far. She rarely spoke of the past, but she had once told Margot that at the age of four, she had fled with her family from the north during the Korean War. Somehow, she had been separated from her parents permanently in that bloody time. Movement for her mother was essentially an experience of loss that Margot, American-born, could never imagine. And yet Margot herself had inherited the same anxiety about driving fast, particularly on freeways. She thought too much about the experience of speed itself, its danger, rather than getting somewhere at last.

Hitting flat straight highway without traffic through farms and fields, Margot untied her ponytail. She could feel herself relax, her shoulders and grip loosening. The sky—an inky ombré of blue and black—stretched wide to reveal a field of stars, twinkling at them from vast distances.

Once, twenty years ago when Margot was six, her mother had packed up their Oldsmobile for a weekend trip to Vegas— the only road trip she had ever taken with her mother, who never took more than a day off work. On the way there, she had driven below the speed limit in the slow lane the entire time, stretching what should've been a four-hour trip into an entire day. Cars and trucks zoomed by, honking. Through open windows, a dry breeze carried an odor of petroleum, mesquite, and sage. Dust powdered Margot's face and arms as she slumped low in her seat.

"Where are we going?" Margot had asked.

"Somewhere very special," her mother said.

"Will there be ice cream?"

Her brown eyes, hard as cabochons the entire drive, softened in the rearview mirror. "Yes."

Driving down the Strip, Margot had marveled at the seductive lights, a wonderland of distraction and pleasure. Here they could have anything—ice cream, games, stuffed animals, cheeseburgers for breakfast, walls made from hard candy that they could lick. But instead they spent most of their one full day in a shabby motel outside of Vegas, waiting for what—or for whom—Margot never knew.

After hours of waiting, they left the next morning. On the drive back, her mother had seemed so utterly deflated that Margot didn't have the courage to ask why they had driven so far. She always assumed that her mother didn't want to talk about the things that hurt her. But maybe Margot was wrong about that. Maybe now as an adult, she was growing into a woman who could understand and support her mother, despite the different languages they knew.

A light every now and then winked from distant points in the black sky and fields around Margot and Miguel. Driving with the road illuminated by the stretch of their headlights made her feel as if she was on a rocket ship, blasting into unknown depths, an infinite spray of stars and planets, tiny galaxies in the void.

She closed her eyes. Why didn't her mother pick up the phone?

The next morning after spending the night at Miguel's parents' house, they were on Interstate 5, listening to a story on the local NPR station about the devastation of the drought. She never knew how much she loved the sun—Los Angeles's interminable light—until she had moved to Seattle where the cold and rain stretched for gray days on end. Growing up, she had often found the light-filled sky oppressive in its ceaselessness, the doldrums of wearing shorts almost every day. That heat, those clothes could be glorious on a day off, but Margot and her mother, who worked long hours at her store six days a week, never had any time for vacation. But now as she contemplated the goldenness of the sun-scorched earth against a backdrop of cloudless blue sky, she could appreciate the warmth and light as if she had escaped a prison.

Hours later as Margot merged onto the 101 South, the sun began its long descent, transforming the sky into a wash of muted blue that blended into bright streaks of hot pink, the glow of tangerine in the west. After crawling along for thirty minutes with other drivers, possessing that quintessential LA—bored and spiritually deceased—look in the eyes, Margot and Miguel exited at Normandie Avenue and drove down the bustling streets of her neighborhood, Koreatown— clusters of signs in Korean, shopping plazas, parents holding bags of groceries and the hands of children, the elderly in sun hats hunched over and hobbling across streets, teenagers with baggy pants and backpacks.

"I don't know if I've ever been to Koreatown before," Miguel said, staring out the window.

"Have you spent much time in LA? You've been a few times, right?"

"Yeah, I've done the touristy stuff. Santa Monica, Venice, Beverly Hills, downtown."

"There's not a lot of reason to be in Koreatown, I guess, unless you're into the food. It's changing now, though." Margot explained how in recent years, developers were carving playgrounds for the fashionable and moneyed, building condos, hotels, and restaurants in the neighborhood. "It's so strange to me," she continued. "Why would anyone want to come here?"

"It's just *different* for people, that's all," Miguel said. "People want to go places that are different. It's slumming, what rich people do for shits and giggles."

Margot shook her head. "For me, being different wasn't a good thing. All I wanted growing up was everything on television—dishwashers and windows that shut properly and a yard."

"You didn't have a yard? Even poor people have yards, Margot. With, you know, like clotheslines and roosters and limping dogs…" He smiled, and Margot laughed.

"We lived in an apartment, the same one my mom lives in now," she said. "We never had a house."

They pulled up to the front of the building that she and her mother had lived in for as long as she could remember—a nondescript, gray stucco three-story complex. The windows on the bottom floor had security bars over them. The large agaves planted out front resembled tired sentinels that badly needed a day off. Margot and her mother lived on the middle floor in a two-bedroom unit with a small north-facing balcony that looked partially out onto another, almost-identical building and back alley.

"Let's sit here for a bit?" she asked. The old embarrassment rose from the pit of her stomach, the shame she felt when she brought classmates home from school to work on group projects. Margot and her mother never entertained or invited anyone inside for fun. No matter how clean her mother tried to keep things, the space always seemed shabby and disorganized—a closet for storage and sleeping and fighting rather than a home. But what else could her mother afford?

It was easy to see now how a place like this, so different from her Seattle neighborhood of green trees and clean sky and open windows without bars, could make her feel embarrassment and shame about her home. Not that life was less confusing in Seattle, but it was much less in her face all the time—the crowd of emotions, the struggle to put food on the table, the fear of being followed down the street at night, kidnapped or stabbed. Always looking behind her. Maybe this was why she couldn't leave the past behind—everything about her life had trained her to look back. By never looking forward, she was always tripping, falling over things.

Miguel touched her arm. "Do you want to call your mom again? Does she have a cell phone?"

Margot took a deep breath and unbuckled her seat belt. "She

has one that she uses for emergencies, but it's never on. It's a flip phone, and she doesn't know how to check voice mail."

"Sacrilège," he said in a bad French accent.

"She's technologically in the Stone Age," Margot went on. "She can't really read English either, and her eyes are kind of bad. My Korean isn't good enough to help her. It always ends in a fight."

How many hours had she spent, words stumbling like stones out of her mouth, trying to explain something in Korean to her mother? A utilities bill. How to work the remote control. A car insurance policy. And in those hours, Margot would always slip, somehow yelling at her mother, as her mother had often done to her as a child when she had misbehaved by oversleeping, by missing church, even by falling ill and needing to go to the hospital.

Her mother had once screamed, "How am I going to pay for this? Why don't you take better care of yourself?" Her mother didn't have time for empathy. She always had to keep moving. If she stopped, she might drown.

"Would you mind waiting in the car?" Margot asked.

The broken security gate shrieked, then slammed behind her. Holding her breath, she climbed the dark, dank staircase, which smelled of wet socks and old paint fumes, to the second floor, where she knocked on the apartment door. The fisheye was empty and dark.

This was no longer her home. Yet with a memory that lived not in her head but in her hands, she turned the key for the dead bolt, which was already unlocked, and then the doorknob. She had spent most of her life, her childhood, dreading the inside of that apartment, not out of fear but out of hatred and spite. Hatred for her mother. Hatred for the money they didn't have. Hatred for her father, missing, gone, a coward. Hatred for her mother's accent. Hatred for the furniture, stained, falling apart. Hatred for herself, her life. She hated it all. She wanted this world to disappear, to burn it all down.

As she opened the door, a dark odor of decayed fruit, putrid and sharp, swelled around her head like a tidal wave. Acid erupted from her mouth onto the arm that shielded her face. She flipped on the light. There was a broken ceramic sculpture of the Virgin Mary on the floor, tour brochures on their coffee table, and in this intimate chaos, her mother facedown on the carpet with her right arm extended, the left one by her side, her feet in sheer nude socks.

Later, Margot would remember the screams and would realize that they were coming from her.

She fell to her knees. The hallway's amber glow was soft like feathers. Face tingling, she lay her forehead on the carpet where the head of a tiny nail pressed against her skin. Miguel's hands abruptly gripped her shoulders from behind, easing her to her feet. They wobbled, weak, down the stairs into the open air, the street.

As the sun disappeared below the horizon, the sky became the longest bruise—purple and blue. The cruel light left its mark.

She rested on the uneven curb, head in her arms folded on her knees, Miguel next to her. Hiccuping through tears, she struggled to breathe.

Maybe she should have checked her mother's pulse, maybe she shouldn't have called the police. What if her mother was only hurt badly, or drunk? No, she never drank and a person that was hurt would not lie on the floor facedown like that. And she couldn't bear the thought of being near that smell, that body, the first time she had seen her mother in almost a year.

That was her umma. That was her head. Those were her feet.

Sirens blared from a distance, getting louder as they arrived.

She directed two police officers and an EMT to her mother's apartment. Another two officers asked her questions. She was appalled at how little she could answer. But she did tell them miscellaneous things about her mother—that she worked all day at this store and that she went to church.

A wiry Korean man in his sixties, perhaps the landlord or even a janitor, spoke to the officers for about ten minutes. Afterward, he stood on the sidewalk, smoking with a few casual observers who had emerged out of the surrounding buildings, curious about the lights and the noise.

They took her body away in a black bag on a stretcher.

Her name was Mina. Mina Lee.

Yes, that was her mother.

MINA

SUMMER 1987

M ina stepped off the plane into a flash of heat, thinking she had made a grave mistake. But it was too
late. The world opened up like a hot mouth devouring her. Yet hadn't it been that way her whole life already?
She reminded herself that this airport, LAX, was actually easier, much more organized than Seoul, or any other great city,
much safer even than her own childhood.

She fought back the memory of the screaming, stampeding
crowd in which she had been separated from her parents while
fleeing the north during the war. Her four-year-old hands
groping to grab them. The rush of bodies. The moment she
lost sight of her mother and father. Surrounded by the distress,
the pain etched into strangers. The dead along the road, the
elderly who had fallen, and those shuddering, hungry people
who did not have anything left to protect.

And in the airport now, her heart throbbed as she waded

through the crowd to get out. She was doing this again, and again she was doing it alone.

A steady stream of people jostled in the same direction—friends and families, smiling, reunited, businessmen in gray and navy suits traveling by themselves. She was in another country, foreign, alone. The breath rushed in and out of her lungs. Her underarms were clammy and cold. What if she fainted now before she could even make it out the door?

On paper, she was on vacation, visiting a friend from work. She had always wanted to visit America. She would be here for a month to see the sights—Disneyland, the beaches, Yosemite. On paper, she would relax, enjoy herself, and return to her life in Seoul, her job as a designer of women's casual clothes.

The papers did not say that she was going to find a job here, that she was going to start a life, that she hoped to find an employer to sponsor her, and if she could not do that, she would stay anyway—invisible, unofficial, undocumented. The papers did not say that she had nothing to return to, nothing that she wanted or could live with any longer. The papers did not say that she did not know how to sit still anymore, that she did not know how to stay in her apartment by herself, that she could not bear the gnawing familiarity of that haunted place, those ruined streets, that ruined home. The papers did not say that everything in her suitcases was now all that she had. Every single one of her belongings had been stuffed compactly inside of them. Selling and giving away most of her life had been an act of self-immolation, whittling herself down enough to stay alive until God took her home, wherever that meant.

A wave of relief washed over her as she stepped outside of the airport into the blast of hot air and sunshine. After loosening the hand-dyed silk scarf, sienna-and-ocher-colored, around her neck, she reached inside her purse for a napkin to wipe her forehead.

She had already secured a place to stay—a small bedroom in a house owned by an ahjumma who lived by herself in Koreatown. Her friend Mrs. Shin, a former coworker in Seoul, had recommended the place after she, her husband, and two children had immigrated and stayed there for a few months themselves three years prior.

On the edge of the sidewalk, Mina raised her hand, hailing a cab. The driver, a tall Sikh man, helped her with her luggage, heaving her two large suitcases into the trunk. She realized that she had never seen a person who was Sikh before. Sweat streamed down her face and neck inside the sauna-like car despite the windows being open. She reached forward, showing him the address she had written in English on a slip of lined paper. The shakiness of the letters, the seismographic script revealed to her how nervous she had been writing down that address, as if signing a contract for the rest of her life.

"First time?" he asked, his eyes smiling in the rearview mirror. His dark turban skimmed the roof of the car.

"Ex-cuse me?"

"First time?"

"Oh." She scoured her mind for English words like a dresser with too many drawers.

"English?"

"No." She shook her head.

"Chinese?"

"Korea."

The driver accelerated onto the freeway, weaving in and out of a brash symphony of traffic. A horn section of big rigs. Brakes screeching. A chorus of road rage. Synthesized pop music, all leg warmers and big hair, blasted from an open window, while records scratched into "The Batterram" one lane over. A man shouted, "Go fuck yourself," like cymbals crashing.

Damp clothes clung to her body. She wiped her face, trying not to ruin her makeup, and gripped the door handle.

As they passed pedestrians in the streets of LA, Mina wondered where the Koreans were. Occasionally, another Asian face appeared in a neighboring car. But here in this cacophonous world of concrete, metal, and glass, in this smell of gasoline and rubber, she could not see herself. She felt disembodied in this new place, where she did not know the language, where the signs, the billboards all blared something in English, gibberish.

She rummaged inside her purse for the photograph that she had always kept with her, one of her, her husband and daughter, both now dead. Hands shaking, she rubbed the edges of his face with her thumb and then the face of her daughter, soft and serene after a day of hiking in the woods. She wanted to kiss the photograph. She thought of the last time she had seen her daughter, and how she had scolded her, for nothing, something so stupid—dropping a dish and chipping it on the ground.

Had she known that would be their final moment together, would she have yelled? No, she would've held her. She would've kissed her. She would've confessed that she was terrified of everything her daughter did, things breaking, objects in disarray, because she could not afford to lose another thing that she loved in her life. She didn't have the strength to rebuild herself.

Then it happened. She lost everything again.

"Here we are."

She had been crying. In the rearview mirror, the driver frowned, furrowing his brow.

He carried her suitcases up the concrete driveway, which sloped gently toward the entrance of the home. The house appeared broken, too, with cracks along the beige stucco, windows held together with tape. Orange and lemon trees and weeds grew wildly. Shingles peeled away from the roof or lay askew. She placed the photograph in her purse and wiped the tears away from her face, carefully, before knocking on the door.

The driver stood beside her, waiting to make sure someone answered. She felt self-conscious standing with this man, not knowing exactly how to thank him, because his silence, his wordlessness, calmed her nerves. She knocked again. The door opened to reveal a woman in her fifties with a short brown bob, gray at the roots. She bowed her head and greeted Mina in Korean.

"Mrs. Lee?"

"Yes." Mina turned to the driver. "Thank you. How... much?"

"Oh, that's okay. Next time." He handed her a business card. "You can pay me next time."

"No, no." She reached into her purse.

He lowered the bags inside the house and walked away, but at the bottom of the driveway he stopped and said, "Good luck. You're going to be okay."

She waved in response, speechless.

"Here, let me take your bags," the woman said. "You must be tired."

"No, I've got it."

They each took one of the heavy suitcases deeper inside the home, dark and cool like a cave. A single fan rotated in the corner, kicking up the curtains with its draft. The house had dirty walls, no artwork except some portraits of Jesus and a ceramic sculpture of Mary.

"Let me show you your room."

M ina lay in her twin-size bed, eager to be doing something—shopping for food, finding work, calling Mrs. Shin—anything. But she didn't have a telephone in her room yet. And the sprawling map of Los Angeles that she had brought, geared toward tourists, confused her—major attractions, such as the Hollywood Walk of Fame, Beverly Hills, and Disneyland, strung together by miles and miles of freeway. She stared at the cottage cheese ceiling, immobilized by the dread of having to decide on what to do next. There seemed to be too much information to learn.

She closed her eyes, taking deep breaths. She didn't want to panic, to feel anything. She was tired of feeling.

She asked God to help her, to tell her what to do.

She had already sold all her belongings, quit her job in Seoul. Without her husband and daughter, there was nothing left for her there in that country, on those streets, in narrow alleyways echoing their footsteps. What else could she do now but surrender to her fate, to the multitude of decisions that brought her right here in this room alone with the windows open, feeling damp from her own sweat in a stranger's clean sheets, staring at a stranger's ceiling?

Knuckles tapped on her bedroom door.

"Yes?" she asked in Korean, sitting up, careful not to crush the map by her side.

"Hello." An unfamiliar woman's voice, husky yet clear.

Mina smoothed her hair down with her hands and opened the door, where a woman, perhaps a few years older than her, with a long face, curly hair, and high cheekbones, smiled generously.

"I live next door." She pointed down the hall. "You just came today?"

"Yes."

"You must be tired."

"Yes, very."

"I'm cooking dinner. Do you want to join me?"

"Oh, no." Her stomach growled. "That's okay."

"Please join me. I have some rice and soup."

Mina's head throbbed between her brows and on the sides of her skull. She wanted to jump back into bed, but she knew that the food would help her, and she had nothing of her own to eat. She didn't know how to get to the grocery store either.

"I have plenty to share," the woman said.

Mina followed the woman to the galley kitchen where in a small dining nook, she had set out banchan—kimchi and seasoned spinach and soybean sprouts—as well as two sets of paper napkins, chopsticks, and spoons. Staring at the objects neatly arranged, Mina realized how little she possessed, and how vulnerable, how small that made her feel. She'd have to buy all those things—utensils, bowls, at least one pot and pan.

"Please have a seat."

Sliding herself onto the dining nook bench, she could see how the kitchen hadn't been renovated or repaired in years. The greasy wallpaper, a pattern of tiny periwinkle flowers, peeled off the walls. Several of the cabinet doors didn't close completely, or hung askew, as if on the edge of falling.

The woman said, "It's very hot," while placing two bowls of rice and kimchi jjigae with tofu and mushrooms on the table. With the steam from the dish rising in front of her, Mina realized it had been close to twenty-four hours since her last full meal. She wanted to dive into the food but waited out of politeness in front of the stranger.

"Where are you from? Please go ahead." The woman gestured toward the bowl in front of Mina.

Mina blew on the soup before tasting what was the most tremendous thing on earth. The brininess of the doenjang on her tongue replenished her body while springtime bloomed like purple wildflowers in her head. It reminded her of the feeling of that first bite of food after losing her parents, when she had been found on the side of a dirt road by an older man, a villager, who had taken her to his house and fed her a single meal of doenjang jjigae before he had to let her go on her own. She remembered how she had cried for her mother as she ate, tears falling into the soup, and how the man with half of his teeth missing tried to comfort her, patting her on the back. Of course, he probably wanted to help her, but what could anyone do during a war, when a child had been another mouth to feed, a liability, when children losing their parents or parents watching their children blown to bits had been the norm?

"I'm from Seoul," Mina said.

"Me, too. Well, not too far from there."

"Oh."

They ate in silence for the rest of the meal. Outside, crickets sang.

They were two women by themselves, living in this house without husbands, and apparently without children, too. Boarders. Too many questions might lead to too much information, too much in common, too much pain.

She dreamed of nothing that night. A purple surrender, the best sleep she had had in months without pills, without drinking, without even prayer.

In the morning, she went to the bathroom that she now shared with the woman down the hall. She unpacked her toiletry bag, laying out her toothpaste and soap at a corner of the vanity without disturbing the other woman's belongings—a folded pink washcloth, a slimy bar of soap, a toothbrush in a bright green plastic cup. In the mirror, her black hair fell to her shoulders in a tangled bird's nest. She couldn't find her brush, so she used her fingers to rake through the mess, discarding stray hairs in the wastebasket.

After a long shower, she lay down in bed again, clean and relaxed, on the edge of forgetting the world for a few more hours. A sweet bird chirped close to her window while a weed whacker, a few houses down, shredded and whirred.

A knock on the door startled her. She rose to answer it.

"Do you need anything?" the landlady asked. Her face was soft and gentle, with a hint of pink lipstick.

"Oh." Mina propped up the towel, slipping from her wet hair.

"I'm going to the store. Do you want to get some groceries with me?"

"Yes, yes. Let me get dressed." Despite the heat, she picked out a long pin-striped skirt, a tan blouse. She applied liquid eyeliner and rose-colored lipstick carefully, as if painting her lips like art. Worried about the wad of cash hidden in a sock under the mattress, she locked the door with a padlock behind her.

In the landlady's car with the windows down and the fan vents blasting air in their faces, they drove for about five minutes through a dusty white light, eyes squinting. The neighborhood was mostly concrete and treeless except for the battered-looking palms with thorny ribs, the tired and curled-leaf citrus trees, and hibiscus plants, with their plate-size blooms and ashy jungle-colored foliage in the dry summer heat.

"Did your friend Mrs. Shin tell you about rent?" the landlady asked.

"Yes, $200, right? I can pay you when we get home."

"Do you know where you're going to work yet?"

"No, not yet." Mina scanned the storefronts, the brightly colored signs in Korean—Drugstore, Books, Piano Lessons. "My friend mentioned some people she knows at a restaurant. She thought I could wait tables or cook. What do you do?"

"I own a clothing store. It's small, but I get by."

"Clothing? What kind?"

"Women's."

"I used to design clothing."

"Oh, really?"

"Yes, I worked for a small clothing company in Seoul."

"Hmm." She sped up, changing lanes. "I wish I could hire you to help me. I need some help. But business has been pretty bad."

"Oh."

"Yes, ever since my husband left, I've been struggling." She pulled into a large lot outside of a freestanding Korean supermarket buzzing with the movements of ordinary life, a kaleidoscope of social statuses (shiny Mercedes Benzes, beat-up Buicks, Ford trucks), mothers with children in tow loading bags of groceries into their cars, working men on break, smoking cigarettes in silence.

"Idiot," the landlady yelled at a car beating her to a spot.

Once they had finally parked, Mina followed the landlady, who, in an automatic gesture, grabbed a shopping cart. The entire place had signs in Korean, too, which comforted her. Everything was Korean, the brands, the language on boxes and packaging.

She picked out some produce for herself—a small watermelon, two oranges, spinach, and a bag of onions—and went down the aisles for staples—rice, ramen, doenjang, and gochujang. Everything seemed surprisingly affordable, even more affordable in some instances than in Seoul.

At the checkout, Mina pulled $20 from her wallet uncertainly, new to the foreign currency. The cashier—who looked in his midthirties, younger than Mina, with a bit of gray at the temples of his thick black hair—lowered his eyes as if to protect her from any sense of scrutiny that might arouse embarrassment. His arms were smooth and lean. She became aware of her chest rising and falling, a fire in the pit of her stomach.

After the bagger had loaded their cart, Mina and the landlady passed a large cork bulletin board by the sliding doors. Among a riot of advertisements for various home and car repair services, banks and churches, a pink flyer spelled in large Korean letters: HELP WANTED.

She looked back toward the checkout where the same man who had rung up her groceries met her eyes this time and smiled. She felt his gaze on her as she turned to leave. She thought of the cold hard coins, the change he had dropped into her hand. Was it the very edges of his fingertips, a flower unfurling, that grazed her open palm? Or had she imagined that detail, that feeling?

Her heart raced. She replayed in her mind the unmistakable curve of his lip, his soft brown gaze, unblinking.

MARGOT

FALL 2014

After she collected the death certificate downtown, Margot drove beneath the gunmetal morning light and weeping palm trees to the brand-new police station. She had never been to a police station before, and for whatever reason had imagined them to be as grubby as her elementary school, which smelled of chemical cleaners, chalk dust, and rubber. In the waiting area, people of all ages appeared anxious or tired. A grandfather, red polo shirt and gold bracelets, crossed his arms in front of his chest, eyes downcast. A mother, strands rising from coppery hair tied in a bun, observed two children thumb wrestling.

Bleary-eyed and weak, Margot had not slept the past two nights—haunted by visions of her mother, that careful bob of hair, that soft extension of her one arm as if reaching for something, or perhaps just an attempt to break her fall, the instinct to create some final grace, some final comfort for herself.

After she had discovered her mother's body, she and Miguel had found a hotel on the outskirts of Hollywood near Vermont Avenue—a nondescript, three-story beige structure—one of many hotels in the area of questionable cleanliness and ornate bedspreads that would not show stains.

She spent most of the next day with the maroon-colored curtains closed. Her chest ached like a bowl made of stone, a mortar in which the pestle of her mind ground down the images of her mother in that living room, *their* living room, a tableau of ordinary life gone awry, the objects that witnessed her final breath—a broken one-foot-tall figurine of the Virgin Mary, a bowl of nuts knocked over, tour brochures for excursions to national parks (Yellowstone, Yosemite, the Grand Canyon) on the coffee table. The smell, that putrid smell, the rot.

When was the last time she had seen her mother? Was it a year ago, last Christmas? The days spent at her mother's store, full of holiday string lights. Margot hung clothes on rounders and racks that glided into place on casters, swept the industrial gray carpet, rang up and bagged purchases at the counter, or helped customers choose the perfect gifts—a crimson sweater embroidered with bells, a pair of bootcut jeans, a slinky dress for New Year's Eve.

Every night, except on Christmas when they'd treat themselves at the local soondubu restaurant, Margot and her mother had dinner at home—the usual stews, a variety of banchan, grilled mackerel or gulbi. They'd sit together in silence underneath the dust-filled overhead light, eating from the jumble of plates and bowls accumulated over the years—romantic and rose-bordered, pastel blue-and-white-checkered, stamped with 1970s brown butterflies and flowers. Their apartment was a testament to the accretion that could happen in a family's life—not through intention but necessity. Objects were acquired while on sale or in thrift stores or as gifts, like flotsam and jetsam as if they had been stranded on an island. Nothing could be thrown away or denied.

But Margot would incinerate it all if she could. She decorated her life in Seattle with austerity and care, leaning toward neutral colors and patternless designs perhaps as a rebellion against her mother, against all that her mother represented to her—poverty, tastelessness, foreignness, uncleanliness, a lack of control.

"Are you going to stay in Seattle?" her mother had asked. The tidy bob, graying at the temples, had been tucked behind her pink ears, revealing the two gold hoops that glinted like metal lures. Her eyes remained downcast as she bit the mak kimchi, tart and scarlet, that she always made at home.

"Yes, I like it there," Margot said in English. She sipped the last of the miyeok guk—anchovy-flavored and lightly briny, beaded with sesame oil—from her spoon.

"But it rains all the time."

"It's not so bad. I'm used to it." That was a lie. She hated the rain. She missed Los Angeles but didn't know how she'd live there. She already had a decent job in Seattle and could afford her own apartment in a quiet residential neighborhood that smelled year-round of spruce and pine. (The only needles she had ever found dropped from trees.) In LA, she would have to move back in with her mother at least temporarily. But she didn't know how to explain this to her, not in Korean, not in English, not in any language.

"Do you have a boyfriend there?" It was a question that her mother had asked more frequently than Margot had liked. Sometimes the inquiry seemed casual, hopeful; her daughter might meet someone responsible and kind, settle down, start a family. But other times the question was carved by a fear that her daughter would do the exact opposite—drink late into the night, meet men who would be reckless with her feelings, her future, her life, end up pregnant and alone—which in a way could've happened at that time.

It had been a month since Margot had begun seeing Jonathan, a much older coworker, a job counselor for people with disabilities. The first time they had kissed, their mouths touched gently, narrow columns of sunlight pressing on the office walls around them. The wet earth from his afternoon cigar, entangled with something else, a clean citrus—a bright decay. His sonorous vintage radio voice saying her name: *Margot*.

But she couldn't tell her mother about any of this. How could her mother understand a relationship that made no sense to Margot nor her friends? The only explanation was one that she could never articulate out loud—that she was lonely and bored and she found him to be thrilling. He was a coworker. He was over twenty years older than her. He was blind. He was a widower. His life was ripe with so much experience, and she could get lost in being around him. He shrank her. He whittled her down. He made her small, so small that she and what she wanted—a more creative life, a more individual sense of accomplishment, of meaning—could evaporate, disappear.

But she couldn't explain this to her mother. Even if she spoke enough Korean, how would her mother understand this—hunger? It wasn't a desire to die, but a need to hide, to delete herself. She wanted to be an artist, and that was dangerous. How could she afford the time and money to have more art in her life? How could she ever be an artist if she had to worry about not only taking care of herself but also her mother one day? All they had was each other in the end. And since she denied herself so much, why not dive into being with Jonathan, who always told her what a wonderful person she was, how smart, how thoughtful, how kind? Jonathan made her feel like the most important person in the world because she erased herself with him. She listened. She supported. She approved. She was like the mother she had always wanted.

So again, she lied. "No, I don't have a boyfriend. I'm too busy with work."

Her mother stood to clear their empty bowls and plates. Not a grain of rice remained.

"I wish you would live near me," she said softly, before turning away toward the kitchen sink where she blasted the hot water to soak the empty pots and pans.

Margot experienced a sense of lightness, relief that topic of conversation had been extinguished for now, yet she could feel the burn of regret for her lies, her ingratitude toward a mother who had sacrificed so much for their survival, her lack of commitment toward learning Korean, even if only to speak to her mother—rising, rising toward her tongue and eyes. They were tears, ones she had hidden from her mother.

That was almost a year ago. In the end, her relationship with Jonathan was only two months long, culminating in the most predictable and uneventful heartbreak. And now her mother was dead.

She had always counted on one more hour, one more day, one more year to explain herself to her mother, to tell her that she loved her more than anyone in the world but could never live around her, never live under the same roof with her again.

Now Margot would never have the chance to help her understand. To help them both understand.

"Margot?" Someone was calling her name. In the waiting room, she looked up at Officer Choi who had been at the apartment two days ago when Margot had found her mother's body. He was young, perhaps in his late twenties or early thirties at most. His hair glistened like black enamel as if he had recently showered or left the gym for work. But the heavy gun and uniform made her nervous, uptight. She couldn't quite meet his eyes. A white mug steamed in his hand. "Would you like some coffee or water?"

"No," she said, standing to follow him.

They passed closed doors down a bright long corridor that smelled of floor wax to reach a shared office, which had a tall bookshelf filled with legal books and manuals. An open file rested on the desk with muted multicolored sheets of paper and a lined notepad.

Margot seated herself across from him. Behind his head, the vertical blinds were half-closed and tilted in a way so that she could still see his face—diamond-shaped with heavy eyebrows and high cheekbones. She realized then that he was handsome, which made her even more anxious, her thoughts pacing like an animal in a cage.

"Do I know you from somewhere?" Officer Choi asked.

"Not that I know of," Margot said. "I haven't lived in LA for years."

"Where'd you go to high school?"

"Fairfax."

"Ah, that's it."

"Really?" He wasn't familiar at all. Actually, she hardly remembered any Korean kids there except herself. Most of her friends had been Mexican, Salvadoran, Filipino.

"Yeah. I *think* you were a few years before me." He smiled. "Small world."

Was she that out of it in high school? She had been too busy experimenting with drugs, a half tab of acid on her tongue, spending her free time charcoaling still lifes of fruit or hiding in the muted red glow of a darkroom. She was artistic and antisocial. He had probably been popular, a jock.

Officer Choi cleared his throat and leaned forward, bracing his arms on the desk. "I'm sorry about your mom. I know this...must be a lot right now..."

Tiny drops of sweat formed on her face. She rubbed between her brows, pressing the pain that throbbed inside her head. She spotted the death certificate on his desk and remembered the black box ticked beside the word *Accidental.*

Margot closed her eyes, inhaling through her mouth as if to protect herself from the memory of the scent of her mother's body. The putrid smell of the rotten fruit—sweet, foul, and gaseous. Acid soured her mouth. She could feel his gaze lingering on her face. When she glanced up at him, his eyes dropped, scanning his notes.

"Died last Saturday or Sunday. Hematoma," he said, scrunching his brow. "Found on Wednesday. All her possessions seemed to be intact, her keys, her Corolla. Cash in her purse. No forced entry. Shoes, slippers by the door."

The outstretched arm. The feet in the nude socks. How tiny she appeared to be on the ground.

A trip. A fall. A horrible way to die. To have survived all those traumas, those hardships—a war, an orphanage, immigration, being a single mother in a foreign country—only to die by something as mundane as a slipper or a shoe. It was terrible. It was all so very terrible.

"Are you sure you don't want any water?" he asked, sitting up in his chair.

"No. No, that's okay."

"I know that this is a lot. It's a lot to process." His eyes softened. "It never makes sense to lose people—especially like this."

There would be no goodbye, no farewell. Her mother's body was in a mortuary, awaiting cremation. There were no plans for a funeral. There was no will. They never discussed her mother's wishes after death. They rarely discussed her mother's desires at all. Margot only knew that her mother wanted Margot to be closer to her. *I wish you would live near me.*

There would only be ash—silent and heavy in a box. What would she do with her mother now?

"Even though this is a closed case… I wanted to make sure that you don't suspect anything? That nothing suspicious was going on, or that there isn't something you want to tell me about."

Finding her mother's body was one nightmare, but sitting in this room with a police officer was another. What good could the police do for her and her mother now? What good had they ever done? There were so many instances growing up when she and her mother needed help—when they had been robbed at gunpoint once, or when a thief had broken into their apartment—but no one ever thought of calling the police. No one ever knew what they would do or whose side they were on, if they could get her mother deported somehow. What did he care? Who cared if he was Korean, too, or went to her high school?

"She went to work. She had a simple life. She worked hard. She was…boring."

Margot believed all these statements to be true. But could she convince *herself* that she knew her mother? Because she didn't. Her world was designed to erase her mother. Her mother was just another nobody, another casualty of this city, of this country that lured you with a scintillating lie.

She had been an inconvenience. A casualty of more important things. Of more important people.

"When had you spoken to her last?"

"A few weeks ago? Something like that." *Business was slow again today. Even all the Korean businesses downtown are closing.* "She…she mentioned that she was struggling at work. She was struggling financially, but none of that is new." Had she been asking for help? Had she needed money?

"And you said her business was in a swap meet down south. Near Bell."

"Huntington Park."

She imagined her mother coming home that night, exhausted, taking off her leather ankle boots. But why was the light switched off? Was it earlier in the day? Was there still light outside streaming in through the window? In Margot's mind, her mother removed her shoes and tripped on the slippers she always kept by the door. There were always two pairs. One for Margot. Or maybe her mother was going somewhere. Maybe she was heading out the door and realizing that she forgot something, turned around and tripped in the dark. How terrible. How infuriating. She wanted to scream, *Why didn't you take better care of yourself?* But there was no one to hear her now.

"Did she have any employees?"

"No, just her."

"Was she friends with any of the neighboring store owners?"

"Yes. Well, there's this woman… She has a children's clothing store across the aisle from my mom."

His pen scratched on the pad. "Did they get along? Did your mom get along with everyone?"

"I think so. When I was growing up, she had some trouble with being one of the few Korean store owners there. She thought the customers and the other store owners might not like her since her Spanish was bad."

Margot remembered how her mother would yell, *Amiga, amiga,* to potential customers as they walked away on the green-painted pathways between the stores. Sometimes they would stop and wave goodbye. Other times they would simply ignore her. Occasionally they would pinch their noses around the Korean food that she brought from home. Her mother had the profound capacity to brush the insults off, but Margot could not. They would haunt her for her life. She had loved her mother more than anyone but was also deeply ashamed of her—her poverty, her foreignness, her language, the lack of agency in her life. She did not know how to love anyone, including herself, without shame.

Tears leaked out of her eyes. She grabbed a tissue from a box on his desk.

"I wanted you to know that you can call me if you need anything," Officer Choi said kindly. "You have my card?"

"I just wish I knew what to do with her now. With her ashes."

"Did she go to church?"

"Yes." The clay Spanish tile roof. The tall creamy white building. The bell tower.

"Could they help you? Could they help you figure out what she would've liked?"

"Yes, of course. I don't think I'm quite ready yet for that."

"Your dad?" He furrowed his brow. "Is he still around? Can he help you somehow?"

The words *your dad* bit at her quick, like an eel hiding in seagrass.

"I don't... I didn't know him." She had often been judged by people at church, at school, who didn't understand how she could survive without a father. *Don't you wonder who he is? Do you think he'd ever come back?* She had been pitied, too. But most of all, she had been excluded, unable to relate to the structure of family, both in America and in what she knew of Korean life. The message had always been that women without men lacked shape, women without men were always waiting for them to appear like images in a darkroom bath.

What would Margot do with all the mundane objects that made up her mother's life? A tangle of rosaries in a dusty ceramic dish. Faded school portraits of Margot with her gapped teeth and the horrible bangs that her mother cut straight across. An old single-CD boom box covered in a fur of dust. A dingy white teddy bear, glossy crooked nose, gripping a stuffed red satin heart. A framed photo of her and her mother on the day of Margot's high school graduation. A box of albums that had gotten so old, most of the images slipped out, no longer held by the ancient adhesives. Closets and drawers full of clothes. She didn't understand why her mother needed so many sweaters and pajama pants and blankets. It was Southern California after all.

It had been about a week since her mother had died and a few days since discovering her mother's body. A part of her wanted to leave everything and go back to Seattle, let the landlord deal with it.

But then her own childhood possessions—her old clothes, schoolwork, photos, immunization records, notebooks— which she didn't even have the courage, the energy to confront in the other bedroom, would be abandoned as well.

Eventually she'd have to go through her old room, which her mother had used mostly for storage, keeping the twin-size bed for Margot's visits around the holidays. As a teenager, Margot would retreat there after dinner, disappear with a notebook and pen, crank up her moody music—PJ Harvey, Fiona Apple, Portishead—to drown out the sound of her mother watching the Korean channel in the living room. Sometimes she'd exit her room and catch a glimpse of her mother nodding her head as if in conversation with the screen. It must've been a relief after a long day in a foreign country to be immersed in images where you belonged just by sound and gesture and face. How much language itself was a home, a shelter, as well as a way of navigating the larger world. And perhaps that was why Margot never put much effort into learning Korean. She hadn't been able to stand being under the same roof as her mom.

But now Margot could see that, despite moving to Seattle, she was everywhere inside of this apartment. It wasn't just her mother's objects covered in dust, but her own—the photographs of Margot as a gap-toothed little girl, the certificates of Margot's grade-school accomplishments framed and hung on the walls, which meant nothing to Margot but clearly were a source of pride for her mother.

It was obvious now how much they depended on each other—for food, shelter, a sense of identity in this world—and how much Margot had resented that. She didn't want to need or be needed by her. Her mother was too heavy with history, with sadness, unspoken and unexplained. She rarely mentioned her childhood and had only sometimes vaguely referenced the variety of jobs—a cook, a textile cutter, a seamstress—that she had been forced to work as a teenager to survive.

Margot knew that at some point her mother had moved from the orphanage into a boardinghouse where she had shared a room with three other young women, either orphans or exiles, without families for shelter—a particularly thrilling time when Mina had finally been free to live her own life, free from the scrutiny of adults.

Margot never felt strong or sturdy enough for the details of her mother's truth. She could barely handle her own. Growing up American was all about erasing the past—lightly acknowledging it but then forgetting and moving on.

But history always rose to the surface. Among the wreckage, the dead floated to the top.

And here now—the rosaries, the dingy white teddy bear, the photo albums.

How could she even begin to separate her belongings from her mother's? Why had she always counted on her mother to be here so that Margot wouldn't have to make any decisions, place any value on the items that were the evidence of their lives—not just of their daily activities, but of what they simply couldn't bear to get rid of, what they simply couldn't bear to lose?

How much had her mother been carrying? How much had she been carrying for them both?

And now Margot would have to bear it all by herself.

Down in the garage—cool and dim and soundless except for the gentle knocking of pipes—Margot backed out of the spot behind her mother's car. A tall figure appeared in her rearview mirror. She gasped and slammed on the brakes, the man scurrying out of the way. As she pulled up beside him, she lowered the window on her side.

"Sorry," she said. "You came out of nowhere."

"That's okay." He stood holding a broom and dustpan in hand. She recognized him as the landlord or maybe the janitor—she couldn't tell which one—who had been there the day she found her mother's body. He was wearing the same gray pullover sweater, pilling and rubbed thin on the elbows. Wrinkled and tanned, he had both the ease and the awkwardness of someone who had immigrated decades ago—a fluent English speaker who had probably grown up on American pop culture but for whatever reason never left Koreatown. He seemed a bit lost, out of place. Margot could certainly relate.

"Hey, I'm so sorry about your mom," he said with a slight New York accent. "She was a good tenant. Always paid rent on time." He coughed and turned to spit on the ground.

"Thank you," Margot said. It struck her that he might have known her mother, seen her more than Margot had this past year. Taking a deep breath to steady herself, she asked, "Do you remember the last time you saw her? What she seemed like?"

"Hmm." He paused. "It's hard to say. She dropped off her rent check a couple days early. Last Friday, I think?"

"Was there—I don't know—anything odd going on? Anything around the apartment or...?"

Scrunching his brows, he ran his fingers through wavy hair, bright white at the temples. "Well, last weekend, I might've heard your mom yelling," he said, biting his lower lip. "At night. But a lot of people fight. A lot of families fight, you know."

"Yelling?" she asked, shocked.

"I don't know. Maybe it was someone else in the building. A Korean woman."

Heart pounding, Margot asked, "Do you remember which day that was?"

"Not really. Saturday or Sunday." He scratched his head, avoiding her eyes. "It's probably a mistake. Who knows? My apartment isn't directly below hers. But my window was open, and I thought I could hear a woman yelling." He shrugged. "I went back to sleep."

"Was it just my mother yelling? Was there anyone else with her?"

He shook his head. "I'm probably mixed up, you know? I heard Korean and there's not a lot of us left in the building, so—I figured it was your mother. But I don't know."

"Did you tell anyone? The police?"

"No, no, I didn't. Honestly, I didn't even remember this until now. Not a big deal. It could've been anyone. I mean, no need to get them involved with that. People fight. People get mad."

"Was my mother usually noisy?"

"No, no. Very nice lady. This has always been a safe building. Very safe. No problems." He dug in his back pocket and produced a Marlboro Lights packet half-wrapped in plastic. Slipping a cigarette behind his ear, he said, "It could happen to anyone, you know?"

Was he being cagey or was it just her imagination? Margot asked, "Are you new?"

"Excuse me?"

"I used to live here," she said. "I don't recognize you."

"My wife owned this building. She died a few years ago and I've been trying to keep it together since then. You have no idea how expensive it is to own a building these days. We used to be the bad guys, you know? Now it's like we can't even make a decent buck, you know, with all the big companies buying everything. The electric bill is so expensive these days. Then you have tenants complaining all the time about the noise. There's crime. Is it my fault? I try my best.

I fix the security door. The next step is to buy a camera, but how much more can I put into this building? How much? It's never good enough. Everyone hates the landlord."

"Well, you own something, right?"

"What is that supposed to mean?"

"At least now that my mom's dead you can raise the rent." Her voice cracked. "Would that help pay for your camera?"

"What are you trying to say? I wasn't complaining about your mom. Your mom was good. She was quiet. She had some visitors sometimes… A man used to come around here. A boyfriend, I guess. Rich guy. Who knows? She had friends. She was fine."

"A *boyfriend*?" Margot's mother had never mentioned or expressed romantic interest in anyone, even the occasional shopkeeper at the swap meet who courted her.

"Yeah, some guy, I don't know. I don't get in anyone's business except when they're parked too close to the driveway or whatnot. Some man. Nice car. Mercedes. I always wanted a car like that."

"Fuck," she said to herself. "Was it the person she was yelling at that night?"

"I only heard one voice that night. The boyfriend, he hasn't been around for a while. Months maybe. Who knows? It was in the summer. I don't like to get involved. It's a safe building. No problems here. I don't like to get involved, okay?"

"You could've told the police," Margot said. "About the yelling."

"What for? I was tired and it could've been anyone. I don't need them snooping around here. Do you? Do you think the neighbors like that? What do you think the police are going to do for you? Do you think they care about your mother? Do you know how many die, get robbed, get killed in this city? I don't need any more problems around here. Young ladies like you should focus on getting married, meeting a nice guy, having a family."

She almost told him to go to hell but instead rolled her window up. Yes, he was right; her mother, and women like her, were an inconvenience.

But if she allowed that story to continue to be told, over and over again—that her mother was a nobody, anonymous, an immigrant who couldn't speak the language, another immigrant who worked a job that no one else wanted, another casualty of more important things, a casualty of more important people—she would be letting them win, wouldn't she? She would be allowing them to sweep her mother away like dirt and dust.

She and her mother deserved better than this. But how would she figure out what exactly happened to her mom?

If only she had left Seattle earlier, bought a plane ticket, she could have prevented her mother's death, or at least found her soon after dying, rather than allowing her body to remain alone in that apartment. Why didn't she try to get there earlier? Why did she brush off the fact that something was weird when her mother was not answering the phone?

As soon as she got back home, she'd leave Officer Choi a message about the landlord and the yelling from her mother's apartment, the possible fight last weekend. She'd scour through her mother's belongings. There might be some clue of who her mother might've been with last weekend. Who visited her? And who was this boyfriend in the summer? A boyfriend. That couldn't be right. Her mother had a single-minded focus—work and their survival.

But could the boyfriend have returned? Could they have gotten into a fight? She'd have to find him now.

As the metal gate of the garage opened, chain squeaking and rattling, she realized with an overwhelming, enveloping sadness that a small part of her always wanted her mother to disappear. Not to die, but to leave her alone. She had imagined that kind of loneliness as freedom, but instead, here she was, treading water, without answers, without any land or any relief in sight.

MINA

SUMMER 1987

On the local bus that grunted down the long roads, Mina traveled to work among a mix of people, mostly Latino, Asian, Black, and an occasional white person, usually elderly. Mina had imagined America to be filled with white people as it was in the movies—all John Wayne, Clark Gable, and Cary Grant. She had never seen such a hodgepodge of individuals in one space. Who knew people could exist in quite this way, and could this project, America, even last?

Still unsure of herself, the languages, the gestures around her, she prayed that no one would speak to her. She tried not to make eye contact but watched peripherally, observing. A Latina mother escorted her two children, a girl and boy of about eight or nine, to school. A Black mechanic, jumpsuit greasy from work, rested his eyes, his arms folded into his body like a cocoon. An elderly woman with a walker, who always wore long dresses like a lady going to church, nodded at Mina. Smiling softly, Mina bowed her head in return.

After the past two weeks of stocking shelves at the supermarket, she learned that she preferred the dry goods aisles, which were not as busy as the produce section where customers zigzagged around with carts, asking questions on where to find this or that.

The same cashier from that first time she had shopped at the supermarket would pass, bowing his head, face square, eyes soft and brown. In the aisles, she would see him once or twice per day. And something about the fact that he would walk by, limbs lithe, acknowledging her without asking for anything, comforted her, put her at ease, unlike the customers or the owner, Mr. Park, who always wanted to chat. Perhaps she simply enjoyed looking at him—handsome, energetic—rushing past, but always stopping briefly to meet her eyes and smile. She still didn't know his name.

On her first day of work, she had showed up in a white short-sleeved blouse tucked into a floral skirt of blues and greens and pinks that reminded her of Monet's water lilies, which seemed inappropriate for breaking down boxes and stocking produce and shelves of dry goods all day. But she didn't care. She didn't have much to wear and wanted to look good. Meeting strangers always made her nervous. Dressing up a little and putting on some makeup boosted the scant amount of confidence she had.

After checking in with one of the cashiers her first day, she had met the owner, Mr. Park, who was only a few years older than her and incandescent like a man who enjoyed the finer things in life—beach vacations, imported cars, golf. Accentuating his tan, he wore a polo shirt of striped pastel colors, a large gold watch.

"You sure you can do this?" he asked, grinning in a condescending way as if observing a small animal who suddenly did something human, like a mouse walking on rear legs.

"Yes, I think so," she said.

"A lot of lifting." He sucked between his teeth.

"I can do it," she said with resolve, unable to hide her annoyance.

She spent half of her first day in the produce section alongside a man in his early thirties named Hector. Wearing an old black T-shirt, sneakers, and jeans, he walked with a small limp, which didn't slow him down as he demonstrated how to stack the fruit so that they wouldn't fall. He carted out the boxes from the back, and she emptied them out, apple after apple, pear after pear—a simple system that worked despite different languages and backgrounds.

At first, the job hadn't seemed so bad in its mindlessness, almost meditative. But after about four hours, exhausted and drinking a 7-Up in the back of the store, sitting, waiting for her next task, she felt utterly dismantled, as if she had been one of those cardboard boxes, unloaded and broken down. Her white blouse had become dirty and wrinkled. She tried not to think at all, tilting her head back and feeling the fizzy drink fill her mouth. But a part of her, no matter how hard she tried, wanted to cry. She felt like an idiot for abandoning her comfortable desk job where she spent most of her hours sketching and designing—yes, boring, but at least accessible— clothes. She missed the coffee and tea breaks and lunches with her coworkers.

But it was only day one. She had to keep trying. She couldn't go back now. She closed her eyes and prayed silently, *Please, God. Please help me. Please let me know that it will be okay. Please.*

After her ten-minute break, she stocked shelves with instant noodles, ramen, and moved on to condiments, soup bases, soy sauce, and doenjang. She sweat as she got up and down on her knees to replenish the bottom shelves. Her skirt became filthy, streaked with dirt over the once-pretty pastels. She felt like a fool now for caring so much about how she looked. What did it matter when all she saw were bottles of sauce, vegetables?

She should get used to the nothingness. It was so much better than being at home in Seoul, her empty apartment, all those reminders of the past. She was free now. She was free.

Mr. Park mentioned that eventually she could move to the cash registers up front. But she preferred the lack of social interaction, the invisibility of working in the back or stocking shelves. In the aisles, she could hide, blur into a wall of doenjang. She could disappear in a vacuum of condiments, bottles, and jars. Only the occasional glance of the handsome Korean man mattered. The fact that he appeared younger than her, in a way, made her attraction feel safe. It was silly and harmless.

Yet she also knew that she could not do this work forever. How many years could she spend lifting and kneeling? She was only forty-one, but still she felt day by day her body getting older, hurting microscopically more and more.

Her body had changed dramatically in her thirties from caring for her daughter. She had become strong, but now all she had were food items to lift, to raise. Now all she had was food. If she thought about it too much while working, she started to cry. So she worked harder and faster to kill the pain, the thoughts.

Once, in the back of the store, she had been lifting boxes of soy sauce off the ground onto a rolling cart. A door squeaked open, a slant of light on the floor. Adjusting his waistband, Mr. Park emerged from his office with a large black canvas bag in hand. The wooden grip of a pistol gleamed at his belt.

"Are you sure you can do this?" He winked almost imperceptibly as if he had dust in his eye.

"Yes, I'm fine. Thank you." She tried not to look at him.

"How are you liking America?"

"It's okay. I'm getting by."

"Tough, ha?" He dropped the bag with a dull thud by his feet. Mina had the impression that it was filled with cash. He was on his way to the bank. The gun.

Bending his knees, he loaded one of her boxes onto the cart. "Well, no matter how hard it is, you got to keep going. Keep trying."

"Yeah."

"I worked hard, *very* hard. And now, I'm the owner. I own all of this." He gestured toward the entire building, the entire universe as if it all belonged to him, too. He grinned so widely she could see the gold tooth in his mouth.

Aware of the gun at his side, she stepped back. "That's nice."

"Yeah, I've been here for—what, let me think…1962."

"That's a long time."

"Yeah, but you see what happens when you work hard?"

"Sure, I guess."

"It pays off." He lifted his brows and bent down to pick the bag off the ground.

She wanted to say, *Really?* She didn't buy any of that. Not exactly. It was impossible to believe in a meritocracy when everyone around her, the women she lived with and the people she worked with at the store, could never own a supermarket no matter how hard they worked. They'd be lucky enough to own anything ever. Like her, they'd be renting rooms in houses. Everything in their lives would be hand-me-downs. Who did this smarmy man think he was? He probably thought she was some lonely woman he could tease and would be grateful for his attention, any attention.

She remembered her husband always had so much faith in her. He would never speak to anyone this way. He treated her like an equal. That may have been unconventional, but that was why she loved him so much.

"Yes, work hard, make money. All goes somewhere. Not a waste at all."

"Okay," she said, trying not to roll her eyes. Bending her knees, she picked up a box from the floor. He grabbed the cart, stabilizing it.

Using her foot, she pulled the cart back from his grip. "I got it." She hauled the box on top and pushed it through the strip door out into the aisles, relieved to get away from him.

Mina didn't know the other renter's name, but that didn't matter much. She referred to her as female friends do in Korea—unnie, "older sister." The other renter spoke English well, with even a bit of a Southern accent, a twang that sounded out of the Westerns Mina's husband had watched. Unnie helped her set up her first phone account and shared all her maps and bus information so that Mina could get around town more easily.

Unnie loved Asian pears and tangerines so Mina would carry home a few of those, as well as something refreshing and cold, such as sikhye—a malted rice drink—which happened to have been her daughter's favorite, too. On a hot night, Mina could drink a gallon of sikhye in a single sitting, but she restricted herself to a glass after dinner when she'd rest sometimes in the dining nook, damp with sweat, listening to the crickets through the open windows and the landlady watching the Korean news.

Because unnie often worked at night, only if their schedules permitted, she and Mina sat down to eat together, once or twice per week. They would talk about the day usually, or America in general, or unnie would translate a document, a billing statement for her, and that was it. They would never go into each other's rooms where unnie read large English novels or listened to classical music that, even muffled through her door, elevated the entire house—notes connected and smooth.

One night in late July about a month after she had arrived in Los Angeles, Mina went into the kitchen, which smelled of onions and doenjang jjigae, to prepare something simple for dinner, enough to fill her stomach so she could go back to bed and fall asleep to the sound of the crickets playing their wings. At the stove, unnie stirred a large stainless steel pot.

"How's work?" she asked.

Mina opened their refrigerator. "Oh, it was okay. It's not so bad—could be worse, I guess. How's work at the restaurant?"

"Eh, everything's the same." She glanced at the egg in Mina's hand and smiled. "I'm making some more jjigae. Would you like some?"

"That's okay, you've been too nice to me already."

"Don't worry about it. You look tired. Let's eat together." She grabbed the egg from Mina's hand before opening the fridge and placing it back in its carton. "Just have a seat. I'll take care of this."

Mina arranged paper napkins on the vinyl place mats along with spoons and chopsticks. Who did this woman remind her of? Maybe one of the nuns at the orphanage? So many of those years, and the people within them, had all been a blur that she had blocked out of her mind—first through work, then through marriage and family.

After eating together for several minutes in silence, Mina asked, "How long have you been living here?"

"A couple years."

"In America?"

Unnie laughed. "No, just in this house. I've been in America longer than that. I used to live in Texas. Do you know Texas?"

"I've heard of it. Yes."

Unnie wiped her mouth. "Why did you come to LA?"

"My friend, a coworker from Seoul, lives here now. I haven't been able to meet up with her yet. She's always at her dry-cleaning shop." She tried to smile. "But I'll see her this Sunday at church. She's going to pick me up." The prospect of reuniting soon with Mrs. Shin, whom she hadn't seen in years, had been a bright spot in her life.

"I see. That's good you have a church."

"What about you? Do you go to church?"

"No."

The silence engulfed them again until the end of their meal when Mina stood to wash the dishes, eager to surrender to her bed.

And as the weeks passed, Mina could understand why unnie avoided church.

Although mostly well-meaning, the women there asked Mina about whether or not she had a husband, kids, as if they had forgotten her vague response from the week before. She wanted to lie and say that she never had either, just to avoid talking with them, but the women, without being explicit, looked down upon those who couldn't marry. How could an attractive woman who had lived all her life in Korea, a country full of Korean men, not meet anyone? Something must be wrong with her. But what?

One Sunday, Mina and her friend Mrs. Shin sat with the other women in the dim downstairs dining area of the church after service for a lunch of gimbap, room-temperature japchae, and kimchi. After bearing their usual prodding questions, Mina finally became fed up with trying to avoid the stigma. She told them the truth.

"They're dead," she said. She said it again, louder. "They're *dead.*"

The women froze, some with their chopsticks raised midair.

"All of them?" the nosiest one asked, food stuck in her teeth.

"Yes, *all* of them." Mina paused. "All two hundred of them." She smiled. "An entire cult. They were all mine."

The women gasped. Beside her, Mrs. Shin choked on a laugh. The nosy one shot her a dirty look and raised her eyebrows at the other women, who fidgeted in their plastic folding chairs.

Mrs. Shin said, "Her daughter and husband are dead. Are all of you happy now? Really?"

After that day, the women avoided her. Perhaps they didn't know how to identify with Mina, a relatively young woman without a family, or they didn't like that joke about the cult. She at least still had Mrs. Shin, who had been in America for a few years already. She was always busy with work, a dry-cleaning business on Vermont Avenue, but after service, they would have lunch at church, or she would invite Mina over to her house where Mina would admire her family, her life. She lived in a large two-bedroom apartment in Koreatown with a funny and kind husband and two awkward teenage kids.

When they sat together eating lunch on Sundays, Mina wanted to tell her all about work but didn't. She wanted to tell her how tired she was, how she hated the boss, but she didn't. Instead, they ate mostly in silence. She asked questions about the kids. But they always avoided talking about Mina's life.

Mrs. Shin hadn't known Mina's husband and daughter well, but enough to imagine what it had been like to lose them. Yet no one knew how to talk about death. As a culture and country, they had so many tragedies from wars already that they persisted in a kind of silent pragmatism that reflected both gratitude for what they had now and an unquenchable, persistent sadness that manifested itself differently in each person. Some had become drunks, surviving off the tenacity of their families in denial. Some had become obsessed with status symbols—luxury cars, designer clothes, and watches. Others worked diligently, a form of numbing the pain that at least had some kind of productive outcome—money in the bank, a roof over their heads, food on the table.

Mrs. Shin tried to fill the silence between them with gossip about people who lived in her building, about women at church. She told Mina about a woman in her forties who cheated on her husband with a younger man.

"She's nuts," Mrs. Shin said. "He's, what, ten years younger than her?"

"*Ten* years?"

"And she's saving up money to run away with him."

They laughed.

"She's crazy," Mrs. Shin continued. "She'll end up pregnant. And then what?"

MARGOT

FALL 2014

The following evening, Margot had returned to the apartment alone after touring apartments for Miguel, close enough to his new job in Burbank, which he'd begin next Monday. He had gone out for a drink with a man that he had met online after Margot assured him she would be okay by herself. He promised to meet her back at the hotel tonight, the same hotel where they had been at since finding her mother.

They considered moving to Margot's mother's apartment in the next couple days to save money. Once Miguel found a permanent place this week, Margot would then stay at her mother's alone until she could finish cleaning and packing or donating their belongings. Her mother had already covered the month's rent, and Margot's supervisor in Seattle had approved extended time off—unpaid.

According to the landlord, her mother had a boyfriend, a

man who visited her often during the summer. Could he be the same person that she had been yelling at last weekend, the same weekend that she had died? Although Margot couldn't quite trust the landlord, he had no reason to lie. She needed to figure out who her mother was with, if anyone, that night. Officer Choi had yet to return her phone call, but she didn't have any more time. She couldn't wait for him or anyone anymore. Her mother's body was proof that sometimes there was not one more hour, one more day, one more week in this life. Sometimes, all you had left was right now—the seconds ticking away.

Margot switched on the overhead light inside her mother's bedroom. Despite the sharpness of the evening air, she had left all the windows open for the past four days to release the smell of death that lingered in her mother's apartment, their apartment, the one they had shared for as long as Margot could remember. She paused to parse through what she could sense outside—a rich red pork pozole next door, a skateboard rattling over cracks in the sidewalk, a woman speaking rapidly on the phone, the exhaust from a choking diesel car—both familiar and strange. This neighborhood had both changed and stayed the same.

Many of the Koreans that she had known as a child had moved out for homes in the suburbs once they had saved enough, and now most of the neighbors were Latino. Yet they all lived here to survive, while longing to be somewhere else. How did the world become a place where jobs and wealth were so concentrated? Why did borders define opportunity? Was it *that* bad for her mother in Korea? Was she more trapped there than here?

Parting the white curtains, Margot looked down at the alley with the garbage bins where the neighborhood kids played soccer and handball up against the side of the building after school and at night. She then looked inside the closet where her mother's clothes hung neatly, unlike Margot's own back in Seattle where every sweater or pair of pants seemed to already be on the floor. Her mother had accumulated and saved so much through the years—nothing of real value but had still meant something to her—a dated leather jacket from the '80s, a cobalt blue dress with large shoulder pads, a simple black sheath, some knee-length skirts from Korea that hadn't fit her for years. Margot dug through the pockets of the pants and jackets, finding coins, faded receipts, a lipstick, small bills.

A pair of black tennis shoes, covered in a fine rust-colored dust, smelled of mineral and sage.

Margot was again reminded of that long drive to Vegas once years ago, more vividly this time. How the hot air whipped her skin through the open windows, caking her face and arms with a fine powder like konggaru on tteok, which she could taste inside her mouth, dry and grainy. Big white clouds hovered above as the world—clay and ocher, brittle and burnt—streaked by. Her mother's eyes, hard as stones, focused on the road. Sweat streamed down the sides of her face and neck.

"Where are we going?" Margot had asked from the back.

"Somewhere very special," her mother said.

"Will there be ice cream?"

"I hope so," she said, eyes softening. "Yes."

"Why are we driving so far for ice cream?" Margot asked in English. She laughed.

"It's not just for ice cream," her mother said in Korean.

"It must be the best ice cream in the world. The biggest ice cream."

Her mother adjusted her collar, cleared her throat. She fidgeted with the radio dial for a minute, frustrated with the shrill sounds, the waves of static, a news reporter's voice, snippets of classical music.

"If you behave well, I'll buy you ice cream. Any flavor you want." Her mother glanced at her in the rearview mirror. A car behind them honked. As he passed on the left, the driver yelled, "Go back to Chinatown, bitch."

Margot flinched as if a stranger had thrown a rock at them. She could see her mother's hands gripping the wheel, knuckles whitening. But she drove on, still dipping below the speed limit.

"Do you want some water?" her mother asked an hour or two later. Margot had fallen asleep.

She was thirsty, but she responded, "No. I'm fine."

"We might…we might meet someone special in Las Vegas." Her voice cracked. "Someone I haven't seen in a long while."

Her mother was trying hard not to cry. Daytime had turned to dusk, a wash of hot-pink streaks and a purple horizon.

"I wonder if this is the right thing to do—bringing you here, on this trip. But I had no one to watch you." It was as if her mother was talking to herself or another adult, rather than attempting to reason with a six-year-old, but only later did Margot realize that as much as she resented her mother for leaning on Margot, her mother was deeply and unimaginably alone.

The only people who did not judge her were God and perhaps Margot as a child.

As they approached the city limits, they stopped at a fast-food restaurant for dinner where they devoured cheeseburgers and fries, much to Margot's delight. When they reached the hotel, her mother collapsed on the bed and fell asleep. It was Margot's first time in a hotel, and she stayed awake all night as if to guard her mother, taking in the new sights and smells. The sheets had a chemical floral scent that was foreign to her. The carpet was extra nubby under her toes. The television appeared huge compared to the one they had at home.

After waiting for an entire day in their hotel room, her mother had seemed so defeated, deflated the next night. Her face and throat were flushed with humiliation. They ordered Chinese food and ate greasy noodles and fried rice, barbecue pork out of the takeout boxes in silence. Afterward, her mother left the bathroom door ajar and ran the hottest water in the tub that she could bear, steaming all the windows, mirrors, glass. She dropped her clothes onto the floor, submerged herself in the tub, her bob tied into a tiny tail, and sweat, glowing red as if preparing herself for a scrub. She lay back, tilted her head, exposing her neck, and closed her eyes.

Margot had been too frightened to approach her mother. She yearned to ask for whom they were waiting, why she was so sad, if she wanted Margot to scratch her back. Margot wondered what she had done wrong, and where was the ice cream her mother had promised her?

Instead she perched on the edge of the couch and watched a PBS show on painting, a bearded man with curly brown hair, dome-shaped, swiftly conjuring the curves and shadows of a dramatic alpine mountain, sublime and white. How foreign, how odd that this landscape, so unlike the one outside their hotel—dry and arid, flame-like on the flesh during the day while sizzling with electric lights at night—could exist on one planet. She fell asleep on the couch, dreaming of the snow, which she had never experienced in real life, splashing her face with the icy water in the clear lake that reflected the peaks above.

The next day, her mother, who wore sunglasses because her eyes were swollen from crying, packed up the car and drove Margot to a Baskin-Robbins, the first time she had ever been to an ice-cream shop. After perusing the marvel of creamy colors—chocolates and pecans and swirls of caramel—she selected one scoop of cookies and cream that dripped down the cone onto her hands, while her mother ordered the strawberry flavor for herself. She had smiled at Margot's delight.

Now, with her mother's dust-covered tennis shoes in hand, Margot went to the living room and picked up one of the travel brochures with a photo of a breathtaking dusky Grand Canyon—all rusty striated peaks and dramatic shadows—that remained on the coffee table. The dust on the shoes matched the specific color of that landscape. Could she have worn these same shoes at the Grand Canyon or a national park? But her mother never would have gone by herself.

Margot would leave a voice mail for the tour company. She didn't expect anyone to pick up on a Sunday night.

But a young woman answered. Her voice was tired and gravelly.

"My mom might have contacted you about a tour?" Margot asked. "And I wanted to see if you had any information on whether she was with anyone or, I don't know, if she went to your office?"

"Uh, I'm not sure we can do that," the woman said, clearing her throat.

"Could you please look into your records? Her name was Mina, Mina Lee." Margot closed her eyes. "She's dead now." Her voice cracked. "And I want to know—"

"Oh, God, I'm so sorry… Hold on." The woman put her on hold for a minute before coming back on the line.

"So, it looks like she took a tour with us on September 12 to the Grand Canyon."

Shocked, Margot asked, "How many days was she there?"

"Three days and two nights."

"Was she…alone?"

"No. She had a guest."

"A guest?"

"We don't have a registered name. She booked a double occupancy room."

"Is there any way—I don't know—is there any way I could talk to the tour guide about this? Maybe someone had seen her?"

"How about I take your number? Is it okay if he calls you back?"

Her mother must have worn these black shoes at the Grand Canyon. But with whom had her mother been traveling? Was it a man or a woman? Why hadn't her mother told her? Had she gotten into a fight of some sort before she died? Why had she been yelling?

Margot felt abandoned and deceived by her mother like never before. What else was her mother hiding? On her hands and knees, Margot searched under her mother's bed, pushing aside shoeboxes full of buttons and spools of thread. In the corner, something shiny flashed. She pulled the wheeled mattress away from the wall, climbed on top, and recognized a condom wrapper. She jumped and shoved the bed back.

Sitting on the floor, she buried her head in her arms crossed over her knees. With an urge to scour, to purge everything, she stood up, wanting to scream. The tacky teddy bear, white but dingy with age, paws sewn into holding a red heart, rested on her mother's bed. She could tear his head off.

Gathering her resolve, she continued to search the apartment. Inside a slouchy brown leather bag, Margot found sticks of gum, church handouts, a small lime-green notebook with some addresses written inside of it. Most of the names were written in Korean and it would take too much effort to read through and try to recognize any of them.

She entered the second bedroom, once hers, where her mother kept bills, paperwork, store receipts, and records. Margot's old clothes remained in the single dresser up against the wall. She needed paper and a pen. She needed somehow to organize now.

In her worn desk that she had purchased in high school at a thrift store, she found a plastic tray full of pencils, color and charcoal, fancy German erasers, sharpeners that Margot had collected and saved, unused, for whatever reason. It was as if she had accumulated all these supplies for the sake of knowing that she would one day use them rather than enjoy them at the time. But what kind of future had she been saving for—the future that she was living in now without any art? She had so many ideas that she had never pursued, so many sketches she had made but abandoned throughout the years. She realized the part of her that dreamed had died somewhere, too, snuffed by a need for practicality, stability, a sense of value in this world, which always seemed to measure you with fixed numbers that had been created for whom, by whom? Not her. Not her mother.

She pulled the tray out of the drawer, stuck half-open, for a better look at what she should take.

Underneath the tray was a business-size envelope with a black-and-white obituary dated in October, cut from the local Korean newspaper inside. The ink of the Korean, which Margot could somewhat read but not understand, rubbed off onto her hands. She struggled, her mind like the fishing net, to catch any word that she could find: *cancer, supermarket, wife, Calabasas, church.*

Even though she had never met him, she knew him in her own face—the squareness of the jaw, maybe even a bit of her own nose and cheekbones. It was like catching a glimpse of herself in a mirror.

Kim Chang-hee.

Here he was finally. Tiny in a black-and-white photo, a stranger she could've passed on the street.

The stranger was now dead. Could he have been Margot's father?

She screamed, shocking herself with the sound that burst from her throat.

MINA

SUMMER 1987

After a month and a half of stocking shelves and carrying produce at the supermarket, Mina felt strong again, the strongest she had been since losing her husband and daughter in Seoul. She felt almost powerful. She didn't necessarily like the way she looked, but she didn't mind. She didn't need a boyfriend. All she needed were the things she had, enough money to get by and save for the future and her health, until it was time for her to die and rise up to meet her family again. That's what heaven was, she thought: the presence of her husband and daughter, the few nuns who had been kind to her at the orphanage, her parents from whom she had been separated in the war.

She remembered vaguely her parents' faces, her mother's smile. The way she would chase after her around the house where she'd hide behind the large dark pillars. The elegant curved roofline. The warmth of the ondol, the heated floors in the winter. The gardens where her mother tended to the cabbage and mu. She remembered the smell of doenjang jji-gae, anchovy stock boiling, the happiness of a sweet red bean porridge. She remembered her mother's voice singing along with music, something vaguely operatic, old. But she had never been able to find that song again. Sometimes she would stop and listen to the radio, waiting again to hear that song, but she never did.

At the supermarket, she had made a few friends, both men and women, mostly Latinos with whom she could hardly hold a conversation. But she learned some Spanish from them, which made her happy. She laughed with them at her inability to pronounce and remember some of the most basic things. She hadn't felt that silly since her husband and daughter had died last October.

Hector, who had been helping her since day one, and Consuela, a stout woman with a thin ponytail, would ask, "¿Cómo estás, amiga?" to Mina, and she would respond, "¿Bueno, y tú?"

"Bien," they would correct her. And they'd all laugh.

They taught her the names of produce—naranja, limón, las uvas.

She had trouble with the letters *l* and *v*. But she recited these words as she displayed the fruit, careful not to let them bruise. It felt good to not take herself too seriously, to see herself through the eyes of someone else.

She tried to reciprocate by teaching them Korean, but they already knew most of the words that would be useful to their work. They knew how to say *hello* and *thank you*. They knew all the numbers (hana, dul, set…), all the names of different produce, the food. She couldn't get over the sight of seeing someone who wasn't Asian speaking her language.

She couldn't get over America.

★ ★ ★

On a Friday morning, two months after she had arrived in Los Angeles, she stood at a cart, wiping sweat from her face before stocking shelves of soft drinks—7-Up, Pepsi, Coca-Cola, fruit-flavored beverages in obscene colors that did not exist in nature. She couldn't believe how much soda people drank in America. She occasionally had a 7-Up when she had a stomachache, but by the looks of it, Americans drank the liquid as frequently as water.

The supermarket owner, Mr. Park, wearing his usual white polo shirt and khakis, approached her slowly with a smile as if he had a little secret to share. Her spine tingled with fear as she froze in place, resisting the urge to run away. He had never done anything untoward, but she hated how he looked at her a shade too long—as if he owned her, too.

"How are you doing?" he asked.

"Fine." The walls of aluminum cans glistened like rounds of ammunition, the bottles like missile shells.

"Making friends?"

"Kind of," she said.

"I heard you're making friends with the Mexicans."

She didn't like those words in his mouth.

"Hector, Consuela," he said.

"Yes, they're very nice." Her legs trembled beneath her.

"They work hard."

"Yes, they do."

"They can't help that they don't, you know...have the business sense." He pointed to the side of his head.

She wanted to ask how he would know that. Did he ever talk to them? He was the idiot, creepy and insensitive. Hanging by her side, her hand tightened into a fist.

"At least they work hard, you know?" he repeated.

"Yes." She exited her body, a shell, as his eyes meandered

down. She fixed her eyes on the linoleum floor, speckled like birds' eggs. Mina had been hiding in the storeroom and the aisles among the boxes and bottles and jars, but in reality, pinned down by his gaze, she had been exposed here, too.

"Anyway, I thought this would be a good time to move you to the cash registers." He smiled. "One of our workers is retiring."

She might be safer surrounded by more people.

"That—that would be great," she said.

"Want to start next week?" he asked.

"Sure." Overcome with relief, her eyes grew wet.

"Just come in and ask one of the cashiers for Mr. Kim, okay? He'll help you." He winked.

"Mr. Kim? Okay."

"Good job." Those words were like hands trying to touch her.

As soon as he walked away, tears fell down her cheeks. She could taste the salt, like the ocean. Hastily, she wiped her face.

Although she enjoyed the company of Hector and Consuela and the other workers who greeted her with a smile, a wave, or a nod every day, she would get paid more as a cashier, a job that would also be easier on her body. She *was* getting older after all. Her stiff joints and muscles reminded her of this daily.

Later that afternoon, she joined Hector in restocking the produce section, which had become quickly depleted earlier that day. As they worked (him grabbing and delivering carts stocked with leafy greens and root vegetables, and her neatly piling them), she thought that maybe she should she tell him that she was leaving the floor. Maybe he would think it would be strange if she didn't tell him, and one day he found out that she was working at the registers. But she didn't know how. She wasn't sure about the words, and she didn't want to offend him.

"I... Monday... I go at cash register," she said in English.

"You?" he said.

"Yes, me."

"Oh, good, good." He smiled with warmth, as if patting her on the back. "Good. You do a good job, okay?"

"Okay."

He stacked the floppy red leaf lettuce with her in silence.

She could sense his resignation. Hector and Consuela had been in their jobs forever.

Dealing with Korean customers directly required the Korean language, sure, but at the same time, Hector and Consuela already knew a lot of Korean, and would learn more if they thought it would make their lives easier. It was obvious why she was getting promoted over them.

She wanted to explain to him, to make him feel better, that she wasn't strong enough to do this job, but both of them knew that was not the truth. The truth was something that would make them both uncomfortable and sad. This was already his expectation. This was already his experience. So she said nothing until the end of her shift.

"Hasta luego." She tried to smile.

"Hasta luego," he said, without quite meeting her eyes.

On Monday, Mina met Mr. Kim, the same man who occasionally greeted her in the aisles, for training. He was indeed a few years younger than her, with his smooth dark skin, square face, high cheekbones, a shy smile that was slightly lopsided on the right. He was not tall, about the same height as Mina, so when he spoke to her, he looked her straight in the eyes, which made her feel self-conscious. She felt dowdy in her slacks and pink polo shirt, her worn tennis shoes.

As he showed her the buttons on the register and the form to fill out for the reports, recording the exact change in the register at the beginning and end of her shifts, she couldn't help but stare at his arms—thin but muscular, covered in a pale down. She always liked arms. And it gave her something to look at besides his face.

On her first day at the register, she was a little slow with the cash, and the customers grew impatient, eyeing her, too busy with their own lives, their own worries to recognize that she was new and trying to learn as quickly as possible.

"That's a twenty. Give me back $3.15."

"Okay."

"No, here. Let me make this easier for you. I have exact change."

She was still getting used to the dollar, the denominations, the feel of it, the way each bill appeared the same but different, the sizes of the coins. Fortunately, the bagger whom she worked with, Mario, with his spiky hair but soft demeanor, was patient. He helped her with the breakdown of the cash or smiled and apologized in Korean to the customers as she stood there, perplexed, having to use a part of the brain that had grown rusty over the years with disuse. He spent his time between customers helping Mr. Kim or the other cashiers lift large sacks of rice or boxes of produce onto carts.

After a few hours, she understood the subtleties of the barcode scanner. She memorized some of the codes for the more popular produce. She received and doled out money automatically.

Although the job was less physically demanding, the presence of all the customers waiting in line for her to do her job quickly while being friendly exhausted her. All those eyes. The nervousness she experienced as a customer watched her scan each item, ensuring that she was charging them correctly. Sure, she would get used to it. Eventually, the customers would become like the bottles of soy sauce that she stocked on the shelves, just another component of the repetitive, ultimately unfeeling nature of her job.

Spinach. Doenjang. Thin rice noodles. Large sack of rice. Garlic. Bean-flavored popsicles. Two oranges. A bag of ginger.

A six-pack of Hite. A bag of potato chips. A bundle of green onion.

At the end of the shift, Mr. Kim, harried and rushed, came

by to check in on her. Sweat ran down the sides of his face. Nonetheless, he tried to be as generous and gentle with her as possible. He asked her if she had any questions, checking the remaining cash in her register up against what she had logged in her binder. He wiped his forehead with his bare arm. She handed him a paper napkin she had in her pocket.

"Thank you," he said in English, smiling.

"No...problem?" She laughed, realizing she still couldn't pronounce the letter *L*.

"Good job today."

"Thank you!" Their eyes met, and she returned his smile.

On the way home, she sat at the front of the bus, staring into space, transfixed, her mind numb. She wanted to go home, shower, and close her eyes. She wished she had a television to distract herself from the sadness that she felt rising within her. Had she made a mistake? Would she be able to survive the glares, the impatience of the customers? Would she be able to handle the steady flow of interaction when all she wanted to do was to be left alone, to not think or feel, with only the physical pain of work transcending to numbness like a drug?

She understood how delicious and easy it was to become an addict. A few times, she had drunk herself unconscious after her husband and daughter died. After burying them, she wanted to throw herself in that same ground. She would drink and end up with a splitting headache the next day, crawling to the bathroom and vomiting.

But she couldn't have gone on that way. The most important thing now was to be good, to work hard, to make it to heaven, where she would be reunited with them someday. That was all that mattered now. Not even Mr. Park, his words like hands lingering too long, could stop her.

Sitting at the front of the bus, swaying with its movement, she told herself that she'd be fine. She'd get used to the registers, the cash, the people, and if not, she could always ask to move back to stocking shelves, or she could go somewhere else. She could find another job. And once she felt a bit more stable financially, she could find a lawyer that would help her stay in the country permanently. Thinking of the darkness of her days in Seoul, that apartment, the streets her husband and daughter once walked upon, she could never go back to Korea.

The place had become a graveyard.

She looked up at the bus driver, a Black woman about her age with a short bob curled inward. This woman had spent her hours within the confines of the bus, trying to do her job, navigating through traffic, yet also having to respond to the steady needs of riders on the bus, who could be either kind and friendly or harried and rude. The woman had the responsibility of driving all these people to their homes or jobs every day.

The driver glanced back at Mina.

"You doin' all right?"

"Me?"

"You all right?"

"Yes, thank you."

Mina wanted to say something else. But she didn't know what or how.

Should she ask how *she* was doing? No, that would be awkward.

Was the bus driver concerned about her? Or had Mina been staring too long at her, making her uncomfortable?

Mina got off the bus as quickly as possible and walked less than half a block to the house. Inside, she unlocked her room where she gathered her pajamas and a towel so that she could shower, rinse the day off (all that currency, the counting, the impatient customers, Mr. Kim's English *thank you*, his smile). She needed to clear her head, relax.

As she touched the knob to open her door, she overheard

the landlady say, "Mrs. Baek," down the hall toward the other renter's room.

That was unnie's name.

MARGOT

FALL 2014

Across from her mother's gated-up shop was the children's clothing store of her mother's friend Alma— likely one of the last people to have seen her mother. Perhaps Alma had noticed something or someone suspicious at that time.

Margot and Miguel stepped into Alma's booth, empty of people. Baby and children's clothes hung from fixtures along the walls and on rounders and racks. Little superhero sweater sets for boys, and princess and pony ones for girls.

"Maybe she's in the bathroom." Margot exited the shop, ducking beneath a tiny white dress wrapped in plastic. Miguel followed.

"Should we wait a little?" he asked.

"Let's open my mom's store and see if we can find anything there. We'll be able to see if she comes back."

Margot's mother worked in a swap meet called Mercado de

la Raza, an old warehouse with a tin roof, high ceilings, and concrete floors filled to the brim with stores. It was located southeast of LA—a dusty landscape of dilapidated factories and fruit vendors gripping bags of oranges on street corners—where a mostly working-class Latino population flourished, carving a community for themselves among the ruins of the defense and manufacturing industries.

Locals gathered on the weekends at swap meets that bumped banda and norteño music. Men with face and neck tattoos roamed the walkways in peace with their children. Families and churches rented a covered corner of the parking lot of the swap meet as a staging area for performances, religious gatherings, quinceañeras.

In this topography intersected by railroad tracks, where garbage and large objects (mattresses, used furniture, broken shopping carts) once destined for landfills disintegrated, Margot's mother, Mina, and other Korean Americans made a living because of the relatively cheap rent for their stores. Even Koreatown proved too competitive and too expensive, so they found themselves adrift in South Central or Bell or Huntington Park, working long hours, sometimes seven days per week, behind counters in places that felt continentally far from both literal and figurative homes.

Margot had detested following her mother to the store on the weekends and weekdays during summer and winter breaks when she imagined children all over the world enjoying their middle-class vacations, tumbling in white sand or green grass. Instead, she had spent her days off from school in the store among plastic hangers and clothing smelling of the factories from which they came, while her mother, in her exhaustion, sometimes even yelled at customers.

Amiga! Amiga! she would holler in her Korean accent to shoppers after they had perused some of the items on the racks and walked away. That image and sound had been seared into Margot's memory—the sight of women's backs in departure while her mother tried to speak in their language. *Amiga! Amiga! I show you something.* The sadness, no, maybe the courage of the unheard. *Amiga! Amiga!* To women who didn't need another friend. The pitch and tone of her mother's voice, during some of their most desperate moments, when her mother hadn't been sure if she could pay the rent or buy groceries, resembled that of a woman thrown overboard, treading water, calling out to other women who drifted by on rowboats.

As Margot navigated the swap meet now, the dirtiness of the surroundings settled into her. She was terrified that Miguel—someone from her middle-class life in Seattle of dishwashers, fleece, and stainless steel water bottles—would finally see this other side of her life, how she grew up. She had been ashamed for so long of her home, her mother's work, her life. But why?

Perhaps sprawling lawns and shopping malls were one version of the American dream, but this was another. She could see that now. Maybe it was not mainstream, maybe it was not seen with any compassion or complexity on television or in the movies, because it represented all that middle-and upper-class people, including Margot, feared and therefore despised: a seemingly inescapable, cyclical poverty. But in actuality this was the American dream for which people toiled day and night. People had left their homelands to be here, to build and grow what they loved—family, friendship, community, a sense of belonging. This was their version of the dream.

Margot unlocked the rusted accordion gate with the lump of keys she had found in her mother's purse, jerking it open enough for them to slide inside—a women's version of Alma's store, jam-packed with clothing. Slinky cocktail dresses, tight tops with shoulder cutouts, and conservative, embroidered blouses for older women hung on display from the walls, along with jeans that had safety-pinned signs, handmade from colored construction paper and permanent marker: sale $20.

On the dusty glass counter, a ceramic Virgin Mary, a twin to the fractured one in her mother's living room, stood by the cash register. Its drawer was empty and open—the sad broken lip. Her mother had always left the machine ajar to ward off thieves, as if to say, *Nothing here. Please go away.*

Margot searched her mother's usual hiding spot for the cash change she kept, underneath a bunch of free holiday calendars in one of her display cases for costume jewelry—rhinestone necklace and earring sets, large beaded hoops, plastic bangles—accessories that she hoped customers would buy to go with the clothing they had purchased. Margot found a roll of ones, fives, and tens rubber-banded together.

"Well, the money's all here," she said, standing up from behind the display case, only to see that Miguel hadn't followed her into the shop.

In the center of the walkway between stores, Miguel was speaking to Alma, who was crying and blotting her eyes with a wad of tissue. Margot stashed the cash in her cross-body purse and joined them. Alma reached out her arms for a hug, and Margot fell into them.

She had known Alma for about twenty years, since after the LA riots—all that shattered glass and black smoke—that had destroyed her mother's first store, a couple miles away in another, much tidier swap meet, where the individual shops each had proper walls and rollup steel gates. Alma had watched Margot grow up across the aisle between their stores—an aisle both narrow with the merchandise racks that overflowed, and immeasurably wide because of the different languages and cultures between them, oceanic in distance. Alma's round face and plump skin hardly seemed to age as Margot went through each awkward stage of her own development—a shy only child with pigtails or a neat bob, a preteen who bleached and dyed her hair navy blue in the middle of the night and smoked cigarettes after school, and a much more conservative college student who understood that getting a degree might be the only way of escaping this life.

Tears spilled from Margot's eyes. Alma pulled away and put her hands on Margot's cheeks and said, "Pobrecita," hugging her again.

"When was the last time you saw her?" Miguel asked in Spanish.

"The last time I saw her was...about two weeks ago," Alma said as they parted. "Before Thanksgiving. Maybe the weekend before Thanksgiving."

Wiping her eyes, Margot could understand most of the Spanish in a casual context, but as with her Korean, she struggled with putting words together on the spot. Her fear of sounding silly or being misunderstood acted as a sieve through which all language had to pass. Any speaking, even in English, often proved difficult for this reason, but foreign languages had a more gelatinous texture in her mind, flowing even more slowly to and from her mouth.

"She took the entire weekend off?" Margot asked in English to herself. "That doesn't make sense." Margot's mother worked on every holiday, including Thanksgiving and Christmas, when she closed the store a few hours earlier than usual. On Thanksgiving Day, they'd sometimes order chicken from KFC—extra crispy drumsticks and thighs that they'd dip in hot sauce. And Wednesday was the only day that the entire swap meet closed on a regular basis. This meant that Alma must've seen her mother last on the Tuesday before the Saturday or Sunday when her mother died.

"Did you notice anything strange or different about her?" Miguel asked.

"She did seem sad these past couple months," Alma said. "Very sad."

"Do you know why?" Margot asked.

"At first, I thought maybe something happened to you, but when I asked her, she said you were fine, that you had a good job, you liked Seattle a lot." She blew her nose. "Then I thought maybe...she was having some kind of emergency, like a family emergency or a death, in Korea, and that's why she's been gone so long." She motioned for Margot and Miguel to wait as she grabbed a box of tissues from her store. "I thought she was in Korea this whole time. Maybe someone in her family had died, or someone was sick. I could tell that she was very sad about something or someone."

The obituary that Margot had found last night: *cancer, supermarket, wife, Calabasas, church.* Seeing the photograph, tiny and black-and-white, was like staring at a ghost of herself. She could feel herself sinking under the waves, the salt of the seawater in her mouth. It was all too much—first, her mother's death, an accident; then, a potential murder; and now, a possible father gone forever. Was her mother grieving him? Was he the same boyfriend, the visitor with the fancy car, the Mercedes that the landlord had mentioned to Margot? Why else would she have saved his obituary? He had to be important to her mother. But if he had died in October, at whom had her mother been yelling?

Was her mother's death really an accident?

In the walkway made narrow by the amount of merchandise displayed by each store, a woman who sold champurrado from a wheeled cart squeezed behind Margot, Miguel, and Alma, leaving a trail of hot chocolate, cinnamon, and masa in the air.

"Did she have any visitors?" Miguel asked.

"No, not that I know of." Alma paused, reaching for Margot's hand. "Do you want some water?"

"No, no, thank you."

"She talked a lot with the Korean lady over there." Alma gestured to a store somewhere behind hers. "Do you know her? The one with the sock shop?"

"The sock shop?"

"Yes, socks, underwear, pajamas, stuff like that." She blew her nose again. "She's kind of new, opened her store earlier this year. They became friends fast, or they seemed to be friends already, very close."

Margot asked Alma if she could keep an eye on her mother's unlocked store as they left to find the sock shop owner. Around the corner, in the maze of mostly makeshift stalls, each store blasted its own genre of Spanish-language music (pop, bachata, banda), punctuated by the distant cry of a caged pet-shop bird or a section of lullabies emitting from plastic toys. At the sight of tiered displays on wheels with stacks of white socks sold in bundles forming half of the perimeter of a store, Margot and Miguel paused.

"This must be the place," she said.

Seductive lingerie hung above the entryways, lacy corsets and nightgowns filled with the breasts of wire-framed hangers shaped into the torsos of women. One pair of scarlet panties, which came with a matching teddy, had a cartoon elephant face and snout at the crotch.

Under the brash fluorescent light, the store owner stood leaning on a glass display case with rows of conservative, pastel cotton panties stacked inside. With her head bowed and a ballpoint pen in hand, she studied the classifieds of the Korean newspaper. She looked up as Margot and Miguel walked into her shop.

Margot couldn't help but start at the sight of her face—elegant, long, out of place. Although perhaps in her sixties, she wore bright red lipstick, which seemed tacky and beautiful and

defiant all at once. Her eyebrows were perfectly penciled crescents, like slivers of the moon. A midnight blue fleece peacoat
with pills along the sleeves swaddled a slender dancer's frame.

Margot bowed her head. "Uh, my Korean is really bad."

"That's okay," the woman said in English with a Southern
accent that surprised Margot. "Can I help you?"

"Did you know the owner of the women's clothing store
over there?"

"Yes. Yes, of course," she said, voice shaking.

"We were just wondering when the last time you saw her
was," Miguel said.

"She—she's been gone for a while." She squinted, laying the
pen down. "I've been worried about her. Why do you ask?"

"I'm her daughter," Margot said. "This is my friend
Miguel."

The woman widened her eyes, then squinted, creasing the
foundation on her face.

"Oh," she said, as if she had just recognized Margot somehow.

But Margot didn't find her familiar at all. She could tell that
the sock lady, like Margot's mother, might have been beautiful
once. The theater of her face told a story, and a rich, sad one at
that. Women like her and her mother were always struggling
to stay above water, their faces floating on top while their legs
treaded frantically underneath. They might wash up dead on
the shore one day—like her mother on the carpet.

"You've changed so much," the woman said, breathless.

"Excuse me?"

"I didn't recognize you at first. Your hair. I guess you
wouldn't remember me." The woman pointed to herself. "Mrs.
Baek?"

"No." Margot shook her head. "I don't remember you at
all."

Mrs. Baek exhaled with a loud puff and smiled tenderly. "We all lived in the same house together until you were maybe three or four." Her eyes softened, revealing a touch of sentimentality that surprised Margot, who had no recollection of that time before the riots, before the apartment that they lived in now. According to her mother, when she had first arrived in Los Angeles from Korea in 1987, she had rented a room in a house, gotten pregnant with Margot, and lived there for a few years until the landlady died in 1991. She had then purchased the landlady's clothing store at a discount from the landlady's adult children, the same shop that would be mostly destroyed one year later in the riots. At the time she had purchased that first store, her mother had moved herself and Margot to their apartment in Koreatown. She had never mentioned Mrs. Baek or any housemates.

"Your mother used to bring you to the restaurant that I worked at, Hanok House. Do you remember? It looked like an old traditional house, lots of wood everywhere."

"I don't remember that," Margot said, a little embarrassed.

For a few seconds, Mrs. Baek's face shattered as if the memory had smashed something open that she had been guarding inside. Her red lips hardened into a line. Margot could sense Mrs. Baek closing off somehow. She had to reel her back in. She needed answers.

"Why did we stop going to the restaurant? Hanok House?"

"Your mother became…very busy after she opened her store. And when she lost that store in the riots…she had to work so much. It was a very difficult time. A lot of people lost everything—their businesses, their jobs. There was no time for anything but trying to recover, to survive. It was almost like living through the war again."

Margot remembered stacks of smoke rising, blackening the air with a noxious chemical smell. A few miles from their apartment, the world had been on fire. On television, there had been a grainy black-and-white video of police officers beating Rodney King, an unarmed Black man, who later said, "It made me feel like I was back in slavery days."

There were somber white men in suits, an acquittal. Bricks thrown, glass smashed, gates trampled. Buildings ignited into infernos that released towers of smoke into the sky. The National Guard stood on street corners in camouflage with large guns.

Her mother cried in front of the television set. Her store, too, had been destroyed. Owning a business where she didn't have a boss yelling at her, a place where she could bring her child to work, seemed too good to be true. All of it would be shattered, too. Because their life would be part of the lie that this country repeated to live with itself—that fairness would prevail; that the laws protected everyone equally; that this land wasn't stolen from Native peoples; that this wealth wasn't built by Black people who were enslaved but by industrious white men, "our" founders; that hardworking immigrants proved this was a meritocracy; that history should only be told from one point of view, that of those who won and still have power. So the city raged. Immolation was always a statement.

Her mother's life was just one life in this wreckage. Margot was there to wade with her in what was left, salvaging together what they could. Their family of two might've been the smallest country, but it was the only place where they belonged in this world.

Margot wept, surprising herself. She didn't think she had any more tears left in her today.

"Are you all right?" Mrs. Baek asked, reaching out and squeezing Margot's hand. "I know that was a difficult time. That was a very difficult time."

Miguel wrapped his arm around Margot's shoulders. She

had been embarrassed about bringing him to her mother's store—that he would see how poor she had been—but now she was grateful he was there. He was like her in so many ways; they could both cry or laugh, *feel* on a dime.

"How'd you end up here?" Margot asked, sniffling.

Mrs. Baek handed her a napkin. "I got tired of working at the restaurant, so I saved and bought this shop in March earlier this year. This was the only place that I could afford. It's hard, but it's a little easier than working at the restaurant. I'm not on my feet all the time." She focused again on Margot. "Your mom hasn't been around for a while. I thought maybe she had gone to visit you, or maybe she had gone to Korea. Is someone sick?"

In eight years, her mother had never visited Margot in Seattle, not even for her graduation, and couldn't afford to miss more than a day off work. To Margot's knowledge, her mother hadn't been on an airplane since she had arrived in the US twenty-seven years ago.

"She's...dead," Margot said, beating back the images that swelled of how tiny her mother had appeared on the ground. How Margot had fallen to her knees, screaming. "She died two weekends ago."

Mrs. Baek gasped, covering her mouth with both hands, eyes welling with tears.

"When was the last time you saw her?" Miguel asked.

"A couple of weeks ago," she said, voice trembling. A streak of red lipstick now on her cheek. She cried, dabbing under her eyes, pink and swollen. Eyeliner streaked gray down her face.

"Did anything seem off?" he asked.

"Yes," she said, catching her breath. "She...had been depressed for a while." She squeezed the napkin in her fist.

"Alma, her friend with the children's clothing store, said the same thing." Miguel glanced at Margot.

"Do you know why?" Margot asked. "Did she mention anything?"

Mrs. Baek's hands shook as she smoothed down the crinkled pages of the classifieds on which she had been leaning. It was obvious that she was considering what to tell Margot, like a grown-up protecting a child. Margot wanted to say, *There's nothing you need to hide from me anymore. I'm an adult now. I need to know.*

"She was struggling. We've all been struggling, you know? There's hardly any customers these days. It's gotten so much worse. Nobody wants to come to a swap meet anymore. You should see the bathrooms, how dirty everything is now. The owner, the manager—no one cares about us anymore." Fresh tears leaked out of Mrs. Baek's eyes. She shook her head. "When did she die?"

"Over Thanksgiving weekend," Miguel said. "We were driving down to LA. Margot found her on Wednesday—"

Mrs. Baek covered her mouth again. "Oh my God."

"She had fallen down somehow. She hit her head."

"Oh my God." She held her head as if she might faint.

"The landlord heard her yelling at someone over the weekend." Margot's voice trembled, recalling the conversation in the garage. "He said she had a boyfriend of some kind, a man who visited her over the summer, and maybe I thought someone would…know who he is, or maybe if he was involved somehow."

Rubbing the space between her brows, eyes closed, Mrs. Baek exhaled out loud.

"Do you know him? Do you know how I can—"

"That's why she was depressed," Mrs. Baek said.

"What?"

"He died in October." She wiped the corners of her eyes.

"So it couldn't have been *him* that was with her that night," Miguel said.

"*With* her?" Mrs. Baek asked.

"That's what we're trying to find out," Margot said. "Who was with her the night she died."

"What was his name?" Miguel asked.

"I—I don't know."

"Was it Chang-hee Kim? Mr. Kim?" Margot asked.

"Oh, yes, Mr. Kim." Mrs. Baek nodded. "I didn't even know about him, their relationship..." her voice rising "...until after he died." She propped herself up, elbows on the counter. "She was so depressed these past couple months, I kept pushing her to tell me what was wrong. Maybe something had happened to you." She shook her head. "Finally, she told me about him." She wiped her nose with a napkin.

"So, she kept him a secret from everyone?" Margot asked.

"She was ashamed, I guess. He was married." Mrs. Baek's voice cracked. "What was she thinking?" She sobbed, grabbing another napkin from inside the glass counter to wipe her face.

What would be the chances of this lover, the man in the obituary, being Margot's father? Maybe Margot had deluded herself into thinking that he would be out there somewhere, that he would appear in her life somehow—dead or alive. Maybe she only wanted to see herself in him to solidify the mythology of her life, to make it real. But the only thing real was her mother's body on the ground, and the knowledge that her mother was in a relationship with a married man, now dead as well.

"Could she have confronted my mother? The wife. Could the wife—"

"I don't know. Maybe? Your mother never said much about her. I wouldn't know that."

"Why would she do that if her husband was already dead though?" Miguel asked. "Why? What would be the point?"

"I don't know," Margot said. "Maybe his wife found out something else, something that pissed her off even more. Or maybe it took a couple months to realize, after his death, that he was cheating on her? So she confronted my mom. Maybe she wanted answers. Either way, we have to find her."

Mrs. Baek nodded as she wept again. Her friend, Margot's mother, was now gone. Her makeup had become a mess—streaks of gray down her cheeks, lipstick smeared. She coughed through her tears, shuddered with a specific loneliness, one that Margot could recognize from her own mother. It was the loneliness of being an outsider.

MINA

SUMMER 1987

As her speed and confidence on the register grew, Mina began observing the different customers and their items. She tried to piece together their lives as she scanned and entered in codes.

White mushrooms. Three packs of tofu. Green onions. Garlic. Dried anchovies. Five Pink Lady apples. A bag of oranges. Toothpaste.

She even invented little games for herself, estimating how much a bag of produce would cost before she weighed it. Or guessing what a customer would make with her purchased items.

Kimchi jjigae. Braised mackerel with radish. Seafood pancakes.

Mario, who must have been only eighteen or nineteen years old, worked with her almost every day now. He said hello, smiled more often. But he still always seemed distracted, running from one task to the next. He meticulously stuffed

purchases into plastic bags, went off to help lift or carry something, and appeared just in time to bag items for the next person in line. He had a whole system for how he would manage
his job most efficiently. All the other baggers in the other
aisles, whom Mina had met several of, seemed to have similar routines. Occasionally, they would stop and say something
to each other, joke, but only for a few seconds before they
plunged back into work again.

During the slower hours, Mario spent his time organizing
and restocking items up front, while Mina restocked and ti-
died the smaller items on display by the registers—the drinks
and candies and snacks. She sometimes saw Hector and Consuela, either at the back of the store or at the registers as they
came forward to do go-backs or grab last-minute items for
customers. They still greeted each other with a nod, a smile,
or an hola, but now never spoke to each other beyond that.
The camaraderie had been lost.

She said hello to the other Korean cashiers in the store, but
they rarely talked as well. All of them seemed bored and unhappy, checking in to do their job and checking out, perhaps
running home to their families. Perhaps her life was easier,
not having to run around all the time, cooking, cleaning,
dropping kids off at and picking them up from school, disci-
plining them, hugging them, kissing them. Perhaps her life
was easier, but she couldn't help but feel an emptiness as she
thought of the lives her coworkers might have. The fullness
that she missed.

Whenever a little girl at the register reminded her of her
own lost daughter, Mina's body trembled with a mix of terror
and exhilaration. Her eyes welled up, but she always caught
herself before she actually cried. Gripping the sides of the
counter, she steadied herself as much as she possibly could.
Staring at the stream of items to enter, the cash to collect and

return, she did not make eye contact with any customers. She spent the rest of the day trying not to think or feel at all.

Once, a girl about her daughter's age with a father, who looked so much like her husband with his long and sensitive face, arrived at the checkout stand. Was Mina imagining this, or were they back again, like specters from the past? She almost ran around the counter to throw her arms around them. Maybe God was giving her one more chance.

But as soon as the little girl said something to her father in English, Mina realized they were nothing like her own family. They were not the same people at all. The father was much taller and younger than her own husband. The little girl had a different face entirely.

During her bathroom break, she ran into a stall where she sat on the toilet and cried. She tried to be as silent as possible but couldn't help the occasional sob escaping from her mouth. She held her face in her hands, gripping it with the pads of her fingers. She couldn't stop. She knew she had to go back up front, but she couldn't control herself. The pain in her stomach and chest overwhelmed her, as if she was being stabbed with sadness itself.

After blowing her nose, she pressed her palms together and whispered, "Please, God, help me. Please, God. Please. I'll do anything you want. Anything. I promise. Please help me. Help me, please." She did not want to admit this to Him, but secretly she was asking God to keep her from ending everything, from throwing herself in front of the bus, which she thought about sometimes. As the bus pulled to a stop in front of her, she wondered what would happen if she stepped out in front of it. Only the fear of hell kept her alive.

Soon after burying her husband and daughter, she stood on the roof of her apartment building, wondering if it was high enough to die if she jumped. As a teenager at the orphanage, after she had been beaten by one of the nuns, she thought of all the places she could hang herself. But she never quite had the courage to do it. She was too scared of the pain she might feel before dying. Wondering what it would feel like, she would sometimes grab a shirt or a pair of pants, and in the restroom that she shared with the other girls, she'd try to choke herself, but she never got close enough to blacking out. It hurt too much. She couldn't stand the pain.

When she was younger, she didn't even care if she had gone to hell. But now she cared. Now she wanted to survive. How else could she see her daughter again?

Those tiny fingers. That perfect face. The high clear voice. The near-black eyes.

When she emerged from the restroom at work with her face red and eyes swollen, Mr. Kim, who had taken her place at the register after she had been gone longer than usual, dropped the closed sign at her register. Mario pretended not to notice and instead busied himself by preopening several of the plastic bags to ready them for the next customers.

Mr. Kim touched her arm, pulling her aside. "Is something wrong?" he asked.

"Oh, nothing. Nothing. Sorry I was gone for so long."

"Do you need to go home?"

"No, I'm okay."

"I can take you home. You don't look good."

Strutting by in his white polo, khaki pants, and visor as if he was coming from a day of golf, Mr. Park asked, "Something wrong here?"

"Nothing, nothing. Everything's fine." She didn't want Mr. Park to see her face. At the register, she removed the sign and waved at a customer waiting in another line. Mr. Kim stood by her side. As soon as she was done ringing the woman up, he asked, "Can I get you something?"

"No, no. Really, I'm fine."

Hours later in the back of the market, she went to her storage basket, where she kept her snacks, jacket, and spare shoes. Unexpectedly, she found a plastic bag full of fruit—bright tangerines, a soothing green Granny Smith apple, a honey-colored pear—topped with two packages of ramen. One of the tangerines wore a little leaf like a hat. The dimpled flesh was clean and bright and sweet under her nose.

Who had left the bag for her?

She didn't see Mr. Kim for the rest of the day.

As she stood in front of the stop watching the bus approach, she recognized the driver, the woman with the round face and neat bob. The bus slid a few feet past her with a rush of hot air, kicking up dust and leaves, before it halted to a dramatic stop.

Showing her bus pass, Mina asked, "You all…right?" The words surprised her as if they had fallen out of her mouth.

The driver laughed to herself. "Eh. I'm all right. You?"

The exchange calmed Mina. She spent so much of her day ignored, an anonymous face behind a cash register, a person who handled items and money, scanned, punched in numbers.

As she sat on the bench seat, she held the bag of groceries with the fruit and the ramen close to her. She closed her eyes, repeating the words in her mind, *You all right? Are you all right?*

In the kitchen, beneath the glow of a single overhead light, yellow and soft, Mina stared at the shiny green apple, the perfection, the evenness of its skin. And without thinking, she grabbed a knife, winding away its flesh, an undressing. She remembered how, after dinner, she would arrange the slices on a plate for her daughter, who with her small hands and mouth would take her time eating each piece. The bright fruit would fade into brown. So much like everything in nature. The color of the fallen leaves that had died, curled on the grass, sweeping the surfaces of their tombstones in the wind.

Mina dropped the knife in the sink, steadying herself on the counter.

She bit into the half-peeled fruit. She filled a pot with water.

Sitting in the breakfast nook, she slurped on the long ramen noodles, comforted by the salty broth, which soothed her even on a hot day with the air stagnant and dense. She parted the curtains and opened the window next to the nook, staring out through the security bars into the darkness. Would she ever forget her husband, her daughter? Would they wait for her? Remember her in heaven? What was the point? She wondered but felt numb from all the crying. She remembered Mr. Kim and imagined how her face must've looked to him, red and swollen.

She cleared the table, washed her dishes, and wiped down all the surfaces, trying to keep the kitchen as clean and tidy as possible. The landlady wasn't neat herself, often leaving food out accidentally or forgetting to clean up spills on the stove. But Mina wanted everything to be as clean as this old kitchen, with the grease on the walls and the broken cabinet doors, could possibly be.

She reached her arms above her head to stretch before lying down in bed, where she stared at the ceiling. She remembered when she had gotten the news that her husband and daughter had been killed in a terrible accident, when the police officers had arrived at her apartment door. All she could imagine was the horror of their excruciating pain. The red blood seeping from their bodies onto the street.

What had she been doing that day at home? She must've been cooking or cleaning. Or had she been watching television? Was it Sunday or Saturday? She didn't know. Wearing an apron, she had opened the door, and seeing the men in uniform, her heart fell to the floor. She wanted to scream but couldn't. Instead, crying, she had fallen, knees and palms on the ground, begging this life for mercy.

MARGOT

FALL 2014

Down residential roads, mostly free of pedestrians at night with an occasional family walking or children playing on the sidewalk, Margot and Miguel drove to Hanok House. Mrs. Baek had said, *Your mother used to bring you to the restaurant that I worked at, Hanok House. Do you remember? It looked like an old traditional house, lots of wood everywhere.*

There was no reason not to believe what Mrs. Baek had claimed about her mother—connecting her mother's recent grief to the death of a lover, the man in the obituary. But Margot still wanted to scope the place out, where she and her mother spent time, a place that both her mother and Mrs. Baek had left behind. And besides, after all she and Miguel had been through these past several days, they needed a feast to reward themselves.

Koreatown, like many ethnic enclaves in major cities, had been changing slowly. White people who had once fled now

edged their way back—particularly youth hungry for cheaper
rent with access to supermarkets, bars, and restaurants. Yet
when areas "improved," did the lives within them get better also, or were they pushed away to somewhere cheaper to
make room for the droves, the new blood? Soon developers
would follow to demolish and build over the place, rebranding
the symbols and the signs of the people who lived there (the
"kitschy" culture and the "foreign" architecture, the novelty
of foods once deemed disgusting). Would her mom have been
one of those priced-out people, too? Or would she have clung
stubbornly, maybe even found a second job so that she could
stay in Koreatown? With her limited English and inability to
drive on the freeway, the choices would be slim.

In a brave mood, Margot had once asked her mother in the
best Korean she could over the phone, "Why don't you go
back to Korea? Why do you live here?" She had always wondered why her mother had chosen this life, which couldn't be
easier than living in Korea where she would at least speak the
same language, possess the same cultural understanding and
history as everyone else. Even though Margot knew very little
about her mother's Korean life—that she was an orphan who
mostly worked in clothing factories from her teens through her
twenties, eventually learning to design clothes—she couldn't
understand why she would rather be in a country where she
had so little power, such few rights.

Her mother had paused for a long while.

"I would be too far away from you," her mother had said.

Margot pulled into the narrow, one-way parking lot of
Hanok House, a stand-alone restaurant in the style of a traditional Korean residence with rustic wood shutters and a
sloped, gray-tiled roof. She had never been to Korea herself,
and although she knew its cities were full of skyscrapers and

electronic screens, she often imagined the homes to still look this way—charming, earthy, and functional.

"Did you ever hear back from Officer Choi?" Miguel asked.

"No, not yet." Margot sighed, pulling the key out of the ignition. "Mind if I give him another try now before dinner? Maybe he's still at work."

"No worries. I'll be managing my prolific Grindr."

Margot laughed while pressing the police officer's number.

"Hey, Margot," he answered. "Sorry I didn't return your call today. Mondays are the worst."

"No problem. Any thoughts on the landlord? The yelling from my mom's apartment?"

"I thought it was interesting. I mean, he wasn't certain where the yelling was coming from and on what day, right?"

"He thought it was my mother. There aren't a lot of Koreans left in the building. He wasn't certain, but it seemed odd to me since my mother wasn't particularly noisy—especially after I moved out for college. Anyway, it seemed suspicious enough for him to bring it up, don't you think?"

"Hmm. I can stop by. I'll try to talk to him this week, see if I can get any more details."

"That would be great," she said, heart quickening. "Also, before you hang up—I know this might sound weird, but last night, I was going through my mother's apartment and found this obituary she had saved. It was from the Korean newspaper back in October. So today I went to the swap meet where my mom worked to see if any of the other store owners had seen anything suspicious around the weekend she died. One of my mother's friends, a woman named Mrs. Baek, said that the man in the obituary was…a man that my mom was seeing over the summer. They were dating and…he was married, so she didn't tell anyone."

"And you didn't know about this guy?"

"No."

"But he's dead now, right? Since October, almost two months ago?"

"Correct," she said. "I don't know if you could do this or if it's related to my mom's death, but is there any way you could find out some more information on him? His name was Chang-hee Kim. I think he lived in Calabasas."

"I could look into it…but let me first talk to the landlord, okay? I'll try to get over there this week." He paused. "But if her boyfriend died back in October, I'm not sure what that would have to do with your mother's death."

"What about his wife? He was having an affair with my mom."

"Hmm, that's a good point. I can look into it."

"Great, thanks. I would…almost want to talk to her myself? Is there a way to get her phone number or address? I tried googling his name, but—"

"I'm not sure that's a good idea."

"What do you mean?"

"To be honest…your mother's death *was* an accident. There's not much we can do unless something substantial happens, some revelation, or we find out for whatever reason that your mother's death is connected to some other activity."

"What?"

"And what if Mr. Kim's wife doesn't know about the affair? What if you revealed the affair to his widow by contacting her? You have no proof that she was involved in your mother's death, so how would we get any information from her without revealing that her husband was cheating on her? There's a chance she doesn't know, right?"

"I suppose so, but—"

"How would you find out whether or not she knows? You couldn't. You'd have to ask her outright, and there would be no reason to ask her about your mom if her husband wasn't cheating in her mind. There's no real other connection. She's a widow. It'd be—"

"I still think we should—"

"I know this is a lot, Margot. You're…finding out a lot of things about your mother, things that she kept from you for a reason, right? Sometimes those things are hard to accept, and you want them to be connected to the hardest fact of all— that she's gone. I get that."

"You can believe whatever you want, Officer Choi." Her voice rose. She could feel Miguel's eyes on her. "But I absolutely refuse to settle for anything but the truth. I need to know what happened that night and why—"

"Margot—"

"You might think we're some kind of *burden* on your workload, but my mother worked her ass off, and she paid taxes like everyone else. She was an honest person. She was kind." Her voice cracked. "Maybe she wasn't a perfect mother or person, but she tried her best to do what was right for me and for everyone else—except herself. People like my mother hold up this sham as much as you."

"Yikes," Miguel whispered.

"That's not it, Margot. That's not what—"

"She deserved to live like everyone else. *You* of all people should know better. 'To protect and to serve'?"

Margot's ears pulsed. Tears filled her eyes. She could hear both Officer Choi and Miguel breathing, startled by her voice. Now was the last chance to stand up for her mother, whom she had been ashamed of for so long. She tried to muffle her crying.

"I'll try to get you some more information, Margot," Officer Choi said, resigned. "I'll talk to the landlord. I'll see what I can find out about Mr. Kim." He paused. "I know you don't think I do, but I understand more than you would know. I get it. I'm just trying to be realistic here. I am sorry about your loss."

"Lord," Miguel said after she hung up the phone.

"Am I crazy?" She wiped the sweat from her forehead, catching her breath.

"Honestly, I think you are right. Everyone else has lost it, Margot." He turned his head as if just noticing the sky—a smoldering tangerine and hot-pink fire. "The world is fucked. But we deserve the truth." He unbuckled his seat belt. "Can we eat now?"

Margot and Miguel exited the car under the last of the day's light. She took a deep breath. She always loved seeing Los Angeles plated in gold by a receding sun, the outlines of palm trees. For a few quiet moments, you might hear birdsong instead of car honks and alarms and trick yourself into believing it was paradise.

Entering the restaurant, she could smell the meat grilling over the gas burners—fat sizzling while flames licked sesame, soy sauce, sugar, onion, and garlic. Nothing could quite connect people like food.

The hostess seated them at a table of glazed wood with raw edges. After ordering beef short ribs and pork belly, Margot showed the waitress—a thin middle-aged woman with pale powdered skin and a short bob, tidy black apron and skirt—the framed image of her and her mother on the day of Margot's high school graduation, the most recent photo that Margot could find. "Do you know this woman?"

"Yes, I think so," the waitress said. "But from a long time ago."

"Do you mean years?"

"Let me ask the owner."

She fetched an older Korean man in his seventies, with

bright silver hair and dressed in an olive green sweater-vest and khakis. A gold watch glinted. With new dentures, he smiled like a false sun.

"We're just wondering if you knew my mother." Margot handed him the photo.

He nodded, lifting his brows. "Looks familiar." His eyes then considered Margot a shade too long.

She made an effort not to turn her gaze away. She immediately didn't like him and she wanted him to know it.

"When was the last time you saw her?" Margot asked.

He scratched his head. "I don't know. So many customers." His nostrils flared. "All look almost same." He grinned—those Paul-Bunyan-statue teeth, cold and white, clinical. "Almost same. Excuse me." Bowing his head, he turned to another table where he greeted a group of boisterous guests—regulars or friends.

"That was shady," Miguel said.

"Maybe he's just confused."

"He doesn't seem *that* old."

The waitress returned with a tray full of banchan, small white plates glowing.

Margot decided to switch tactics. "Do you remember a woman named Mrs. Baek? She used to work here. Red lipstick?"

The waitress smirked. "Oh, yes, very red."

"When did she stop working here?" Margot asked.

The waitress glanced behind her shoulder. "Earlier this year. Spring, I think."

After switching on the tabletop grill's gas burner with a click and a hiss, the waitress hurried away, empty tray in hand. Around the low blue fire, they munched on banchan—seaweed salad, mak kimchi and kkakdugi, lightly pickled mu, seasoned spinach, potato salad. A feast for the senses.

"Well," Margot said. "At least we know Mrs. Baek was telling the truth about opening her store in March."

Elbows on the table, Miguel played with his chopsticks as if pinching the air in front of his face. "After the riots, what did your mom do?"

"What do you mean?" Margot tasted the kkakdugi, perfectly crunchy and a little sweet. Her face tingled, hot from the flames in the center of the table.

"Your mom stopped talking with Mrs. Baek then. She was busy. But it seems kind of pivotal, right? That they stopped talking, and now suddenly, just this year, they became friends again? Seems coincidental."

"After the riots, I think my mom worked at some fast-food restaurants. She took on random jobs until she could save enough—a couple years later—to start a business again." The seasoned spinach smelled of fresh sesame oil, which melted in her mouth. "I just remember it was *very* rough. She was able to save some of the merchandise and hangers and stuff from her old store, and we lived with those clothes in boxes in the apartment since we didn't have any place to store it. We ate government food—like canned pork, powdered milk. The Salvation Army gave us toothbrushes."

She tasted the seaweed salad, one of her favorites, which suppressed some of the sadness she could feel rising inside of her. Its delicate gelatinous acidity, its brininess satisfied her. How she yearned for the ocean right now. As a teenager, she would ride the bus on her own to the beach and spend hours walking or sitting on a bench, reading and watching the water. "It was hard. It was really hard back then."

The waitress returned to the table with a platter full of raw meat—the marinated short ribs and pork—to grill. Soy sauce and sugar, ginger and garlic caramelized, dripping fat into the fire. With an intense feeling of gratitude, Margot moved the galbi and slices of pork belly to keep them from sticking to the grill. How joyful, how abundant life could sometimes be—despite the disappointments, the tragedy. Every meal, even a somber one like this, was a celebration of what we had left, what remained on this earth to taste and feel and see.

She imagined her mother at the Grand Canyon, the dark shadows pressed against red-and sand-colored rock striated over billions of years by wind and water. She thought of Las Vegas, her mother's hands gripping the steering wheel, the open windows, and the fine powder that caked their faces and arms.

"During that time was when my mother drove us to Vegas."

"Vegas? I thought your mom didn't go anywhere?"

"It was just once. I was probably about six years old. She had never driven on the freeway before, I don't think. She was really slow." Margot laughed. "I'm surprised we were never pulled over. Anyway, we were supposed to meet up with someone there. I think this was right before my mother opened her new store, the last one, in the swap meet."

"Interesting." He finished the last of the seaweed salad. "I guess it could've been anyone that she was meeting up with? She didn't have any family, though, right?"

"No," Margot said. "But… I don't think any of this has to do with Mrs. Baek. I mean, I believe Mrs. Baek now, but it is odd that my mother would've just cut her off that way, right?"

"Well, it probably wasn't intentional," Miguel said. "Sometimes people grow apart, or maybe your mom just didn't have time for friends—only church and you, I guess. She was trying to survive, right?"

Once the meat had browned, Margot laid pieces on Miguel's plate, like her mother would've done, before serving herself. A heaviness gathered in her chest. She wrapped a bite of warm white rice, soft pork belly, and ssamjang in a red lettuce leaf, still wet, and crammed it into her mouth.

As a teenager in restaurants, she had often glanced around her at larger groups in their booths, envying the volume of people, the generations that could be brought into a single period of time and space, the architecture of a family over shared food. There was a kind of rigid hierarchy between parents and children, older and younger siblings. But the politics protected a sense of togetherness and place, a statement that read in the silence of subtle gestures (the pouring of another's glass, the use of two hands, the serving of others first): *We will always protect each other.*

Yet despite those gestures, those fragile attempts to express their feelings, she and her mother couldn't get along, relax. Were they too foreign from each other?

Or was it the intensity of two women alone, two women who would be mirrors for each other, for each other's sadness, disappointments, rage? If one would experience joy, the other would feel not her own joy rising but a pang of jealousy rooted in a fear of abandonment that would cause her to strike the other down. And where did this fear of loneliness come from? Was it universal or specific to her mother? Or maybe even specific to being Korean?

Her mother, as a child of the war, would have surely died alone if she had not been found. And the whole world told women every day, *If you are alone, you are no one. A woman alone is no one at all.*

Miguel had only spent a few days in LA here and there on vacation, so they decided to see the city after dinner. They could use a break, a diversion. Anything to get her out of her own head and heart, which by now had become flooded with details of her mother's life. She did everything for so long within her power to avoid the reality, the pain of her mother, and now it came down on her in a deluge of confusing facts, images, and emotions. The sock lady, Mrs. Baek, red lips smeared. The obituary of her mother's lover, who resembled Margot as well—the squareness of the jaw, maybe even the eyes, the cheekbones. The restaurant owner's brand-new smile. Her mother facedown on the carpet. The dark smell. A gas. The smell she could not get out of her nose and mouth.

"Let's drive to the ocean," Margot said, starting the car. "We can walk around the pier a little, then we can come back and go to a bar, or there's this old salsa club downtown. We should check it out."

"Hell yeah," said Miguel.

Fifteen minutes later they reached Pico Boulevard, named after the last governor of California under Mexican rule, which stretched all the way west from Los Angeles to Santa Monica, getting richer, cleaner, and quieter toward the coast.

Although chilly and damp from the ocean, Margot cracked open the window for some air. She had always loved coming to the beach, oftentimes by herself so that she could plop down on the sand, bury her toes, and watch the waves crash, or walk along the old creaky pier and play Galaga at the arcade. As a teenager, she would ride a local line to Rimpau station where she hopped on the Blue Bus for an easy, hourlong commute to Santa Monica.

She had been mesmerized by the smell and the sound of the waves and the vast expanse of murky blue that was not only a moving color but actually a well of living organisms—fish and algae and octopuses and whales—all moving through their lives unaware of the terrestrial world above it. Knowing also that somewhere at the end of the ocean an entirely different continent of people stared into the same abyss of water

and distance and time comforted her. A universal aloneness
and yearning.

"I would be too far away from you," her mother had said.
And now she was gone forever.

On Ocean Avenue, they parked beside the bluff with well-
maintained grass, robust palm trees, and a recreational area
for a retirement center. Homeless people lay down in their
bundles on the benches.

"Do you want to walk around a little?" she asked.

They opened their car doors and flung themselves into the
cold, biting wind. Already pitch-black outside, carnival lights
danced on the pier where floodlights touched the surface of
the ocean with a mottled yellow glow. Walking to the pier,
tourists bundled up in coats and sweaters, filling the darkness
with a cacophony of voices and languages—accents, tones, and
rhythms from across continents. The cheerful crowd floated
like a diaspora of desire, seeking the thrill of new experiences, the satisfaction of hunger with funnel cakes, hotdogs,
hamburgers, and fries. Arms outstretched for selfies. Local
couples and families moved at a slower, more contemplative
pace; they, like Margot, had come here for comfort, for the
familiar sights and sounds, a part of the patchwork of memories that we touched when life and the future felt uncertain.

Margot zipped up her jacket as the wind cut their faces and
ears. Stopping at the bottom of the stairs that took them to
the beach itself, they removed their shoes. The soft, cold sand
swallowed their feet. She rolled up her jeans. They stomped
arm in arm through sand, shivering as they pressed their sides
up against one another. The wind whipped Margot's hair in
her face, clinging to the balm on her lips. As they stood twenty
feet or so from where the ocean licked the shore, Margot released a great big sigh.

"Isn't it beautiful?" she asked.

"It's freezing, but...yes, there's something magical here."

Her cell phone rang. She flinched. An unknown number.

"Hi, this is Tom from Ko-America tours."

"Oh, yes?"

"You wanted some information? About Mina Lee. September, Grand Canyon?"

"Yes, do you know who my mother was with during that trip? Do you have any information on her or him?"

"Yes, um, I have his emergency form. Hmm, no phone number, but the name is Kim Chang-hee. I have address only, in Calabasas."

Margot remembered the black tennis shoes she had found in her mother's closet, covered in a fine rust-colored dust, the smell of mineral and sage. She had finally made it to one of the national parks, after all these years of work, and she had not been alone, but with a lover.

"Could you give me the address? Or any other information."

"Uh...who are you again?"

"I'm her daughter. I'm Mina Lee's daughter." The words carved into the heaviness inside her chest, which being by the ocean had only partially relieved. Was she still a daughter if her mother was dead? "She died a week or so ago and... I wanted to get in touch with him to let him know. I thought he would want to know."

"Oh, I'm so sorry about that."

"Could you text me his address? Will you do that now? I don't have a lot of time. I have to leave soon," she lied. "I live in Seattle and I have to go back to work."

As soon as she received the text with the Calabasas address, she jumped with excitement.

"He sent it," Margot said. "What next?"

"No phone number, right?" Shivering, Miguel danced his feet in place.

Margot shook her head. "We could drive there maybe?"

"Yeah, this week for sure. I gotta go to the Valley anyway to look at apartments. But would we just knock? We can't do that, right?"

"What if Officer Choi is right and she doesn't know about the affair, or who my mother is?"

"I think we should go check it out anyway. I mean, we'll be in the Valley already. We don't need to knock, just kind of scope it out. I mean...this would be the former residence of your mom's boyfriend. And...do you still think he could be your dad?"

"Maybe, but it just all seems too coincidental at this point." She shrugged. "But I think there's something there. My mom never ever had a boyfriend to my knowledge while I was growing up. What would she be doing with this specific man? A married man...with cancer. It was doomed."

"And the wife—she had to know, right? I mean, c'mon."

"Yeah, he went on a goddamn recreational tour with my mother. She had to know."

"We'll figure it out."

"I'm just glad. It's weird, but I'm happy that she went on that trip." The ocean rippled under the full silver moonlight. "I never saw her on a real vacation. Ever. I'm relieved she got to do that before she died."

For the first time since discovering her mother's body last week, she felt hopeful—as if somehow, slowly, her persistence might be paying off. She dropped her shoes to the ground and ran toward the ocean, which appeared calm and placid. The cold air rushed in and out of her lungs, whipped her hair out of her bun, all over her face. She had felt so trapped her entire life in that apartment, at that swap meet, inside her mother's life. And temporarily she could free herself here, right now; there was so much space and hardly anyone around.

Her feet splashed into the icy water. She screamed, then laughed, realizing she had chosen this for herself. With her teeth chattering, she ran out and back in again, deeper, up to her knees. A dip in this water was a kind of insanity. But she felt free.

She had always been a little scared of the water, of getting in too deep and being swept away. She never learned how to swim. There were no swimming pools where she had grown up, no extracurricular classes for kids. Water was always something she walked in and feared for its power.

On the pier, roller-coaster riders screamed. Red and white lights danced in a black sky. The salt air smelled like safety, the longest sigh of relief. The Ferris wheel spun and blinked, throbbing lightheartedly, its spokes like many arms outstretched in the night.

As she stood knee-deep in the water, a tangle of weeds wrapped around her ankles, tickling the skin. She could trip and fall into the dark foaming water, and the strands would wind around her, squeezing the last breath out of her body, until she belonged to no one, not even herself. She would belong to the sea. In a panic, she lifted her feet in a dance, retreating toward the sand, to free herself from what was, upon closer inspection, not actually seaweed, but a thin rope, no, a net, a piece of fishing net, gummy and laced with kelp leaves and pearl-like polyps. Maintaining her balance, she dragged the net out of the water and picked it clean as she walked toward Miguel. Her nose ran from the cold, and she wiped her face on her sleeve.

"Are you okay?" Miguel asked.

"This thing wrapped around my legs."

Margot held a corner of net out to the sky, up against the

shape of the Ferris wheel on the pier in the distance—blinking in black, many-spoked, turning slowly, aglow. She imagined all the tiny silver fish that would swim through the weave—like her mother's words, no, her mother herself, shimmering, liquefied, slipping through every hole.

MINA

FALL 1987

W hen she finished her shift on most days, she found something small waiting among her belongings— two bananas, a pack of gum, a head of lettuce, a small box of chocolates. It was hard to tell what the logic of each selection was, or if there was any at all. Depending on her mood, each item seemed entirely thoughtful or utterly meaningless. She looked forward to seeing what had been placed in her bin, and on the days when she didn't receive anything, she went home sullenly disappointed, as if that was the inevitable end to a streak of good fortune. But then the next day, she would find something again—a package of ramen, a small container of doenjang, the most exquisite Korean pear, perfectly shaped and freckled—and the world seemed to open up a little once more, a crack of light seeping into darkness.

She knew it was Mr. Kim. He had seen her that day, after she had rung up the father and daughter who reminded her so much of her own, after she had run to the bathroom and emerged with her face red and swollen. He had given her *that* look, silently acknowledging her pain, and later that day, she had discovered the fruit, that beautiful green apple, and the ramen in her bin. Since then it had been clear in their quiet and polite exchanges that he wanted to help her somehow, that somehow in her loneliness, her despair, he recognized something. Maybe a bit of himself.

A part of her wanted to reject everything, to confront him and ask him politely to not leave her anything anymore. She didn't need or want any sympathy. And it confused her. What was the point of these gestures that couldn't lead anywhere for her?

At the same time, the idea of not receiving the little gifts, which often served as the highlight of her entire day, terrified her. Maybe it was the tiniest of things, at times, on a consistent basis, that kept us alive, and if she could not create such kindnesses for herself, couldn't she allow someone else to do so for her?

After a couple weeks of the monotony, the accretive familiarity of the cash and the coins in her hand, the dull flashes of courtesy between her and the customers, punctuated only by the gifts she received at the end of most days, Mario disappeared.

On a crisp autumn day, Mina approached her register, where a teenager, maybe eighteen or nineteen years old, was working with Mr. Kim on the front-of-store tasks that Mario usually did on his own. As soon as Mr. Kim noticed Mina, he tried to smile and walked away to the back of the store. She said hello, acting as natural as possible with the new employee who introduced himself as Daniel.

Where was Mario? Perhaps he had the day off, which, for whatever reason, seemed odd to her. He had quietly guided her through many of her more difficult days as a cashier. Something about the whole scene seemed askew. But she reminded herself that he could be sick or on vacation. Who knew?

Daniel learned quickly, had certainly worked in a supermarket or grocery store before. During the slower hours, he would ask if she needed help with anything, which she didn't. She went around tidying the registers, trying to ignore him because she couldn't quite think of anything else for him to do. Mario always kept himself busy. She looked around to see if Mr. Kim was anywhere, but she didn't see him, nor the owner, Mr. Park, at all for the rest of the day.

At the end of her shift, a Korean pear wrapped in its Styrofoam sleeve waited in her storage bin. She inhaled the dappled skin of the fruit, which smelled of fall, crisp and sweet. She cradled the pear in her two hands and, for a second, pressed it to her chest.

Mina had come out of the restroom and gone down the soft drinks aisle to pick something up for herself when she noticed Mr. Kim, who had seemed to be avoiding her, walking away toward the other end of the aisle. Finally she had the chance to ask him about Mario. For a second, she thought to proceed slowly; she didn't want to run into him, but at the same time, she was tired of not knowing, and something about his avoidance pained her, made her question the items in her bin, and whether or not she had mistaken his politeness, his kind nature toward everyone for something else.

"Mr. Kim," she called.

He turned around. His face was haggard, tired around the eyes.

She walked closer to him but stayed far enough away to not appear suspicious to anyone passing by.

"Is he sick?" she asked.

"Who?"

"Mario."

"Oh. No, he…" He turned his head to see if anyone was coming from behind. "He got sent back. To Mexico."

At that moment, she felt the distance between them—cold like the aluminum can in her hand. She had the sudden urge to throw it and break the cruel, fluorescent light.

"Why?" Her voice cracked as she fully realized what he meant. They would probably never see Mario again.

"I don't know. I tried to… When I found out, I thought maybe I could send him some money for a lawyer."

"How could he get sent back?"

"He didn't have his papers. I don't know."

"Oh." Her eyes dropped to the floor. Could Mr. Kim tell that she, too, didn't have her papers, or at least not yet? Was it obvious to others? Or had Mario somehow gotten himself in trouble, and in the process been caught?

"His mother and his brother and sisters are still here. They all live together."

"So, that's it? He just gets taken away."

"It's happened before. I don't know why, what triggered it."

"But he's been here all this time, right?"

"Yes. It doesn't matter, though."

"But…there has to be something. How could he disappear like that?"

"I spoke to his mom. That's how I found out. He just didn't show up, so I knew something was wrong. I think he was the only one supporting his family. His father had been killed going home one day. Shot out of nowhere." Tears welled up in Mr. Kim's eyes. "It's not all right."

"Is there anything we can do for them?"

"I'm not sure, but I think I'm going to start collecting some money." Mr. Kim slipped a pack of cigarettes out of his shirt pocket. He had never given off any indication that he smoked before. "I went by last night with some groceries. There was a little baby, a couple girls, a boy. She has some family, I think. A church. But I'm gonna start collecting some money here. I haven't told anyone else yet."

"Okay, let me know," she said. "I want to help."

He tapped out a cigarette, holding it softly in his hand. She wanted to hold that hand now.

One week later outside of the supermarket, Mina wrapped her sweater around her body before climbing into the passenger seat of a large white van, which smelled of exhaust, damp cardboard, and overripe fruit. In the driver's seat, Mr. Kim switched on the radio to a sudden blast of pop music. He flipped through different stations until he found some oldies—the Shirelles' "Dedicated to the One I Love." After turning onto the street, he eased into the steady flow of early Saturday night traffic, bopping his hand on the steering wheel and mouthing the words with the enthusiasm of someone younger, someone unharmed by life.

She smiled at this morsel of joy, despite the heaviness of their task. Swaying a little to the music, she stared out the window as they drove south through unfamiliar neighborhoods. She tried not to look at him. It made her nervous to sit so close to him. She could reach out and touch him, and no one would see. No one would know.

In front of a two-story apartment building, windows barred and cracks crawling up the stucco like vines, Mr. Kim unloaded the bags of donated food from the van and carried them to the top of the steps. He pressed one of the unit numbers on the intercom, and when a woman answered, he introduced himself. For a second, Mina wasn't sure if she would open the door until a loud obnoxious buzz let them inside.

Mario's mother stood in front of her apartment door like a woman accustomed to bad news. Her orangish blond hair, dark at the roots, had been pulled into a loose, high bun above a heavy face with vertical lines carved between her brows. Her black T-shirt was stretched at the neck, revealing fragile collarbones.

"Hola, Lupe," Mr. Kim said. "Uh, tenemos comida, uh… fideos, leche, jugos…para ustedes."

Lupe clapped her palms in response. She reached to help Mina with the bags, but Mina refused as Lupe guided them inside of her apartment. On the sunken couch sat three ebullient children of different ages glued to a Spanish-language game show on TV, erupting into squeals of laughter at every joke or wacky stunt. The oldest, a girl of about ten or eleven, held a baby with the downiest brown hair on her lap. The baby sputtered, and she wiped the baby's mouth with a cloth.

Mina smiled thinking of her own daughter at that baby's age—her pink face, the little closed eyes, the nose, the tiniest fingers and toes, the creamiest folds of skin, and that smell, that sweetest of smells, soft and powdery.

"¿Quieren algo de beber?" Lupe asked, gesturing for them to sit.

Mr. Kim rested the bags on a round dining table and slid two chairs out for themselves while Lupe poured glasses of orange juice. Thirstier than she had thought, Mina sipped gratefully as Lupe sat down with them, observing the children watching television, laughing. The eldest daughter lowered the volume.

"No saben lo que le pasó a Mario," Lupe whispered. "No sé cómo decirles."

Mina recognized enough words to piece together that Lupe hadn't told the children about what had happened to Mario.

"¿Cuándo fue la última vez que…escuchaste de él?" Mr. Kim asked.

Tears spilled out of Lupe's eyes. Mr. Kim pulled a handkerchief out of his shirt pocket. The second girl, without the baby, and the boy rushed to her, putting their faces on her back, their arms around her shoulders.

Unsure of what to do next, Mr. Kim and Mina stared at the dining room table. When Mina glanced up to see the mother and children holding and comforting each other, she could feel her heart, which she had worked so hard to ignore, tear in two.

"Lo siento," Mina said. "Lo siento." One of the expressions she had learned from Hector and Consuela.

When Lupe finished blotting the tears from her face, she inhaled deeply through her mouth. Her daughter wiped away the hair sticking to her face and kissed her mother on the forehead with such tenderness that Mina felt a heat rise from her chest and she couldn't help but cry. Mr. Kim's eyes rested on Mina—a shade too long.

He now knew. This was her sadness, too. She was mourning someone, a family.

The following week, Mina and Mr. Kim sat side by side on the couch as Lupe served leftover chocolate cake on paper plates printed with rainbow confetti. Yesterday had been her eldest daughter's birthday. The two girls ran in circles around the small living room, bopping each other with helium-filled balloons, while the little boy, five or six years old, held the baby.

Lupe had received a phone call from Mario at a detention center in the morning. Describing the conversation, she clapped her hands, eyes upward, thankful to God. Tears leaked out of her eyes. Having heard stories of briberies and beatings, even murders, she only needed to know that he was still alive.

Mina could sense Lupe's guilt, the guilt that perhaps all parents feel when somehow they lose their child, no matter the age or the circumstance. That guilt was a vertical and endless wall made smooth from hands and feet attempting to climb it. Occasionally a memory together—the laughter, the squeaky voice, a kiss on the cheek—would serve as a kind of ridge on which to hoist yourself, but still you'd fall somehow. There was no way to rest.

As they left the party, Mina pulled herself into the van beside Mr. Kim. "Does she know yet how long he'll be there, in the detention center?" Mina asked him.

"No. But could be weeks, months." He turned the ignition a few times. The engine choked. "I spoke to Mr. Park about getting her a job at the market."

"Oh, that's good," she said.

"She has a neighbor, a nephew who'll help her with the kids while she works." He tried again. This time, the engine groaned to life. "It'll be hard, but it's not hopeless."

"What about her? Is she or the kids at any risk? Of being deported?"

"Yes, of course."

Outside the car windows, men cruised on low bikes. Tires glinted like the steady throb of lighthouses in the dark. Mina couldn't help but wonder what each person living in this city did to get by. How many of them lived like her, underground, and how many had stories like hers? How many risks did people take, on and off paper, to survive the brutalities of what they could not change about their lives? America, to many abroad, represented the only way out—not a solution but a chance to keep hope alive and burning.

But some days she felt like she was living inside of a lie.

"Do you want me to take you home?" Mr. Kim asked, breaking through her thoughts. "Or back to the store?"

"Oh. Are you going back to the store?"

"I don't have to, I can also just go home. I can drop you off."

"Okay, well…"

"It's not a big deal."

"If…if you could take me home, that would be nice." She was hesitant to tell him where she lived. She didn't know why. "I live near Wilton and Olympic. Is that out of your way?"

"No, not at all."

"I can take the bus."

"No. It's fine."

She asked him to turn right onto the dark, tree-lined street on which she lived. She became self-conscious of being in this car alone with him, a man—concerned that either the landlady or Mrs. Baek might see her and get the wrong idea.

But what was the wrong idea? What would be so shameful about her and Mr. Kim or any man for that matter? She was an adult. She could take care of herself, make choices about her body. But still her heart raced. Perhaps she was simply terrified of wanting more from this life—more feeling, more joy, more pleasure—knowing that it could all be taken away at any moment and that still she'd have to survive. Was she strong enough?

"A couple blocks on the left," she said, pointing. "Right there."

He pulled up in front of the house, which had all the lights off inside. The landlady must have already gone to bed.

"Thank you," she said.

"No problem." His hands remained on the steering wheel as he stared through the windshield. He gulped. Was he sweating?

As she opened her door, Mr. Kim said, "Do you...do you want to get dinner sometime?"

"Oh. No. No, thank you." She smiled, hopping out of the van.

"You're not married, are you?"

"No. I just—"

"Just thought I'd ask." He nodded, lips pursed. "Have a good night."

She shut the van door and waved goodbye through the window. She walked up the broken driveway to the house, afraid to look behind her because she knew he was still in his car, making sure she got inside safely. She opened the front door and rushed toward her bedroom.

She switched on her lamp and lay down, face pressed against the pillow.

She liked Mr. Kim. His polite, big-hearted demeanor. His warm smile.

The smooth skin of his arms. The thick black hair on his head.

But why would anyone want to be with her, a widow who had lost her child? She was damaged goods, as far as she could tell. It would be too much work to get involved with anyone now. Besides, she could never afford to lose anyone again.

She couldn't sleep at all that night, thinking about him, about Lupe, her children, Mario, and then about Mr. Kim again. Her mind, like the streetlights, let off a steady beam until the morning, when she could hear the birds singing, and the sky turned purple and yellow, like a fresh bruise outside. That was when she finally closed her eyes.

★ ★ ★

Mina caught glimpses of Lupe in the store, stocking items as Mina had done when she began working at the supermarket. They'd wave at each other or smile and say hello with a silent understanding that they shared something, something that might be too significant, even dangerous to speak of. Mina yearned to ask her about Mario but didn't quite know how.

She had wanted to learn Spanish for many reasons and now for this one in particular. How would the shape of her feelings, thoughts change if she could say them out loud? If she could hear them? If someone else, who might understand, could hear them, too? By only speaking Korean, her world, and the world of what was inside her, felt limited to the few people she spoke to each day, or the people whom she couldn't quite trust at church. How could the shape of her life change if she had more people that she could reach with words?

She'd have to learn on her own. She could get a book. But, no, she should learn English first.

But why should she learn English when no one around her used it? Every single person at the supermarket spoke Spanish or Korean or both. Perhaps Mr. Kim and Mr. Park, the owner, spoke English, but that was it. In Koreatown, she managed to do almost everything in Korean. And since she rented her room under the table, completed all her transactions in cash, she didn't even need a bank account yet. Even if she did open one eventually, there would be a Korean bank to help her, a Korean accountant.

At the end of her shift, she walked to a bookstore a few blocks from the supermarket, where she picked up a Spanish language book. Standing at the bus stop, she flipped through the text, trying to decipher the diagrams.

Dorothy swims in the lake. / Dorothy nada en el lago.
Dorothy drinks orange juice. / Dorothy bebe zumo de naranja.

A sudden gust of wind, speckled with dust and dirt, devoured her as the bus approached. Mina showed her pass to the woman with the round face and perfect bob.

"Aren't you cold?" the driver asked.

"No, no. It's okay."

"It's freezing out there." She mimed shivering, crossing her arms to keep herself warm.

Mina smiled, making her way to the back where she could study her book.

"It's freezing out there," she repeated to herself.

Once she got home, she reheated a pot of doenjang jjigae while skimming the text and flipping through the lesson plans. It seemed that with about thirty minutes per day, she could get through at least half of the book over the next month, completing all the exercises and assignments along the way.

In the dining nook, she closed the book and blew on a spoonful of soup before taking a bite and realizing then how cold she actually was in that house. She needed to put on a sweater but felt too lazy and hungry to move.

Mrs. Baek emerged from her bedroom in a drab gray T-shirt and loose matching pajama pants, yawning as if she had just woken up. The night before, she had probably worked the graveyard shift at the restaurant where she cooked for late-night diners and partiers who had been out drinking and craved a comforting bowl of soondubu jjigae or a cast-iron platter of bulgogi.

"I haven't seen you in a while," Mina said. "I made dinner already, some doenjang jjigae. Do you want to join me?"

"Sure, let me take out some more banchan."

Mina ladled her some soup and scooped rice while Mrs. Baek laid out a stack of little bowls—gosari namul, kkakdugi, panfried dried anchovies—covered in Saran wrap from the fridge.

"I make these *every day* at work," Mrs. Baek said, unwrapping the banchan and releasing the rich, comforting scents of sesame, onion, and garlic. She sat across from Mina as if she were on the floor, lifting one of her legs and placing the bottom of her foot on the bench. Unlike so many women, Mrs. Baek didn't seem to mind taking up time and space, spreading herself out, which both irked and fascinated Mina.

"I'm so thirsty," Mrs. Baek said, chewing. "I don't know why."

"Let me get you some water." Mina ran the faucet, trying to remember how many years Mrs. Baek had lived in America. Five, ten, twenty?

Mrs. Baek flipped through the Spanish textbook absentmindedly, as if strolling through the glossy pages of a women's magazine. "You're learning Spanish?"

"Trying. I figure it'd be easier to, you know, talk to people." Mina laughed. "I guess I should learn English one of these days, too. I can't always depend on you."

"Oh, you'll learn eventually." Mrs. Baek smiled. "It takes time."

"How long have you been here, in America?"

"Many years. Almost twenty."

"No wonder your English is so great." Mina mixed rice into her jjigae.

"Yes, yes. I read a lot, too. I was also an English literature major. Do you like to read?"

"To be honest, I hate reading." Mina smiled. "I was never a good student."

"You can watch television or movies then. I think if you take in the culture, it's easier, you know?"

Mrs. Baek impressed Mina with her college degree, her English skills, and her cooking, yet something about her was also deeply unsettling. Mina couldn't quite understand how this woman would've ended up in the same house as her, at a restaurant cooking food, when she could get a higher paying job in an office somewhere. Was she running from something or someone?

She couldn't ask that. Still, she had a sneaking suspicion that Mrs. Baek, like her, was hiding from the world. But from whom?

In the back of the store at a long folding table, Mina nibbled on her packed lunch, a bento of leftovers—rice, seasoned spinach, kimchi, a few bites of bulgogi. She thought about the Spanish words she had learned from Daniel, words about the weather—nublado, viento, soleado—which sounded beautiful out of his mouth but funny and garbled out of hers. She still couldn't quite get the sound of the letter *L*.

As she formed her tongue and lips, trying to find the shape of that sound—*L… L… L*—Mr. Kim entered the break area, stopping to bow his head toward Mina before heading to the restroom. Now that Lupe worked at the supermarket, Mina and Mr. Kim no longer had a reason to visit her and her children. He still left food items for Mina in her storage bin, but as the days passed, she saw him less and less. Perhaps he now felt embarrassed after asking her out to dinner a couple weeks ago. Who could blame him?

He exited the restroom, turning away.

"Mr. Kim," she said, not knowing why or what she would say.

He stopped in his tracks. "Yes?" His voice was tired and gravelly.

"I've never thanked you..." She cleared her throat. "For the things you put in my basket."

"Oh." He turned around, staring at the floor a few feet ahead of him, waving dismissively. "No big deal. Sometimes, we have these leftovers, can't sell them or anything, so...no big deal." He lifted his hand to acknowledge her words before turning again.

"Mr. Kim."

"Yes?"

"Is something wrong?"

"No, nothing. Everything is fine." He glanced at his watch. "I have to run now. But thank you."

For the rest of the day, she thought about his downturned face. The tenuous bridge between them was eroding. She imagined herself shouting for him as he walked away, but she didn't know what she would say. She couldn't explain how frightened she had become of life, knowing that at any moment it could be taken away and that there were no lessons, no meaning that she had found in loss, only pain. How could she explain this to him?

At her register, she scanned and punched the numbers, barely acknowledging the customers, anyone around her.

"¿Qué pasó?" Daniel asked.

She feigned a smile. "Nada."

But she couldn't stop thinking about him. She wished there was something she could do for him, leave something in his office. But what? What would he need? How would she know? Maybe it didn't matter. Maybe any gesture would count.

At the end of her shift, she grabbed an Asian pear from the

produce section, paid for it, and rushed toward the back of the store. She placed the fruit on his desk in his tiny office, which she had never entered before and smelled musty and slightly sweet from paper and ink. She heard a noise behind her and turned around. He stood at the door.

"Is that for me?" His brown eyes softened.

"Yes." She caught her breath. "I just thought—sorry, I probably shouldn't be in here."

"That's nice of you. You don't have to do anything for me."

"You just looked...tired."

His gaze dropped toward the ground as his mind seemed to calculate what and how much to say. "A lot going on around here."

A pair of feet shuffled behind him as the store owner walked over. Facing them both, Mr. Park said, "Hello, hello. Am I interrupting something?" He lifted his eyebrows.

Mina cringed inside. The office seemed to shrink in size.

"No, Mrs. Lee wanted to talk about her schedule."

"Oh, any problems?" Mr. Park craned his neck, trying to catch a glimpse of her behind Mr. Kim. "You're not in any kind of trouble, are you, Mrs. Lee?" He winked, almost imperceptibly.

"No, everything is fine," she said in a steely voice. "I just wanted to...talk to him about my hours. I'd like to work more hours."

"Oh, I see," he said, grinning at Mr. Kim before patting him on the shoulder. Walking away, Mr. Park added, "By the way, good job, Mrs. Lee. You've been doing a good job."

"Thank you."

Mr. Park went out the back door, either to smoke or leave for the day.

Mr. Kim faced her again. "Well, thank you for the apple," he said with a smile.

"It's a pear."

"Oh, that's right."

"Um…" She touched the corner of the desk with the tips of her fingers, steadying herself. "Do you still want to have dinner?"

MARGOT

FALL 2014

L ast night had been Margot and Miguel's first night sleeping in the apartment, about a week after they had discovered her mother's body. Margot had slept in her mother's room while Miguel stayed in Margot's. After brewing a cup of coffee with a French press that she had bought her mother many years ago, Margot sat at the dining room table, staring out the window at the alley that separated their building from the next. Her mother had never used the French press, preferring instead the packets of instant coffee, pre-mixed with sugar and creamer from the Korean supermarket. Her mother had even kept it in its box as if preserving it for someone.

How many times had Margot gazed out that window?

She and her mother would sit at that table, at breakfast, at dinnertime, silent. How she had wished her mother would ask her how she was feeling more often. How she had longed for her mother to ask her what had happened that day, if it was good or bad, or if something about it had surprised her.

But maybe the questions themselves frightened her mother. Not because she didn't care about Margot, but because the questions were the same ones that she was never willing to ask or answer about herself. It hurt too much to know. *How are you doing? How do you feel?*

Margot finished what was left in her mug, chewing the crystals of sugar that hadn't yet dissolved.

Wearing a white undershirt and black jeans, Miguel emerged from the bathroom with a hand towel, drying his wet hair. She realized then that she hadn't taken a shower herself in days, not even after she had walked on the beach and submerged herself in the ice-cold water. She placed the kettle on the stove top now to brew Miguel a cup of coffee, too. The electric coil glowed orange, deepening to red.

Miguel grabbed a razor from his overnight bag and closed the bathroom door. Her phone rang.

"Oh, hi," Officer Choi said. She could hear background noise of him rummaging through papers, folders. "Hope it's not too early? I've got some stuff for you."

"Is it...good?"

"Well, couple things," he said. "I finally reached the landlord. I spoke to him yesterday afternoon."

"Oh, great."

"Unfortunately, he said he didn't remember anything odd about the weekend that your mother died. He said that he had no idea what you were talking about, the yelling, your mother's voice—"

"What?"

"He said it was just like any other weekend. Your mother had been a quiet tenant."

"I know I'm not imagining what he said."

"So I tried knocking on some of the doors of your neighbors."

"And?" She paced back and forth in the kitchen.

"Only one of them answered. And she said she wasn't home at all over the weekend. She's lived in the building for a few years and your mother has always been very quiet."

"God, I can't believe this," she said to herself. "I swear, he told me... We were in the parking lot, the garage. I know what he said. I have no idea why he wouldn't tell you..."

But she remembered the landlord's words after she confronted him about not talking to the police: *What for? I was tired and it could've been anyone. I don't need them snooping around here. Do you? Do you think the neighbors like that? What do you think the police are going to do for you? Do you think they care about your mother?*

"Damn it. I'll have to talk to him again," she said. "It's bullshit."

"I'm not sure what else we can do, Margot."

"There had to have been someone else around." She gritted her teeth. Her eyes darted toward the electric coil—red and hot. She could hear the bubbling inside of the kettle now.

"I looked into the obituary, too."

"You did?" she said, somewhat relieved.

"Your mother's boyfriend, Kim Chang-hee, was a pretty big deal in the Valley. Rich. Donated a lot to the church. He had this small supermarket chain, Super San. Ever heard of it?"

"No," she said, leaning on the edge of the counter next to the stove. "I guess I just don't know the Valley."

"Wife. No kids." He paused. "Pancreatic cancer. He died in October."

"I see." Should she tell him that she saw a resemblance between herself and Mr. Kim? No. It was silly wishful thinking.

"His widow lives in Calabasas. They have a home there."

She knew. The tour operator had given her the address.

"I don't really see a connection to your mother or her death," he said. "You found this obituary at home without any explanation?"

"Yes, I… I found it in a drawer that I was going through."

"I mean—"

"What was her name? The widow's name?"

"Mary Kim."

"Do you have a phone number?"

"I really don't think we should go down this route."

"What do you mean?"

She could hear men's voices in the background. "Your mother." Officer Choi lowered his voice. "She had a lover. He died. And then—later, *she* died as well." He paused. "It's terrible and sad, but there isn't a point in hurting anyone else, right? I mean, none of this information will bring your mom back."

"*Hurting* anyone else?"

"The widow. Mr. Kim's wife. Why bring her into this? She might not even know about the affair."

"But what if she does?"

"How are we going to figure that out? Ask her? Why would we be asking questions about your mother? We'd have to tell her." He sighed. "I don't really see what else I can do here, Margot. As far as your mother's death goes—which was terrible, I'm sorry—it's an open-and-shut case. It was an accident, and there's not much more I can—"

She hung up the phone. The kettle screamed.

She turned off the burner as Miguel reemerged from the bathroom, freshly shaven, clean and minty, and strolled into the kitchen.

"Did you hear any of that?" Margot asked, pouring the hot water into the French press.

"Yeah, I did." He shook his head. "So the landlord is now just acting like he didn't hear anything. Of course."

After stirring the grounds in the water, she said, "I'm gonna talk to him. I'll try this afternoon."

"The landlord?" Miguel leaned on the kitchen counter. "Do you want me to go with you? Do you feel safe?"

"I'll be okay, I think." She pressed the grounds down and poured the coffee into a mug. "You have errands to run. I'll try him today, and we can still go to Calabasas this week, right?"

"Sure, how about tomorrow? Or Friday?"

"Sounds good," she said. "I can't believe the landlord lied. This is so frustrating."

"Maybe you should go down there now? I'll go with you. Or do you have his number?"

"Yeah, I do." She grabbed her phone again. "I *should*, or actually—it's here on the fridge, I think." Her mother had taped up a piece of paper with the phone numbers of important people—Margot, the landlord, her church, Alma, the manager of the swap meet—in case of an emergency.

She dialed. When the answering machine picked up with a generic recording, she didn't bother to leave a message. She had a feeling that he would be avoiding her now.

"Maybe take a break?" Miguel said. "I have some appointments at apartments today. How about we do that and then go out to eat something? We could drive around Burbank for a bit, get away from this place."

She nodded and said, "I'm just so fed up with everything right now."

"Too bad hot Officer Choi turned out to be such a bummer."

"Predictable," she said. "All of this and that landlord are so fucking predictable."

"Why not surprise them?" He sipped his coffee. "I think we should surprise them, don't you think?"

"What do you mean?" she asked.

"We roll up our sleeves and figure this shit out on our own. You don't need him for anything else, right? *Delete* him."

He was right. She didn't need Officer Choi or the landlord. None of them were on her or her mother's side, dead or alive.

Normally, she would've deferred to their opinions. Their doubts would've wormed their way through her own intelligence, her own instincts to defend what she knew was right. But she now realized that their power relied on her ability to undercut herself. And she was tired of doing that. She and her mother deserved more. She wouldn't stop until she found the truth of her mother's life.

Two days of searching for an apartment had gone by before Miguel scored a modern one-bedroom in Burbank early Friday afternoon. After a late lunch at an Italian chalkboard-menu eatery blocks from his new place, Margot and Miguel endured the stop-and-go down the 101 for almost twenty-five miles to the hills of Calabasas, west of the San Fernando Valley.

The plan was to check out Mr. Kim's house where presumably, his widow, Mary Kim, still lived. Margot wanted to find out as much information as she could about Mr. and Mrs. Kim without actually confronting her. Otherwise, Officer Choi was right; she might be revealing the affair unnecessarily to her. And in Margot's mind, although Mary was once the only person who might have a motivation to harm her mother, the landlord, who had lied to either her or Officer Choi, had become increasingly suspicious; his answering machine now indicated that he was out of town for a family emergency. How convenient.

"Do you want to stay with me on Sunday night—after I move in?" Miguel asked. "Are you comfortable at the apartment by yourself?"

"I think I'll be okay," she said. "Besides, I probably should stay at my mom's and find that landlord. Finish stuff up. Burbank *is* far."

Of course, she was happy for Miguel, but she envied how organized he was, how easily he seemed to manage the logistics of life. He had found a better job in another state that gave him more options to pursue his passions, his dreams. He now had an apartment with stainless steel appliances in a LEED-certified building located close to his workplace, an acting studio, shops, and restaurants. Why couldn't she get her life in order, too?

What was wrong with her?

She couldn't stand her job as an administrative assistant— the data entry, the proofreading, creating brochures in that tiny appendix of an office with the adobe red walls, the single, dusty task lamp she used every day. She couldn't bear the weather in Seattle. After a life in Los Angeles, she had never adjusted to the gray winters.

And when she did catch a glimpse of the things she wanted (a more creative job, art classes, a stronger sense of community outside of work), those things would disappear before she could touch them, back into the mess of her mind. She'd get distracted by other lives—the problems of men. Her two-month relationship with her coworker Jonathan last year had been disastrous. His self-absorption combined with his generic flattery—the compliments about her thoughtfulness, her empathy and intelligence—was seductive. She had this keen feeling that if she could support him endlessly—through his grief over his deceased wife, his adult son who struggled with addiction—she would be rewarded with his attention, his admiration forever. She could disappear around him and still feel good about herself.

But of course, he broke her heart. He was an it-hurts-me-to-hurt-you, an I-love-you-but-I'm-not-in-love-with-you kind of man. It was all so dull and predictable in the end.

And now that her mother was dead, there was no one to run from except herself. She wasn't even a daughter anymore. She'd have to become someone else.

Her foot cramped in its stop-and-go position over the brakes. This slow miserable parade.

"Look at that sunset," Miguel said.

Her mind shifted to the riotous sky, its mesmerizing wash of pinks and oranges. She had always loved those sublime colors that suggested both the beginning and the end of everything. The sun in LA could be a real drama queen, quietly blazing in a tulle of smog all day until the evening asked her to leave, and she became all flourish and flames.

Exiting the 101 later in twilight, the car wound up hills, past expansive homes of varying architectural styles—Mediterranean, Tudor, Cape Cod—complexes of both good and bad taste but mostly expressions of large bank accounts, impenetrability, power. Manicured lawns, a pristine green, not a leaf or twig or stem misplaced, maintained by armies of workers who lived and traveled far daily from much poorer parts of the Valley and LA, who spent hours in the sun, working while remaining invisible.

Margot couldn't believe her mother had a lover who lived with such wealth less than thirty miles away from her in Koreatown. Could he also be her father? Perhaps she not only wanted to find out more about Mary Kim but also whether or not Mr. Kim could be her dad. It seemed absurd to follow an impulse toward such an elaborate story. But why else would her mother be dating this wealthy man all the way in Calabasas? What would they have in common with each other except the past?

Growing up, she only knew that her mother had worked at a supermarket when she had first moved from Korea and met a man there who disappeared after she became pregnant. Her mother never explained why and refused to give away any details about him—his name, his personality, his face. Eventually, Margot stopped asking.

Margot had always imagined her father as a quiet, nondescript person who still worked at a grocery store, and potentially had his own children and family, or had been a perpetual bachelor, breaking hearts wherever he went. She had preferred the latter, someone cruel. That way she never had to wonder why she and her mother had been abandoned, discarded like the peel of a fruit.

But now she couldn't resist the potential of this story—that Mr. Kim could be her father, that her mother had found love in the final year of her life, that a vengeful wife had confronted her mother, maybe even killed her, whether on purpose or by accident. As far-fetched as this scenario seemed, it made more sense to Margot than her mother randomly falling in her own apartment, only to have her out-of-town daughter find her body days later. She understood that both life and death could be random, unnecessary—but she needed more from her mother's story. And now that her mother was dead, Margot was no longer afraid of any truth.

They pulled up in front of the address Margot had received from the tour operator earlier this week. It was a white two-story Mediterranean-style home, expensively kept with its dense lawn and swaying palm trees. All the lights were on, blazing in the evening dimness. A tiered stone fountain gushed water indefinitely as if the drought, or any other problem of this planet, could not touch this blessed house and land. In the driveway, a brand-new Lexus SUV and Mercedes sedan posed as if straight out of a holiday car commercial.

"Maybe you should go down a block? So they don't see the car," Miguel said.

"Yeah, my car's just a *little* out of place." She pulled forward along the curb. She said in a grande dame voice, "Hello, 911, there appears to be an average-looking automobile outside the grounds at this time."

"We could be housekeepers."

She laughed despite the pounding in her chest. What if a neighbor saw them? Were they trespassing, breathing in the citrus blossoms, the new car smell of this neighborhood? She felt foreign and alien.

After parking down the block, they strolled down the sidewalk through the bronze gate that had been left wide open. Perhaps a car had pulled in temporarily, or the residents always left the gate ajar, which seemed odd but worked in their favor that night. As they approached the house, Margot and Miguel ducked, scampering across the lawn until they reached a row of boxwood to hide behind while they peered through a large window into the silent, empty house. Elegantly unlived-in with mostly monochromatic holiday decor—pine cones and boughs painted platinum and white atop a mantel covered in silver photo frames. An ivory tufted sofa and armchair with clean, inviting lines.

"It's nice in there," Miguel said. "Like in that Anna Wintour kind of way."

"It's like a magazine."

"Do you want to look around the back?"

"No, I don't think we should—"

Margot froze as a pearl-skinned woman of an indeterminate age appeared in the center of the living space. In her long creamy nightgown, she cradled a crystal of whiskey with slender fingers crowned by oxblood nails. A lithe, compact body, eyes kept low. She moved in and out of their sight line, pacing like an animal in a cage as if possessed.

Margot closed her eyes, afraid she might faint. She had an impulse to run now, forget everything. She never had a father. She never needed one. She had her mother at least—a mother who was often unavailable but nonetheless protected her, perhaps protected her too much, but she had done so because she had known how sensitive Margot could be, how emotional. But now that her mother was dead, Margot had been thrust into seeing her, into seeing them both for who they really were—women who survived on their own. They thrived in their own country of two. They were in a way, despite how they might've appeared to the outside world, perfectly fine.

Miguel tapped her arm. A man in his forties—handsome, chiseled as a movie star—entered the room. Wearing a black crewneck sweater and dark slim-fit jeans, he smoked a cigarette with an intense Tony Leung face. He perched himself on the edge of the white sofa as if unable to relax, unwilling to get too comfortable. They appeared to be in some intensely somber discussion—brows furrowed, prolonged silences between words.

"Damn, he is fine," Miguel said.

"We should go," Margot said. "I don't think—"

The man stood, snuffing out his cigarette in an ashtray.

Margot and Miguel ducked behind the bushes. Edging her face upward, she caught a glimpse inside of the couple kissing in an embrace.

"Let's get out of here." Margot pulled Miguel's sleeve, and they scrambled away, low to the ground. As soon as they emerged out of the open gate, they slowed down, trying to appear as casual and ordinary as possible, as if they were only two people out on an evening stroll. The cold air burned her lungs. A queasiness rose from her stomach up into her chest. She could taste the bile at the back of her throat.

"Whew," Miguel said, shutting the car door. "I guess widows just wanna have fun?"

"Somebody traded in for a new model."

She pulled away from the curb, making sure no one followed them.

Down tree-lined roads, branches veined the night sky between stately homes lit like welcoming lanterns. But the images of the woman and man kissing, her sullenness despite the airy perfection, the heaven of that house, had been burned into Margot's head.

"I wonder how old she is?" Margot asked. "That had to have been his wife, right? Officer Choi said he had no kids."

"How old was her husband?" Miguel asked.

"Sixty-four, I think."

"I feel like the oldest she could be…would be forty? Maybe fifty?"

"Do you think she just found this guy?" Margot asked.

"Maybe. Or he could've been her lover from the get-go."

"You mean, while her husband was alive?"

"A little side dish," Miguel said.

"But then she would have no reason to fight with my mom, right? I mean, why would she care?"

"Money?"

"What do you mean?"

"I don't know, but that's the only thing I can think of."

Soon they sat in a thick silence with only the ticking of the turn signal, the hum of the car's engine between them. For the rest of the drive, Margot sped home through the dark, thinking of the woman's face—a perfect oval that shimmered softly like a pearl. The man's hands on her waist.

Mary and her mother had such different lives, and yet it was as if Margot could hear Mary suffocating under all that rich light, straining as if she'd been trapped like a perfect specimen inside of a jar.

MINA

FALL 1987

In Mr. Kim's blue station wagon with velvety seats, a paper pine tree dangled from the rearview mirror. The moon glowed silver and bright, peeking behind a faint cloud. Staring out the window into the dark, Mina wrapped her sweater around her body. She realized now how sullen she had been the past couple weeks when Mr. Kim had been avoiding her after her rejection of him following the last time they went to visit Lupe. As a result, she was learning Spanish to distract herself from how unhappy she had been, how impossible life could sometimes be.

The air freshener hung like an amulet. She yearned for some sign from the universe that said, *You are doing fine.*

"So, where do you feel like going?" Mr. Kim asked, breaking the silence. "Do you feel like anything in particular?"

"No. I'm okay with anything."

"There's a restaurant that I like, Hanok House. They've got pretty much everything—galbi, jjigaes."

A longing to somehow touch him crept up, like vines attaching her to this man beside her, to this world. She wished she could incinerate the shoots and tendrils, but she would risk destroying herself. What was she doing? It had been a year since her husband and daughter had died, since burying them in the ground, a single tombstone, together. What was she doing in this car, far away from them, far away from home? She wanted to ask Mr. Kim to turn back, but as soon as she looked at him, the inside of her mouth felt parched. She couldn't. She wanted to be here now.

As they pulled into a narrow parking lot, she almost clapped her hands at the sight of the restaurant that resembled a traditional Korean house. Its decorative wooden beams and curved, gray-tiled roof were charming and lovely compared to the drab concrete and graffitied stucco of Los Angeles.

Inside the restaurant, which smelled of seafood, peppers, onion, garlic, and sesame oil, Hahoetal masks grinned on the walls beside booths made out of dark slabs of glazed wood. Early still for dinner, the restaurant was mostly empty except for another couple in a far corner of the dining room and an older man, sleeves rolled up, carefully sipping from a boiling-hot jjigae by himself.

As they sat down, a waitress greeted them with two sticky laminated menus. Mina studied hers, avoiding eye contact with Mr. Kim.

"I'm having the maeuntang," he said. "I always get the same thing."

"Oh, that sounds delicious."

"What looks good to you?"

"Ahl jjigae." Her mouth watered at the thought of fish eggs

boiled with tofu, onion, and mu in a spicy stew. "I haven't had that in a long time."

"One of my favorites, too." His arm moved on the table as if resisting the impulse to hold her hand.

The waitress returned with a pot of barley tea.

"So, how long have you been in LA?" she asked.

"Gosh, over ten years, I guess. I came here after college." He brushed his full black hair back with his hand. "I was going to do my master's degree, but that didn't last long." He smiled, crinkling the skin around his soft brown eyes. She loved looking at him.

"How come?" she asked.

"Oh, just wasn't my thing. It was an excuse to get over here." He winked. His lips were perfectly sized. A sensation of warmth pressed her chest like the sun shining on new leaves—tender and bright green. She could feel the sap coursing through her body. "It sounded good to my mother. My poor mother." He shook his head, pouring her tea. "How about you?"

"Me?"

"How come you're here? Or why does your family *think* you're here?"

Steam rose from her cup of barley tea. She closed her eyes and could feel the grip of her mother's hand, and then the sudden absence of that pressure on her skin. Even if she had her own family, a husband, a daughter, for several years, she didn't belong in this world it seemed. She never did.

"You don't have to tell me," he said. "I'm sorry."

The waitress returned, spreading banchan on the table—mak kimchi and kkakdugi, seasoned soybean sprouts and spinach, soy-glazed lotus root. With his metal chopsticks, Mr. Kim sampled the spinach, chewing thoughtfully as if admiring its composition—garlic cloves, green onions, soy sauce, sesame

oil. The tanginess of the mak kimchi, which she always tried
first, opened her palate. She bit into the candy of the lotus root,
crunchy and chewy, for comfort. There was a startling familiarity to the banchan as if she had tasted the specific character
of each dish, every different taste and texture, someplace else
recently, but she couldn't name where.

"What did you study?" she asked, pouring him tea.

"Economics," he said. "I guess I still kind of ended up in
economics. Business, sort of." He smiled again.

"Not quite what you expected, though."

"Nope, but that's okay. That's how it is." He sighed. "We
come here thinking that we'll work hard and sometimes it
works out, sometimes it doesn't. That's life."

"You're still young."

He blushed. "Young? Not really. I haven't been young for
at least ten years."

"Well, young enough. If you wanted to start over, you
could."

"That's true. I'm not tied down or anything."

"Were you ever married?" The words slipped out of her
mouth.

"Yes." He sipped his tea. "For about a year. Not long."

Hands shaking, she lifted the pot to refill his cup.

"She passed away," he said, eyes downcast. "She had stomach cancer."

"I'm sorry." She exhaled out loud. "That must have been
very difficult."

The waitress arrived with two heavy stoneware bowls filled
to the brim with piping hot stews redolent of the earth and
sea—snapper, fish eggs, and clams, zucchini, ginger, and garlic. Mina watched hers bubble while Mr. Kim, adventurous,
spooned a bit of his soup, blew on the broth, and sipped. She
bit her lip, wishing she could scarf down her ahl jjigae. So

much of Korean food was about patience as the volcanic soups settled down, building the diners' anticipation with the bright colors of the red pepper and green onion, the smells.

"Is it good?" she asked.

"Yes, try some." He nudged his bowl toward her.

"I will in a little bit. Please, go ahead."

The broth burned her tongue but tasted like it would at any restaurant in Seoul, perfect in its depth and brininess from the roe. The fish eggs crumbled inside her mouth, and she washed them down with a spoonful of delicate mu that had become perfectly translucent.

"You?" he asked, not looking up from his bowl.

"Yes?"

"Did you ever marry?" He sniffed from the heat of the spice.

"Yes," she said, surprising herself. "He died, too." Those words wrung her heart. If she were to mention her daughter, she would completely fall apart. She would run out into the street screaming. She would beat the bottom of her fists on the ground, as if trying to break her daughter free. She never intended to tell him about her husband and daughter at all, as if she had been ashamed of the tragedies that had rent her life, her family. Wasn't that how most people treated her back home—like her sadness was a disease that could spread?

"I'm sorry," he said.

She wanted to get out. But she couldn't. On the walls, the Hahoetal masks seemed to be laughing at her. How could she leave now?

"Are you okay?"

"I need to use the restroom. Excuse me."

Standing at the sink, she cried, wiping her eyes. She splashed her face with cold water and waited a few minutes until she caught her breath and most of the red had left her skin. She couldn't. She couldn't do this. She didn't belong in this life, this dream. Her husband and daughter's deaths were proof of this fact. She was made for nightmares. She would work and go to church until one day she died and went to heaven. That was all there was left to hope for, that was all there was left to long for in this world.

She returned to the table where Mr. Kim had refrained from eating in her absence. Her ahl jjigae had gone lukewarm.

They drove back home in silence. The pine tree deodorizer swung like a pendulum. The night had ripened into a starless black while the streetlights glowed amber on steel and glass. From the periphery, she watched his arms, thin and muscular, guide the steering wheel, his leg press on the gas. She could say something. She could tell him everything. But what? What would that something be? What could she say without falling apart, revealing how broken and unlovable she had become? She had already told him too much.

As he pulled up in front of her dark house, Mina said, "I'm sorry about earlier. I just—"

"No worries. I understand."

"I'm… It's all so new." She was ruined now, wasn't she? She couldn't even have a meal out and enjoy herself.

"Of course. Don't worry about it."

"I'm sorry." She wanted to run out of the car. "Thank you for dinner."

Before she shut the door, he said, "You're very nice and pretty."

She didn't know how to respond.

"I mean that. You're very nice."

"Oh, okay." She resisted the urge to cry. As a widow who had also lost her child, it seemed she had again become as invisible as she was growing up—alone without a family, a leftover from a war, an unwanted girl.

"Can we have dinner again? Next Saturday?"

She nodded. In English, she said, "Good night."

Inside her room, she lay on her bed, thinking of Mr. Kim—his warm smile, the sadness of his eyes, his smooth arms—then her husband, the peck of his lips as he departed each day for work, and she buried her face in her blanket.

Tears leaked out of her eyes. She tore at the fabric with her hands, not ripping but gripping, wings flapping over a marsh at dusk, purple and glassy, until she was too tired to realize she was falling into a soft miracle, insects skimming the surface, of sleep.

Autumn settled in the city. The nights grew colder, dropping down to the fifties at times, which seemed chilly in a place where houses and apartments didn't have much for insulation and heat. The drafty home in which Mina lived felt colder than it was outside at night, and she bundled up in sweaters and blankets as she listened to the Korean radio or stood by the stove, cooking something for herself. Some of the local trees had lost their leaves, but the palm trees lining the streets persisted, ragged, swaying in that bright, smog-filled sky.

At the supermarket when no one would notice, Mr. Kim, lips curled, winked at her with an almost comedic force. Mina laughed, covering her mouth, when she wanted more than anything to kiss him, feel his warm animal breath. She wanted her face to tingle, her heart to thump against her chest. Be wild, like rubbing oneself in the dirt or plucking flowers and pushing them in her hair.

After that awkward first date, he still left gifts in her bin—a Hershey's bar, a bag of salted peanuts, a Valencia orange with the most perfect navel—objects that aroused some softness, like a rabbit's fur against her face. To know that he was there, to know that he was thinking about her was a strange but marvelous relief from the hardness of every day.

At the beginning of their courtship, her husband, with his long sensitive face, relaxed eyes, and mischievous smile, had brought her flowers and chocolates like the main character in an American movie. His kindness continued throughout their marriage, but not with the same intensity, of course. After so many years together, raising a daughter, too, their lives had turned toward the practical, to the questions of how they would provide the best life they could for her, what they would have to sacrifice.

So the romance had left them, but never the love. Every morning, he dropped in to kiss her, like a seagull diving into the ocean, before he rushed out the door. She would be eating breakfast by herself or getting ready in the bathroom, and he pecked her on the cheek or sometimes sloppily like a farm animal to say goodbye. He loved rituals, organization, patterns.

But to encounter these small objects—these ordinary gifts—now from Mr. Kim revived something in her that she had forgotten, stirring the coals of a small fire that she had believed had long since died. She began wearing lipstick—soft pinks and berries—which she purchased at a drugstore near the house. She still wore the same blouses and slacks, but she brushed and combed her hair, checking herself in a pocket-size mirror she kept in her purse throughout the day. She lined her eyes black with the tiniest flick at the end. All of this happened so quickly, within a week, that even the landlady, who rarely said anything about anyone's appearance, noticed.

"Somebody's *living*," she teased.

With Thursday off, Mina, exhausted from a late shift the night before, slept in until noon, when pots and pans, metal surfaces, banged against each other. She hated loud noises, especially sudden ones, striking like the universe crashing down, and she didn't know in which direction she should run. In her pajamas still, she exited her room and peeked through the open door of the kitchen, which always smelled of garlic and green onion.

With her pale and bony legs, Mrs. Baek stood in a gray T-shirt-like nightgown, clicking a burner on the stove. Her bun of curly hair hung low on her neck. Her forehead and nose gleamed in the room half-lit by sun.

"Ah, it's been a while," Mrs. Baek said, drizzling oil onto a pan.

Mina feigned a smile, yearning to return to bed.

"Are you hungry?" Mrs. Baek asked. "I was just about to make something."

"I might wait a little bit." She placed her hand on her stomach.

"You sure? Sit down." Mrs. Baek lifted a large bowl on the counter. "I have all this pancake batter. Fresh squid."

Mina loved the hot crispy pajeon or bindaetteok fried in the open-air markets back home. The anonymous bustle and then the comfort of sitting on a tiny plastic stool as she waited to be fed. The women who cooked in each stall always seemed harried and gruff, yet their mannerisms were also distinctly soothing—as if underneath their no-nonsense approach was the tenderness of the family that they were each charged with providing for. They were women of great power and importance, and they knew it.

"I have some rice from yesterday," Mina said. "Want me to heat that up?" She reached into the refrigerator for a large round Tupperware, cracked open the lid, and placed it in the microwave, where she stood watching the stove with Mrs. Baek.

"I saw you the other night," Mrs. Baek said in a low voice, smiling as she tilted the pan to spread the oil.

"Where?"

"At Hanok House."

"You work there?" Mina remembered the calming familiarity of the banchan—the spinach and soybean sprouts, the crunchy lotus root.

"Yes, I was in the back. I noticed you sitting with a man. I didn't want to interrupt."

"I see." Mina leaned her hip on the counter. "I knew I recognized the banchan from somewhere."

"Who is he?" Mrs. Baek asked. She ladled the batter onto the hot pan where it cooked almost immediately, the edges hardening.

"He's a coworker. I work for him." Her stomach rumbled.

"Oh, that makes sense," Mrs. Baek said, still focused on the pan.

The microwave dinged. Mina scooped hot rice into two bowls from her drying rack.

"Do you like him?" Mrs. Baek nudged the pajeon with the spatula so that it wouldn't stick.

"I don't know. Maybe." Mina settled in the breakfast nook, the wood benches cold despite their cushions. The smell of squid and scallion pajeon, hot and crispy, filled the kitchen. With her pale bird legs, feet covered in red house slippers, Mrs. Baek shuffled toward Mina carrying a heavy plate and a small bowl for the dipping sauce. The pajeon was perfectly golden and browned, sliced into quarters.

"Go ahead and have some. Let me clean up a little bit."

Mina waited until Mrs. Baek slid onto the bench in front of her.

"Go ahead," Mrs. Baek said.

"No, you first, please. Thank you for sharing."

Mrs. Baek picked up her metal chopsticks, lifted a piece of the pajeon onto her bowl of rice. "He's handsome." She raised her brows.

Mina smiled, dipping a piece of pajeon into a tiny bowl of soy sauce and vinegar. "He is."

"Is he nice?"

"Yes, so far, but it's hard for me to trust anyone, I guess." She sighed.

"I'm the same." Mrs. Baek nudged the mak kimchi, Mina's favorite, toward her. "You can never tell with men, you know?"

Mina nodded, tasting the mak kimchi. Perfectly tangy and ripe.

"I don't think I'll trust any man again," Mrs. Baek said.

Mina wondered about what kind of history Mrs. Baek might have had, but she could tell by the resentment in Mrs. Baek's words that to resurrect those experiences here might only shatter the safety, the precarious lack of judgment between them—two women, adrift in a foreign country, without any apparent family.

After eating in silence for a couple minutes, Mina said, "Everything you cook is delicious."

"It's hard to cook for one, you know?"

"I agree. I only make ramen or the same jjigae nowadays." Mina remembered her daughter's favorite meals—kalguksu, sujebi, braised mackerel in the fall and winter, naengmyeon in the summer—and how much time and care she put into feeding them all back then. She wanted her daughter's life to be full so that she would never suffer, so that Mina could erase all the hardship and deprivation she had herself endured. But the past always had a way of rising back again when so many of the questions had remained unanswered, wrong-doings remained unacknowledged, when a country torn by a border had continued for decades to be at war with itself. Both the living and the dead remained separated from each other, forever unsettled.

"Were you ever married?" Mrs. Baek asked.

In Seoul, by now, the leaves hanging would be their brightest, their most beautiful against a gray sky. The gingko and maple would glow yellow and red down the streets and up the hills. The crisp fall air would pierce her mouth, her throat, her lungs. She and her daughter ran through the fallen leaves, kicking and laughing.

But she hated those red leaves now, the season that took her husband and daughter away from her, too.

"He died," Mina said.

"Oh, I'm sorry." Mrs. Baek placed her chopsticks on the table. "Was he sick?"

"No. It was an accident."

Mrs. Baek reached out and squeezed her hand, the first time Mina had been touched with purpose in a long time. She could feel something sprouting inside of her chest as if Mrs. Baek's kindness was the amber-colored light stretching longer and longer each day in spring.

But it was still only autumn. A season of dying. And when she thought about those trees, how they must look at this moment—the saturation, the brightness—ablaze, all she could imagine was the blood that must have been in the road, after a reckless driver, rushing on his way to work, mowed her family down.

MARGOT

FALL 2014

U nderneath vaulted ceilings and stained glass catching the faintest of morning light in delicious jewel tones, Margot could feel how beautiful and safe a church could be—the sinuous burn of incense, the calm lemon oil on wood, the rituals, the incantations and song. It had been years since Margot had gone to church herself. In her teens, she had fought with her mother about what she viewed as the oppression, the boredom of worship. But seeing the windows now, she remembered how as a child, she would stare at the stained glass and think of pieces of candy like Jolly Ranchers. She had wondered what the windows would taste like if she could climb up and lick them.

The Irish priest greeted the gathered in Korean with a bit of his native lilt. The pipe organ played and the choir sang clearly. Every cell in her body vibrated with music. She couldn't understand the lyrics, but she could feel their meaning, the se-

duction of their gentleness, their meekness in front of a God
who would reward them, a God who would always restore
order and peace to this world.

She closed her eyes. Did her mother believe in any of this?
Or did she just need to belong? Did she only need to return
here every Sunday to restore order to her spirit and mind? She
could understand why her mother needed to believe there was
a heaven after all of this—after all her anxiety, her loneliness,
the frailties of a body that could be taken from her, apparently,
at any moment, this body that suffered, that belonged to and
dissolved into the earth like that of any animal.

And her mother's ashes. What would she do with them?
What would her mother have wanted for herself?

Whether she was in heaven or simply gone, Margot ached
for her mother. Umma. Tears streamed down her face, dripped
from her chin onto her chest. She licked the salt away from her
lips. *Amen* hummed around her. While the priest read from
the scripture, his Korean calm and fluid as a creek, she kept
her face lowered, collecting herself. She wished she could understand the words, but instead the Korean washed around her
like water, chest-deep. Her head spun from the frankincense.
She couldn't sit still any longer.

After the homily, more prayer, she stood to receive the communion, but instead of walking toward the altar, she bolted
out the front door into the morning light where she could
finally catch her breath. The sun glowed through haze and
smog like an ember dying. She sat on the cold concrete steps
as finches flitted and chirped through trees. Pigeons cooed
under roof eaves.

After all those years of fighting with her mother who feared
Margot would go to hell one day, Margot was now here
searching for what everyone else was—answers, safety, relief.

She had hoped to speak to the priest or a deacon after the

service, find out what she might do for her mother, her ashes. At the same time, she was embarrassed by the fact that she couldn't afford to do anything proper for her mother. First she had to sell her mother's store and car. Suddenly, she felt a profound sense of shame—as she had always felt around most other Korean Americans—that she had grown up fatherless and poor. Among Korean Americans, many of whom were Christian and from middle-to upper-class backgrounds as a result of status-filtering immigration laws, a child out of wedlock, a missing father, seemed to be particularly embarrassing when family success represented all that you had in this country far away from home. Anyone who failed was defective. She and her mother had been defective—not the dream, not the conventional shape of a family and success.

Their existence was criminal. Her single mother was undocumented. Margot was fatherless. Shame, shame on them all.

The heavy wooden doors crashed open as the parishioners emerged. Margot stood at attention, searching the crowd that streamed around her. With a jolt, she recognized Mrs. Baek dashing by in the shuffle. Margot almost said something, but instead she followed her to the congested one-way parking lot where groups of people, mostly middle-aged and elderly, chatted, while cars backed out of spots with care.

Mrs. Baek had reached her car and went to unlock it when Margot caught up with her.

"Mrs. Baek," Margot said.

She jumped and turned around with her keys, sharp, sticking out of her hand, while teeth flashed between her red lips, the edge of a snarl. Startled, Margot raised her hands up in front of her chest as if protecting herself. Why was Mrs. Baek so scared?

"Oh my God," Mrs. Baek said, eyes wide, catching her breath. "You scared me."

"Sorry, I was happy to see you. I don't know anyone. You go to this church?"

"I just started," she said. She smoothed the bun on top of her head and loosened her grip on the keys. "I never really did, but my first time was last week."

"I see," Margot said, wondering why she had begun attending.

"Did you go to church with your mom?"

"While I was growing up, but not recently."

Mrs. Baek nodded. "Are you going to have a service?"

"I think so, still trying to figure it out. Her ashes are at the mortuary. I don't think I'll be able to have a service until after I sell my mom's store, her car. Maybe at the end of the month, or in early January."

Mrs. Baek fixed her eyes on the cracked asphalt of the parking lot. "She never told you or asked for anything, right? She never had any requests?"

"No, not that I know of."

"She wouldn't want you to spend so much money." Mrs. Baek reached out and squeezed Margot's arm. "Now that you're alone, you have to take care of yourself, right?"

Margot nodded and tilted her face upward to blink back sudden tears, noticing a white trail in the sky like a scar. She looked back at Mrs. Baek, whose eyes had softened into dark brown pools that shimmered in the morning light. Despite the distraction of her red lips, she had the soulful face of someone who felt deeply. She was the kind of woman Margot would want to be one day—stylish, genuine, self-possessed, and confident.

"There are ways to honor your mom privately, don't you think? I think that makes the most sense. It would probably just be me and Alma, you know, if you had a service. Maybe some people from church." She smiled. "But she wouldn't want you to spend a lot of money."

Margot suddenly remembered what Miguel had suggested about Mrs. Kim after snooping around the Calabasas house on Friday night: that if she had fought with Margot's mom, who was having an affair with her husband, her only motivation would be money. She already had a lover. She couldn't have been jealous romantically. But if Mrs. Kim was motivated by money, a desire to protect herself financially, what could that reveal about whether or not Mr. Kim was Margot's father? Could her mother have been seeking support? Maybe Mrs. Baek would know.

As Margot was about to ask, Mrs. Baek turned away toward her car. Opening the door, she said, "I miss your mom." Her voice trembled, eyes downcast. "Maybe—maybe that's why I came here, you know? I just had this impulse to come here." She glanced at Margot before wiping tears from her cheeks. "Maybe I was hoping to see your mom? That's silly, I know. She was always here on Sunday."

Margot hesitated, deciding it wasn't the right time to question her.

After shutting the door, Mrs. Baek started the engine and backed out of the spot. Margot watched as the windshield reflected a plush solitary cloud in the gray-blue morning sky, obscuring Mrs. Baek's face. Her hands, slender and long, guided the steering wheel. Her tires squealed unexpectedly. Finches flew, a flurry of tan feathers, before landing and pecking again at the asphalt, whatever scrap they could find.

L ate afternoon the next day, Margot returned to the swap meet to ask Alma and the neighboring store owners if they knew someone who might want to purchase her mother's store outright. Earlier that morning, she had gone to the bank with her mother's death certificate, and since Margot had been listed as a beneficiary, she was able to withdraw her mother's funds—$562—and close her account. But she needed more than that to cover her mother's cremation and unpaid bills.

In the parking lot of the swap meet, large speakers vibrated and bumped to banda music. A man in a cowboy hat grilled chicken in a cloud of delicious smoke. Inside the old warehouse structure, merchandise overflowed into the aisles where people perused and picked over items for sale. Her mother's store had remained untouched, the gate still padlocked, undisturbed.

Margot couldn't help but worry that someone, knowing that her mother was gone, had broken into the place and taken everything. And now that her mother was dead, how much was her store—the clothing, the racks, the display cases, the hangers, which her mother had worked over twenty years to acquire—worth? Margot had enough of her own savings to cover rent in Seattle but not enough to remain in LA past the holidays.

As Margot unlocked the accordion gate, Alma emerged from her store—jam-packed with Christmas decorations— wearing a Santa hat delightfully askew. Strings of flashing multicolored lights and metallic tinsel garlands dazzled in the overhead fluorescent light. Alma hugged Margot, kissing her on the cheek, a benediction of sorts. "Ven conmigo."

She offered Margot a mug of champurrado, easing Margot's mind with the familiar smell, the taste of hot chocolate, cinnamon, and masa kept warm for hours.

Sitting down together, Alma pointed to her mother's store. "¿Mi hermana quiere comprar la tienda?"

"¿Tu hermana?"

"$6,000?"

Margot had no idea how much her mother's store was actually worth, but what could she do about that now? How much time and energy did she have? $6,000 was plenty, enough to cover her mother's cremation and help with Margot's expenses since she was taking unpaid time off work. And she knew that Alma and her sister would take good care of the store and customers.

"Next week? Dinero," Alma asked.

"Okay. Sí. Can I call you?" Margot finished the last of her champurrado and motioned for Alma to add her number to her phone. "I'll come back next week?"

A wave of sadness engulfed Margot. She couldn't believe it had all come down to this, all those years her mother had spent protecting and growing her store. All those years, she had yelled, *Amiga! Amiga!* at the women's backs as they walked away, swept the floors, complimented strangers after they had tried on clothes, *Bonita. So young. Joven.* All the women who had stood in the makeshift dressing room mirror, observing themselves from different angles, considering who they were and how they looked.

Alma embraced Margot, rubbing a circle on her back. Of course, this was how her mother would want things to be. How complete.

After placing her mother's notebooks, receipts, and the foot-tall ceramic Virgin Mary in the biggest cardboard box she could find, she locked up the store.

Now that she had some money coming her way, she realized that maybe she should take Mrs. Baek out to dinner this week. They could go to Hanok House again. Her trip to Calabasas with Miguel hadn't answered much about Mr. Kim—other than that his wife, Mary, already had another lover—and maybe Mrs. Baek might know more about him. Maybe she even might be able to answer the question of whether he was Margot's father.

Margot strolled through the maze of shops decked out in tinsel garlands and flashing holiday lights. Children ran, screaming and laughing. Loud speakers in another section of the swap meet blasted "Feliz Navidad," entangled with the music of various electronic toys for sale.

Margot thought of the years she had spent hating this place, resenting the work, the dirtiness, and the trash that accumulated in the aisles.

"I don't want to go to work," Margot, as a teenager, had yelled. "I want to stay home. It's my weekend."

"Do you think I want to work?" her mother asked, voice cracking. "I need your help. I can't do everything alone."

"It's not my fault that you have to work. Why do I have to go there? You're fine there by yourself."

"I need your help. Do you understand? I can't do everything alone."

And Margot almost always caved to preserve what little sanity, what little order could be kept in their home of two people struggling to understand each other, preserve what little control they could have over this world that seemed to shun them—poor immigrant outsiders. Yet Margot could witness now that this store, this swap meet, where her mother spent six days a week, was an extension of home, and the homes of all the people who worked here, including Alma, not just for money but because of love, the love they had for their families and friends, raised and supported here and abroad. Love, in all its forms, could look this way, too.

Margot stopped at the sight of the racks and display carts, once stacked with socks and underwear, stripped bare. The lingerie hanging from torsos made of metal wire, all of the merchandise had disappeared. A FOR LEASE sign hung on the wall.

"Oh, shit," Margot said to no one, almost dropping the cardboard box. Mrs. Baek's store was gone.

Margot went straight to Hanok House, where she met with Miguel for dinner after his first day at work.

She'd have to press someone there further to find Mrs. Baek now. It seemed like a good place to try since Mrs. Baek had worked there up until earlier this year. Why would she shut down her store without telling Margot yesterday at church?

Lone men in rolled-up sleeves slurped noodles. Families spoke in low hushed tones. Closer to the holidays, Korean immigrants, who often owned small businesses or worked long hours in the service industries, depended on this time of

year, when people dined out and shopped more often, to survive. No one appeared to be celebrating anything at all. The
scent of meat licked by flame, fat dripping on fire lingered,
but tonight was a night of hardy, inexpensive dishes—jjigaes,
kalguksu, yukgaejang. Tonight was a night of getting by, ful-
filling oneself after an especially hard day, finding comfort
and home in food.

"Is the owner here tonight?" Margot asked the same waitress from last week.

"Mr. Park? No, not today." Her face was unpowdered and
pink around the cheeks and nose from the heat of the food.
In her opaque black tights and sensible ballet shoes, she strode
toward the kitchen in the back.

So many customers. All look almost same, the restaurant owner
had said about her mother. He had grinned with those Paul-
Bunyan-statue teeth, cold and clinical.

The myulchi bokkeum, chewy and sticky stir-fried
anchovies—tiny eyes, gills broken, bodies twisted in death
throes that had disgusted her growing up—were now satis-
fyingly briny and sweet in Margot's mouth. It was like a bite
of the sea but candied, pure luxury.

Miguel sampled the myulchi bokkeum himself. One of
the tiny fish slipped out of his chopsticks' grip onto the table.

"How was work?" Margot asked.

He picked up the fallen myulchi with his fingers, placing it
in his mouth. "Oh, it was fine. Met everyone on my team."
He sipped from his glass of water. "Nothing much to do today.
Got my laptop, all my supplies and everything. *So* many pens."
He opened his eyes wide. "I've never seen so many different
types of pens. Rollerball. Gel. Classic ballpoint..."

"A little different from working at a nonprofit?"

The waitress delivered two earthenware pots of soondubu
jjigae that boiled and bubbled at their table.

THE LAST STORY OF MINA LEE

"Excuse me," Margot said.

"Yes?" The waitress lowered her head.

"Do you…happen to know how I can get in touch with Mrs. Baek? She used to work here—until earlier this year."

The waitress paused, inhaling deeply. She glanced around the restaurant.

"I tried going to her store at the swap meet today," Margot said. "It was completely gone. She—"

"No, I don't have any information," the waitress interrupted with a tight-lipped smile. "I'm sorry." She turned away with her tray in hand.

Margot resisted the urge to call after her. Maybe she should try asking one of the other waitresses? Biting back her frustration, she turned to the food. Through steam from red pepper, onions, and fish broth, they cracked an egg on top of their jjigaes. Margot picked at more banchan—seasoned spinach and soybean sprouts—waiting for the soup to settle down.

How this jjigae must've provided the perfect comfort on a cold Korean night. She had never been to Korea herself, never had enough money to travel on her own, but through the vigor and brashness of this comfort food, she could imagine the brutality of a winter, or even a history and culture itself, that needed this kind of balm. She needed this right now.

Where was Mrs. Baek? Margot could go to church again this Sunday, but could she wait almost a week until then? And what if Mrs. Baek wasn't there either? Then what? Shimmering like a school of the tiniest fish, she was slipping through the net.

"Have you decided what to do about Calabasas or Mrs. Kim?"

She sighed. "I feel like I've hit a dead end with that. Unless I'm willing to just go to her and ask her outright about her husband, there's nothing much I can gain, especially now that Mrs. Baek is gone." She dipped her spoon into the soup, mixing the ingredients—the clams, mussels, and shrimp, zucchini and onion.

Margot felt a light tap on her shoulder and turned to see the waitress, who leaned forward and asked, "Could I talk to you? Outside?" Bowing her head slightly, she gestured toward the door. Margot followed her out.

The fog of their breath rose from their faces as if smoking cigarettes together on break. The waitress hugged the empty tray like a shield, pressing the round surface to her chest. Margot jammed her hands into her pockets. Lint rolled at her fingers.

"You're looking for Mrs. Baek?"

"Yes." Margot's chest again was a dark mortar, the pestle grinding.

"Everything okay?" Mascara clumped the waitress's lashes into sharp ends. Cigarette butts littered the somber parking lot, which glittered with specks of broken glass.

"No." Margot shook her head. "My mom—she's dead."

"What?"

"My mother is dead. She died about two weeks ago. And… I wanted to ask Mrs. Baek some questions about her. They were friends for a long time. She might be able to answer some questions about my mother."

The waitress touched Margot's arm involuntarily as if both offering comfort and steadying herself.

"I went to Mrs. Baek's store today and she wasn't there. She sold her store, I guess. She left. Do you have her number or address? Some way to contact her?"

The waitress squeezed the tray to her chest again and shook her head. "I don't know if I can give that to you. I'm sorry."

"Why not?" Margot asked.

"When she quit, she also… She told me to never tell anyone where she lives."

"Why? My mother was her friend for a really long time. I don't think it'd be a problem if—"

"Yes, but…" She slid the tiny cross around her necklace.

"But what? It doesn't make sense. I don't have any problems with Mrs. Baek. I saw her yesterday even, at my mother's church. We're fine. I just need to ask her some questions." Margot's voice grew hoarse. On the verge of tears, she said, "She's the only person I have left right now. I don't have any family. No one else can help me."

The waitress closed her eyes and frowned.

"I don't have anybody to help me," Margot said. "Please."

She opened her eyes and met Margot's gaze. "Do you know why Mrs. Baek left?" The waitress pointed toward the ground, meaning the restaurant.

"She said she couldn't be on her feet all the time," Margot said.

"She quit when Mr. Park bought the restaurant."

"Wait, who's Mr. Park?"

"Mr. Park bought the restaurant to be closer to her," the waitress explained.

Mr. Park must be the owner Margot had spoken to the other night. His eyes lingering on Margot's face too long.

"I think maybe they had a few dates or something, but she was not interested in him. And he bought this restaurant to be closer to her, you see? He was already retired for a while."

"Oh, shit." Margot covered her mouth.

The waitress glanced at her watch. "I have to go."

"Wait." Margot touched the waitress's elbow. "So he's been following her, or…stalking her?"

She nodded. "She had to move, too. She told me not to tell anyone anything about where she lives now. When you came here last time, Mr. Park was here so I couldn't say anything in front of him."

"Do you know where she lives? I promise that I won't tell anyone. I would never tell Mr. Park or anyone else. I would never put her in danger like that."

"I—"

"I really need her help."

"I will write it down for you before you leave, okay?" Her eyes were full of fear. "Don't tell her I told you, okay, about Mr. Park? Don't tell anyone, okay?" She squeezed Margot's arm before she reentered the restaurant.

Hard breaths billowed fog. Streetlights glowed off the glass of parked vehicles in the lot.

Margot returned to the table to find Miguel slumped in his seat, texting someone on his phone. He had finished most of his jjigae.

"Sorry about that," she said, sliding herself onto the bench. "God."

"Something wrong?"

Margot planted her forehead in her palm. "Mr. Park, the owner of this place?" she whispered. "He's been stalking Mrs. Baek. That's probably why she left the store. Maybe he found her there?"

"Oh my God. Shit."

"I know, I know. I knew something was off about him."

"I hope she's okay."

"Me, too. The waitress is supposed to give me her address. She's writing it down."

"What are you going to do?"

"I'm going to her place—tonight."

"What if she's already gone?"

"I have to find out what she knows about Mr. Kim. She's the only one who knows. I know it. I just know."

The waitress slipped a small folded piece of paper on the table in front of Margot.

Her jjigae had gone lukewarm, but she didn't care about eating anymore. She had to find Mrs. Baek before it was too late.

MINA

FALL 1987

With the sun hanging low, a dusky and molten landscape of clouds striated and stretched thin, and the dark silhouettes of palm trees backlit, Mina and Mr. Kim, on their second date, drove west in his station wagon down Olympic Boulevard, one of the longest streets in the city. It was lined with stores, restaurants, and shopping plazas through Koreatown but rapidly dwindled down to a residential area with mostly single-family homes around its intersection with Crenshaw Boulevard.

Staring out the window, Mina marveled at how much her life had changed in the past several months since moving to America, how large and strange the world now seemed in this foreign place of warm weather and cold surfaces—cars, speed, metal, and glass between people. She missed Korea and its quiet alleyways, snow melting into clear water, the mustard-colored leaves of gingko trees, undulating stone shingles on roofs, despite coups, military rule, wars, a border that was not a scar but an open wound.

And how could she remove the memory of the physical beauty from the memory of her losses, the tremendousness of that pain? Absence was always present. Thunder, bombs dropping. Now she had only this dull ugliness, this dull drone—the charmless buildings, the boring roads, the battered buses, drooping palm trees gone brown—spectacularly lit.

"Are you cold?" Mr. Kim adjusted the temperature with the dial.

"A little. I'm okay."

"Let me know if you want me to turn the heat up some more."

"Okay."

"How was your day today?"

Earlier, Mina had slipped into his car, afraid that someone might see her from the store. She had been at work all day, distracted, ringing up items twice or giving the incorrect change. She had been unable to sleep the night before.

"It was fine," she said. "Yours? I didn't see you at all."

"I took the day off." He cleared his throat. "I wasn't feeling so well this morning."

"Are you okay?"

"Yeah, totally fine. Just some stomach problems I sometimes have." He sighed. "Been really busy at the store."

"Yeah, seems that way."

"I guess, that's a good thing. More customers, maybe more money."

"Or maybe just more work."

He laughed. "Yeah, pretty much. One of these days, I'm going to own my own place."

"What kind of place?"

"Grocery store. I'm a grocery man."

She smiled. "You make it sound like that's your destiny."

"Why not? I mean, what else? The only thing I like better than food is books. But what am I going to do, sell Bibles? What kind of books do people buy in Koreatown?"

"There's a bookstore near the market."

"Have you ever been in there?"

"Sure." She thought of the Spanish textbook she had bought a couple weeks ago.

"It's Bibles and English and Spanish books. And maybe some other stuff, but no one has time to read anymore. All we do is work... But everyone has to eat."

"I hope so," she joked.

"The grocery store is the future."

"The grocery store is now." She cracked up, covering her mouth with her hand.

"I've been saving, but probably in a few years I'll start a store somewhere else, maybe in the Valley, so I'm not..."

"Directly competing with the boss," Mina finished.

He grinned. "Exactly."

Driving down Olympic Boulevard toward a wide sky of hot bright streaks of citrus pink, he turned down a residential street with small but well-maintained homes and green lawns with rose bushes still in bloom, shapely ornamental shrubs, trees pruned into pleasing forms, arms stretched open. He appeared to be taking in the surroundings and admiring the houses until they hit Pico Boulevard, where they turned right to continue west, the farthest she had been from Koreatown since that day in July when she had landed at LAX.

"So where are we going?" she asked.

"The beach."

"The beach? What is there to do at night?"

"Oh, restaurants, games, rides, all kinds of things. You haven't been yet?"

"Nope."

"How long have you been here again?" he asked.

"Few months."

"Well, you don't have a car. I'm only surprised you haven't been with one of your friends."

She thought of Mrs. Shin, her kids, her business. "Everyone's too busy."

"Do you like the beach?"

"Yes." She remembered sitting with her husband on the smooth hot sand at Naksan Beach, watching their daughter play in the waves, who seemed so tiny then in her shell pink swimsuit and floppy white hat. A much-needed weekend trip, a relief from the oppressive heat of the city. Mina loved the smell of the ocean. But she remembered also feeling guilty for wanting, for whatever reason, despite how much she loved them, to be alone. "I love the beach," she said. "You?"

"One of my favorite places." He smiled. "Reminds me of my childhood."

After parking on the side of a palm tree–lined road, already lit by the hollow glow of streetlamps, she opened the heavy car door to the surprise of a teeth-chattering wind that whipped her hair everywhere. She wrapped her sweater around her body. Despite the cold, the sharp salt and seaweed in the air cleared her heart and her head. Here she could forget LA's soot-colored sky like the aftermath of a constant fire, a perpetual burning. Here she might breathe again.

"Do you want my jacket?" he asked, walking by her side.

"No, that's okay. I'll get used to it."

"Are you sure?"

She nodded. Approaching the water, she read a high arch over a wide driveway lit up with words she didn't quite understand—*Santa Monica, Yacht Harbor, Sport Fishing Boating*,

Cafés—a beacon in a darkening sky. She recognized *fishing* and *boating* and *cafés*, but what was *yacht?* Was it a name?

"I thought we could just grab something on the pier," he said. "Something easy. Hot dog? Hamburger?"

"Sure." Seagulls chirped overhead.

"And then we could walk around, check out the Ferris wheel?"

"Um, I'm scared of heights." She smiled, embarrassed.

"You are?"

"Yeah. I don't want to fall."

"You should try this, though. It's going to be beautiful."

Down the walkway to the pier in a bustle of all ages and races, she thought about the first and last time she had been on a Ferris wheel when her daughter was four or five years old. Mina had closed her eyes the entire time. All she could imagine was them plummeting down from that wheel into the crowd below. The screams and the crash. She hated the creaking sounds that the seats made lurching in the wind. She swore to herself that she would never go up there again. She would stand back and watch on the ground where she belonged.

"What do you feel like eating?" he asked.

"Oh, anything."

"There's a pretty good place right here, off to the side. It's not fancy or anything, but they've got hamburgers and hot dogs."

She had tried American food a handful of times in Korea but never enjoyed the flavors—the taste of dry beef, bread, and cheese, the odd mealy tomato, the flappy lettuce. But tonight, she felt a little adventurous, ready to plunge into something different—American food in where else? America. She had already enjoyed Mexican food from a taco truck parked a few blocks away from the market; she craved the bright salsas, the lime squeezed on meat, the soft, moist tortillas.

"What do you think you'd like?" he asked as they stood before the menu board of a simple and low rectangular building, weather-beaten on the pier.

"What do you recommend?"

"Really anything. I think I'll get a cheeseburger."

"I'll have the same."

He stepped toward the counter while she stood there watching him—the flex of his arms as he reached to pull his wallet out of his back pocket, the way his thick black hair faded into his neck. The smooth lines of his back, his waist. When he turned around, she couldn't help but smile, still looking at him.

"Busy night," she said. "So many people out."

"Yeah, people love this place."

"Do you come here a lot?"

"I used to come here all the time, but now I come every now and then. Sometimes I just walk on the pier. I like to see the ocean. It always clears my head. We'll have to come when it's light out sometime—that's nice, too, but different."

Behind the counter, a woman called their number. After thanking her, he picked up the tray with two cheeseburgers, a pile of fries, and two cans of Coke. From an empty table by the window, they could watch the water as the sun slipped below the horizon.

"Sorry, I forgot to ask what you wanted to drink. I got you a Coke, but I could get you something else."

She popped the can open and sipped. "It's good."

She wasn't sure how to eat her cheeseburger, so she picked at it with her fingers, tearing off pieces to put in her mouth and enjoying the taste of the lettuce and tomato, the greasy meat and cheese between the bread. She watched him dip his head to the burger, ripping with his teeth and chewing. American food seemed so barbaric. Where were the chopsticks?

She took a bite, mimicking Mr. Kim, and covered her

mouth with her hand as she chewed the massive amount of food. She tried hard not to laugh at herself.

"Are you okay?"

She motioned with her finger that she needed a minute. After she had swallowed the food, she asked, "How do Americans eat like this?"

"Is it good? Is everything okay?"

"Yes, it's all delicious, but…messy." She grinned.

"You'll get used to it. I try not to eat it too much. Not the healthiest, but I do love french fries." He grabbed a couple, gesturing for her to try.

She dipped one in the tiny cup of ketchup and popped it in her mouth.

"I can get used to this," she said.

"Ha, I know. I gotta be careful." He patted his stomach.

"You don't have anything to worry about. You're so thin."

He laughed. "You think so?"

"Yes."

"Skinny?"

"No, not skinny. Just right." She blushed, looking down at her cheeseburger and taking another bite. Eager to change the subject, she asked, "So you went to the beach a lot growing up?"

"Yes, I did. I grew up in the south, Busan."

"Oh, that's supposed to be nice. Never been."

"It is. I think about it a lot." His eyes locked into hers. She looked away, pretending not to notice. "I guess this isn't a bad place to be, though." He stared out the window, admiring the carnival lights.

"No, it's not." She wanted to reassure him, to reassure them both.

"Lots of work," he said.

"Yeah." Her gaze rested on the salt and pepper shakers, the fries.

"Are you not sure about being here, in America?" he asked.

"I haven't figured it out yet."

"Well, something I learned is you don't have to know where you are going to, you know, enjoy yourself a little, have a good time."

Tears filled her eyes. She picked up one of the last fries and placed it in her mouth, chewing slowly.

After finishing the food, Mr. Kim threw away their trash. A blast of mist and wind struck them as they ducked out of the café onto the worn boards of the pier. The rough surface pressed through the soles of her shoes to her feet, still throbbing after the day at work.

"Here, take my jacket." He took off his windbreaker.

"No, that's okay. You'll catch a cold."

"Please take it." He held it out to her, insisting. She reached for it, but instead he helped her put it on from behind. She slid her arms through the large jacket and zipped it around her body. The warmth engulfed her.

He suppressed a smile. "You look funny in that," he said.

"Thanks."

"No, I mean, you look cute."

She couldn't help but chuckle, wanting to hit him playfully on the arm. But she felt conscious of how close they stood together, how he could reach out his hand and grab hers as they walked past the carnival games, the wild pulsing lights, the stuffed neon animals. How his fingers would feel between hers.

He stopped in front of a tent with basketball hoops. "Should we play a game?"

"Oh, I'm no good."

"Here, let's try this one. I'm Magic Johnson." He pretended to dribble and mimed a sloppy jump shot.

She laughed. "I'm terrible, it'll just be a waste of money."

"Let's try." At a red-and-white-striped booth, he purchased a handful of tokens. After handing them to the vendor, they threw the ball wildly, missing each time. Mina screamed when she almost shot her ball into another person's hoop. Finally after several rounds, both Mr. Kim and Mina scored, one after the other. They jumped up and down, high-fiving like children, victorious and giddy.

They each won a small white teddy bear, holding a red heart between its paws.

"I'll give you mine, if you give me yours?" he asked.

"Why should I? I like mine better."

"They're the same."

"No, they're not. Mine is more symmetrical."

"Okay, fine. Yours is more symmetrical." He pouted playfully.

"I'm just kidding. Give me yours." She took his bear and placed hers in his hand. For a second, they held them together, admiring their silly faces—the bulbous snout and half-moon ears, the saccharine heart.

"Thank you very much," he said in English.

"You're welcome very much." She couldn't help but laugh.

Through the maze of people, mostly younger than them, her self-consciousness twinged. She squeezed the bear in her hand. Was she cheating on her husband? In their fifteen-year marriage, there had been only a handful of times when she had come close to even thinking about another man. Nothing had actually happened. She had met an attractive new coworker, or she would pass someone on the street, and she would imagine what it would be like to be with that person—a dinner, an embrace, a kiss. It flashed in her mind like a projection on a movie screen. When she thought about these moments, she hated herself. But why should she? Hadn't her husband ever thought about someone else—a pair of legs passing, a pretty smile? How was it possible, human, to not imagine the possibilities?

She panted, breath quick and shallow, questions seated on her chest. Her mind, like a fine fishing net, strangled the details around her, the sounds: a shriek of laughter, children screaming, a man singing in a Spanish baritone, the thumping bass of a boom box.

"What do you think?"

Without her realizing it, they had reached the Ferris wheel line.

"Wanna try?" He raised his dark brows. His eyes, however, appeared sympathetic, ready to be turned down.

As she lifted her face toward the sky, the questions unseated themselves; her brain was less of a tangle. The wheel seemed gentle, a spider's web made from steel and light. "Okay."

"Are you sure? You don't have to if you don't want to." He smiled.

"I think I'll be all right."

As he walked toward the ticket booth, she waited, watching him, still holding the bear. Black beady eyes. Red heart. Thinking of her daughter's stuffed animals, she hugged the bear to her chest. She could almost cry. She didn't want to think about her anymore. But if she stopped thinking about her, would that be a betrayal? How could she manage to love and honor people without those feelings tearing her apart? How could she continue to hold on to them without it destroying every bit of her, shredding every possibility and hope she might dare to have?

He returned with the tickets. "Are you okay?"

"Yes. I'm fine."

They walked to wait at the end of the line. "Are you cold still?"

"A little."

"I wish I had more layers to pull off," he said.

"Ha, that's okay."

"Wait here. I'll get us something to warm up."

The crowd, bodies like bees in a hive, swallowed him. A mass, strange faces and limbs.

An explosion blasted inside her mind. Her knees almost buckled as she clung to that rope inside her brain. She had been holding her mother's hand, and suddenly she was not. She was lost. Frightened, she had cried out at the people, rushing by her to get out. She had fallen to the ground, smoky and sulfurous, the earth's shards stabbing her, had been almost trampled except that a man, a stranger, had helped her, had picked her up and placed her on top of his shoulders even though blood ran fresh from his scalp.

Mr. Kim returned with two Styrofoam cups, startling her out of the memory. "Have you had hot chocolate?"

"No, never," she said, relieved he was back.

"I think you'll like it."

She blew on the drink before sipping. "Mmm, that's good." She wanted to gulp it all down, but it was too hot.

"I guess you have a sweet tooth."

"Didn't realize it until now." She'd always liked chocolate but had never had it melted into a drink before, a comfort. She leaned her head back, entranced by the Ferris wheel, the swaying cars, the lights dancing, winking at the world.

"You're going to be cold up there," she said. "You don't want your jacket back?"

"I'll be okay."

As they walked up the line, the attendant said, "You have to throw away those drinks."

She took a final sip before he placed their two cups in a trashcan nearby. "I was hoping we could hold on to those."

"Me, too."

As she climbed on, the entire car rocked as if they could flip over and she squealed sitting down.

"Don't worry," he said, grabbing her hand gently. She squeezed his hand back as they rose higher and higher into the black sky. The crowd below them receded, shrank in size. Shivering, she sat the closest to him that she ever had, the side of her hip pressed against his.

"I'm going to close my eyes," she said.

"Okay. Don't worry."

While the wheel rotated, gliding up and over and down and under, she squeezed his hand harder, eyes closed. Her heart thumped against the wall of her chest. Teeth chattering, they huddled together closer. He reached his arm around her shoulders. The cars creaked gently around them.

"Are you okay?" he asked.

"Yes, just keeping my eyes closed." She laughed. "I know it's childish."

"Don't worry. It's a big step for you. Be happy that you made it this far."

"You mean…"

"On the Ferris wheel. You didn't have to get on, but you did."

His breath was close to her ear, her neck. She turned her head toward him, and he touched his lips against hers. She kissed him, tasting chocolate, the salt in the air around them. She became nothing but a body, far away and light, built for flying.

And when he lifted his face from hers, she opened her eyes to the contrasts of the world below—bright and sparkling, deep and dark, everywhere, magnificently, breathtakingly around her.

MARGOT

FALL 2014

L amplights glowed steady and unflinching while television screens flickered behind gauzy curtains, closed windows. A chorus of dogs behind fences and walls accompanied the howls of sirens. Sweet corn masa toasted on a griddle somewhere. Regardless of temperature or season, there was always something burning in Los Angeles—a bacon-wrapped hot dog, a roach of weed, short ribs sizzling, the rubber of tires in the heat, an entire neighborhood crackling with sparks in July, an entire forest on fire. You'd never forget the flames.

Sitting in her car, parked beside a strip of dying lawn with succulents and cacti in battered ceramic pots, Margot gathered herself, breathing through her mouth. Twenty minutes earlier, the waitress at Hanok House had slipped her this address near MacArthur Park. It was still only Monday.

Through the open courtyard, Margot ascended the first

flight of stairs to Mrs. Baek's apartment. Unit 211. Her knuckles rapped on the door. The pads of her fingers lingered on the smooth gray surface as if touching an animal.

A shadow filled the muted light of the fisheye on the door.

"Who is it?" Mrs. Baek asked, gruff and harsh.

"It's Mina's daughter, Margot."

The door creaked open to reveal a brass chain bisecting Mrs. Baek's face—pale and ghostly without makeup, hair wrapped in a salmon-colored towel. She squinted and asked, "What are you doing here?"

"Could I talk to you?"

"It's late. How'd you get my address?"

"I...googled you."

She sighed, unlatching the chain. "I was just about to put on a sheet mask."

The cramped living room smelled of a used bookstore—a dust-covered breakdown of paper and ink—and thick cucumber cold cream. Stacks of books and newspapers on the coffee table resembled a fragile skyline that could topple to the ground. A fire hazard.

Margot sank into the velvet of an old hunter green couch—a vintage curbside piece that had been cleaned and now animated a space that resembled more of an office or a storage closet. On the flat-screen television between the living and dining areas, the Korean news had been muted.

In a gray dove-colored robe over a pink sleeping gown, frayed hem kissing her bony knees, Mrs. Baek crossed her arms beneath her chest, remote control in hand. Without her armor of makeup—the red lipstick, the eyebrows penciled into the slivers of a moon—she resembled a tropical bird plucked of its feathers.

"I wanted to ask you some questions," Margot said.

Mrs. Baek crossed her arms. "About?"

The claustrophobia of the room closed in on Margot. What was she thinking coming here? But she thought of what she was searching for and steeled herself.

"Mr. Kim and my mother," Margot said.

Mrs. Baek tightened the towel wrap on her head.

"I went to the swap meet today," Margot continued. "Your store was gone."

Mrs. Baek planted a dining chair in front of Margot and sat down. "I'm done."

"With work?"

"For now." She bit into a hangnail. "Did you see any customers there?"

"No."

"I've been losing money for a while."

Business was slow again today. Even all the Korean businesses downtown are closing.

The waitress expected Margot to refrain from mentioning Mr. Park, but she wanted to know if Mrs. Baek was safe. Even if her business had been doing poorly, it seemed odd that Mrs. Baek would close down her store right before the holidays— the most lucrative time of the year.

"Any other reason why? Seems like you closed things down pretty quickly."

"I've been…planning this for a while."

"What will you do now?"

"I'm not sure. I'll survive. Don't worry about me."

"Will you go back to Hanok House?" Margot asked, knowing the answer but hoping that she could provoke some response.

"No, not there. Never again." Mrs. Baek adjusted the knot on her robe's belt.

Margot examined a stack of books on the coffee table, novels that she had read in high school and college herself. Difficult books. Beautiful books. George Eliot. Edith Wharton. Pages on pages like teeth once white, now yellowed. How a book was kind of like a mouth. Did stories keep us alive or kill us with false expectations? It depended on who wrote them perhaps.

"You read these?" Margot asked, noticing Thomas Hardy's *Tess of the D'Urbervilles*, one of her favorites, in a pile. A pang of sorrow filled her as she thought of that story, and its end. "My mom never read."

"She hated reading." Mrs. Baek leaned back in her chair. "Believe it or not, I majored in English. Like you."

Those words, *like you*, wrung something in Margot's chest. How much *had* her mother talked about Margot? Had she been proud of her?

Mrs. Baek planted her hands on her knees, ready to stand. "It's getting late," she said. "My sheet mask is calling."

"Could I ask you about Mr. Kim?"

"I don't know that much, to be honest." Her voice trembled. "Like I said, she didn't tell me about him until *after* he died."

"Was he my father?" Margot's heart thumped inside of her chest.

Mrs. Baek widened her eyes in shock.

"I found his obituary at our apartment. There's a picture of him. He looks like me."

Biting down on her lip, Mrs. Baek remained silent.

"It doesn't make sense that they would be together otherwise. I visited his house in Calabasas, you know? He had this beautiful house, a beautiful life. His wife is stunning. He was living in an entirely different world. How could they have met? What would they have in common except for the past?"

Mrs. Baek inhaled deeply, staring down at her lap.

Margot leaned back, hands on the velvet couch again. "He owned some supermarkets. I remember my mother said that my father worked at the same supermarket as her when she first came to America. Why else would he—what else would the connection be between them? Or maybe they were just friends from back then? But every time I look at his picture—" Her voice shook. "I swear—"

"It's him," Mrs. Baek interrupted, brows furrowed. "You're right. He was your father, Margot."

"Why didn't anyone tell me?" Her heart broke. She needed air.

Mrs. Baek shook her head in response.

"Why didn't anyone tell me?" Margot shouted—angry at her mother, Mrs. Baek, the world. Crying, she rose to her feet.

"Because your mother thought there was no reason for you to know. He was dying. There was no reason to tell him about you as well. What would be the point?" Mrs. Baek tightened the towel around her head. "*She* made that decision."

"But it's not fair. I would've rather known. I wouldn't care that he was dying."

"Maybe she just didn't want to tell *him*," she responded fiercely. "It's a tough thing to find out when you're sick. He had cancer. She was trying to protect you both." She burst into tears and sobbed. "She was trying to protect you. She was trying to protect everyone." She wiped her nose on the sleeve of her gray robe.

Margot plopped down again on the couch. Mrs. Baek stood and left the room, returning with a box of tissues that she handed to Margot.

"I still don't understand." Margot blew her nose. "And now—what? What do I do with all this information? It's useless to me now. They're both dead."

Mrs. Baek sat next to Margot, held her hand. "The past is…" She winced, her eyes fixed on the carpet. "Sometimes, it's better to forget. You have still so much ahead of you, okay? You have to… *We* have to move on, okay?"

"But I don't want to, not until I understand. Whether it was really just an accident."

"Your mother's death?"

Margot nodded. "I'm not going to—to move on until I understand. I can't move on until—"

"Until when? Until you realize it was not your fault?" Mrs. Baek's eyes glistened. "Do you feel guilty?"

Margot's cheeks burned. "I should've checked on her more often, visited her more often. Maybe I wouldn't have…prevented anything, but also maybe I would've known what was going on in her life. I could've—"

"It wasn't your fault, Margot." Mrs. Baek squeezed Margot's wrist. "It was an accident. A very bad accident." Wiping the corners of her eyes, she said, "We all wish that we could've done something differently, right? But it's not really worth revisiting. We all could've done things differently." She focused on the piles of books in front of them. "That's the problem with memory."

Her mother could crack open a moment with her memory as if the present was nothing but an eggshell, spotted and frail. As a teenager, Margot had begged her mother once to attend a concert (she couldn't even remember the band now). Even if Margot had secured a ride with her friend's parents, which was a lie, her mother did not want her out at night.

"Do you know how hard I work?" her mother had yelled in Korean. "Do you know how hard I work? I haven't done anything fun for years. Fun?"

"Why won't you let me be happy?" Margot yelled in English with little care for her neighbors next door.

"You should be doing schoolwork. You should be at home.

Do you know how lucky you are? Do you know what I was doing at your age?" Her mother jabbed her own chest with an index finger. "I worked in a factory all day as a child. Do you know what that's like? I got sick all the time. Terrible things happened to children like us. We were all burdens. We were all mouths to feed. I had to learn to feed myself. There is no fun. There is no fun in this world."

But her mother's harshness was designed to protect Margot from what her mother considered to be a universe without shelter, without much kindness for kindness's sake. Of course, her mother would perceive the world that way—so much of her identity was about the past. She was floating, like all of us, in history. Yet the taste of hers was particularly foul and dark, filled with smoke and flame.

Tears streamed down Margot's face. She had to get out of this room. Clawing. She needed air. Gripping the arm of the sofa, she stood and moved to the door.

"Sorry to come by so late." She placed her hand on the doorknob.

"Your mother... She was very lonely when she first came here." Mrs. Baek offered this—a departing gesture perhaps to help Margot forgive herself, forgive her mother at last.

But Margot didn't turn. She hated that word, *lonely*. She wanted to ask, *What about me? It's not my fault she was lonely. It's not my fault that I was born. I was lonely, too. I was lonely. Nobody wanted me.* But she remained silent, clenching her teeth.

"She was like a lot of us. Lonely. But that's what it's like for women like us. That's why...we were the way we were. That's why we make the decisions that we make. So that we can survive. We can get by. We can protect each other." Mrs. Baek sighed. "She would've done anything for you. You kept her safe. You saved her."

Margot couldn't hear any more. Gasping for air, she stepped out of the apartment, descended the stairs, and rushed through the courtyard into the street. She waited in the car, catching her breath. A single lamp beamed onto the vacant sidewalk.

Women like us.

Margot's brain was a wild animal, clawing out of her head. The net that wrapped around Margot's ankles, threatening to drag her into the sea.

You saved her.

But she hadn't. She had been too late.

Margot wound her way past MacArthur Park, its black lake glowing with smeared reflections of light, toward 10 West, realizing now that she never owned a car in Los Angeles, that her whole life until she moved away at the age of eighteen had been confined to buses, walking, and riding with her mother on surface streets. And yet she could always find the freeway, at least I-10, as if the signs toward them had somehow been imprinted on the map of her memory, the bones of her hands and feet that drove this car now to the ocean.

She had never taken a car onto the pier, which jutted like a driveway onto the sea toward the horizon, a visual cliff. The wheels rumbled beneath her over the boards. She imagined gassing it, a *Thelma & Louise* end, flying through the metal handrails and over the edge. She'd be weightless and free before plunging into the terrible deep. Inhaling the salt and water would be both the end and a great relief.

In the pier's parking lot, she turned the car off and stared at the dark ocean and the Ferris wheel, a many-spoked strobe that throbbed like the heart of this place, dreamlike, up and over and around, dipping the rider back into life and out again. She got out and jogged toward the ticket booth, empty at this time of night. Standing in line for the Ferris wheel, alone, the salt air and the carnival food cleansed her head.

After stepping in one of the tubs, which swung beneath her, she waited as the others boarded, and she rose into the black night, light, eating air.

MINA

WINTER 1987–1988

Mina thought about the first night they had kissed on the Ferris wheel, how the car had swayed beneath them as they revolved again and again at a steady pace, floating in the night sky. Teeth chattering. Salt air and hot chocolate. His breath close to her ear and neck. She had been terrified of both the ride malfunctioning and the free fall of plunging into the depths of what she could feel, her body and her lips pressed against his.

She had been taking an inventory of his kindnesses—the way he had given her his jacket that night, brought her a drink to keep her warm, hadn't teased her for closing her eyes when the wheel started to turn. Her husband would've done that, not out of cruelty, but because he enjoyed innocuous jabs, jokes, laughter—a quality that appealed to her more serious self.

But what if this was a ruse, this thing between her and Mr. Kim? What if she allowed him to get close, showed him love, only for him to change? What if she were to lose herself in the feelings, the illusion of potential happiness again? What if, what if, what if?

Since riding the Ferris wheel, they had spent many nights together, even a weekend celebrating the holidays in Las Vegas—a neon place of lush, dizzying distraction. She had played the slot machines, lost money and won it back again, witnessed a kangaroo box with a man in a circus ring as cowboy clowns chased each other around the stage. At a dinner buffet, they gorged themselves on American food—breaded chicken, grilled steak, macaroni and cheese, all kinds of potatoes (baked, fried, roasted). She refused to drink, mostly because she didn't like to, but also because she had become afraid of losing herself again.

After her husband and daughter's deaths, she had spiraled out of control for almost a week, crawling around the apartment on her knees and elbows, only to throw up in the restroom. Drinking was the lone response she had for pain. And drunkenness gave her permission to express her anger, her rage in flashes of tearing clothes or smashing plates. When she couldn't drag herself to the store, the cough syrup in the medicine cabinet could bludgeon her mind enough to get her through a night.

But now, with Mr. Kim, in a tangle of sheets on the bed, at restaurants, by the turquoise pool of a motel, she hadn't felt this good in a long time. She often caught herself smiling for no reason, checking her hair and makeup in mirrors that she passed by.

Both Mrs. Baek and the landlady noticed the shift in her appearance, her demeanor, and habits. The landlady bestowed upon her a knowing smirk or a nod of approval every now and then, but Mrs. Baek never shied away from asking direct questions, even though Mina didn't feel ready to talk about Mr. Kim yet.

Some nights, Mina didn't have the energy to avoid Mrs. Baek. They shared the same kitchen, the same bathroom. Less than ten feet separated their bedroom doors.

"I grilled some mackerel. Do you like mackerel?" Mrs. Baek asked two days before the end of the year.

"Yes, I do." Mina loved the fish's oily and sticky smell, the beauty of its dark stripes, the crispiness of the skin when grilled.

Mrs. Baek had prepared a feast—seasoned spinach and soybean sprouts, baechu kimchi and kkakdugi, pickled perilla leaves, and two types of jjigae—compared to their usual meals of maybe two or three banchan and soup.

"Go ahead." She motioned to Mina.

Picking up her chopsticks, Mina tasted the kimchi—rich and tangy with hints of pear and shrimp.

"How's your boyfriend?" Mrs. Baek asked, adjusting her position on the bench.

Mina tried to smile. "He's okay."

"Has he been nice?"

"He's been fine. Yes. He's nice." The mackerel's flesh slipped away from the bones, melted like butter in her mouth. How this fish tasted like comfort on a winter night even here in Los Angeles. "How about you? Are you interested in anyone?" Mina only now remembered that Mrs. Baek had once said, *I don't think I'll trust any man again.*

"No." Mrs. Baek laughed to herself. "I have books. I have music. I don't need a boyfriend. I'm busy."

"What is that supposed to mean?"

"I mean that you seemed bored before, that's all. All you did was work. I'm not bored. I'm never bored."

"I see, because you're so interesting." Mina placed her hands on the table. "Educated."

"I didn't mean it that way," Mrs. Baek said. "I wasn't talking about you. I was referring to myself."

Mina slid off the bench and cleaned up her side of the table.

"Just leave it there," Mrs. Baek said. "I'm sorry."

"No, I'm sorry. I'll put this soup back. I haven't touched it."

"Don't do that."

She grabbed the bowl and Mrs. Baek pulled it back.

"Please sit down. I'm sorry."

Mina realized then how much she had been a little frightened by Mrs. Baek—her quick mind and mouth, carefully drawn brows, her relaxed sense of self, sprawling like the city itself. But at the same time, Mrs. Baek had been too generous, too helpful, and, yes, maybe even too interesting to deny from her life. And she made some of the most delicious banchan. Something as simple as a leaf fermented could create a moment, a meal that resembled a home, even if you never really had one.

Mina sat down again, gazing at what remained of the mackerel—the brown meat at the belly, the clear bones pronounced.

"Anyway, I was wrong, okay? I didn't mean what I said. It has nothing to do with you. I'll never trust men. I don't know how anymore."

"Were you married before?" Mina asked.

"Yes, yes, I was." Mrs. Baek's face grew red. "He was terrible."

"Do you talk to him still?"

"No, God, no." Her nostrils flared. "He lives in Texas."

"You ran away?"

"Yes. I didn't have a choice." Her voice trembled. It was the first time that Mina had seen Mrs. Baek this vulnerable.

Mina reached out her hand and rubbed Mrs. Baek's wrist with her thumb.

"Maybe I'm just a little bitter sometimes," Mrs. Baek said. "I wasted so much of my life. And now what?"

"You're still alive," Mina said, both to Mrs. Baek and herself. "Isn't it a miracle? That we're still here?" Tears filled her eyes. "No one would have expected this of us. We surprised them. We surprised ourselves."

Entering the kitchen, the landlady said, "That smells good."

"Do you want to join us?" Mrs. Baek asked, pulling her arm gently away from Mina, who lowered her head, wiping her face.

"No, I'm fine. I already ate. I'm just making some soup now for tomorrow."

After dinner, Mrs. Baek, as a kind of peace offering, peeled and sliced two golden apples, which they enjoyed together in silence. Mina swallowed the fruit—bright and sweet and tart as if just plucked from the branch—with an intense satisfaction.

Despite all their efforts to forge their own lives in this foreign land as individuals, it was obvious: they needed each other. They reminded one another with shared food or words that life, although mostly mundane and sometimes painful, was still spectacular, full of wonder, especially when we pushed ourselves toward the edge, beyond our fears, as Mr. Kim had asked Mina to ride the Ferris wheel, and imagine another life, with him.

At his one-bedroom apartment off Normandie Avenue in Koreatown, Mina and Mr. Kim would eat dinner after work and then—arms draped, thighs touching, fingers laced—they would watch the Korean news and occasionally an American show. Eventually, they would make their way to the bedroom to make love. Lying next to each other afterward, with Mr. Kim snoring loudly, Mina would sometimes stare at the ceiling, wondering what had become of her life, how it had all happened so quickly.

A couple months into their relationship, a TV special aired on the local Korean channel about the temporary reunification events for Korean families separated in the North and the South without any ability to communicate with each other for decades since the Korean War. These families had been torn apart, members lost, in the process of fleeing the violence and death that erased millions of people. How could they have known that one day their country would be split in two, severing them from their mothers, fathers, brothers, sisters, children, without any palpable end in sight?

And the reunification opportunities were scarce. Tens of thousands of families remained on the waiting lists, hoping to be chosen by the lottery, not knowing if they would die before they got the chance to see their loved ones again.

Mina closed her eyes, yearning to change the channel. She couldn't bear the volume of feeling, the faces stretched with a violence of so many emotions, the raw complexity in response to so many years lost between members of the same family on the screen. Grandmothers in hanboks wept, holding the faces of each other between wrinkled and spotted hands. Grandfathers cried and begged for forgiveness at the feet of the children, now adults, whom they had left behind, not knowing that the war and border would separate them forever.

But Mr. Kim remained transfixed by the screen, red creeping up his neck and face.

From a box that he kept on his coffee table, Mina handed him a tissue. Her heart cracked. "I'll change the channel," she said.

"No. I want to see this."

On the television, the elderly offered testimonials on who they were missing and how much they hoped to hear from or see them again before dying. Tears streamed down so many faces. Hands clutched handkerchiefs and tissues as the reunited, dressed in their best suits or hanboks, dropped to the ground, grabbing each other as if checking to make sure that the bodies of the lost were real. A single human being could live an entire continent of pain and worry and longing.

"Do you ever wonder if your parents might still be there, in North Korea?" Mr. Kim asked.

"What do you mean?"

"When you lost your parents—where were you when you lost them?"

"I don't remember. I only remember there were hills, dirt, people fleeing. That's all I remember."

"Do you ever think that maybe they never made it across?"

"No, I've never thought of that." Heat rose from the pit of her stomach through her lungs and throat.

"But maybe that's why they never found you," he said, disturbed.

"Maybe. I guess there's nothing to do about it now." She stood to change the channel.

"No, not yet."

"I don't want to watch this anymore."

"Just let me finish this, please."

"I'll go and sit in the bedroom."

As she entered the bedroom and lay down, tears spilled from her eyes, soaking the pillowcase beneath her head. Why was he doing this to her? What did he know about her parents? How dare he assume that they hadn't made it through? What kept her alive all these years was the thought that they were fine, maybe they had moved on without her, maybe they had another child, but they were fine. They were fine.

They were somewhere in South Korea. They had normal lives. They had moved on. They were fine. Fine. Fine.

She wanted to yell this to him. She wanted to scream, but she didn't. She couldn't afford to lose him now.

Ten minutes had gone by until she heard him stepping toward her. With her back facing the door, her body tilted like a canoe as he sat on the bed by her feet. He put his hand on her leg, which he squeezed in the softest way as if testing the reality of her presence in his life.

"I'm sorry," he said.

"Don't worry," she said, trying to disguise in her voice that she had been crying.

"I'm very sorry."

A sharp sob escaped his mouth like a hiccup as he wept. She turned to see his face above hers, broken, before he covered it with his hand. She wanted to touch his face but didn't know how, not at that moment.

"I... I should have told you this before," Mr. Kim said softly. "I was hoping that I would see my father. Every time anything about North Korea is on television—I always hope to see my father."

She sat up in bed. He bowed his head, staring at her legs, which were a kind of border between them.

"My mother, when she was pregnant with me, left the North with her brother and parents. My father had to stay behind for work. He wanted to take care of everything, the home we had. He didn't want to just leave, but she never saw him again after that." He paused to wipe the tears from his eyes. "No one knows what happened to him. My mother tried, but who knows? So many people back then, everyone just trying to get out. Maybe he made it. Maybe not." He wiped his nose on his sleeve. "Anyway, I like to believe that if I saw his face, I'd know it was him. I'd know—there's my father. That's why I watch the TV."

She reached to touch him as tears leaked out of her eyes. She wanted to be strong for him, but she couldn't hold herself together.

"She raised me by herself," he continued. "It was very hard. She did all kinds of things, just so we could get by. She could've lost me, too, when she was pregnant. There was so little to eat. It's really a miracle that I'm alive. She was a very good mother."

"Where is she now?"

"In Busan. Getting old, though."

"She never remarried?"

"No. As I got older, I tried to convince her, but she always seemed to think that one day, she would see my dad again, and she wouldn't want to tell him that she had remarried. I guess, she's waiting. She's been on the list for a while. But she doesn't even know if he's still alive or what. No one knows. It's all a mystery."

He wiped his eyes before lying down on the bed. She joined him. Her hand rested on the side of his face where she could feel the sandpaper of his stubble under her palm, her fingertips on his cheekbone. This man's kindness emerged out of the cruelties of their lives like birds hatched on fields ruined by mines and barbed wire. She wanted to be kind, to be gentle, too. He was showing her that it was okay to try.

"I thought one day, I'd get rich." His eyes brightened as if laughing at himself inside. "I'd come to America, get rich, and go back, you know? And if I had enough money, we could find him. But that doesn't seem to be going to plan either. I'm sort of trapped here now."

"We're trapped together," she said with a smile.

"At least I met you."

"There's still time."

"Yes, there's still time, but we're getting old. All of us. Especially my mother."

"How old is she?"

"She's in her fifties."

"She's still young."

He lowered his eyes. The tips of his fingers trailed her arm.

"Have you tried prayer?" Mina asked.

"I have, but God gives me the cold shoulder."

"That's not true." But she felt that way on most days herself.

"I'm sorry about what I said earlier," he said. "I'm sure your family is fine."

Pipes tapped on the walls as the shower ran. In the next apartment, a neighbor snored.

Mina couldn't fall back asleep. Her mind turned over Mr. Kim's words like stones that clacked soothingly on a shore: *She always seemed to think that one day, she would see my dad again, and she wouldn't want to tell him that she had remarried.*

What if his father was dead already? All those years his mother would have wasted, alone. But then again, what if the hope of never having to move on was what kept her alive? Maybe the tragedy of waiting was the only way she survived?

Would Mina be able to face *her* husband in the afterlife?

Would he be angry about Mr. Kim?

In heaven, if they were all dead, would they awkwardly have to see each other? Or would heaven mean that she could have two lives? Was heaven a world in which she could have them both but separately? She wondered if her brain and her heart could even handle the different iterations of her life, the many ways a song could be played. A change in lyrics, a different tempo and pace.

Perhaps thinking she was still asleep, Mr. Kim tiptoed toward his closet from which he pulled out his day's outfit—his polo shirt, his khaki slacks. A eucalyptus scent from his aftershave, clean and fresh, filled the room, which had become a bit musty from the windows unopened in winter. With her eyes half-open, she observed him slide on his underwear and pants, admiring the muscles in his back and shoulders.

"You should keep your shirt off more often," she said.

"Ah, you're up." He turned around and sat on the edge of the bed, his hand on her leg. "Hope I didn't wake you."

"No, I had trouble falling asleep."

"Are you not feeling well? You could call in sick?" He slipped on his shirt.

"I wish."

"Do you want me to find out if someone could cover for you?"

"No, I don't think so. I'll be fine. I have at least five more hours. I'll get sleep now."

He kissed her wetly on the cheek.

"Ew," she said, wiping her face, laughing.

After she heard the locks on the front door click shut, the knob tested, she closed her eyes, thinking of him, trying to stay focused on him, them, the feel of his hand on her leg, the feel of his face beneath her fingers, now. But she couldn't shake the feeling that this couldn't last. Nothing did—good or bad.

Fifteen minutes early, Mina grabbed a can of 7-Up for the dull ache in her stomach and made her way to the rear of the store. She hadn't eaten lunch yet but wasn't hungry at all, so she stashed the ham sandwich and Fuji apple that she had packed for herself in her storage bin and returned to the registers up front.

For as long as she could remember, whenever upset or depressed, she couldn't force herself to eat. She could skip a few meals easily, unable to free herself from the weight of the sadness in her chest or the gnawing of a dolorous mind. Her emotions, like a long pin holding an insect or a butterfly into place, could control her in that way.

On her first day at the orphanage in front of a meal of beans and barley, her stomach had closed like a fist as if protecting the most vital, the most mysterious part of herself. All she could do was sip water until the nuns allowed her to leave the table after over two hours. Only after a few days of settling into the routines, the faces around her, could she finally ingest an entire meal, a watery doenjang jjigae, heavily boiled with summer squash. At her first bite, her entire body from head to toe tingled in a riot of sensations—a plant bulb buried in the most brutal winter scorched with a startling summer heat—and she had to fight herself from devouring the rice and soup like an animal.

At the front of the store, Mr. Kim, with his sweaty hair flopping and falling onto his forehead, appeared as if he had been running around all morning. When their eyes met, he flashed the most subtle yet knowing smile before jogging away to some task—a customer complaint, a shipment delayed, a bottle shattered on the floor in aisle three. Perhaps they had been understaffed that day.

She imagined him owning his own supermarket and how much pride she would have for him, knowing that he could help his mother one day. Maybe his mother could move to America, and they could take care of her together. Or maybe his mother would want to stay in Korea, but Mr. Kim could buy her a nice house and visit her once a year, lavishing her with gifts—chocolates, new shoes, and clothes.

How often did he go back to Korea these days, if ever at all? He never spoke of traveling despite his feelings for his mother. Could he not afford to take time off, or was he not able to fly freely because of his immigration status? How much could they ever know about each other?

Two bundles of green onions. Doenjang. Large sesame oil. Package of dried seaweed. Dried anchovies. Flour.

Six pack of Hite. Dried cuttlefish. Two boxes of Choco Pie.

She felt dizzy after a few hours, having to steady herself on the counter. Acid rose from her stomach to the root of her tongue. The flow of customers had slowed down, so she rushed to the back of the store, afraid she might faint or throw up.

Through the doorway of long rubber strips that slapped together as she passed through, the darkness and the drop in temperature revived her. She stood bent over, hands gripping the front of her thighs, catching her breath before she headed to the restroom. Arching her head backward, she gulped air through her mouth, worrying that she needed to go home. Maybe all she needed was rest—in her own room, on her own bed—alone.

Behind the door of Mr. Park's office, she heard chairs slide violently on the dusty floor. A woman shrieked.

Mina froze, startled by a fear that grabbed her by the throat. Unable to approach the sound, she ran back into the aisles, searching for Mr. Kim. Near the registers, he stood with an elderly woman. As soon as he saw Mina's face, he excused himself and followed her to the back where she pointed toward the door. He listened, then shouted, "Mr. Park." Silence. "Mr. Park!" He tried the knob and pushed inside.

Standing about fifteen feet away at a sharp angle that obscured the inside of Mr. Park's office, Mina heard a woman scream again. The men shouted, soon followed by the crashing sound of bodies colliding.

Mina didn't know what to do. She wanted to rush inside, but she was frozen in place, terrified. Should she hide?

"You son of a bitch," Mr. Park yelled from the room, panting as if catching his breath. "You're fired. Get out of here."

With his arm around the shoulders of a woman bent in pain, Mr. Kim limped through the door.

It was Lupe.

Mina's heart sank. The room spun. Foul acid rose in her throat.

"Let's get out of here," Mr. Kim whispered to Mina. "Before he sees you."

"What?"

"C'mon." He grabbed her hand. "Lupe, c'mon."

Together, they walked out the heavy back door into a cruel white sunlight. "My purse," Mina said. "My keys."

"We'll get our stuff later. I'll call Daniel and have him grab everything. We'll get it all later, okay?"

Opening the station wagon door, Mina motioned for Lupe to sit in the front seat where she sobbed uncontrollably with her face in her hand. Red ran down the side of Mr. Kim's jaw, dripping onto his shoulders, onto the polo shirt he had put on that morning in front of her. From the back seat, Mina searched the car for napkins, something to blot the blood but couldn't find anything. She removed her sweater and reached forward, holding it to his head.

"I'm—I'm so sorry," Lupe said in English, coughing, almost choking.

"No, no le preocupe. Le llevaremos a casa, a su casa," he said.

Mina reached to squeeze Lupe's shoulder, an attempt to say what she didn't know how to say in Spanish or English: *It's not your fault. None of this is your fault.*

Trapped in the back, unable to attend to Mr. Kim's wounds, unable to comfort Lupe, Mina's heart and mind raced as she scrambled to put together what had just happened. Swallowing the taste of her own vomit, she didn't want to think about what would happen to them now, later, tomorrow. She tried to calm her breath, closing her eyes.

"Son of a bitch," Mr. Kim hissed to himself.

Arriving at her apartment, Lupe tried to compose herself, wiping her face dry with her sleeve. Mina vomited on the strip of grass next to the sidewalk as soon as she opened the car door. Neither Lupe nor Mr. Kim noticed. For a second, Mina became distracted by a long trail of ants devouring a snail that had been smashed.

Body covered in bruises, forehead and hands bandaged, Mr. Kim lay on the bed, staring at the ceiling.

"What's going to happen now?" Mina asked.

"I don't know." He had described how he had walked into the office on Mr. Park holding Lupe down. Upon seeing him, Mr. Park pushed Lupe aside. She hit the corner of the desk as she went crashing to the ground. Mr. Kim punched Mr. Park in the face until his hands bled. And when he reached to help Lupe, Mr. Park shoved him into a bookshelf. Objects toppled onto his head.

"You son of a bitch. You're fired." Mr. Park had spit the words out of his bloody mouth.

Imagining Lupe's horror—that fear and entrapment and disgust—Mina yearned to kill Mr. Park. A box cutter to his neck. She remembered him emerging out of his office to help her while lifting cartons off the ground. The grip of a pistol had flashed at his side. *Are you sure you can do this?* He winked. Chills ran down her spine. Fists clenched. *I worked hard,* very *hard. And now, I'm the owner. I own all of this.*

She could break him down like one of his boxes, stuff his words back in his mouth. He deserved the worst kind of ending.

Mr. Kim sighed. "There's a chance…"

"A chance of what?"

"That he'll call the police on us." He squeezed his eyes shut.

"You? Why?" Her voice had grown hoarse.

"He has friends."

"What do you mean?"

"He has friends. Just… If he really wanted to…he could get rid of us all."

"But he already fired you." Her heart pounded in her chest, her head.

"If that's enough for him."

"What do you mean?"

"I don't know for sure, but my sense is that he had something to do with Mario getting sent back."

"What?"

"I don't have any proof. Maybe I'm just being paranoid." He shook his head. "The other day, he made this comment about what a good worker Lupe is. Then he said something about Mario not being able to keep himself out of trouble, that he wasn't smart enough to mind his own business." A tear leaked out of Mr. Kim's eye. "I didn't press him any further. But it's like he was trying to tell me something. It was like a warning. I don't know."

"Why would he call the police on *you* when you're the one who was trying to help Lupe? He's the criminal."

"Because he knows that *she* would not call the police. She could risk being deported. He could make up some kind of story about how I *assaulted* him. She has children. She would never go to the police."

"But I would say something. I could say something. I was there for everything."

"He's more powerful." His nostrils flared. "It's his story that gets heard, you see?"

Carefully, she pressed the adhesive of the bandage peeling off his forehead. The cotton had grown brown. She closed her eyes and an explosion blasted in her head. There was no mercy. Even the silence itself was preparation for the most horrible sounds. She had cried out at the people, desperate to save themselves, rushing by her. *Umma*, she had screamed through her tears. *Umma*. She couldn't get the screams and the whistles of the bombs out of her mind. The earth stabbed her knees when she fell to the ground.

She imagined blood spurting out of Mr. Park's neck.

"I better lie low for a while." Mr. Kim gripped her hand, nudging her back to the present.

"What do you mean?" She touched his arm in a gesture that urged him to lie back down with her.

"Hide. I don't know." His eyes wide. "I should call Lupe first, make sure she's okay."

"What? Where are you going to go? This doesn't make sense."

"I don't know." He covered his face with his hand.

"Are you thinking of leaving town?"

"I don't know."

"You can't leave town." She wanted to say, *You can't leave me now.*

"I can't get arrested. I can't…"

"Nothing will happen. Why do you keep thinking something like that could happen?"

He rubbed between his brows. "I never—I never told you this. When I first came to this country, I came on a student visa, and I let it expire. By then I had given up on everything, and then I found this job."

"You're not supposed to be here?"

Neither was she. And the concept of who was and who was not supposed to be here perplexed Mina. Hadn't he been working all this time? Hadn't he been paying his taxes, too? Hadn't the wars, the uprisings, the slaughter in the streets that had destroyed their families and homes, driven them here to this country that glittered untouched by the bombs it dropped everywhere else, been enough? And why did the law take any opportunity to either lock people up or kick them out when the worst kind of people, like Mr. Park, should be in prison rather than getting rich off the labor of everybody else, the terror of everybody else?

Rushing to the bathroom, she knelt in front of the toilet. Nothing came, only a trail of mucous that clung to her mouth. She hadn't eaten at all that day. The square pink tiles spun as she tried to steady herself standing up. She remembered those days after her husband and daughter died, those days of palms and knees dragging on a wet floor, of brushing her teeth with an index finger because she had already thrown all their toothbrushes in the trash. There were pills in the cabinet that she had jammed in her mouth, forced dry down her throat. Yet here she was, six thousand miles away, still confused, still lost. Would she ever find home?

Entering the bedroom, she jumped at the sight of Mr. Kim seated on the edge of the mattress in the low glow of the lamp, holding a gun—small, black, and matte.

"What are you doing?" she asked, breathless. "Put that away."

"I want you to have this," he said. "I'll show you how—"

"No, I don't want that. What do I need that for? I'm fine. I'll be fine. Please put that away."

He contemplated the gun, shook his head, and returned it to its holster and bag on the bed.

"Why do you even…" But she didn't bother finishing her question. Of course he owned a gun. She had never seen so many guns on men who were not in the military until coming to America. From what were they all protecting themselves? He could hurt himself, if not someone else. She had to take it away from him somehow. It was too easy to hurt someone. She couldn't lose him. She couldn't lose anyone again. "Could you please—put that away somewhere? I can't be in this room with it there."

He slid open his nightstand drawer, tucked the bag inside.
She closed her eyes, inhaled, and placed her head in her
hands. "Should I go to work tomorrow?"

He sighed. "Yes, I think you should."

"I can't. I can't ever go back." Her lips trembled. She
couldn't hold in her tears anymore.

"I think you should pretend that…you weren't there. You
have no idea what happened. Did he see you?"

"I don't know. I don't think so."

"That's good." He paused. "I think it's better if you pretend nothing happened so that he doesn't think you were
there, right?"

"I can't do that."

"You have to." His eyes glowed wet with fear or some profound resignation or both. "His face was bleeding. I probably
broke his nose. I doubt he'll be there tomorrow. If you don't
feel safe, leave, okay? But I think if you're missing from work,
everyone will assume you were involved somehow, and we
don't want that right now. We should keep you out of it. We'll
keep you out of it, okay?"

"Why? Why should I go?"

"You need the work for now." His voice cracked. "We can
all find different jobs later, but you need the work, okay? I
know this is terrible. I know, but someone has to… We can't
all not go back."

"I know."

"Can you do it? Can you go back to work tomorrow?"

MARGOT

FALL 2014

The morning after visiting Mrs. Baek at her apartment—the cramped living room that smelled of used bookstores and cucumber cold cream—and then riding the Ferris wheel at the pier by herself, Margot woke up early to once again drive to Calabasas, which might take almost an hour in weekday traffic.

The question of her mother's death zigzagged in Margot's mind. Regardless of what Mrs. Baek had said—that she had closed her store because she had been struggling financially—her stalker, Mr. Park, with his fake smile and lingering eyes, seemed increasingly dangerous, capable of physically harming someone. But even with the yelling that the landlord had heard the night of her mother's death, she couldn't connect Mr. Park with her mother yet. And if she dug deeper into Mr. Park's life, if she confronted him somehow, could she be responsible for him retaliating against Mrs. Baek and the waitress who had disclosed his behavior? These women were doing their best to navigate their own lives within circumstances driven, stories told by men. Margot also had to protect them.

She was also still upset that, in those final months of his life, her mother had not connected her with her father, as if she had been hoarding him all to herself. Perhaps her mother had everyone's best interest in mind, but why did her mother get to decide? And she had left unexpectedly the tangle of this net for Margot to unravel by herself.

With her foot on the accelerator, Margot needed to know her father now.

She wanted to know what he had done all those years after he left her mother and why he had fled Los Angeles. These were hard questions, questions she wasn't even sure she was ready to ask out loud. But she had been presented with this rare opportunity, and in a way, she had been preparing for the answers her entire life.

Maybe that's what she had been doing this entire time— hardening herself for the truth. Some questions were never meant to be answered, yet ideally, pursuing them might at least shed light on how much you valued yourself, the need you might have to tell your own story, however fragmented it might be. It was okay to yearn for the impossible every now and then as long as in the yearning you discovered something about yourself.

And she was admitting to herself now that all those years of not caring about who her father was, brushing off the idea of him, was a mask she wore to deny what she really wanted— to learn more about him and her mother, to understand her origins. Were her parents in love? Was it a one-night stand? An affair?

How human, how beautiful even our mistakes could be.

Once again the bronze gate had been left open. The same

two cars—glistening and new—had been parked in the drive-way along with a muddy landscaper truck. A weed whacker whirred in the distance.

The creamy white two-story house appeared even more dreamlike during the day. The sun drenched the surround-ing foliage in a honey-colored light, and well-fed birds flitted playfully on the dense grass. The tiered stone fountain gushed water as the palm trees rustled against each other in the breeze.

She tapped the heavy brass door knocker, and the very handsome and chiseled man from the other night answered, wearing a soft gray cashmere sweater and perfectly fitted dark slacks. He smelled like a Dolce & Gabbana ad, and from what she could tell, had the body to match.

"Can I help you?" he asked.

Her knees almost buckled beneath her from nerves. "I'm here to see Mrs. Kim?"

"Can I ask who you are?" His brows furrowed.

She gulped. "I'm someone from…her husband's past."

"You mean a friend? Or a relative?"

"Kind of," she said. "Um, yeah, a relative."

"One moment." He shut the door as she waited. Behind her, the landscaper dumped bare branches into the back of his truck. She waved hello at him, and he nodded back under his cap. The cold morning air smelled like fresh-cut grass.

A minute later, Dolce & Gabbana reappeared. "Come in," he said.

After walking through the entryway where she left her shoes, embarrassed about the condition of her dingy socks, Margot perched herself on the edge of the ivory tufted sofa in the living room that she had peered in on the other night. The air felt impossibly crisp and clean inside the house as if she had been sealed in a vacuum of perfect temperature and humidity and light—both wondrous and eerie.

"Can I help you?" Mrs. Kim asked as she entered. She tucked her silky black hair behind her ear, revealing a large iridescent pearl like a full moon, hypnotic and silvery. Her fingernails were shiny, oxblood-colored. She wore a voluptuous sweater, snow-white, a pair of heather gray leggings, and chic mule slippers made out of the most impractical velvet.

"You look lovely," Margot said out loud, involuntarily, as she stood up like a suitor in a Victorian novel.

Mrs. Kim smiled and patted herself on the cheek, blushing as she sat on the armchair beside the sofa. "I try to take good care of my skin. Please, have a seat." She raised her brows. "Could I offer you something to drink?"

"Oh, no, not right now, thank you."

"Is there something that I can help you with? My driver mentioned that you might be related to my husband. A relative?"

"Well, that's one way to put it," Margot said, realizing that her lover was the driver. She couldn't wait to tell Miguel about this.

"And we've never met? You...do look familiar." Mrs. Kim's face was indeed beautiful, in the most idealized Korean way—line-free and luminescent, narrow chin and jaw and nose, creased and doe-like eyes—but immobile the entire time as if she didn't quite feel anything anymore, or as if there was a human being trapped behind the skin. She was like the perfectly constructed woman—from an alien planet, luxurious and fur-covered.

Suddenly, Margot became very self-conscious about her socks, the lack of makeup or any color on her face, her ragged nails.

Margot took a deep breath and began. "I don't really know how to say this, but—"

Mrs. Kim's driver-slash-lover reappeared. "Would you like something to drink? I'm making myself some tea."

"Oh, no, no thanks," Margot said. "Well...what kind of tea?"

"Green tea?"

"Sure."

He nodded. Mrs. Kim stared at Margot's face as if she recognized her from somewhere.

"So, a couple weeks ago..." Margot cleared her throat. "I found my mother's body in her apartment in Koreatown. She was dead. And going through her things, I found your husband's obituary in an envelope."

"What?" Mrs. Kim's mouth dropped open.

"Well, let me backtrack. I never knew my dad. I grew up in Koreatown. My mom was working at this supermarket in the eighties, and someone she worked with got her pregnant, and he left right after. I never knew anything about him, but when I saw his picture in the obituary—"

Mrs. Kim froze, eyes open wide.

"And then my mother's friend confirmed that he is my dad."

"What's your mother's name?"

"Mina. Mina Lee."

"Oh my God," she said, slapping her hand down on the cushion of her seat. Her face grew red, jaw clenched. "So, that's who she is."

The driver reappeared. "Here's your tea," he said, handing the delicate, bone-colored cup on a saucer to Margot then exiting the room.

An awkward pause fell before Mrs. Kim finally spoke. "My husband and I... We were not exactly...conventional."

"Okay."

"We have always been very open."

"You mean..."

"Open about our relationships with others."

Margot almost spit the tea out of her mouth. "Like swingers?"

"No, not like that." She gave a small laugh. "But we were… flexible."

"Open relationship?"

"Yes, basically."

"Wow. Modern." Margot placed the cup and saucer on the glass coffee table next to perfectly positioned, untouched books like monuments to a very predictable taste—Richard Avedon, Chanel, and black-and-white Paris.

"Anyway, my husband got very sick over the summer. He had cancer. And I had seen this…" her voice broke "…woman's name that he had been calling a lot. Mina. Your…mother. I didn't care much. So what, he's dying. 'Go for it. Have fun.'" Tendons pulsed in her neck. "But then after he died, I realized—" Her eyes widened. "Do you know *how much* he spent on that woman?"

"My mom?"

"Yes, your mom. Sorry. I'm sorry for your loss. I mean—" She gritted her perfect teeth. "Do you know how much he spent?"

"No. No, I don't. I don't know what you're talking about at all." A heaviness built inside of Margot's chest. What money? None of this made sense.

"He hired an investigator that he had been using, for himself, to find out some things for her. I found all these receipts—"

"What?" Margot exhaled, letting all the air out of her lungs. She had been holding her breath. She picked up the saucer and drank some of the tea that had cooled and now tasted faintly metallic. "What would she have been using this investigator for?" She shook her head. "It's not like he spent money on her for *stuff.* There's nothing of value where she lives."

"This investigator works with people all over Korea to find missing people, missing families, like the ones who were separated by the war. My husband found out about his own father that way." She sighed. "Not that your mother or her family didn't matter, but to me, she was just a stranger, see? Some random woman that he just met."

"Do you know what she found out? Or what specific information he would've—"

"No. And I tore it all up. I didn't want to look at it anymore." Frustrated, Mrs. Kim pinched between her brows with her fingers.

Margot felt a pang of remorse that she would never know what the investigator found.

"Why would he spend so much?" Mrs. Kim asked. "But now...now it makes sense."

"I don't think he knew about me."

"But she was someone from his past then. It was some kind of deeper relationship. Maybe he even...loved her," she said, biting her lip as if ashamed of herself.

Margot didn't know what to say. "Why did you marry him?" she asked. "Did you ever love each other?"

"Yes, I suppose so. But you know, it just made the most sense. He was rich, and I wanted security. I had had my heart broken so many times before then."

"By other men?"

"By all kinds of people," she said. "I used to feel so much, you know? But feelings are dangerous."

"Wouldn't life be meaningless without them?"

"Ha, you're very sentimental. Like your father." Mrs. Kim nodded. "I never understood him much, to be honest. He was so different from everyone else."

"How?" Margot could feel the grip of her muscles loosening, relieved to learn even this tidbit about him—what they might have in common. For a few seconds, she felt less alone. It was wondrous to be *like someone*, to be carrying someone else in your blood and bones. People whom you might not have even met.

"Oh, in so many ways. I can't really talk about this right now." Mrs. Kim wiped carefully at the inner corners of her eyes with her fingertips. "I do miss him." She exhaled out loud. "I'm sorry, but I have this terrible headache."

"Can I get you something?"

"No, no, that's okay." She shook her head. "It's been difficult for me, now that I'm on my own." She opened her eyes. "He took care of everything, you know? The finances, the bills. Now what? I'll probably sell all the supermarkets, and then?"

The driver stood by the wide doorway, waiting and watching Margot. She could feel the hair on the back of her neck rising.

"I should sell everything and travel the world, don't you think? I could go to Machu Picchu. I've always wanted to go there. Have you been?"

"No, I've never been."

"It's supposed to be magical."

"Could I—could I get your number?" Margot asked. "Maybe when things settle down, we can talk again, before you go to Machu Picchu. I'd love to learn more about him. I know that it brings up a lot, but there are still so many things I don't know, like what he was doing all those years after he left Koreatown, why he left my mother in the first place."

"To be honest, there are so many things that I don't even know about before we—before we were married. Sungmin, give her my number, okay?"

The driver, Sungmin, nodded.

"Thank you for visiting. What was your name again?"

"Margot Lee." She stood.

"Thank you. What a lovely name," she said. "Sungmin will walk you out." Mrs. Kim left the room, rubbing her temples.

Following Sungmin to the entryway and lacing on her sneakers again, Margot pulled out her phone for him to enter Mrs. Kim's information. After he opened the door, on an impulse, Margot asked, "Do you happen to know anything about my father? When did you start working for him?"

Sungmin shook his head. "Please leave." He tried to smile politely. "We have a lot to get done today."

With his hand, he gestured like an usher toward the exit.

Margot stood at the doorway, facing the driveway into the honey-colored morning light. She felt a hand on her shoulder and then a small shove.

She gasped and looked back at him as the door shut. He had touched her. It had all happened so quickly she didn't even have time to react. The tiered stone fountain gushed water indefinitely. She smelled the fresh-cut grass and the undercurrent of something foul like manure or compost in the air.

He had pushed her. Not hard but in a way that still alarmed her with its abruptness, a hand out of nowhere. And she could still taste the tea, that metallic taste in her mouth.

The Virgin Mary's face was half-smashed, revealing the creamy bone color inside. Her single dreamy eye and delicate mouth, pert and peach-colored, appeared unbothered. Beneath the drape and the folds of her sky blue cape bordered by gold, her arms stretched forward. A bare set of toes peeked out the bottom of her diaphanous white dress, like that of a Greek goddess, on top of a serpent flicking a tongue.

Margot had been in bed for the past two days sick—dizzy,

sore, and tired, immobilized yet frustrated by how much she still had left to do. She now sat on the living room couch, exhausted, contemplating the Virgin Mary in her hand. Margot recalled how upset Mrs. Kim had been about her husband spending so much money on the investigation of her mother's family. If she called Mrs. Kim, would she provide her with the investigator's number so that she could figure out what kind of information he had found? Would she know enough Korean to speak with him?

And the push, that final push on the doorstep by the driver? Why had he done that? Was it a warning? The green tea had tasted a bit metallic in her mouth. Poison seemed too far-fetched—plus she was still alive—but the timing was odd. Was this all about money? Was Mrs. Kim out for revenge?

Should she call the police, Officer Choi again? But he had said that he didn't think they should be contacting Mrs. Kim. And his hands were tied. He couldn't get further involved: *I don't really see what else I can do here, Margot. As far as your mother's death goes—which was terrible, I'm sorry—it's an open-and-shut case. It was an accident.*

As she turned the statue in her hands, Margot inhaled through both the sadness and a grave feeling of responsibility since she had found her mother's body two weeks ago. It was as if she was living for both of them now—thoughts spinning, heart racing wildly—but what if she never found any answers?

Her phone rang. "How are you feeling?" Miguel asked when she picked up.

"Better. Not dead."

"You've been working pretty hard over there. Visiting Mrs. Baek, visiting Mrs. Kim. Maybe you should relax a little."

"I guess now that I'm sick, I kind of have to."

"Could I get you something? I could drive over later tonight?"

"No, no, thanks. If I don't feel better by tomorrow, I'll find a doctor. I'll be fine."

After hanging up the phone, she went into her room, retrieved one of her old unused notebooks from her desk drawer, and sketched the broken Mary—fragments of her face, her toes, the serpent's tongue at her feet. Her pencil pressed onto paper the big blue eye, thin round brow, the perfect Cupid's bow mouth.

It had been years since Margot had been compelled to draw. Despite her lack of technical skill, she had a way of juxtaposing images unexpectedly. She always suspected she might have a knack for something more three-dimensional, something akin to mixed media or assemblage, which required more space and would be difficult to describe. The point was that it would tell its own story, invent its own dimension and time. But all of this sounded so high-minded and ridiculous for a woman like her to pursue, a woman who had grown up poor, who had been surrounded most of her life by people struggling to keep the lights on and food on the table.

Yet, everyone needed art. Why else did her mother assign so much care into the fruit that she sliced, that long peel of skin, a ribbon that revealed the tenderness of the flesh inside? Or the tiny flick of her eyeliner that she angled perfectly in the mirror, the arrangement of the outfits that she hung on the walls of her store. Her mother, who was in another life a clothing designer, had sometimes caught Margot drawing. Once when Margot was in the sixth grade, still young enough to not understand how distant her own tiny family had been from ideal, she had been sketching a portrait of her mother's face—the high cheekbones, the narrow chin, the soft brown eyes that shone as if on the verge of tears, water lapping at a lake's edge.

"Let me see." Her mother grabbed the drawing. Squinting,

she held it to the yellow light above the dining table. "Am I this old already?"

Margot didn't have a response. Her mother was the most beautiful person in the world.

It became difficult for Margot to understand what to create. As a child, she hated to upset her mother. Instead she stuck to close-ups of flowers or trees—evergreen in winter or deciduous and mustard yellow and blood orange in the fall—pastoral landscapes that she copied out of wall calendars, which bored her, but what else could she do? She hated to draw her own face—a face she couldn't quite recognize in her mother or anywhere else on TV or in the movies—the face of a stranger, a foreigner, anonymous and plain.

Later as a teenager, abstract sculpture like that of Ruth Asawa and Lee Bontecou, assemblage, and installation had captured her imagination. She would have the urge to topple trashcans over, scour for materials, but how could she explain this to her mother? And where would she store all her projects? Their apartment was too small. Of course, she'd have to run from this place.

But after she had finally left for Seattle, after college, her student debt had grown and she settled into a desk job, the first one she could find that also might benefit society. At the nonprofit, all of the clients and many of her coworkers were blind or had low vision and navigated the world in ways that startled her—a white cane and GPS, Braille watches, software that read screens out loud.

The first year or so had been almost inspirational, a marvel, but quickly her administrative tasks had become insurmountable piles, deadening levels of repetition on her desk. Her life smelled of printer toner, sounded like the gulp of the water cooler, the beep and whir of the copy machine. Of course, after three years of this, her relationship last year with

Jonathan, a coworker, had been thrilling—the warm animal breath, the pulse, the tiny hairs on her arms rising. She needed danger. The thrill of sex drowned out her burning questions, replaced the real dangers that, when pursued, might actually kill her. Who was she? What would happen if she were unafraid of herself?

Margot had always guarded the different parts of her life from each other—her mother, her friends, past boyfriends, coworkers. If none of those things touched, if she could keep them in isolation, she could never be hurt or destroyed entirely. The constant yet quiet construction of separate rooms, compartments around her. But most of the time, she felt alone in the center of that building. Lightless and airtight.

Her mother's death had burned that structure of Margot's life to the ground.

She attempted now to draw her mother's face again on a blank page—the soft brown eyes and narrow chin, her hair in a bob—just as Margot had remembered her the last time she had seen her. And then on the opposite page, she drew her father's face as best as she could from her memory of the obituary. She carved the outlines of their faces in pencil, the wrinkles around the eyes and between the brows.

When she stopped to rest, exhausted, she realized that when she closed her notebook, pressing together the pages, they would nearly kiss again—features overlapping each other's.

MINA

WINTER 1988

With Mr. Park, Lupe, and Mr. Kim gone, the day passed with a silent and intense melancholy. Word had gotten out, and although no one said a thing, no one acknowledged what happened or what could've happened, Mina could feel the tension, the sadness as thick and inescapable as the city's smog.

Everyone sensed that neither Lupe nor Mr. Kim would ever be back and that if they, too, wanted to keep their jobs, they better avoid getting in the way of Mr. Park. Perhaps it had been that way all along and Mina only noticed it now, naively. When she thought about everyone's interactions and air around him, they each had already been taking their precautions as most people do around powerful people in even the tiniest universe of a supermarket. Perhaps they each silently knew that their positions were always tenuous, that they could each become someone's prey.

Standing at the register, heavy as a sack of grain, she tried not to think about Mr. Kim or Lupe, or the gun that she had taken from him this morning. She had crept up to him, still snoring. She yearned to smooth the creases between his brows where she kissed him, inhaling his morning breath, which she had never minded. It was the smell of his comfort, his rest. She slid the drawer open beside his bed. The gun bag was lighter than she had expected. As she rode the bus to work, she kept her large brown purse on her lap, cautious about putting any pressure on it, as if it possessed a wild animal, a snake, tranquilized for now but vicious and unpredictable.

Now Mina listened for the beeping sound and stared off into space, only paying attention when she received cash from the customer and doled out change. At this point she had memorized most of the produce and could enter the codes without having to look at the keypad.

During her break, she called Mr. Kim on a pay phone outside of the supermarket. No one answered. Who knew what he was going through now? Was he already in jail? She wanted to contact Lupe but didn't have her number. She, too, must have been figuring out what to do, how she would find work to help Mario, to feed her kids.

Mina wished she had a cigarette to smoke so that she had a reason to be outside, feeling self-conscious after a few minutes of standing as if waiting, but waiting for what? She went inside. Avoiding the rear of the store altogether, she didn't even use the restroom. She would wait all day until she got home.

Later that night at the bus stop, she stood, light-headed and nauseous, by the transit sign alone. She had almost forgotten about the gun in her purse. She sensed that things would never be the same again, that Mr. Kim would have to find a new job, that she, who wouldn't be able to look at Mr. Park, had to find a new one, too. How could she get into this kind of disaster so quickly, after being in America for less than a year?

As the headlights of the bus approached, she had the sudden urge to step out in front. Just one foot.

Like a deer in the road, crossing, unaware. It would be that simple and pure. An erasure. Another body in the morgue.

The bus swerved, screeching to a halt. The driver, her eyes wide and mouth open, appeared shocked, sad, then upset.

Mina thought to run away but where? How could she keep running?

Instead, she got on the bus with her head hanging, eyes on the ground.

"What are you doing?" the driver demanded. "Are you trying to get yourself killed? You're trying to get us *all* killed?"

Mina walked through the center aisle, past the perked ears, the watching eyes. She wedged herself between two passengers, one who didn't care at all, and the other an older woman who was in shock.

Mina glanced forward to see the driver raise her hands in exasperation, letting them fall at her thighs with a slap. In the rearview mirror, the driver's face softened into a broken heart, as she mouthed, "Fuck," to herself. She shut the heavy doors, driving toward the next stop.

In the kitchen, Mrs. Baek stood at the stove, stirring a pot.

Trying to go unnoticed, Mina slipped off her shoes and headed toward her room. She yearned to disappear. She hadn't slept at all last night. But before she could reach her door, Mrs. Baek asked, "Did you eat dinner yet?"

"No, not yet. I'm very tired."

"You don't look so good. Are you getting sick?"

"Maybe."

"Do you want to join me?"

"That's okay. I have a phone call to make."

Mrs. Baek suspended the wooden spoon in the air, like a baton in a marching band. "Why don't you join me after your phone call?"

"Um…"

"I can wait. Go ahead and make your call."

Without any energy left, Mina unlocked her bedroom door, and once inside, dropped all her belongings on the ground. She picked up the phone on her nightstand and spun by memory Mr. Kim's number on the rotary dial. No answer.

After using the restroom, she sat in the breakfast nook across from Mrs. Baek, who had been sipping on a mug of barley tea, waiting.

"You don't look good at all," she said.

"I've been working a lot," Mina replied. "Stomach problems."

"Like what?"

"When I get stressed out, I have trouble eating. And when I do eat, I want to throw up."

"Your boyfriend—everything okay?"

"Yes."

"You sure?" Mrs. Baek placed her hand on top of Mina's. "Maybe you have some kind of stomach bug? You look very pale."

"Yes, that's probably what it is."

"Let me make you some rice porridge," Mrs. Baek said, standing up.

"Don't trouble yourself. Thank you. No, really."

"Don't worry. It won't take long. Why don't you go back to bed? I'll wake you up when it's ready."

Mina dragged herself to her room again where she lay down and cried, blotting the corners of her eyes with her blanket. She didn't want Mrs. Baek to see her that way—just another woman sobbing in a room by herself. But that's what she was, wasn't she? She had this crushing feeling that she'd never see Mr. Kim again. How could she feel like this, how could she allow this to happen?

She closed her eyes and drifted off to sleep until she heard a knock, maybe ten or thirty minutes later, she couldn't tell. Before she could say anything, Mrs. Baek poked her head in through the door.

"Sorry to wake you up," she said. "I have your porridge."

"Oh, that's okay. Thank you." Mina tried to rise up from the bed on her elbows in time to meet Mrs. Baek, but her arms collapsed beneath her.

"Oh," Mrs. Baek said, approaching to help. "When was the last time you ate?"

"I don't remember. I don't think I ate yesterday."

"You have to eat something before you fall asleep then."

Mina slumped over on the bed, leaning against the wall. Mrs. Baek held the bowl of porridge with a metal spoon, contemplating Mina's face.

"Here, take a bite," she said, holding the spoon up to Mina's mouth.

The tenderness of the gesture made Mina's eyes water again. Tears rolled down her cheeks, and she couldn't help but cover her face, as if to shield herself from the kindness of someone else.

The phone rang, waking Mina from a deep sleep she had achieved only after a few hours of tossing and turning and pounding the mattress with her fists in sadness and in rage. She grabbed the receiver, suddenly wide awake.

"Mr. Kim?" she asked.

"Yes." His voice was weary.

"Are you okay? Where are you?" she cried. "Where are you? Are you leaving me?"

He took a deep breath. "I'm... I'm at the airport."

"What? What are you doing there?" She couldn't control herself. She knew what he was about to say. She knew this was going to happen. She kept repeating this over and over again to punish herself, to teach herself a lesson. Just like the women at the orphanage who would punish her when she was bad, when they caught her stealing, when she spoke up against them. She knew this was going to happen. *This is why nobody wants you*, they'd say.

"I can't talk long. I went to see Lupe yesterday. She's going to be okay. She has some people at church, family to help her, so don't worry about her, okay? She's going to be fine. Worry about yourself, okay?"

"What about you? Where are you going?"

"I've got a cousin in Chicago. I'm going to...leave for a little while."

"How long?" she asked.

"I don't know yet."

"A while?"

"Maybe."

"Can I come with you?"

"No, I don't think that's best for now."

"Why don't you take me with you? Why don't you take me with you?" Her voice rose, echoing throughout the house. She didn't care who heard her. "Why don't you take me with you?"

"It's not that easy. I would. There's just... It's too dangerous right now. I'm sorry." She could hear him crying. "I never wanted to hurt you. I never wanted to hurt anyone. I didn't think—"

"Then take me with you. I have nothing here. Take me with you."

"I can't. It'd be easier to hide by myself. It's safer for you this way." He paused, gulping breath. "Did you take the gun?"

She didn't answer, heart racing.

"Be careful with that. It's loaded, okay? Don't take it out of the bag unless you need it. Protect yourself, okay? Be careful."

"I can handle him myself." Her voice shook like an earthquake, rattling every bone in her body.

"Just, be careful. I'm—I'm sorry. I love you." He hung up the phone.

She threw the receiver, which hit the wall with a loud crash. The sound of the dial tone drove her to pick the receiver up and smash it into the phone with a *crack, crack*, a hollow plastic sound. She didn't care anymore if she broke it. This was the time now. This was the time to end it all. She could hang herself in her room. She had sheets. She could tie them around the door, slip them around her neck and end everything, the way she should've ended things before coming to this strange country, before Mr. Park could ruin all of them, before, before…

Before the Ferris wheel, before the salt in the air, the taste of hot chocolate, once again, falling prey to the dazzling deception of the world, the blush and the bloom inside her chest.

But she could kill Mr. Park before taking her own life. She could find him in his office. She had the gun. She could end him. She could end him in front of everyone. Who knew how many he had terrorized? How many he had cannibalized for his own gain? How many of them had he hurt? How many more lives could he ruin? She had nothing to lose now.

Someone pounded on the door.

Mina cried out, "Not now."

"Are you okay?" Mrs. Baek asked.

"Go away."

She could tell that Mrs. Baek still stood on the other side, waiting for her, for anything.

"*Go away,*" she screamed. She grabbed a pillow and threw it at the door.

Mrs. Baek tried the knob. Finding it locked, she pushed her way through the flimsy wood.

Shock and terror distorted Mrs. Baek's face at the sight of Mina on the floor.

Mina saw herself through Mrs. Baek's eyes. She wanted to kill herself even more.

Mrs. Baek knelt to the ground beside her, trying to help her stand up.

"Get your hands off me." Mina vomited a yellowish fluid, right onto her own chest.

Mrs. Baek wrapped her arms around Mina, dragging her to the restroom where she had her sit on the floor beside the toilet. Mina threw up the sad remains of last night's paltry dinner, the rice porridge. Mrs. Baek grabbed a towel and wiped down Mina's face, covered in tears and snot like a child's. She then handed the towel to Mina, who blew her nose.

She couldn't stop crying, her breath rushing in and out.

Both of them knew as they sat on the floor beside the toilet that Mina was pregnant.

MARGOT

WINTER 2014

The Monday before Christmas, Margot was finally feeling better. She had been in bed for the past several days, overcome by weakness and nausea. Was it simply grief and exhaustion, the beginnings of the flu, or poisoning? Miguel had offered to drive her to a clinic or hospital, but she had refused, unwilling to deal with the worries of insurance, in-or out-of-network.

And for the first time in a while, she woke up early this morning with the urge to prepare breakfast, sunny-side up eggs on rice. Afterward, she cleaned out her mother's kitchen, emptying cupboards and drawers, still sticky from a life rushed between work and home. The nutty dark amber of sesame oil—heavy and clinging—remained in a half-full bottle. A squeeze bottle of honey—crystallized into sugar, rough on the tongue—had glued itself down, leaving a dark footprint, a sweet oval on the lining of a shelf.

Margot had already touched most of everything in the kitchen with a practical intimacy her entire life—no secrets, no other lives. But even the utensils, a hodgepodge of stainless steel, became tiny monuments—sharp, reflective, serrated, and curved with feeling.

Growing up, she had hated using chopsticks. She had refused them, seated at the table with her mother—different instruments in their hands—as if the inches between them were as expansive as a continental divide, the dark rift of an ocean. And yet, despite this daily breach, this rupture between mother and daughter, hands posed around shapes foreign to each other, she remembered the bowls of rice her mother had fed her, the banchan, the stews, the fruit she had meticulously peeled and sliced, and how food was perhaps the most practical and necessary means by which Margot could access the stories and memories, the sap running inside her mother.

They had spoken different languages—drifting further and further apart as Margot had gotten older. Margot's mother never learned much English in Koreatown, didn't have to, and Margot, who spent so little time with her mother besides working long hours at the store, distanced herself from Korean culture, which she associated with alienness and poverty and war. She wanted to live like "real Americans" on television with their clean surfaces, their walls without cracks and chipped paint, their dishwashers and shiny appliances. She wanted to live like they did in books—those precarious and fragile skylines in Mrs. Baek's apartment, paper like teeth once white, now yellow—with beauty and complex feelings, agency, choice interrupted by fate, and vice versa.

Her mother's life seemed to have little self-determination at all, only the burden of getting by, knowing that no matter how hard she had worked, she would never leave that apartment. And that was exactly what had happened, wasn't it? Her mother never left that place. A woman, alone, fallen to tragedy and fate, men who would leave and destroy her.

She was like a lot of us. Lonely. But that's what it's like for women like us.

The foul stench of the body—bile and rotting fruit.

But was it an accident? Or intentional? There was still Mrs. Kim and her driver, Sungmin. The surprising push of his hand, as if Margot was just an animal who had wandered in off the street. And where was the landlord still? He couldn't be trusted either.

Retiring to the couch, Margot sketched in her notebook a single fork on one page and a set of chopsticks on the next so that she could flip between them, their shapes. She wanted to live somewhere in that movement, like the beat of a dove's wing.

There were so many things that she could never explain to her mother. Even if they had spoken the same languages, the chasm that divided them would have still been too great. In some ways, Margot's success in this country, her independence, relied on this distance from her mother—her poverty, her foreignness, the alienation of her life, the heaviness of her thankless work, the hours and minutes, ignored and even reviled by the world. And there were so many ways to be crushed, to have your heart broken navigating that canyon between them—what they could not say, what they had said to wound each other.

But maybe only here in these pages, in these drawings, if Margot had shown more commitment to their relationship, if she had been unafraid of commitment, could her mother have understood: that Margot would never leave her in the end, that she would, despite the distance that separated them, never let go of her hand.

★ ★ ★

After finishing the kitchen, Margot cleaned her mother's room, where she once again found the sneakers covered in fine dust, the condom wrapper beneath the bed. She threw the discarded, forgotten objects away and placed the shoes in the garbage bag, knowing now that these were remnants of her mother's reunion with her father, Mr. Kim.

On her mother's bed, that sad teddy bear, dingy with time, clung to a satin red heart attached to its round cartoon paws. She squeezed the heart and felt something hard inside. Her pulse began to pound. She tore apart the seam, sloppy and hand stitched.

A piece of paper with a box number and a bank's name and a small key fell out.

She ripped open the rest of the bear but didn't find anything else. She scavenged through her mother's belongings, checking the pockets and the linings even more carefully now for anything, any clue that could somehow not eliminate but ease the pain, the barrage of questions clawing inside her head. She wanted answers now. She wanted her mother to be alive so that she could finally ask her all the things she had always wanted to ask, all the things she found herself too frightened to ask before this. Her mother's life and her past had always been so carefully guarded. It always felt like the wrong move, look, touch, or words would break her mother forever.

As a child of four or five seated in the lukewarm tub of milky Dove soap–scented water, scratching the petals of the anti-slip stickers beneath her, Margot had asked, "Where is my father?"

Her mother, knees on the bathroom floor, had winced, pausing to reflect. "I don't know. He left us a long time ago."

"Where did he go?" Margot asked the ceiling above, sloshing the water with her feet.

"I don't know." Her mother adjusted her legs, hands covered in foam. "I never had a father, too. You ask too many questions." A tear slid down her face, quick and silent.

Tilting her head back as her mother poured water from above, careful not to splash her face, Margot yearned to push the tears back in her mother's eyes. It was excruciating to watch her mother, who worked tirelessly and silently day after day, emote, expose herself at once. In these rare moments of great tenderness and fragility, their sanity rattling like glass cups in a cupboard during a quake, Margot learned that families were our greatest source of pain, whether they had lost or abandoned us or simply scrubbed our heads.

All of these feelings had turned into a kind of rage when Margot became a teenager, when the world demanded answers: *Where is your dad? You don't have a dad? What does your mom do for a living? You've been living in that apartment for* how *long?* Questions that were judgments around what she and her mother could not afford or control.

It was all about control, wasn't it?

Money could make the world intimately spotless. That was the illusion.

Kneeling on the carpet, Margot contemplated the small key on the table beside her mother's bed. A key was such an obvious symbol, yet sometimes the truth was always there, right in front of your face, until you were ready to swallow its shape and all its edges, until you knew you were strong enough to bear its weight.

It had been eight years since she had moved to Seattle, eight years of half-understood conversations over the phone and visits during the holidays that revolved around work. Margot had believed they could go on this way forever, that this distance hurt them both the least.

But she now knew there was so much truth undisclosed.

Like a tree that had lost its leaves, silently bracing itself against wind and cold, the sap inside of them could, under the right conditions, push the green, those tender revelations, out of them once more.

With her mother's safety-deposit key and papers in her purse, Margot opened the apartment door and looked behind her to observe the condition of her mother's home—donation bags everywhere and piles of junk in the center of the room. The scene both satisfied and terrified her at once. She had finally found a way to get rid of this place, this apartment that had taunted her with its sadness, its poverty, with the dirty windows, the misshapen and faded couch and the coffee table with rings from mugs like wet footprints that had dried on the surface. But then another part of her wanted to throw her body onto those piles and stay there forever like a waiting room until her mother came back, or until the universe somehow delivered the answers that she needed to make decisions, get on with life like the rest of the world. She locked the door behind her.

In the dark and musty stairwell, the landlord climbed the steps, gripping the handrail.

"Excuse me," she said. "I left you a message about my mom?"

"Oh, yes, yes, sorry. I've had so much going on—"

"Why did you lie to the police officer?" Margot interrupted.

"*Lie?*"

"The police officer?" She folded her arms across her chest. "Officer Choi? He said that you didn't hear a thing from my mother's apartment. You told me—"

He smiled as if amused and combed his hand through his thick gray hair. "Didn't I say that the police weren't going to do anything? There's no need to get them involved. I don't need them hanging around the building, scaring my tenants. What good is that going to do for your mom?"

"But don't you think—"

"We don't need police around here."

"Yeah, but what about my mom? Don't you think if someone could've *killed* her, that your tenants would *care* about finding the guy?"

"Shhh," he said, annoyed. He came up the stairs closer to her. "I'm just trying to run a business, okay? It's not like I don't care."

For a few seconds, she imagined pushing him down the stairwell. His thin-limbed body tumbling to the ground. His head cracked against a step. She flinched at the image, the cruelty. It would look like an accident.

"I just don't think you can trust the police," he said. "Why risk yourself? Why get involved? Don't you think enough people have been hurt? Enough people have been hurt already."

"You made me look like a liar."

"Listen, I'm sorry about that. I'm trying—" His voice cracked. "I'm trying really hard to keep things together. Believe me. I'm always about to lose this place." Tears filled his eyes. "If I thought talking to the police would help your mother, I would, I really would, but I honestly don't think it would make a difference. I've seen a lot in my years."

Margot hesitated. Her mother might've done the same. She might've felt the same way.

"Maybe I don't do the best job around here, but I'm trying my best," he continued. "I know no one likes the landlord. I didn't even want to get into any of this—it was my wife's idea. And now I'm stuck like everyone else. What else can I do? No one would hire me now. Nobody wants a guy like me. Nobody wants any of us, you see?"

"What do you mean?" Margot asked.

"If they could have their way, they'd tear down the whole thing, make it into fancy condos or something. Get rid of us all. They like the work that we do, but they don't like our faces or language, you see? It's a big conspiracy and now we're all stuck. There's an episode of *Twilight Zone*—you wouldn't remember—but the one with the toys that are all trapped in a bin, a big cylinder. That's us."

"Well, I can see that," she said. It was obvious that she had reached the limit of what the landlord could provide regarding her mother's death and he didn't seem particularly guilty or capable of harm himself. And now she needed to get to the bank, before it closed, with the safety-deposit key and papers, ripped from the teddy bear's heart. She climbed down the stairs past him. "Let me know if you remember anything else, okay?"

"She has a friend, right? Lady. Red lipstick. Maybe she can help you?"

She paused, turning to face him. "She has. She already has."

"She has problems, too, or something, right?"

"What are you talking about?"

"I just remember, one time, she was here—maybe in September or October, something like that. I saw her park on the street and it looked like an older man was sitting in his car, waiting for her. You know? Like he was following her."

"An older man?"

"Yeah, a different one. Not your mom's boyfriend."

"Did he have a kind of…square head, big white teeth, big gold watch—"

"Exactly."

"So he followed the woman with the red lipstick to this apartment?"

"I think so. Yeah, I'm pretty sure of it."

Margot's heart pounded in her chest. Mr. Park knew where

her mother lived. But would he want to hurt her? Unless somehow her mother had tried to intervene in his behavior, tried to stand up to him? Maybe he had gone to her apartment, asked her where Mrs. Baek lived or worked now, and she had refused to answer. Her mother would do anything to protect Mrs. Baek.

Would this be enough for him to fight with her? Push her?

Margot couldn't go to the restaurant and confront him now. It might be too dangerous and could jeopardize the waitress as well. If she needed to question Mr. Park, she'd have to find him somewhere else and she'd have to ask Miguel to go with her just in case. Where would he be other than the restaurant? Someone had to know. She couldn't ask Mrs. Baek because she would be too concerned for Margot. Perhaps Margot and Miguel together would have to follow him after work.

She ran down to the parking lot and opened the car door. Catching her breath, she glanced at the rearview mirror to make sure she was alone. Chills ran down her spine as she thought of the driver's hand on her shoulder, the push. Maybe that's all it had taken. There was blood that had pooled and pressed against her mother's brain. She was getting too close. Mr. Park followed Mrs. Baek to her mother's apartment. The net had wrapped around her ankles.

A safety-deposit box. A bank that would soon close. A door closing. Margot was on her own.

There were now too many people who might be angry at her mother—Mrs. Kim and her driver-slash-lover, Sungmin, also Mr. Park—too many people who might want to hurt her. Perhaps that was the life of any woman like her mother, a woman who was poor and in so many ways powerless but nonetheless persisted like a kind of miracle, a defiance against the world.

But who would want her mother dead the most?

MINA

SPRING 2014

After a dinner of doenjang guk, myulchi bokkeum and kimchi as banchan, Mina, in an automatic gesture, turned on the television. As soon as the elderly faces—wrinkled and scrunched in pain beneath men's hats covering balding heads, grandmothers in hanboks squeezing out tears from behind glasses—appeared (footage of last month's daylong reunion, the first in three years between families separated in North and South Korea), she fled to the kitchen where she slumped down onto the laminate floor.

News of the seemingly endless negotiations between governments for these fleeting reunions—the lunch, the afternoon, when these families who had waited their whole lives, sometimes over sixty years, for each other—had this time, more than any other, driven her to the brink. She pressed her forehead and free hand against one of the cabinets as she inhaled all the years in this place, as if this apartment had been a kind of lover, who kept a roof over her head, who had no opinions but provided, despite its sorrow, a certain kind of strength. How long had it been? Over twenty years.

Time was wearing her down. She was approaching seventy years old now and could see herself in the faces of the elderly reunited, the hair around her temples whitening. She could see herself in those reunions—her vulnerability and pain—rubbing the sadness away from her already worn face.

How much could the body, how much could the heart take?

Twenty-six years ago, not long after she had first arrived in Los Angeles, she had caught a similar TV special on these painfully scarce family reunification efforts with Mr. Kim on his couch after a dinner of—what was it?—something simple like shigeumchi or baechu doenjang guk. Like the memory rising now, the crimson crept up the smooth skin of his neck, his face as tears welled in his eyes, which she had yearned to push back inside of him.

Do you ever wonder if your parents might still be there, in North Korea? Mr. Kim had asked.

No, I've never thought of that.

But maybe that's why they never found you, he said.

That was the evening before the end. On the floor of her kitchen now, she sat leaning against the cabinets, eyes closed, breathing hard through her mouth, tending to images from the past: Lupe's face on that day that she had been attacked by Mr. Park, how she sobbed in the front seat of the station wagon, the red blood running down the side of Mr. Kim's face, the smell of iron, Mr. Kim seated in the low glow of the lamp, holding a gun—small, black, and matte.

Mina still had that gun.

She had never heard from Lupe again. She prayed that she and Mario had been reunited somehow, but no one knew.

No one at the supermarket spoke of them, as if silence was a form of protection.

Mr. Park had mostly ignored her. Every now and then, she would catch him glancing at her, but he never said a word, as if she were now invisible, an inanimate object. She had no idea if he knew of her involvement in what had happened to Lupe that day, but he had been suspicious about her relationship to Mr. Kim perhaps.

She had worked at the supermarket, *his* supermarket, up until the very day that her water broke. That late-June morning had begun like most others with her lumbering to the bathroom, eating breakfast alone in the kitchen's nook, and making her way through a gray malaise of smog to the bus stop. She climbed the stairs onto the bus and eased herself onto one of the seats up front. Staring out the windshield relieved her nausea.

After only an hour at the cash register, her stomach, already bulbous and uncomfortable, hardened into a fist. A sharp bright pain sparked. Her water broke as she hobbled to the back of the store. The warmth ran down her legs onto the floor. She placed a maxi pad on her underwear in the bathroom, collected her belongings for the very last time. Exiting the rear door, she waddled around the building to the front of the supermarket, where she called Mrs. Baek at the pay phone. Breathing through the pain, she waited for thirty minutes under a hard sky of sun and haze, the color of laundry water, for Mrs. Baek to drive her to the hospital downtown.

During two days of agony, mostly alone except for when Mrs. Baek could get off of work, except for the few hours when Mrs. Baek held her hand, consoling her, Mina screamed at the world that threatened every day to tear her apart. Her body was consumed in flames, like a saint's burned at the stake. Until finally, she held her baby, red and howling, covered in white wax.

A monster.

A monster, like her, born into a world, hollow—without a family, without aunts and uncles, cousins, grandparents, without even gravestones to call their own.

Mrs. Baek named the baby Margot, a name that she loved.

Mina had already suffered months of the other Korean women at the supermarket, observing the stretch of her stomach into a bulb. Of course, they gossiped about what kind of lewdness would lead to her pregnancy, the pregnancy of a single Korean woman in her forties. Mina had quit church as soon as she began showing, out of fear of the shame she would bring upon herself among the women there, even Mrs. Shin, whom she trusted, but couldn't expect to understand what it would be like to come to this country as a single woman, a widow, and fall in love, despite all the best intentions, only to end up again alone.

At home, Mina cried in bed while Mrs. Baek cared for the baby. She never thought she would ever stop crying, as if she could exhaust herself to death that way. Weeks passed, and she would still burst into tears, without warning sometimes, as she waited her life out, unable to work. She had enough savings to pay for rent, groceries, formula, diapers for a few months, and Mrs. Baek and the landlady helped by preparing her meals, tending to the baby while she slept.

She couldn't get out of bed some days. With the light outside, the blue sky, the birds she could hear in the backyard, chirping, the world seemed to move on without her, as she cried, hardly able to bathe and feed herself, let alone her baby. She contemplated leaving the baby somewhere safe and running away, but where would she turn to next?

Argentina? The San Fernando Valley? New York?

She didn't have the energy anymore.

Yet how could she raise this baby by herself? She couldn't rely on the kindnesses of Mrs. Baek and the landlady who had their own long hours of work, their own worries, forever.

After almost two months at home, she dropped her daughter off at the apartment of a local grandmother she would pay to take care of Margot. She worked for a year washing dishes, and then at a fast-food restaurant where she assembled chili dogs, deep-fried corn dogs—bizarre American foods. She worked and worked and worked until she could figure out what to do with her life.

But as the years passed, and the landlady died, her house sold by her children, and Mina lost her first store in the riots, and Mina and Mrs. Baek went out on their own and lost touch with each other, and her daughter's limbs became long and loved to draw, and her face grew into questions and thoughts, Mina forgot Mr. Kim's face.

She saw only herself in Margot, as if she could not bear to see her in her entirety, as if she was a puzzle with pieces missing forever. She refused to see the entire girl.

She had moved on that way. When she had saved enough money to buy another store, she didn't have to worry about a babysitter when Margot was not at school. She could bring her to work. She could teach the girl to help her. At the swap meet, Margot would make friends. Margot would become a woman one day, and she would leave Mina, too. They would all leave her. Her daughter, an American, who spoke English, could hardly say anything with depth in Korean, who would go to college in Seattle. Her daughter had not forgotten about her, but Mina knew that she wanted to forget. Who wouldn't want to forget all those years of work and pain? To her daughter, this apartment, her apartment was dirty, not suitable to her new tastes, her new life as an actual American.

Something about this country made it easy to forget that we needed each other.

The phone rang and she sprang from the kitchen floor into the living room where she gripped the receiver in her hand. It was her. Mina's body tingled as if reanimated by Margot's voice, which—despite its clear frustration in its struggle to mix Korean and English—tethered Mina back to this world.

"What did you eat for dinner?" Mina asked.

"Some pasta. Spaghetti," Margot said. "What about you?"

"Doenjang guk." For years, Mina would wake up before sunrise to make her daughter a large pot of soup or stew for the day. She couldn't bear her daughter coming home from school and not having anything nutritious to eat, so she filled her food with as many vegetables as she could afford—zucchini, carrots, peppers, and onions. Even though her daughter craved American meals, she wanted her daughter to always think of their home as, if not the most comfortable place, a shelter in which she'd never go without food. Wasn't that the most heartbreaking thing for any parent in the world? To know their child was hungry. Sometimes she wondered if perhaps being separated from her own mother might've protected them from enduring the pain of watching each other whittle away until they became nothing—bones in the dirt that would be broken by bombs, by soldiers' boots.

But no, nothing was worse than losing each other; nothing was worse than being lost. It was as if she and her parents were both half dead and half alive—haunting each other at once. It was almost worse than death. Purgatory.

"Everything okay?" Margot asked.

"Yes, everything okay. You?"

"Busy. A lot of work," Margot said in Korean.

"That's good. Being busy is good."

"How's the store?" Margot asked.

She didn't want her daughter to worry, her daughter who, despite her upbringing and how little Mina could provide, managed to go to college and find a nice office job. She knew that her daughter had college loans to pay, her own rent and bills. And Mina was proud of her, too. At church or at the swap meet, she bragged about her, the one that got away, concealing the wound of abandonment beneath her pride.

"Business is slow, but it's okay," Mina said. "I get bored a lot. Not a lot of customers these days."

"Why don't you learn English? Do you want me to buy you some books so that you can learn?"

"It's too hard for me now."

"Why don't you try? You can learn," Margot said in English. "You have time."

Her daughter would never understand why she couldn't make the time to learn a language that would never accept her—especially at her age now. What would be the point? She was in her sixties and couldn't find a job anywhere except at a swap meet or at a restaurant in Koreatown. She didn't know a single English language speaker except for her daughter, who only visited once per year. What was the point of learning a language that brought you into the fold of a world that didn't want you? Did this world want her? No. It didn't like the sound of her voice.

"Why don't you learn Korean?" Mina asked sharply.

"I'm not bored." Margot paused, formulating her words in Korean. "There's no time. I don't have a use for it."

Mrs. Baek laughing flashed in Mina's mind: *I have music. I don't need a boyfriend. I'm busy. I'm not bored. I'm never bored.*

Would Margot ever realize that when Mina said she was bored, she was trying to say that she was lonely? Bored was a much easier word to say, wasn't it? She was tired of fighting with her daughter to move back to LA, to come back home.

And she didn't need her daughter to lecture her. She had been through enough already. What did her daughter, American-born, know about time, about survival, about usefulness? What did she know about *boredom*? About loneliness?

Mina had spent so many years dedicated to her business, growing and tending the inventory like her own garden, earning pride in something she owned. But now that there were fewer customers, she had little to distract herself anymore. She couldn't afford to replace broken or old hangers anymore. The racks and rounders had grown bare of clothes. Now only the poorest of customers remained, the ones who haggled and walked away because they could sense her desperation, her fear that she, in her age, would have to again find another way to keep the roof over her head. For their essentials, the other customers drove to big-box stores where they knew they could always get the best deals, where they might become, in some ways, finally American, where the exchange of items—money for shampoo, a new dress for a first date, cough syrup, a sweater for Grandma—might come without any emotional response, familiarity, or bond.

She had felt the slow creep of sadness overwhelm her as she realized now that all she had built could not survive. Her business had become her child, hadn't it? What would or could she do next in this life with so little money and so little time?

"Okay, well, take care of yourself. Get some rest soon," Mina said before hanging up the phone.

She had diverted herself with work all these years. How could she tell her daughter, who had such a limited understanding of Korean, what she had been through, why she couldn't learn English, why she had chosen this life, how much she loved Margot, how much she was both proud of and frightened by her daughter, who was sharp and quick and strong? Her daughter had to be, of course, because of how she had been raised. They had raised each other in a way. She loved her daughter. She would do anything for her.

But she would never, ever learn English. She didn't care. She hated the way the language sounded in her mouth, out of her lips—stilted and childlike. And when she did attempt to speak to someone on the phone, or at the DMV, she often got dirty looks or harsh, condescending responses. She didn't need a language that wasn't big enough for her, didn't want to make room for her.

She had been through enough, hadn't she? She had church. She had God. She was fine. She didn't need anyone at all. This *was* her language. This was the story she told herself to survive.

After another sleepless night, Mina rushed back to her shop from the restroom, washed coffee mug and dish soap in hand, and bumped into a small yet powerful figure. She appeared out of nowhere like a sudden earthquake.

Mina's insides swayed like hanging lights. The mug smashed to the ground. "Mrs. Baek?"

Together they bent to recover the pieces scattered along the painted walkway where merchandise hung above or leaned on display carts in an explosion of goods from children's toys to sneakers, diet green teas, herbal tinctures.

As she cradled the half-broken mug, filled with its shards, in one hand, Mina unconsciously grabbed Mrs. Baek's arm with the other. It surprised her how tight her grip was on this now stranger, and Mrs. Baek didn't even flinch. She was that strong.

"Do you work here?" Mrs. Baek asked, eyes wide.

"Yes." Mina could feel herself slipping below the surface

of the water. She had tried not to think about their past for so long—and here she was now.

"I opened a store around the corner," Mrs. Baek said. "A sock shop."

How many years had it been since they had last seen each other? Over twenty. Her voice—urgent and husky—had remained familiar but her face had ripened into a theater of surprising beauty with lips perfectly lined, a striking shade of red. They seemed to float in the sky toward Mina like an object of surrealism in a mind that had become so heavy and gray, thick as the smog in LA.

She must have used makeup to conceal the circles under her eyes, the dark circles that Mina had seemingly always had, even in her twenties. Or Mrs. Baek had been blessed with good genes, or the ability to sleep well at night, or maybe because she didn't have children. How much, despite the years of Mrs. Baek's intimate knowledge of Mina's life, the care of Mina's own baby, did she really know about Mrs. Baek? Where had she been since they last saw each other?

And what was she doing here now?

"You left Hanok House?" Mina asked, a pang of sorrow in her chest. She remembered her first date with Mr. Kim—the slabs of dark wood as tables, the Hahoetal masks that laughed, grains of ahl on her tongue—and how later, after Margot's birth, Mrs. Baek would invite them there for a free meal, piping hot jjigaes and tangs, brothy and slow-cooked. How much Mrs. Baek had nourished them. It was a house after all, wasn't it? It was a home that none of them could have, where food was safety, temporary shelter from the darkness of the world, the hours of mindless work, the fear that it could all be taken away, any day, at any moment.

"Yes, I left Hanok House. Earlier this year."

Mina wanted to ask why but didn't. There were many reasons why a woman fled—boredom, fear, frustration, a desire to get ahead. But it was hard to tell whether owning a sock shop was for Mrs. Baek an improvement in the quality of her life or a type of banishment. Surely she couldn't make much more here than she had at Hanok House where at least she would always be fed.

"I've—I've wondered about you," Mrs. Baek said, her eyes filling with tears.

Mina nodded. "It's strange that we ended up under the same roof again."

"There aren't many places left these days for a small business, I guess."

"Yes, yes, that makes sense," Mina said. "I should…get back to my store." She forced a smile to obscure the quickening of her heart, the rising nausea, the cold sweat on her neck. "I'm sure I will see you around?"

Not that Mrs. Baek had wronged her in any way, but rather she represented a time that Mina had no reason to relive, a time during which she was particularly vulnerable, when she had first moved to America, when she had been so naive to think that she could run away from the past, when she had replaced the sorrow of losing her husband and daughter with the sorrow of losing a lover, a father to her child, when all the sorrows in her life threatened to undo her, and Mrs. Baek, the entire time, appeared so put together, so confident, educated, and thoughtful.

As soon as she entered her store, Mina sat down on the floor behind her counter, tending to that history: *It's not your fault. None of this is your fault*, how she had longed to say this to Lupe in the station wagon on that day, the blood running down the side of Mr. Kim's jaw, how she had thrown up in the toilet and Mrs. Baek wiped down her face like a child's after his final phone call.

Mrs. Baek had entered her life one more time, like a ship that passed, churning water. But perhaps what terrified Mina the most wasn't a resurgence of what happened, what could have happened, what had never happened, but instead something that Mrs. Baek threatened to offer—friendship again.

Why had Mrs. Baek fled Hanok House? Did she need her now?

Later that afternoon, Mina searched the swap meet for Mrs. Baek's store—a sock shop—which turned out to be less than a minute away, around a corner she never passed, down one of the aisles toward the rear of the building. Both conservative pajama sets and lacy lingerie hung outside the store's perimeter constructed, like Mina's, of gridwall panels. She caught a glimpse of Mrs. Baek near her glass counter, organizing bundles of athletic socks.

"Mrs. Baek," Mina called from the center of the walkway. Her heart was racing, as if she had been walking straight into the waves for someone who had been washed away, who couldn't swim back to the shore by herself. For the past several hours, she had been steeling herself for this moment.

Mrs. Baek lifted her face, and upon seeing Mina, motioned for her to come forward.

Trembling, Mina threaded between tables, piled with undergarments, to the glass counter.

Her eyes couldn't resist the pull of Mrs. Baek's lips—red and perfectly lined. Now she remembered. A poster of a painting that she had seen once. The long lips stretched across a wide sky spotted with clouds in a faint snakeskin pattern. Women like herself rarely wore red lipstick, not only because a woman who wore it called attention to her face—carved with lines by a life of working long hours—but because red lipstick required the wearer to be vigilant about where they placed their hands on themselves, so as not to mess up or smudge their mouths, vigilant about the lining of their lips so that the color wouldn't bleed into the tiny cracks that formed as time went by, as they had on both Mina's and Mrs. Baek's.

But she admired the effort Mrs. Baek had put into herself, apparently *for herself*. Mina wondered with what color she would adorn her lips. Not red. She always preferred soft pinks and berries—like the ones she used to wear when she was young.

"Everything okay?" Mrs. Baek asked.

Mina could not feel her feet, as if her torso and head levitated, legless, above the dull gray carpet. For a moment, she fixed her eyes on an English novel on top of the glass counter—Thomas Hardy, *Tess of the d'Urbervilles*.

"Yes, it's been such a long while," Mina said. "I—I was wondering if you wanted to get dinner sometime?" The shyness of her own voice surprised her. Why was she so afraid?

"Yes, of course," Mrs. Baek said, as if she had been waiting all these years for Mina to ask.

A weight lifted off Mina's chest. "How about tonight or tomorrow?" she asked.

"Yes, yes, anywhere is fine," Mrs. Baek said. "Just not—"

"Hanok House." Mina smiled.

"Yes. Somewhere else." Mrs. Baek smirked. "Tonight is fine." Her neck appeared to grow red. "I was only planning on finishing that book." She tilted her head toward the counter.

"Is it any good?" Mina thumbed through the pages, impressed by Mrs. Baek's ability to read so many English words. She didn't know a single person who loved novels like her.

"Yes, I read it a long time ago. In college," Mrs. Baek said. "It's sad but beautiful."

Mina set the book back down and rested her hand on the cover as if she could absorb through its flesh some of her friend.

"But it's full of terrible men," Mrs. Baek said, shaking her head. "And I always hated the end."

Short ribs, sugar, sesame, and garlic caramelized over flames, sizzling around them, accentuated by the sharpness of kimchi jjigaes and fish stews boiling in earthenware pots. Mina hadn't had a meal at a restaurant in ages it seemed, not since she had dined with her daughter last Christmas. The assortment of banchan—seasoned soybean sprouts, acorn jelly, potato salad, tofu jorim, fried fishcake, grilled gulbi, kkakdugi—strummed her senses like pure sunlight pressing on seedbeds.

"Do you remember the banchan I used to bring home from work?" Mrs. Baek asked.

"Yes, of course. They were always the best." The potato salad melted like a mousse in Mina's mouth.

"I loved working there, in a way," Mrs. Baek said. "I could just cook and it was simple. I guess everything was simpler back then."

"The hours were very hard, though, right?"

"Yes, but I didn't mind."

Mina tasted the soybean sprouts—that delicate crunch between her teeth, the gentle sting of garlic and green onion, the mouthwatering sesame. "Why did you leave? I thought maybe you were tired of the restaurant."

Mrs. Baek sipped ice water, staining the edge of the glass with her lipstick. How she left her mark, a signature of sorts, wherever she went. Mina's own lips felt dry as she rubbed them together. She peeled a bit of dead skin off with her teeth.

"It's complicated." Mrs. Baek tapped the ends of her chopsticks on the table before gripping a cube of kkakdugi that disappeared in her mouth.

An unease ripened between them in the pauses of their speech.

"What is Margot up to these days?" Mrs. Baek asked.

"She lives in Seattle now. She went to college there. She works in an office, a nonprofit."

"That's wonderful."

The waitress set the green bottle of soju and two glasses on the table.

"Would you mind bringing us some more banchan?" Mrs. Baek asked. She poured the soju with two hands. "Do you think she'll move back to LA?"

Mina hadn't had a drink in years, not since leaving Korea, but with her heart pounding now, her palms sweating, she gulped down the clear fluid, bolting toward some relief, the comfort of a blunted mind.

"I don't know. She seems to like it there," Mina said.

"Kids will do what they please these days. But she'll be back, I bet. I'd love to see her again." Mrs. Baek grinned. In the overhead light, her eyes were dark and dull as charcoal.

Mina filled both their glasses.

"Did you ever hear from her father?" Mrs. Baek nudged the plate of grilled gulbi toward Mina, who shook her head. The fish's open mouth revealed the tiniest teeth. "What have you been doing these past years?"

"Working. Going to church. What about you?"

"Same. No church, though, of course." Mrs. Baek's chopsticks split the skin, gathering a bite off the bones. She laughed. "I never understood how you could hang out with the women there. So judgmental." She slipped a translucent bit of bone out of her mouth.

Mina adjusted herself in her seat. "I never see them really except on Sundays."

"That's right." Mrs. Baek nodded. "What ever happened to the lady who was your friend back then? Your friend from Seoul?"

"Mrs. Shin?" Mina asked. A pang of sadness. "While I was pregnant, I stopped going to church for a while, remember?" She exhaled out loud. "Eventually, I changed churches. We didn't keep in touch after that." An unacknowledged tension had risen between her and Mrs. Shin as Mina's growing stomach became more and more apparent. The disgrace of it all. Even if she cared for Mina, Mrs. Shin couldn't have a woman like Mina around influencing her children. She was ruined, wasn't she?

But with Mrs. Baek, Mina could be, for once, human. They cared for each other despite their flaws, or idiosyncrasies, which were—in a certain light, even in the smallest gestures like Mrs. Baek's red lipstick—acts of defiance and courage. They need not erase themselves.

"Will you retire soon?" Mrs. Baek asked.

"To be honest, I'm not sure. I'll probably have to work until I can't anymore, until I'm too old. I can't really afford to retire."

"Same here." Mrs. Baek sighed.

The waitress carried two heavy earthenware pots of soondubu jjigae. Steam rose between them, clouding the air with the scent of kimchi, sesame oil, garlic, anchovy, shrimp. They cracked their eggs onto the jjigaes. The yolks throbbed on top.

Mina rubbed the space between her brows, partially covering her face. "You know, I have to be honest. When I first saw you, I was sort of terrified of the memories that you might bring up. I've grown so accustomed to being alone after Margot left, you know?"

"Yes, I understand. I felt the same way, I think."

Mina pressed her palms on the wooden bench below her.

"I don't know if you know this," Mrs. Baek said, eyes low. "But back then, when you were going through so much, that's how I survived in a way—by helping you and Margot. That

way I didn't have to think so much about my own problems
anymore. I felt like I had escaped mine and that I had to be
strong. For you two." She sighed, crinkling the paper sleeve
of her chopsticks.

Mina wanted to thank her for helping all those years ago.
When having a child should have been impossible, Mrs. Baek
had fed her and tended to Margot when Mina couldn't do so
herself. Maybe that was what made Mina so uncomfortable
about Mrs. Baek. She had never experienced this kind of love
before; this was family.

And yet she realized that she had never known much about
Mrs. Baek. In the past, Mrs. Baek had mentioned a husband
in Texas. What problems had she escaped by helping Mina
and Margot? Mina couldn't ask her about them now, could
she? Maybe one day she would. She wanted to help her, to be
of some use to her, too. Who had Mrs. Baek left behind, or
who had she been fleeing from all those years ago?

"Did you ever—your husband—did you ever speak to him
again?" Mina asked.

Mrs. Baek's eyes darkened into coal. "No, no, of course
not. He was terrible." She sighed. "Thank goodness we never
had children together."

"Did you want to have children?"

"No, I did not," she said. "To be honest, I never wanted
my own."

"Is that why you had to leave? Did he want them?"

"Yes, he did, but—that's not why I left. When we first met,
he was so much fun. Isn't that how they all are? But once we
married, I realized he was very bad. He…he couldn't control
himself." She shook her head. "But I didn't have a way out
until I became a citizen, so I stayed with him for years. I had
to survive, you know?"

"Yes, of course," Mina said. Sadness crept up from her

chest into her face. She wondered how many women had been trapped—in terrible marriages, terrible jobs, unbearable circumstances—simply because the world hadn't been designed to allow them to thrive on their own. Their decisions would always be scrutinized by the levels at which they were able to sacrifice themselves, their bodies, their pleasures and desires. A woman who imagined her own way out would always be ostracized for her own strength. Until one day they found each other by some kind of magic or miracle or grace—here now. They were safe.

Tears filled her eyes. "You've done well," Mina said.

"Me?"

"Yes, we've done well. Don't you think?"

Mrs. Baek smiled with a dull glint in her eyes. Pulling the rest of the gulbi's flesh off the bones, she said, "You and I, we've always been stronger than anyone else." She nudged the plate of fish toward Mina. "At least we have each other."

Mina stared at the objects in front of her—the banchan, the jjigae, the metal spoons, the chopsticks. For a moment, as Mrs. Baek delicately spooned her soup, Mina contemplated the matte rouge that managed, despite the eating and drinking, to remain perfectly lined with only a patchy fade, a charming pinkish stain on the lips.

So much of Mina's life had been driven by the need to survive in a world created by and for someone else. What would the world look like if she made it her own, even temporarily, for a moment, fleeting, so that she could experience again the throb, the hunger of being alive, eyes wide, teeth showing?

The color, the mark on the rim of a glass of water. *I am here, I was here*, it said. Makeup expressed a desire to be seen while providing some camouflage as well. But what else was Mrs. Baek hiding? And how could Mina help her now?

MARGOT

WINTER 2014

On the floor of her mother's bedroom, Margot pored over the contents of the safety-deposit box—a large envelope of documents in Korean and mostly black-and-white photographs extending over decades. For the first time, she saw her mother as a small child—her oval face and clever gaze—posing by herself in front of a traditional Korean house with its elegant tiled roof and dark wooden beams, then her mother as a young teenager, defiantly unsmiling at a communal dining table. All of these images had faded through the years, which reminded Margot, almost, of the Seattle sky in winter, all those layered gray washes of muted softness and light.

She could begin to imagine what her mother's life might have been like at the orphanage, from which she had never been adopted and which she had almost never discussed.

But what stood out most, what startled Margot with waves

of uncertainty, were several color photos, in particular one of her mother as a woman in her late thirties with a husband and child, a pigtailed daughter in a red T-shirt and leggings. With its yellowish tint, warped surface, the photo had been thumbed, touched through the years repeatedly like a worry stone.

The husband had a long sensitive face and an easy smile, standing in a relaxed, open stance with one hand on his daughter's shoulder and the other arm around Mina, fashionable in her wide-legged jeans and floral blouse. She stood stiffly with a slight smile on her face that shone without a single wrinkle or line. In the background, a tree-covered hillside revealed a slip of blue sky at the top of the frame. A sunny remarkable day in the woods or the country. Dust from ambling on trails covered their shoes.

The little girl in the photograph resembled Mina with her high cheekbones and narrow chin, more than Margot did herself. And the strangers, the husband and child, had an innocence and clarity about them, untouched by the hardness of Mina's orphan past and her future immigrant life.

Margot had always thought of Koreans as workaholics, religious and pragmatic, yet at times showy and status-oriented when they had the means. But studying those relaxed faces in the photographs, those dusty shoes, Margot could see someone else, *Koreans*—not Korean Americans, not immigrants hardened by the realities of living in a foreign country, who like her father in Calabasas had stubbornly "succeeded," achieving a sheen of perfection while obscuring his actual complexity, an isolation from the self. Or like her mother, who had worked tirelessly yet had never amounted to more than the long days, the long hours, alone.

What did this country ask us all to sacrifice? Was it possible to feel anything while we were all trying to get ahead of everyone else, including ourself?

And how could her mother have abandoned this other family to live in America, where her life had been tough in this cramped apartment, working an often soul-crushing job, as she yelled, *Amiga! Amiga!* to strangers walking away, as she raised Margot day-to-day, month-to-month, by herself? Unless, for whatever reason, the husband in this photograph had been worse, this family, this life had been worse. But how could that be possible?

Of course, her mother might've wanted to tell Margot about all of this one day—another family, another country, a half sister somewhere. But when and how? Perhaps her mother, like herself, didn't know what to do with life sometimes, hadn't made any decisions yet. Her mother had kept the key to the safety-deposit box inside the teddy bear's silly heart, which she had assumed no one would ever steal or touch. She, too, might have been under that spell, the illusion that delaying one's decisions, one's actions was the same as prolonging life. But then—unexpectedly—she died.

Who could help Margot understand this all now?

In the stairwell, the landlord had said Mrs. Baek had been at her mother's apartment in September or October, when he had seen Mr. Park waiting for her outside.

We all lived in the same house together until you were maybe three or four. Your mother used to bring you to the restaurant that I worked at, Hanok House. Do you remember?

Only one person knew her mother well enough.

MINA

SUMMER 2014

In her bathroom mirror, Mina applied the dusty rose–colored lipstick that she had purchased with Mrs. Baek from one of the swap meet's dollar stores. Earlier that day, as they were sharing a lunch of rice and various leftover banchan on top of the display-case counter of Mina's shop, Mrs. Baek had said, "You look so tired these days. Remember back in the day, how much you cared about your looks?" She smiled. "I remember you even wore those long, flowing skirts to work. Weren't you stocking shelves?"

Mina couldn't help but laugh at herself, how naive she had once been. "I wanted to make a good impression," she had replied, recalling the first time she had seen Mr. Kim—the edges of his fingertips as he had dropped the change, the cold hard coins, in her open palm, the pink flyer that spelled HELP WANTED, his eyes, smiling.

"Why don't you wear some makeup?" Mrs. Baek asked,

snapping her Tupperware closed. "You look like a grandma and you're not even a grandmother yet."

"Do you know how old I am?"

"So what? Do you know how old *I* am? I'm older than you."

"What do my looks matter?"

"Maybe when you look in the mirror, you might be happy. I feel that way. When I'm drawing my lips or my eyebrows, I feel alive, like I'm taking care of myself. I feel like I'm controlling my life in some way. Like I'm in control."

"Maybe you're right," Mina said.

"Let's go to the dollar store over there and get you some color."

Together, they stood close, the sides of their arms touching as they lingered over the small selection of lipstick on a stand covered in cosmetics—foundation, powders, and blushes. Mina tested several shades on the back of her hand until a flash of dusty rose appeared and Mrs. Baek said, "That one. That's it."

"You think so?"

"Yes, it's subtle but pretty, don't you think? You could start off slow."

"Eventually, maybe I'll graduate to red." Mina placed her fist on her waist and popped out her hip.

Mrs. Baek laughed. "Maybe," she said. "But by then we'll be on our deathbeds. Twins, I guess."

Now, in the mirror's reflection, Mina inserted an index finger into her mouth, puckered, and pulled the finger back out through her lips—a trick that Mrs. Baek had taught her to keep the color from her teeth. She smeared the waxy color onto her cheeks, brightening her face. All she needed was a bit of under-eye concealer, and despite her age, she could be beautiful, or at least, lively again.

Through an open window, she could smell a neighbor grilling carne asada—the smoke of animal fat, citrus, and garlic.

Her stomach grumbled. With toilet paper, she wiped the color off her mouth.

The phone rang. Was it her daughter? Or was it some pesky salesman, trying to sell her something in English?

She rushed to the living room. "Hello?"

"Mrs. Lee?" a man said roughly. "Mrs. Lee."

It was him. She would know that voice anywhere.

She gasped and slammed the receiver down with a crash.

Mina had grown terrified of the sound of unexpected knocking on doors, which would always remind her of when the police officers came to her apartment in Seoul. And so when she heard a knock the next day, she stepped back for a second, thinking that she could pretend she wasn't here, but then the knock came again, and she realized that whoever it was could hear her television. She crept toward the door, avoiding the fisheye, knowing that whoever it was might see her.

A minute passed. "Who is it?" she asked.

"It's me." A throat cleared. "Mr. Kim."

Oh, no, oh, no, oh, no. "Go away," she screamed, surprising herself. "Go away."

She slumped onto the floor, crawling on her hands and knees toward her bedroom, where she waited until she could not hear a thing anymore, only the drip of the faucet in the bathroom, the flush of a neighbor's toilet. She didn't know for how long she hid.

When was the last she had seen him? Over twenty-six years ago. He seemed to be speaking to her from the past, from the Ferris wheel where she had opened her eyes, observing the beauty of this world that, for a few minutes, promised not to harm her. Like the Ferris wheel, the entire world, her life had pulsed—ripe and bright—with the smell of the ocean bathing away her pain, the grief that kept her up most nights.

Over twenty-six years ago, she had taken the gun from Mr. Kim's drawer, slipped it into her purse, and gone to the supermarket like any other day at work. She could've killed Mr. Park then, but he wasn't there. The gun bag was in her closet, which she had hidden in an attempt to keep Margot safe, to submerge that part of her life as best as she could.

After a long bout of silence, she checked the fisheye. He was gone.

He had pushed a note through the bottom of the door.

Please call me. I don't have a lot of time left. I have cancer. I'm dying. I can help you. I want to help you with your family.

She turned toward her coffee table and slapped the Virgin Mary statue, a twin to the one at her store. The statue tipped to its side, tumbling to the ground with a crack.

As daylight ended in the grapefruit-and-orange glow of sunset, Mina called him almost two weeks after his visit. A part of her hoped he would disappear and die, unable to bear the idea that he was alive, and another part of her could not tolerate the idea of him not existing in this world at all.

Within these two weeks, trapped in this limbo between calling him or not, she avoided Mrs. Baek. She thought all day and night about what choice she would most regret. Would he help her? What would that mean? Could she trust him enough to let him in her life again? Or was this all a ruse to humiliate her, as he had done when he abandoned her, as he had done when he had failed to meet her in Las Vegas? What was the excuse then? How much more humiliation could she take?

Twenty years ago, she had driven to the desert for him. He had found her, in their apartment, mailed her a letter asking her to meet him in Las Vegas if she could.

I am going to be in Las Vegas for one week. Can you come and meet me? I will be at this hotel. Ask for me at the front desk. Please do not let anyone know.

She planned to introduce him to Margot, six years old then. She didn't understand what he had been doing in Vegas, or why, but she remembered their trip there together a long time ago, when they had gorged themselves on American food at the buffets, gambled on penny slots until the crack of dawn, made love in the dim light of the sun still rising, and slept soundly until lunch.

Mina had packed up the car with her daughter, who sat in the back by herself, unaware. She had no idea what to tell Margot and decided to not say a word about Mr. Kim, in case, for whatever reason, he either didn't show up, or he had changed or didn't want to have anything to do with them, or perhaps the correspondence had all been a terrible mistake.

That had been the first and last time she had ever driven on the freeway. She drove below the limit. Despite the cars around her honking, all she could remember was not the dry arid landscape and the fear that she should've felt driving alone for such a long distance, but the way her heart throbbed in her throat thinking about Mr. Kim, their time together in bed or on the Ferris wheel, and the pleasure, the joy she had felt around him for the first time since her husband and daughter had died.

But he never showed up. The hotel where they were supposed to meet didn't recognize his name. She hadn't heard from him since.

Until now. Chewing her fingernails, she dialed the long-distance number on the note that he had slipped under the door. What had overcome her? Perhaps at the end of his life and toward the end of hers, she needed to hear his voice again. She needed to know that their time together was not an illusion that she had tucked somewhere inside of her brain. She needed to know that it was all, in some way, real.

"I didn't think you'd call." His voice, worn and raspy, startled her.

Did she dial the wrong number?

"Hello?" he asked.

She remained silent.

"Mrs. Lee?"

She placed the receiver down on her lap, contemplating if she should hang up the phone. She couldn't stand to be reminded of the life that she had lived without him, yet she couldn't bear to let him go again. She hated the universe, even God, right now. Why couldn't He make life simple and clean? Hadn't she suffered enough? *Enough*, she wanted to scream.

"Mrs. Lee?" She could still hear his voice, muffled on her lap.

Trembling, she lifted the receiver to her ear again. "Yes?"

"Can we talk? I can help you, I think. I can help you."

"How did you get my number?" she asked. "How did you find me?"

"The house that you used to live in? The landlady who died, her kids? I called them. You bought a store from them, right? They had your new address, your number."

"Why would they have—"

"I told them I was dying, that I wanted to reach you, that I could help you before—"

"I don't want your help."

"I know that—you probably wondered all these years."

"What about Vegas?" Her voice cracked. "What about then?"

"Yes, I know. I'm sorry. We were…so young then." He cleared his throat. "I was—I was in Chicago at the time. There was a conference in Vegas. I worked for my cousin's import business." He sighed. "But my wife—"

"I don't want to know," she said. Her heart raced.

Breathing deeply, he said, "Okay. But I can help you, before it's too late. Your parents. What if they are still alive?"

Your parents. She almost dropped the receiver.

"I don't care anymore," she said, her voice rising. "I've already moved on. What if they're dead? What is the point?"

"I can help you find them. I have someone, an investigator in Seoul that I use."

"I don't want to know." She hung up the phone. "Don't you think if I would've wanted to know, I would've tried myself," she said out loud to no one but herself. "I would've stayed in Korea and waited like your mom. Why would I want to know them now? For what? So I can bury them, visit their graves? What is the point?" Tears streamed down her face. She wanted to throttle someone. She wanted to throttle the universe.

The phone rang.

"What?" she asked, relieved that he had called back.

"Meet me," he said. "Why don't we go somewhere?"

She breathed hard through her mouth.

"We can talk. That is it. I promise… I'll be there. It's different this time."

She didn't want to ride in his car, nor did they want to be seen in Koreatown together, so she agreed to meet at the end of the pier on Sunday night. Of course, she knew that he had chosen the place not for its seclusion, but because of the memories aroused by the air, the salt of the ocean, the lust of the carnival lights, and the rough wood boards that squeaked beneath her feet, providing the illusion of walking out on water.

She didn't know if she would even recognize him and kept thinking to run away before it was too late, before he would pull her in like the waves, out into the ocean again. She had agreed that she would only meet him if he did not ever bring up the past, if he did not ever bring up where he had gone, what had become of his life since he had left LA, how long he had been living in the area, why he never made it to Vegas—especially his wife. She didn't want to hear any of it. All she wanted to know was what he could offer her now, what he knew or could know, and how he knew it.

As she walked closer to the end of the pier, the screams on the roller coaster whooshed by, and she stared up at the Ferris wheel, flashing red and white. Tears filled her eyes. She hadn't expected to cry. She hadn't been to this pier for years. Her daughter would sometimes come on her own, but Mina refused to step foot again in this place, where she had let herself feel again. And here she was once more, overcome with an emotion that made her mouth dry, hungry for the sweet burn of the hot chocolate she could smell by memory, the first time she had had hot chocolate in her life. She thought for a second she must turn around, or jump off the side of the pier, amid the jostle of bodies around her, the street musicians. The water was calling her name.

But before she knew it, she had reached the end of the pier. Underneath the white glow of a tall lamp, a man sat on the bench, shriveled in a large black wool coat. She walked closer to him. He turned around and she, alarmed and desperately, sadly happy, caught a glimpse of his face. The world tilted beneath her feet. They bowed their heads at each other.

She could collapse, but she gripped the back of the bench as quickly as she could. She sat two feet away from him as if they were strangers.

She crossed her arms in front of her belly, ashamed of her body, and wept.

She could sense him trying not to look at her, although he

wanted to comfort her. He reached into his coat pocket and offered her a handkerchief. She wiped her eyes at only the corners to not disturb her eyeliner, the makeup she wore. The tears, springing from her heart's heaviness, the heaviness of a lifetime, almost seventy years, streamed down her face, and she didn't care if anyone could see her.

She faced the ocean. The moon glowed, shimmering on its surface. She couldn't glance at him again. She couldn't see his face.

"You're still cute," he said.

Surprised, she couldn't help but smile.

"You're still pretty," he said. "I don't know if you're nice anymore, though."

She laughed, gently dabbing her cheeks with his handkerchief. "Why should I be?" she asked.

"You are right about that." He sighed. "I'm so sorry for… everything."

A tightening in her throat. She fell silent for a while. From the corner of her eyes, she watched him cross and uncross his legs. The water lapped the pillars beneath them. She tried not to shiver or appear cold in front of him.

Finally, she asked, "Did you ever find your father?"

"Yes, I did," he said. "But it turns out, he died…a long time ago." He cleared his throat. "Actually, I found out that he died shortly after we left him in the North. A bomb had been dropped near our house."

Mina gasped and closed her eyes momentarily.

"I never had the heart to tell my mother that," he said. "I always thought it'd be best to…let her wait it out. So… she died thinking that he might still be alive somewhere, or maybe she would meet him in heaven. But I couldn't let her know that she had waited all those years for him…for nothing. That would've broken her heart, more than anything else, don't you think?"

She could feel him watching her. For a second, she glanced back. The sight of him, old and small in his long coat, pained her. She remembered his arms, how she loved his arms, and she could see that he had grown thin, wasting away. She could hardly recognize him except for the softness of his eyes beneath his curved brows, the gentle line of his lips.

He cleared his throat. "Do you...do you want to know the truth? About your parents?"

Your parents. The words stung, stirring the ashes inside her heart. "I don't think the truth matters anymore."

"How is that?"

She held back tears. "Like for your mother. Why would the truth have mattered to her? Why would the truth matter now?"

"Because you have time."

"There's hardly any time." She wanted to say, *I'm almost seventy. What time do I have left?* She wiped her eyes with the soft white handkerchief balled up in her fist.

"You still have time."

How did we measure what we had left? Not in days or years for Mina, but with what strength remained. His days were numbered. He had said the cancer would overtake him before the end of the year. She wanted to hold him, but didn't know how, after all this time had passed. Their bodies had changed so much. She could hardly recognize themselves under the weight of all the years—twenty-six of them—and what time could do to the body and the heart.

He placed his face into his hands, shaking.

"What is worse than the truth is where your mind goes," he said. "How it wanders, how it refuses to let go. The things you imagine that could've happened. At least you have an answer. At least you can stop thinking at night. My mother was at the point where there was no more moving forward—all she had left were her dreams to keep her alive. You still have time. You still have so many years left, but also, no one has enough time. I just wish... I wish I had come here sooner. I could've tried to help you earlier, but...life..."

"You didn't know."

Of course, she couldn't tell him now about Margot. What would be the point? Judging by the gold band on his finger, he was married now, might have kids of his own. The idea of Margot might shatter him. She would keep him from that knowledge, as he had protected his mother before her death. She would spare him.

And for Margot to have a father now, how could that help her, when he was on his way out of this world? She couldn't trade the grief of not having a father for the grief of one dying. At least she had gotten used to the former, a familiar sadness rather than something frightening and unknown. Mina would spare them both. And she would allow him back into her life on her own terms.

Mina stared out into the wide ocean of obsidian, scintillating under the white moonlight. Once, behind them, they had ridden the Ferris wheel in a riot of light flashing in the still blue glow of night. Back then, every delicious second mattered. Every single breath.

MARGOT

WINTER 2014

After Margot had gone through the contents of the safety-deposit box on Monday night, she resisted the temptation to rush to Mrs. Baek's apartment and sleeplessly waited until the morning. Only Mrs. Baek could help her understand the photograph from the safety-deposit box—her mother, a woman in her late thirties with a husband and child in Korea. Where was the other family, the pigtailed daughter in the red T-shirt and leggings?

But yesterday, when Margot knocked at Mrs. Baek's door, no one answered. And now, Wednesday, Christmas Eve, Margot had only one place left to search.

Margot and Miguel drove past houses decorated with holiday string lights and plastic Santas to her mother's church, which would be having separate services in Spanish, Korean, and English. Afterward, they'd have dinner at a Oaxacan restaurant that neither of them had been to but had heard good things about—rich red and black moles and live music in an oilcloth setting.

Despite the circumstances, both of them felt the need to do something for Christmas. In a place as warm and bone-dry as Los Angeles, the holiday season still seemed chilly, especially at night, when locals donned boots and down jackets and sweaters. And the festivities provided at least a hearth of togetherness and activity—shopping, cooking, the resurrection of plastic trees, the ribbons, the lights. The smell of pozole and birria, meats long-simmered in chilies and herbs, and traces of Korean food with its piquant kimchi and stews and bulgogi filled the hallways of her apartment building. Christmas cacti decorated drab balconies in fuchsias. Supermarket poinsettias flourished, brazen and flaming red. The children off from school ran around at all hours.

Outside of Margot's car, men on bicycles zoomed by in traffic; commuters chatted at the bus stop, plastic bags bulging with groceries; street vendors sold everything from oranges and peeled mangoes served on a stick to shiny boom boxes and soft polyester blankets printed with teddy bears and cartoon hearts.

"Do you think it might be time to call Officer Choi again?" Miguel asked, sitting in the passenger seat. "I mean, we know what we know about Mr. Park, right? He's been stalking Mrs. Baek. He was apparently at your mom's apartment."

"I would think that if Mrs. Baek wanted the police involved, she would've called them already," Margot said. "She might be scared that he'd retaliate somehow."

"But he already could've hurt your mom. Isn't that enough for us all to be scared?"

"We don't know that for certain yet. I just hope Mrs. Baek's at church tonight. If we see her, we could let her know that the landlord saw Mr. Park at my mom's apartment. I don't even have to mention what the waitress told me about him buying the restaurant and stalking Mrs. Baek, right? I'll ask her about Mr. Park, if I can call the police. I just don't want to do anything that could harm her." She sighed. "I wish—I wish this wasn't happening all at once. I feel like I'm falling behind, like I'm not fast enough. I'll never be—"

"You were sick last week," Miguel said. "Your mom died. You just figured out the identity of your dad. This would be too much for literally *anyone*."

Tears filled her eyes.

"It's a miracle that you're still standing after all you've been through. You're tough."

It was the first time anyone had told her that, and she believed him. She had always thought of herself as sensitive, fearful, even passive at times, but he was right. She had gotten her strength from her mother. Her mother was bold—moving to this country where she didn't know the language and laws, falling in love, raising a daughter by herself.

And in these past few weeks, Margot alone had knocked on unknown doors, sold her mother's store, stood up to a police officer—actions she couldn't have imagined doing even a month ago. Her life had seemed so banal back then: managing to avoid Jonathan, her coworker with whom she had that relationship last year, sorting years of paperwork in her boss's office, scrolling through endless dating profiles online, editing and obsessively adjusting clip art in a program newsletter. Now she was driving around the city, searching for the truth of herself, the truth of her mother, of whether she was murdered.

"So when I got sick last week?" Margot said. "I have a sneaking suspicion… I know this sounds really paranoid, but it's almost like that guy—the driver, the hot one?—it's almost like he *poisoned* me. That tea didn't taste right."

Miguel covered his mouth in shock. "I swear to God, I

was thinking the same thing when you told me. But I didn't want to scare you."

"Shit. You can't trust people who are that good-looking."

"Do you plan on calling her, too?" Miguel asked. "Mrs. Kim? I mean, I know this could all be separate, but... I guess, if you wanted more info on your dad? Or are you too creeped out?"

"I'll call her. I was thinking after the holidays, let her settle down a little." Margot sighed. "For now, I think it's best that we find Mrs. Baek. She's the only one who could know about my mom's other family, the husband and daughter. And I'm afraid that because of Mr. Park, she might disappear or go somewhere else."

After circling the block a few times, they nudged their way into a tiny parking spot, questionably close to a defunct-looking hydrant. Walking up the front steps of the Spanish-style church, they went inside to see it was completely full of families dressed in their best. Heads bowed, everyone listened as the Irish priest, speaking Korean, led them in prayer.

At the rear of the church, Margot and Miguel wedged themselves between strangers and leaned against the cold walls. The smell of incense, old paper, and dust intermingled with the personal fragrances, the perfumes around them—a heady mix of florals, evergreen, and spice. This devotion to the senses, to the sounds of scripture and song, the fragments of color that could barely be seen from the stained glass windows at night, coalesced in this space where ritual and practice among strangers created a community. This was why her mother had returned here each Sunday, because she could insert herself and, without a word or even a glance, belong.

The last time they had gotten into an argument about church, Margot had been fifteen or sixteen years old, mutinous and loud enough to scare her mother. That was about the same age when she had fully given up on learning Korean, too, the same age when her defiance was the only thing she had to feel alive. And anything about her mother—her foreignness, her poverty, her powerlessness—became only a mirror for what Margot did not want to be or become.

"I don't believe in God," Margot had said in English, washing dishes after dinner. "I don't want to go to church tomorrow."

"You don't believe in God?" her mother replied in Korean, wiping the table. "Do you know what happens to people who don't believe in God?"

"Yes, of course."

Her mother approached, cornering Margot. "Do you want to go to hell?"

Despite her fatigue after a long day of work, twelve hours or so of running around downtown for inventory, courting customers who mostly ignored her, who sometimes called her "china," laughing at her face, her mother, in an argument, drew words from her deepest well, her deepest fears.

"I don't believe in hell." Already exhausted, Margot rinsed the pot under the hottest water, steam rising, tickling her face.

Her mother's hand slapped the counter. "Do you want to go to hell?"

"If there was a God, He wouldn't let us suffer," Margot shouted, turning off the tap. "He wouldn't let so many of us be poor." Her voice had risen in English, and she couldn't tell how much her mother would understand, but it didn't matter. She needed to say this out loud. "He wouldn't make life so hard for us. There wouldn't be war. He wouldn't make life hard for so many people." Tears gushed out of her eyes. She couldn't stop herself now.

"What about when you die? Uh?" Her mother gestured

to the ground as if they would all be buried right on the spot under the beige linoleum of their floors.

"When I die, I'll be dirt. It doesn't matter."

"What about when you die?" Her index finger, shaking, pointed toward Margot's chest. "How will people find you? Uh? How will you find the people you lost?" Her mother, who rarely cried, sobbed. "How will you find the people you lost?"

At the sight of her mother's face cracked open, Margot rushed past her into the bathroom where she perched on the toilet, weeping about the impossibility of living with her mother, tyrannous but every now and then, unexpectedly transparent, leaking light from the disasters of her life—her single motherhood, her childhood as an orphan, the war, the hours and hours without a proper day off, without a vacation, that she put into the store.

Margot never knew what to do with the bright flashes of who her mother was that would threaten to burn them all to the ground.

She could hear the squeak of the carpeted floor as her mother stood outside the bathroom, listening to Margot cry. Margot imagined her now—her fingers pressed against the closed door, her head leaning forward, her hand curled in a fist to knock, but then she retreated.

How afraid they were of each other. How impossible they seemed together. But if only her mother would've knocked, and Margot's response wouldn't have been, *Go away.* If only they had a way to embrace each other and say, *I don't understand you, but I'm trying my best. I am trying my very best.*

And now being in her mother's world was like stepping into a wildfire, the edges of which she might not ever contain or even know. An immolation that might clear dead brush, bring seed trapped in perfect pine cones down to the soil.

At the end of the prayer, the crowd stood, flipping through

the onionskin pages of black vinyl-covered books, clearing throats to sing. The gentleness of their song above organ music elevated the room, as if their spirits could skim the vaulted ceiling, filling the rib cage of the church. She didn't understand the words, but her body hummed with the sound, a sound of kindness and belonging, maybe even forgiveness, too. Tears filled her eyes and she wiped the corners with the sleeve of her sweater before they could fall.

When she looked up, she saw the side of a familiar face about twenty feet in front of them.

The red mouth.

Margot nudged Miguel urgently.

"What?" he whispered. The sermon had begun. The priest in his robes spoke with gentle but firm words, stirring the church like a fire. Margot could only catch in the net of her mind the Korean words for *giving*, *love*, and *God*.

"Mrs. Baek," she said. "Over there."

"Where?"

"Gray scarf." A man standing beside Margot shot her a dirty look.

When communion commenced and her row had been called, Mrs. Baek, who wore a deep navy blouse, rose from the pew. Her long blue skirt, closer to indigo, swayed with her body. She bowed when receiving the wafer in her mouth. Margot imagined the taste and texture, the dryness before it dissolved on the tongue, down the throat. She leaned against the wall, looking at the gilded altar above which Jesus hung, pale and lanky, arms spread on the cross.

Returning to her row, Mrs. Baek glanced up and, for a second, Margot thought that she had seen her and Miguel. Of course, they stood out. But then she picked up her songbook and seated herself as if nothing unusual had happened.

At the end of the service, Margot watched as Mrs. Baek

354	· NANCY JOOYOUN KIM

gathered her belongings in a black canvas bag from which she pulled out her cell phone. Reading her screen, she stumbled out of the nave, oblivious to her surroundings.

Margot signaled to Miguel, and they followed, maintaining their distance. Before exiting the building, Mrs. Baek turned and descended a flight of stairs into the church's basement. Stepping as quietly as possible, Margot and Miguel went down into a dusty storage area and waited behind several tall columns of cardboard boxes. They could hear Mrs. Baek speaking with someone, a man in Korean whose voice sounded familiar.

"You look so nice tonight," he said. "Let me take you out for dinner. It's Christmas Eve."

Margot and Miguel glanced at each other as they crouched down lower to the ground.

"How did you get my number?" Mrs. Baek asked.

The man laughed. "What's wrong with you? Come here."

"Stay away from me. Don't ever call me or come here again."

"I thought maybe you might be looking for a job," he said. "I could help you find a new one."

"I don't need anything from you. Why won't you leave me alone?"

"Shhh, lower your voice. You're like an animal," he said. "Ha, that's what women are like when they don't have men around. They're like animals."

Mrs. Baek said something, which Margot couldn't understand, through her teeth.

"What do you mean by that?" he asked.

"Mrs. Lee." Her voice cracked.

"Ha, which one?"

"Lee Mina."

"I don't even know who that is," he said. "Come here."

Swiftly, she grunted. He yelped in pain.

"Don't touch me," she spat. "I'll kill you."

Margot peeked around the boxes to see Mrs. Baek rushing out and Mr. Park following her, cradling his shin.

"Shit," Margot said, looking at Miguel. "Let's go."

They ran up the stairs and out of the building into the cold night, which had rapidly blackened into a street almost empty of people. At the other end of the church's parking lot, Mrs. Baek slammed the door of her battered gray Toyota Camry and drove off. Mr. Park had disappeared.

"She's probably going home," Margot said, catching her breath. "We should make sure she's okay?"

Why did she say her mother's name? Did he kill her?

Driving toward Mrs. Baek's apartment, Margot remembered the stacks of books and magazines in the living room, the layers of paper and text, tenuous skyscrapers, and Mrs. Baek's face without makeup, the wash of pale skin, and the eyes—intense, defiant, a little terrified. A steady and slow state of shock. She had imagined her in that apartment, poring over books, completely alone.

But Margot had been wrong about both her and her mother: their loneliness was not special, or any worse than anyone else's. In fact, they each had their own universes, small but constructed in their own way. Who was to say that in their devices, in their plots, they were different from other people?

Margot, who could only see her mother as the impossible foreigner with her rapid-fire Korean and embarrassing, halting English, who could only see her as an oppressive prop in Margot's own story, realized more and more that, in actuality, her mother was the heroine. She was the one who had been making and breaking and remaking her own life. And in the end, she might've paid for it.

MINA

FALL 2014

On the Saturday prior to Thanksgiving, almost one month after Mr. Kim's death, Mina entered her daughter's musty bedroom, folded newspaper in hand. She had attempted to snag a copy of the paper every day on her way to work while stopping for inventory at one of the wholesale businesses downtown. Sometimes there would be an unread newspaper on a counter that she would slip into her purse, or she would ask if she could take a look inside for an obituary. A friend had just died. Finally, one of the business owners offered her a stack of newspaper that he had kept from the past few months—saved for the bottom of his birdcage at home. Inside of her parked car, she scavenged through the pile until she found the one from October, the one with Mr. Kim inside.

Now on top of Margot's desk, where Mina mostly stored her own records and bills, she grabbed a pair of scissors from a wide plastic purple cup jammed with all the pens they had collected over the years. She imagined peering over the shoulder of her daughter, sitting at this desk hunched over a sketchbook with pencil in hand.

Mina lay the newspaper on that desk and flipped carefully through the pages until she found again the black-and-white photo of Mr. Kim, Kim Chang-hee—a slightly younger but much more vibrant manifestation of the man with whom she had traveled to the Grand Canyon two months ago in September.

Hand in hand, they had stared at the largest chasm they could find.

Dark shadows pressed against red-and sand-colored rock striped over billions of years by wind and water. The purest golden light saturated large swathes of the green brush and trees clinging to walls of hard mineral against a soft and hazy azure sky. The warm breeze smelled of pine. The earth was rich.

This was what she had always wanted—a return to feeling minuscule, tiny yet safe somehow again. Here she was so small that she could elude the cruelties that she had endured. Here she could go undetected. Nature in its most extreme forms taught us that there was a design greater than us, and we could unburden ourselves briefly from our individuality in this world, our self-importance. Wasn't that the relief?

The closest proximity to which she could attain this feeling in her everyday life must have been under God's roof in a cathedral, where the vaulted ceiling, that arch, was a refuge in which the entire universe, in the form of prayer and song, hummed. Beauty was safety. Beauty kept us from harm.

Cumulus clouds above projected shadows, dark silhouettes, deepening the drama of the peaks. The ornate striations of color and light made the spectacle of yesterday's overnight stop in Las Vegas—which they had finally experienced together again after all these years—laughable. Standing in front of this chasm was like looking up at heaven and into the deepest part of the earth—its soul, the violence and agony of its billions of years, and the resulting splendor—at once.

And then three weeks later in early October, he had delivered in a clean manila envelope the information on the whereabouts of her parents, papers that she now stowed in a safety-deposit box along with what she had left of her past— a few photographs from her time at the orphanage, her old identification documents in Korea, the only image she had left of her husband and daughter on that day they had gone hiking together.

Here now in front of this black-and-white photo of Mr. Kim—his face still glowing, eyes warm and soft, the gentle curve of his crooked smile—she experienced an unburdening, a rush of relief as this obituary confirmed what she had known when he had stopped answering his phone weeks ago: that he was gone forever. Now, she could reassemble her life, placing Margot's items—any photographs or mementos of hers that Mina had hidden from Mr. Kim these past few months— where they belonged before Margot's next visit.

Margot would never know he had been there, or who he was. And vice versa.

Carefully, Mina cut around the edges of the obituary's text, the straight lines.

In their few months together, despite his weakened condition, despite the fact that their bodies had changed, hers rounding and softening, and his revealing more bone and angles, they loved each other. He kissed her on the mouth in her bed. They felt young again as if they had just moved to America, as if they had always been in love. They could somehow erase the past. She had forgiven him. She did. She was so relieved to forgive someone.

But nothing could prepare her for the hole that Mr. Kim's death could leave in her life.

She found an empty envelope, folded the obituary, and slipped the paper inside for safekeeping. She opened the drawer and slid the envelope underneath the tray of her daughter's art supplies. To her knowledge, Margot never went inside that desk anymore. Mina had actually not seen her daughter sketch anything in a very long time.

She closed the drawer, sat on her daughter's chair, and wept on top of the newspaper that remained spread on the desk. She lowered her face onto the empty rectangle from which she had removed Mr. Kim's life, soaking the print, gently stamping the side of her face with smears of ink.

"**M**ina?" Mrs. Baek said on the phone, relieved and angry. "Where have you been? I've been trying to reach you for days. Haven't you been listening to your messages?"

For the past week since she had cut the obituary from the newspaper, Mina had been ignoring the phone, the sound of which made her heart pound in her chest. She had been overcome by the most profound exhaustion, recalling all those days of relentless grief, years and years ago when her husband and daughter died, like so many waves, pounding against her.

Mr. Kim was gone. This truth had knocked her down into the icy water, tossed her body around, and she found herself gasping for breath on the shore. She needed sleep. She needed rest and warmth.

"You haven't been at work in what—a week?" Mrs. Baek asked.

Until today, the weather had been balmy. In the seventies

and eighties during the day. Outside now, the sky was black, and the ground shimmered, wet with rain. The season was turning again.

"I'm fine," Mina said, rubbing the space between her brows.

"Are you sure? I thought maybe you might be with Margot or something for Thanksgiving but...it's been too long. I've been worried about you these past few months. What's wrong? Can you tell me what's wrong?"

"You've done enough for me, unnie." Mina's voice cracked as she remembered, all those years ago, Mrs. Baek rushing through her bedroom door, helping her to the bathroom, the toilet. How many times had Mrs. Baek held her hand? "Please do not worry about me. I just need some rest. I'm very tired these days. I'll be back at work tomorrow. I promise. We can talk about it then."

Silence on the other end.

"Hello?" Mina asked.

"No. No. I'll come over, okay? Have you eaten anything?" Mrs. Baek's voice softened. "You sound weak."

"No, I don't need—"

"I'll bring you some food. I'll be over in an hour, okay? Wait for me. I'll be there soon."

As they sat on Mina's couch, the broken figure of the Virgin Mary watched and Mina, finally, after twenty-six years, shared why Mr. Kim had fled. She told Mrs. Baek about what had happened to Lupe that day—how the supermarket owner had assaulted her and Mr. Kim intervened, causing him to disappear for fear of deportation. Mina confessed about Mr. Kim's reappearance in her life, their affair over the summer, their trip to the Grand Canyon, the information he had gathered about her parents by using a private investigator, his death.

"Does Margot know?" Mrs. Baek asked, picking up a

framed photo of Margot as a child, six or seven years old, her bangs straight across, on the couch's side table.

"No, she does not," Mina said with a heaviness in her chest.

"I don't remember this photo." Mrs. Baek scanned the room. "There's another one there, too. I remember thinking that you didn't have any photos of Margot—the first time I came here. In the summer."

"I hid all of them. I didn't want Mr. Kim to know."

"You never told him?" Mrs. Baek appeared confused.

"No."

"All those years," Mrs. Baek said, eyes lingering on the photo in her hand. "But Margot. Look at that face. Don't you think she would want to know? Don't you think—"

"It's better this way." Mina mustered all the strength she could to say those words. Did she believe them? She had but now she wasn't so sure.

Mrs. Baek nodded, setting the frame down on the table. Scrunching her brows, she appeared lost in her own thoughts, her own memories. A deafening silence bloomed.

What would Margot gain from knowing that her father had reappeared and died, only months later? Margot had already given up on him long ago. She had moved to Seattle and apparently was doing just fine without him, without Mina, too. But what if Mina was wrong about her daughter? What if—

Abruptly, Mrs. Baek stood, paced back and forth. She stopped, turned toward Mina, and asked, "The owner of the supermarket, the one who attacked Lupe—whatever happened to him?"

"Mr. Park?" Mina sighed. "Nothing to my knowledge. After I had Margot, I left. I never wanted to think about him again."

"His name was Mr. Park?"

"Yes, why?" Mina noticed the quickening of Mrs. Baek's breath. "Are you okay?"

"I just realized something, that's all. I need some water." Mrs. Baek rushed toward the kitchen. Mina heard her grab a glass from the drying rack and fill it from the tap. A moan of sadness escaped Mrs. Baek's mouth.

Mina found her slumped down on the laminate floor, leaning on the cabinets, and Mina was struck with the feeling of staring at a version of herself. How many times had she leaned on those cabinets alone?

"Unnie," Mina said, bending down to the ground beside Mrs. Baek. "What's wrong?"

Covering her face, Mrs. Baek wept. Mina had never seen Mrs. Baek cry before, and she had the sudden urge to hold her, to wipe the tears from her face.

"Unnie." Mina gently helped Mrs. Baek to her feet. "Unnie, please have a seat. Sit in the living room."

Mrs. Baek rested again on the couch, leaning forward with her head in her hands.

"I'm sorry," Mina said. "I'm sorry if I said something, I'm sorry if I said—"

"No. It's not you." Mrs. Baek shook her head.

Mina grabbed a roll of toilet paper from the restroom and handed it to Mrs. Baek.

"I just—I just realized something," Mrs. Baek said. Terrified, nostrils flaring, she looked into Mina's eyes. "Mr. Park."

"Yes?"

"I think he's the same man who's been following me." She breathed through her mouth.

"Following you?"

Mrs. Baek nodded. "He's been making my life hell. When you said that he owned the supermarket, I realized that the man—the man who's been following me, he's the same Mr.

Park. He told me about it, the supermarkets that he owned." Her voice grew hoarse. "For whatever reason, I couldn't connect that with where you had worked—back when you first came to America." Tears streamed down her face. "I never connected that until now."

"What do you mean?"

"Don't you just hate how small this world is?" Mrs. Baek asked with a depth of sorrow that Mina had never seen in her eyes. Her red lipstick had been smeared to the right of her mouth. Mina had the urge to erase it from her cheek with her thumb. She knew exactly what Mrs. Baek meant.

"He bought Hanok House, you know?" Mrs. Baek said. "That's why I left."

Mina gasped. "Mr. Park? I thought... Why didn't you tell me?"

"I didn't realize, I hadn't made the connection—"

"No." Mina shook her head. "Why didn't you tell me that someone was following you?"

"I couldn't. I figured it'd be best to not involve anyone else. I didn't want you, or anyone, to worry. Or what if—what if he retaliated against me if I did, or if someone else called the police? I thought I could deal with this on my own." She blew her nose. "I've been through worse."

"Does he know where you live?"

"I moved after I quit the restaurant. I had to change my number, too, earlier this year. I've been hiding. I can't walk around the park or the lake anymore. I drive far—all the way down Wilshire—to go to the pharmacy. I go to the grocery store during off hours. I'm always looking in the mirror behind me." Her eyes opened wide. "I don't even know why... It's like he only wants me because I rejected him, because I said *no*."

Mina closed her eyes, remembering the fear on Lupe's face, how Mina had the gun in her purse at the supermarket the next day, how she could've killed him before she quit. She could've finished him back then.

She went into her bedroom, where she switched on the light. Trembling, muscles tense, she retrieved the gun holster, which she had recently moved to the drawer beside her bed. She had never intended to use it, but in the dark aftermath of Mr. Kim's death, she had become fascinated with its power, its smell of brown leather, the way it felt in her hands. She could hear nothing but her own breath.

On the tour bus back from the Grand Canyon, the sides of their bodies pressed against each other, their fingers laced, Mr. Kim had asked, "What did you do with the gun?"

"I still have it," she said, heart racing. "I never knew how to get rid of it."

He nodded, staring ahead at the back of the seats in front of them. "Do you know how to use it?"

"No, I don't. I always thought I could figure it out myself if I needed to."

"You might want to take it to a shop and get it cleaned, checked out one day. Just in case. I could help you do that. I could show you how to use it."

Now in her hands, the gleaming brown leather appeared made for a man—belt hooped, redolent of cowboys, the West. Although still strange and foreign to her touch, the gun animated her with thoughts of revenge. She could be anyone she wanted to be with this gun. She could be young and powerful again. In this country, it was easier to harm someone else than to stay alive. It was easier to take a life than to have one. Was she finally an American?

Mina remembered the tenderness with which Mrs. Baek fed her on that night years ago, before Mr. Kim had called, leaving her in the morning. That night, she had dragged herself to her room where she lay down and wept.

Sorry to wake you up, Mrs. Baek said. *I have your porridge.*

Mina had tried to stand in time to meet Mrs. Baek. But her arms collapsed beneath her.

Here, take a bite, she said, holding the spoon up to Mina's mouth.

Turning toward the bedroom door, Mina noticed on her dresser the last printed photograph she had taken with Margot, the one of them together at her high-school graduation. How proud and terrified Mina had been that day, knowing that Margot would soon be on her own—all the way in Seattle. These past eight years, they had rarely taken any pictures since all of their time together had been working at the swap meet over the holidays. Maybe this year, they would not only pose at her store, but she would ask that Margot have the image printed and mailed to her once she returned to Seattle. Mina missed having something physical to hold.

She entered the living room with the holster in her hand.

At the sight of the gun, Mrs. Baek gasped, jumping to her feet from the sofa. The broken Virgin Mary, which she had been contemplating, fell to the rug. "What are you doing with that?" she asked. Her eyes were white. "Put that away." Her voice rose. "Have you lost your mind?"

Mrs. Baek seemed to be talking through water, gulping for air. The holster grew heavy in Mina's hand. A bomb whistled in her head. Her ears rang. She could smell the sulfurous earth, the blood that dripped down the head of the man, a stranger who carried her on his shoulders, the flash of red. Mrs. Baek's lipstick was still streaked on her cheek.

"He's still the same," Mina said.

"Mina," Mrs. Baek said. "Mina, please put that away." Mrs. Baek closed her eyes, mouth trembling.

"Who knows how many people he has hurt?" Something jostled inside of her like an earthquake. Her voice was the glasses rattling in the cabinets. "You need this now, unnie. To protect yourself. I want you to protect yourself. Don't you think you should protect yourself?"

She couldn't lose one more person in this life.

The acid rose in her throat. A long trail of ants devoured a snail that had been smashed outside of Lupe's apartment. The spoon at her mouth. Back then, she had imagined the thrill of killing Mr. Park. She had imagined cornering him at the supermarket. She could've ended him in front of everyone. Who knew how many he had terrorized? How many he had cannibalized for his own gain? How many of them had he hurt? How many more lives could he ruin? She needed Mrs. Baek to save herself.

The lust of the carnival lights flashing. The salt air and the smell of hot chocolate on the breath. She and Mr. Kim rising. A stage. But they didn't need an audience.

And then again underneath the white glare of a lamp, they sat on that bench at the end of the pier, like strangers. The moon glowed, shimmering on the water's surface, and she realized that life beneath a certain light—despite its sadness, its tragedies, its disappointments—was often still stirring, arousing the germ of a fresh seedling that might, with enough warmth, unfurl, like the tips of Mr. Kim's fingers as he dropped the change in her hand.

Holding the gun holster still, Mina said, "It's loaded." It was the fall, nearly one month before winter. But her hands trembled like a branch pushing the green buds out of the flesh, offering itself to the world. Together, they could finish him. "Let me show you how it works."

MARGOT

WINTER 2014–2015

Outside of Mrs. Baek's door, Margot stood to the side of the fisheye, heart in her throat. Christmas Eve revelers in the next apartment laughed, blasting banda music. Sweat glided down her face, neck, and back. She knocked again, this time with more force, as if pounding on a drum. Paint flecked onto the floor. In the basement of the church, Mrs. Baek had said to Mr. Park, *I'll kill you.*

Margot and Miguel had wasted nearly fifteen minutes finding a spot for their car. The evening—its voluptuous mix of sermon and song, smoke and incense, houses netted by string lights—felt urgent as if an exit had been closing, trapping Margot in the dark.

"Who is it?" Mrs. Baek yelled from a distance inside the apartment. Her voice grew closer, asking again, "Who is it?"

Margot sighed with relief. Mrs. Baek was home. Mr. Park hadn't followed her.

"UPS," Miguel said, startling Margot. "I need your signature."

"Leave it at the door."

"I need you to sign this."

"How come I can't see you?"

The lock unlatched. The door cracked open.

Margot pushed herself into the apartment as Mrs. Baek screamed, stumbling backward toward the coffee table, revealing a long beige slip under the same gray dove-colored robe. Margot sprung forward to help. Shooing her away, Mrs. Baek wrapped the thick fleece around her body, tightened the belt at her waist, and groaned.

"You hurt me." She clutched her hand and wrung it with the other. She had removed her lipstick, mouth still flushed, but her eyebrows, the dark crescents, remained intact.

"Sorry," Margot said, catching her breath. Miguel shut the door behind them.

"I can't—I can't do this right now," Mrs. Baek said, squeezing her hands together, knuckles whitening.

Two olive-colored suitcases were splayed open on the floor, filled with shoes, clothes, and books. The apartment still smelled of paper and ink and dust, but the stacks of newspapers and novels had disappeared. Only the furniture and some miscellaneous items—a CD boom box, the flat-screen television, empty glass vases—remained.

"Are you going somewhere?" Margot asked.

"None of your business."

Miguel stood by the door and shrugged, unsure of what to do next.

"If you're going to leave," Margot went on, "could I ask you some questions first?"

"I'm in a hurry."

"Can I contact you?" Margot asked.

"She's dead." Mrs. Baek's face grew glossy and red as she shook her head. Tendons in her neck pulsed. "What does any of this matter to you?"

"I found a safety-deposit box." The ache in Margot's chest, the mortar. "Some photos, photos of another family." Tears gathered in her eyes. The apartment blurred. "My mother with another family—a husband, a child—in Korea." She couldn't believe those words: *another family*. How could her mother have kept this information from her? Why didn't her mother tell her about this family, or her father's obituary in the drawer? Could the past have hurt that much?

Mrs. Baek winced from the pain of her hand. "Hold on." In the kitchen, she opened the freezer with a suctioning sound. She returned, plopping her body down on the hunter green couch with a bag of frozen peas and carrots for her hand.

Margot half sat on the arm at the opposite end. Miguel waited by the door, swaying a little to the Christmas music playing through the walls of the neighboring apartment.

"There was another family," Margot said. "Before me. Do you know anything about them? There's a photo." She wiped her eyes with a sleeve. "A husband, a little girl. It must have been in the seventies, or the early eighties—before she came to America."

"It makes sense." Mrs. Baek sighed, closing her eyes. "She never wanted to talk about the past. I always figured it was because...she was an orphan, the war." She opened her eyes again and looked at Margot. "But she mentioned a husband once, that he died in an accident."

"What?"

"That's all that I know. I didn't press it any further than that. She only brought it up once."

"Do you think that she could still be alive? The daughter?"

"I—I wouldn't know." Mrs. Baek rubbed between her brows. "Were there any papers? With the photo?"

Margot nodded yes.

"The only thing I know about—you promise to leave me alone after this, right? She found some papers. Your father helped her. He worked with an investigator. He helped her find some information on her parents, the ones she had been separated from in the war."

"What? Her parents?" Margot asked, breathless. Her mother had never spoken of them, as if she had given up. But she hadn't. She had found them after all.

"Her mother survived, I think," Mrs. Baek said. "Your mother had these papers. That's all I know, okay? Were they in the safety-deposit box?"

Margot nodded, remembering the pages of Korean words, illegible, inside that manila envelope—forms, documents, handwritten notes.

"So, she had another family," Mrs. Baek said to herself. "A husband *and* a child in Korea. That makes sense." She tossed the frozen peas and carrots onto the coffee table and squeezed her fingers as if they still ached.

Margot rose from the couch to find something for Mrs. Baek's hand. In the narrow kitchen, which jittered under the fluorescent light and smelled faintly of bleach, she filled a plastic bag on the counter with ice cubes from the freezer, empty except for some dumplings and stiff gulbi. As she walked by the round dining table beside the kitchen, she noticed a red satchel had been tipped over, exposing its contents—a passport, lipstick, pens, a wallet.

Margot picked up the passport. Neither she nor her mother ever had one of their own. Mrs. Baek half smiled in the photo. The name read *Margaret Johnson*.

"Who's Margaret Johnson?" Margot asked.

"None of your business," Mrs. Baek said, lunging toward Margot. "Get away from there." Miguel came forward from the entryway and grabbed Mrs. Baek's arm. "Get away from that bag." Her eyes flared.

"Margaret Johnson," Margot repeated in a low voice. "But...isn't your last name Baek? And your first name is Margaret?"

She snatched the passport out of Margot's hand. "It's my legal name. I never liked the name Margaret, but my husband thought it was a good name... Margaret like Margaret Thatcher."

"Your husband?"

"Yes, but... I always liked the name Margot." Her eyes softened. "I helped pick your name, you know. I guess you wouldn't remember."

Margot shook her head. The irony of being named by a woman who had been named by a man. How many names could one person have? And why did she now refer to herself as Mrs. Baek? Was it her maiden name? Or a fake? Could she have been hiding from someone else besides Mr. Park?

"Remember, we lived together in the same house when your mother first moved to America. I had... I had just left my husband in Texas."

The Southern twang. Another life entirely. Almost another country.

Margot sat with her elbows on the dining table, forehead pressed into her palms. "What happened? You just didn't get along with your husband?"

"No." She shook her head. "He was the worst kind of person."

"And Mr. Park? We overheard you fighting with him. At church," Miguel said.

Mrs. Baek gasped, stunned.

"Has he been following you?" Margot asked. "Why did you—why did you meet him down there?"

Mrs. Baek burst into tears, covering her face with her hand. "You were there?" she asked.

"Yes, we heard everything," Margot lied.

"I wanted to tell him once and for all to leave me alone." She gathered herself, wiping her eyes with the sleeve of her robe. "I didn't think I'd be...in any danger at church. I didn't even think he had my number. I changed it. But during the service, I got a message from him, letting me know that he was there, that he wanted to talk to me."

"Is that why you closed the store? Is that why you're leaving?" Margot asked.

Mrs. Baek nodded.

"Was my mother with Mr. Park?" Margot asked. "On the night that she died? Do you think it could've been Mr. Park who pushed her? He seems like—"

"No, no." Mrs. Baek coughed.

Margot steeled herself. "The landlord of my building said that he had seen you—and Mr. Park following you—at the apartment, my mother's apartment. He couldn't remember when. In September or October."

"What?" She opened her eyes wide.

"So Mr. Park knew where she lived," Margot said, voice rising. "Was she with Mr. Park? Do you think she could've been with Mr. Park on the night that she died?"

"No. No." Tears spilled down her cheeks.

"I don't think she was alone that night. He heard yelling, the landlord thought he had heard her fighting with someone." Margot's heart raced. "Could he have pushed her?"

A grimace of pain appeared on Mrs. Baek's face, shattered.

"Maybe he was trying to find you," Margot said. "He could've pushed her, right?"

Mrs. Baek tossed her passport, slapping the surface of the table. She thrust her hand into the red purse and pulled out a black handgun.

Margot jumped. The last time she had been this close to a gun was when she and her mother had been robbed as they had parked in front of their apartment. Her mother had surrendered her purse to the stranger, whose face was covered. Any wrong move would result in bullets, blood sprayed on shattered glass. At ten years old, Margot had remained in the back seat, frozen—still as a deer swallowed in headlights.

She remembered her mother shaking and crying after the man had left. Her arms folded over the steering wheel, her head down, her hair disheveled. Margot had been too terrified to comfort her mother, who could never call the cops for help. She could never trust the police, never knew what she could be deported for and when, what could happen to Margot if she were taken away. She had worked so hard in this country for so little, which could be destroyed at any moment—either by criminals on the street or men in uniforms.

"Look familiar?" Mrs. Baek asked, checking on Miguel behind her. Holding the gun, her hand trembled. "Do you recognize this?"

Margot shook her head.

"This was your mother's." Her voice cracked.

Of course. Who else would protect them but herself?

"She wanted me to keep this in case—in case Mr. Park—" Mrs. Baek wept, her face bright red.

"What?" Margot glanced at Miguel, immobile by the door, frozen with fear.

"She tried to give this to me, to protect myself," Mrs. Baek said, gently setting the gun on the table. The room relaxed. Margot could breathe. "They all worked at the supermarket together, before you were born. Mr. Park was the owner."

"The same one where my father worked?"

"Yes."

"So my mother knew Mr. Park from back then?" Margot stared at the muzzle of the gun, lying down but pointed in her direction.

"One day...there was a woman in his office. She had been screaming. Your mother said that your father stopped Mr. Park as he was attacking a woman named Lupe. Your father hit him."

Margot covered her mouth with her hands.

"Your father left LA after that. He didn't want to get in trouble." Mrs. Baek's eyes met Margot's. "He didn't have his papers. Maybe Mr. Park might've reported him."

A beat of silence passed as Margot tried desperately to absorb this information. Finally she asked, "Did you know the entire time that you were dealing with the same Mr. Park, the same Mr. Park from her past?"

Mrs. Baek shook her head as she sat down at the table, where the gun rested between them like a border. Margot joined her and sat on one of the dining chairs. She had the urge to turn the gun so that it faced the wall instead of her. But at the same time, the idea of touching a potentially loaded weapon, reaching for it, and how that might cause Mrs. Baek to react, unnerved her. The gun remained where it lay—silent and volatile.

Sweat beaded on Margot's face.

Miguel backed himself onto the couch, about ten feet away from them.

"When did she find out about what Mr. Park was doing to you?" Margot asked.

"After your father died, she finally told me about her relationship with him. How they reconnected this summer, what had happened to him and her and Lupe before he disappeared.

She never told me that story before. I don't know why. Maybe she was ashamed?" She rubbed her forehead with her fingers. "I told her the truth about why I had left Hanok House—Mr. Park bought the restaurant to be closer to me."

"Did you ever go out with him?" Margot asked.

"We went on a few dates at the beginning of the year. I never returned his calls. He bought the restaurant and started showing up everywhere—downtown, the park where I used to walk. So I quit working at Hanok House." She groaned, exhausted. "I've spent so much of the past nine months looking behind me."

"Why didn't you tell her earlier?" Margot asked. "Maybe she could've helped you somehow? Have you told *anyone*?"

Mrs. Baek shook her head. "We hadn't seen each other in over twenty years. What could she do? All she would do is worry about me. I wanted her to be happy. I wanted us...to start over again." She placed her head in her hands, elbows on the table. "But after your dad died, and she told me the truth, your mom and I—we realized that it was the same person. Mr. Park is the same man who tried to rape Lupe years ago. Who knows how many people he has hurt?" Her voice broke.

She lifted her face, revealing the depth of how crushed she had been, how so much of her life had been about finding beauty and wholeness, the kind of meaning that stories gave us, gluing herself back together—the perfectly lined red lips, the dark crescents for brows, the shimmering brown eyeshadow on her lids—after being smashed by the circumstances of her life over and over again.

Margot closed her eyes. How each of these women deserved so much more from this world.

"She told me to take the gun." Mrs. Baek wiped her nose on the sleeve of her gray robe. "But...every time I look at it, I—I feel sick." Her voice grew hoarse.

Margot's heart thumped. If she could reach for the gun, what would she do with it in her hand? She had never held a gun in her life.

"She said she didn't need it anymore, that I needed it to protect myself, but I kept trying to explain... I couldn't explain to her..." She cried, covering her face again.

"What couldn't you explain?"

"That...that my husband..." Mrs. Baek lowered her hands. Her eyes bore into Margot's. "He would get so angry sometimes, so angry at the world. He would—he hit me in the face." She grabbed her throat as if protecting herself.

"God, I'm so sorry," Margot said.

"One day, he—pointed a gun like that at me." She stared at the gun on the table. "It looked exactly the same. And I grabbed my purse and ran. I never went back. I left forever. He was going to kill me."

Margot imagined Mrs. Baek in her car like her mother, eyes hard, as she steeled herself for the long drive, that long drive once to Las Vegas. Mirrors and glass obscured by films of dust. Margot had never been to Texas, but she could picture the bright and wide landscape—all yuccas, breathtaking mountains, ocher land, and sage—as Mrs. Baek fled for her life.

There was a sudden stillness as if the whole room was holding its breath at once; the silence before a tidal wave crashes down.

"How did you end up with the gun if you didn't want it?" Margot asked. She reached forward to touch Mrs. Baek's hand, but she pulled away.

"I was trying to... She was reaching toward me, to give me the gun." Mrs. Baek closed her eyes, her face crumpling. "I changed my mind. She...she was so stubborn."

"Did you push her?" Margot asked.

"I didn't think... It all happened so quickly." Her voice broke.

"Did you push her?" Margot repeated.

Mrs. Baek nodded yes.

Margot burst into tears.

"And you left her there to die?" Miguel asked, wiping his eyes.

"I didn't know what to do. I never wanted to... I couldn't..." She sobbed weakly, covering her face with her hands. "There was no way to save her. She was gone."

Margot finally knew the truth. It *had* been an accident.

"And you took the gun?" Miguel asked.

"I didn't want to leave it there in case...it would look suspicious." Mrs. Baek hiccuped through her tears.

Margot's ears rang in the exhausted silence that followed. She was both heartbroken by her mother's death and Mrs. Baek's life and relieved to know that, in the end, Mr. Park hadn't harmed her mother, that there was no malicious intent. In a way, her mother was now free. She had died trying to help someone she loved, her friend.

"What are you going to do now?" Margot asked.

"I don't know. I'm leaving town." Defeated, Mrs. Baek stared at the ground. "Margot, I'm so sorry about what happened. I didn't think—she never mentioned that you might be coming home." She sniffled, wiping her nose on her sleeve. "If only that Mr. Park would've just left me alone." She gritted her teeth. "This is all his fault."

"Should we call the cops?" Margot asked. "I mean, after you leave. We can't just let him get away with doing this to everyone. You and Lupe, you can't be the only ones, right?"

Mrs. Baek shook her head.

"I think we have to call the police," Miguel agreed. "We

don't have to say anything about your mom's death. It could just be about him, his stalking, *his* behavior. We could just—"

"You don't understand," Mrs. Baek said. "It doesn't work that way."

"I don't think you have to leave," Margot said. "It'd be better if you stayed. We could do this together. I'm sure there's other women, maybe at Hanok House, or from the supermarket back in the day—"

Mrs. Baek seized the gun with two hands, knocking the dining chair down behind her as she stood. She pointed the barrel at Margot, then backed herself into a corner, arm trembling from the weight. It was the shaking of that arm that terrified Margot the most, as if Mrs. Baek was mustering all her strength to not shoot them all right now.

Margot held her breath as if underwater. She imagined them all submerged, tumbling in the waves, trying to hold on to each other. But this time she wasn't worried about her mother. She was worried about herself. She was worried about Miguel. She would do anything to save them.

"I'll figure it out, okay?" Mrs. Baek said, gasping. "I need you to—I need you to leave now."

Was that a faint smile? A glimmer appeared in her eyes as if she had designed a solution. As if this gun, Mina's death, had been part of her story, its symmetry, all along. Its purpose was clear.

Mrs. Baek lowered the gun and said, "I am ready."

A day after Christmas, Margot stepped outside of her apartment building into a bright yet hazy late-December light—an atmosphere with that specific quiet deflation after a major holiday, as if the air had been let out of the world until the impending celebration on New Year's Eve. The sulfurous smell of leftover fireworks mixed with exhaust added to the afternoon's malaise, like the entire city was hungover.

Margot had spent most of yesterday at her mother's apartment with Miguel discussing what they should do after the incident at Mrs. Baek's. She had a gun. She had killed Margot's mother. But they couldn't call the police, could they? It was an accident. And Mrs. Baek could've harmed them if she had wanted to, but she hadn't. Instead, Margot and Miguel had slid out the door and run downstairs into the car parked on the street.

Mrs. Baek had clearly suffered enough. She needed freedom. She didn't deserve any more pain than what had already threatened to break her—an abusive husband, a stalker, a dead best friend. Crime and punishment. She would have to live with herself somehow, and escape Mr. Park, this city that sometimes chewed you up and spat you out.

Margot wished that she had gotten Mrs. Baek's number so that she could contact her somehow, make sure that she was safe. But it was too late. And although she had been relieved to finally understand what had happened on the night of her mother's death, she still didn't have answers about her mother's life—the safety-deposit box.

Who was the other family—the husband and child, pigtailed in a red T-shirt and leggings? Did Margot have a half sister somewhere? And where was her mother's mother, Margot's grandmother, who Mrs. Baek said had survived the war? Was she still alive? Did Mina ever contact her? Would she want to know about Margot, or would she be ruined by the death of her Mina, the daughter she had lost in the war?

Now haunted by the weight of these questions, Margot finally felt like an adult.

Choosing if and when and how to share the truth might be the deepest, most painful necessity of growing out into the world and into yourself.

Sometimes we wrongly guessed how much others could bear. It was in the curve of a question mark—should I or shouldn't I?—in which we all lived. In the end, her mother had decided to keep Margot and her father a secret from themselves, to protect them both. Margot would need to forgive all of them—Mina, her father, Mrs. Baek—so that she could one day begin to forgive herself.

After several minutes of feeling the sun on her face, Margot untied her gray hoodie from around her waist. She walked with purpose, although she had no idea where she would end up—which direction and where. Like a fire, she needed air. She even had the urge to run for the hell of it.

She passed a small park with a playground. Children rode the swings high or chased each other down slides, laughing and running, a commotion of joy. She walked in front of a gas station, then a Korean grocery store, and found a strip mall with several businesses, including a salon, huge posters of women with '80s hair in the windows.

Her mother used to cut Margot's hair in the dim light of the dining area next to the kitchen. She laid sheets on the floor, draped a towel around Margot's shoulders, and, with a comb and scissors in hand, worked her way around Margot's head.

"Your hair is so shiny," her mother said. "So soft."

Margot never knew how to receive her mother's compliments because she had grown accustomed to her barbs—about her acne, her wrinkled clothes, her creaseless eyelids, the beginnings of a double chin. It was as if her mother believed that any ego at all would be too big for this home, too big for this family. Her fundamental responsibility was keeping Margot in check.

But every now and then, her mother would direct her attention to herself, brandishing a quiet and devastating memory— a cold injection, almost a relief, a reprieve from her gaze, into Margot's veins.

"When the nuns cut my hair, they never cared," her mother once said. "They never made it pretty."

Or: "There was a girl at the orphanage who would beat me," she said. "She told me that she was going to destroy my face, set fire to it."

Margot never knew how to respond to these intense sudden offerings of the self, bottomless and rare, as if the state-

388 NANCY JOOYOUN KIM

ments had been at the edge of her mother's psyche, the edge of her mother's survival, and any further conversation could push her over the brink, plunge her head underwater. Instead, as her mother cut her hair, Margot waited in silence for the signal that she had finished—removing the towel as a cape, brushing Margot's shoulders, picking off the bits stuck to her face. And then Margot was temporarily set free.

Inside of the salon, which smelled vaguely of hair dye and perms, a slim young woman with chestnut-colored hair, a French-striped shirt, and trendy chunky white sneakers, greeted her eagerly. Margot sat in the waiting area where she noticed, among the one-inch-thick beauty and lifestyle magazines, a copy of the local newspaper in Korean. On the cover was an image of Mr. Park, sympathetic, genial with his Paul-Bunyan-teeth smile. Margot seized the paper, trying to decipher what she could—the photograph of him and the image of a silver Mercedes sedan parked on a dirt road.

"I'm ready for you now," the stylist said, both gracious and curious about Margot, like a visitor from a foreign planet. She never paid much attention to her looks and it was obvious.

Margot held out the newspaper. "Did you see this? Do you know what happened to this guy?"

The stylist peered at the front page and said, "Oh. They found him dead yesterday afternoon."

Margot gasped. "On Christmas?"

She remembered Mrs. Baek's arm trembling from the weight of the gun, Margot holding her breath. Her smile, the glimmer in her eyes, as if she had figured out the solution to this mess—Margot's mother, her friend dead, a stalker with a past of terrorizing women, abusing his power. *I am ready*, she said.

"He was retired but owned a restaurant in Koreatown. A rich man." She motioned for Margot to rise.

"What happened?" In the black pleather chair, Margot faced herself in a clear mirror, wide and ceiling-high.

The stylist draped a gray cape over her body and untied Margot's long hair—releasing the tangled mess that it had become. She grabbed a wide-tooth comb and tried to break apart the knots without tearing too much.

"A jogger in Griffith Park. She found some clothes on the road, a wallet, keys, cell phone. So she called the police."

Margot tilted her head, following the motions of the comb. Her heart raced.

"They found his body. He was less than one mile away, in the bushes." The stylist raised her brows and smirked as if amused by the calamities of men. Margot liked this woman at once.

"The bushes?" Margot asked. She imagined the dense gray vegetation in the hills—the mixed chaparral and sage scrub. The sunbaked and herbaceous scent. The dry fuel.

The hairstylist lowered her voice. "Naked."

"What?" Margot cringed.

"He was naked." She escorted Margot to the sink to wash her hair. "Someone shot him in the leg."

"In the leg?" Margot tilted her head back. "But how did he—"

"The animals ate him." The stylist adjusted the towel under Margot's neck. "One of my customers said that his whole face, arm, almost *everything* gone," she said, before the blast of warm water.

Margot could feel they were both trying their hardest not to laugh. Yes, death was sometimes funny. Maybe it was a Korean thing, but after these weeks of pain and stress, she couldn't help but delight in the absurdity of it all. It was almost a piece of performance art.

Bravo, Mrs. Baek.

★ ★ ★

Standing on the sidewalk, Margot called Miguel as soon as she left the salon—hair angling down toward her chin in a sharp bob. The sun had begun its descent, blasting wildly from the west. She shielded her eyes with her hand, inhaling the exhaust of cars zooming by, kicking up the dirt and bits of dried leaves that would stick to her skin. A ragged palm tree across the street basked in the last of the golden light before the city bathed in a soft dream of pinks and purples—changing and fleeting—and the brash glare of street-and headlights, the adrenaline, the thousands of feet on the gas, ruined the romance.

After she filled Miguel in, he said, "They found his body on Christmas Day? Lord. She *fed* those animals."

"I mean, it had to be Mrs. Baek, right?" She hurried down the street toward her mother's apartment. "Not to be messed up, but... I'm glad we didn't call the police." She ducked under a scattering of pigeons, wings flapping treacherously close to her head. "I am still worried about her, though."

"What do you think happened?"

"She lured him somehow to take her up there. He was naked. Ugh." She shuddered at the image. "Maybe she tricked him into thinking that she changed her mind, that she was interested in him and wanted to hook up or something? People go up into the park for that, you know."

"What else is nature for?"

She laughed. "Maybe she told him that they had to go into the bushes."

"And she shot him in the leg?" Miguel asked. "This story is a gift, Margot."

She crossed the road before a car careened in front of her.

"And no one heard his cries?" he asked.

"Maybe it was kind of remote. In the middle of the night," she said, catching her breath.

"And the animals *ate* him?" Miguel asked.

She tripped on an uneven part of the sidewalk and couldn't help but laugh at both herself and the absurdity of life. She had for whatever reason imagined a Disney-animated version of all the wildlife—Snow White's friends, round and wide-eyed—flitting and dancing around Mr. Park's body.

"And they haven't caught her, right?"

"Nope, not from what I can tell. I googled it. He parked his car, got out, and removed his clothes at some point. Someone in the online comments thought it might be the mob or a gang or something. Anyway, I hope she's okay."

"What are you gonna do now?"

The sun disappeared behind the buildings and the world appeared to be melting around her. Bathed in the sharp air of the oncoming night, Margot inhaled the faint aroma of a left-over pork pozole reheated on a stove through an open window. She still dreaded returning to the apartment.

"I'm pretty exhausted," Margot said. "I think I'll sleep until the new year."

"Do you want to go out on New Year's Eve next week?" Miguel asked.

"I don't know." A part of her wanted to head back to Se-attle as soon as she could get rid of everything. She could take the contents of the safety-deposit box with her. She had Mrs. Kim's phone number; she could always reach her later to find out more about her father. She didn't need to stay in LA anymore.

But the other part of her longed to remain in this city to recover something she had left behind—not just history or her past or her mother's, but whom she had always dreamed of becoming. She had abandoned that side of herself here, too.

"Maybe you could use a distraction?" Miguel asked. "This guy I met invited me to go drinking downtown with some friends. I'm thinking dancing afterward at the salsa club. You'll come?"

Margot stood outside of the apartment building as the sky glowed sapphire, and she turned to find the sliver of a moon. She could see inside people's lives through windows—the flickering of television sets, bodies walking behind curtains, a little boy's mouth, fishlike, pressed against the fingerprinted fog of glass. She could imagine the gills on the side of his face. She laughed.

"Nah, I don't think so," Margot said. "This is all you."

He paused. "I know you've been through a lot, but it'll be fun. You should come. I want you to come. If the guy turns out to be a dud, I'll need someone to dance with, right?"

"You always dance with strangers anyway," she said.

"But I want to dance with you," he said. The sweetest words she had heard in a long while.

She closed her eyes. She felt as if he understood her, they understood each other, precisely at that moment.

There was nothing left to say except, "Okay."

Wasn't that the thing with words? It wasn't just their surfaces—sometimes serene and shimmering, others violent, crashing, and brash—but what they, when carefully considered, conveyed: we are more than friends. We're family.

On New Year's Eve, Margot loaded up on snacks and booze at the nearest Korean supermarket, whatever she could get her hands on to feed the crew that would come over—Miguel and his new friends, a group of five or six people. Instead of imbibing at a crowded bar, they'd hang out at her mother's mostly vacant apartment and carpool to the salsa club afterward.

Growing up, she and her mother had never invited people to their home. There was hardly any room, both physical and spiritual, for entertaining when her mother had spent six long days out of the week at work. The seventh day was always for running errands—grocery shopping, preparing meals, mailing payments for bills, or waiting in lines at the bank. There was never time for rest or celebration and Margot now wanted to change that if she could.

She maneuvered a cart through the produce section, which featured boxes of fruit as gifts, amping up the volume and variety this time of year. She packed several Asian pears in a plastic tear-off bag, then moved on to the most perfect Fuyu persimmons, smooth, orange, and firm. She had always been embarrassed when her mother had given people such odd and practical "Korean gifts"—the boxes of apples or even laundry detergent—when in reality, outside of America, these objects might have some rich symbolic relevance that perhaps Margot didn't understand.

If she thought of the labor and resources that went into each piece of fruit—the water, the light, the earth, the training and harvesting of each plant—a box of apples could be special, a sacred thing. Perhaps in this land of plenty, of myth and wide-open spaces, trucks and factories, mass production, we lost track of that: the miracle of an object as simple as a pear, nutritious and sweet, created by something as beautiful as a tree.

As Margot considered the large pile of napa cabbage, the grooved white to pale green heads, a hand reached over in front of her. She jumped back and turned to see Officer Choi there. He looked different in his casual clothes—a heather gray V-neck sweater, a collared shirt underneath, and a pair of dark blue jeans.

"Oh, I'm sorry. Was that your cabbage?" He smiled.

"No. Actually...yes, that was my cabbage."

"Here, allow me." He grabbed the head, placing it in a bag for her.

"Wait, that one was... I don't know, not cabbagey enough. How about that one over there?"

He laughed. "Okay." He picked up the cabbage he had placed in her cart, put it in his own. He palmed another one at the top of the pile. "This one?"

"Actually, Officer Choi—the other one, the one with all the leaves."

"Oh, I see. The one with all the leaves." He crossed his

arms across his chest. He looked clean and handsome, like a J.Crew model that wasn't too snobby and also wore Hanes. Boxers or briefs? She blushed at the thought of his underwear.

"Call me David," he said. "I quit."

"What?" She gazed at him and, for a second, forgot how to use language entirely. "The police?"

"I mean, it wasn't easy, but...new year, new me." He shrugged.

"How come?" she asked, relieved.

"I was kinda burned-out anyway." He inserted his thumbs into his pockets. "And something about what you had said to me... I realized why I joined in the first place." He scratched the back of his neck. "You were right."

Her three favorite words. "Really?"

"That first phone call? Remember how upset you were?"

She nodded, remembering most of the words. *You might think we're some kind of burden on your workload, but my mother worked her ass off, and she paid taxes like everyone else... People like my mother hold up this sham as much as you.*

"Because you wanted answers, and you didn't feel like you were getting any," David said. "And that your mother deserved better."

"Yes, I remember."

"She did. She does." He avoided her eyes. An ahjumma nudged her shopping cart into Margot's. They moved away from the napa cabbage as she passed with a *hmph*.

"Why *did* you join?" Margot asked.

"I had an older brother who died when I was a teenager. Everyone thought it was suicide, but... I couldn't believe he killed himself. So I wanted to help people if I could. There weren't a lot of Korean officers—at least not back then. And I thought the cops were just blowing my family off because my parents didn't speak English."

"I see. I'm sorry," she said, a heaviness building inside her chest.

"That's all right." He sighed. "I've spent the last couple years doing boring-ass paperwork, busting people who are trying—maybe in not the most legal or 'moral' ways, but trying—to survive. I wasn't helping people in the way that I want to. And to be honest… I'm tired all the time. *Really* tired." He shook his head. "Anyway, this is way too much—"

"No, it's not. I'm glad to know. I'm just happy that you realized all of this."

"What about you?"

What should she tell him now? "I think I'm…accepting it. My mother's death. I'm getting there at least, knowing what I know about my mom now. I got a kind of closure from all this. Maybe an opening, too."

"Good." He rested his hand on his cart.

Silence grew between them and they exhaled at once.

"Are you making kimchi?" he asked, pointing his chin toward the cabbage.

She *could* make kimchi this week? "Ha, I wasn't planning on it, but I guess now I am? I wasn't even sure how long I'm staying."

"Where?" he asked.

"Koreatown."

She paused. Around them, last-minute shoppers perused and collected vegetables—yellow and white and green onions, chili peppers, knobs of ginger.

"Are you hosting tonight?" he asked. Another ahjumma bumped her cart into Margot's.

"I've got friends coming over," she said. "What about you?"

"I don't have any real plans, so I'm going over to my parents' house. My other brother will be there with his kids. It'll be nice and chill."

How does Officer Bae not have any plans? "How many kids does he have?"

"Two. You wouldn't believe that he's actually four years younger than me."

Two grandmothers turned over the heads of napa cabbage, disappointed. One of them tore off a piece of leaf, popped it in her mouth, and nodded. Her hands were powerful and wrinkled—so much like her mother's. How much Margot loved those hands that would create the long peel of skin before slicing the fruit for her. How much she missed those hands.

"Well, I've got a few more things to pick up," he said. "It was nice seeing you."

"Likewise." She couldn't help but smile.

He freed himself from a traffic jam of carts, bowed his head to other shoppers, excusing himself.

"David," she called, self-conscious about her loud English voice in this space.

"Yeah?"

Startled, an ahjussi shot them both dirty looks. Those voices. American kids. How rude.

Smiling, she abandoned her cart temporarily, threaded herself through the crowd, and stopped a couple feet from him. "Now that you're unemployed—could I ask you a favor?"

After exchanging phone numbers with David, who could help her translate her mother's documents, Margot paid for her groceries and headed back toward the parking lot where amber floodlights illuminated cars and customers pushing carts. She had only a few hours to clean and prepare for her guests, who would arrive at nine. She rushed toward her car with a sense of levity, a giddiness about the new year and the possibility of living in Los Angeles.

She'd find a new place, a smaller one, maybe a studio in

Koreatown or Echo Park, or she could rent a room in a shared house just like her mother when she first moved to America. She'd fly to Seattle to pack up all her belongings and ship what she needed down. But the thrill of starting life over again animated her.

She couldn't quite see herself transplanting her same behaviors in an office job from one city to the next. She always knew that she wasn't cut out for it—the hours indoors in front of a screen, the data entry, the filing, the water cooler outside her door—but what else could she do with so little experience, no connections, and an English degree? She'd have to do something fresh, reinvent herself. She could work at a coffee shop or a restaurant or in retail while she went back to school for art.

Margot was struck by the memory of holding the corner of the net out to the sky, up against the shape of the Ferris wheel, imagining all the tiny silver fish—like her mother, shimmering and liquefied—that would swim through its weave.

But she and her mother were now both free yet forever woven into each other. They could be both—separate and inseparable. They were not a rotten net but something more deliberate like threads of color, variations of blue, plaited, one after the other. Her mother's death was not a knot but a temporary undoing. Her mother had been carrying the burden of so much truth, truths that she had protected Margot from, and now Margot knew: she, like her mother, could handle anything—even love, even family.

Accelerating onto the 10 in a Friday night snarl of traffic in the middle of January, she wondered if moving back to LA was, in fact, a terrible idea. She hated driving. She gazed at the sad disco of taillights, with her mother's ashes in the passenger seat, thinking about Mrs. Baek, wherever she was, driving off to start all over again. What if she hadn't made it anywhere far? She could hide in this city. It was easy to be anonymous, to find some nook within one of the suburbs, or even in downtown LA, to lie low until the trouble had passed. How would anyone know?

Margot thought about how she could one day run into her, that perhaps driving down the street, she could glance at a car stopped beside her and notice a woman in the driver's seat and wonder if that was Mrs. Baek.

After a dinner of kimchi fried rice two weeks ago at his apartment in Echo Park, David translated some of the documents from her mother's safety-deposit box. With the help of

the investigator hired by Margot's father, her mother had de-
termined the identity and location of her parents in Gunpo,
a city south of Seoul. Only Mina's mother, now ninety-two
years old, survived. But what was not obvious from the documents was whether or not Mina had ever reached out to her,
or whether knowing her mother lived was enough.

"Would you want to meet her?" David had asked.

"I don't know." Margot stared at the grain of his wood dining table. The whorls reminded her of thumbprints.

"We can call this investigator, Mr. Cho." He studied the
papers. "Maybe, if not about your grandmother, maybe he has
some info on this other family?" His eyes were glossy. "The
little girl with the pigtails, if she's still alive."

"Oh, God, I don't know. I'd have to sit with this for a bit
first."

Afterward, she drove home and cried for her mother and
father. She cried for her grandmother. Why did this world
break so many people apart? Why was it so hard to be together? Would her grandmother be relieved to know what
had happened to her daughter, or would she be struck by the
kind of grief that could kill her, too? How did we decide how
to live without breaking each other?

She wept for days and could hardly eat at all. The following weekend, Miguel delivered groceries and made a dinner
of enchiladas for them at the apartment with a red mole sauce
that he had purchased from the restaurant they never made it
to on Christmas Eve. They sat in silence mostly, which was
just what she needed. All the things she felt were terrible and
heavy. All the things she felt were different variations of pain.

She had then finally mustered the courage to call Mrs.
Kim, who had at first not answered, but returned her call
two days later.

Sitting on her mother's couch in the living room which was

now mostly bare except for the most necessary of furniture, Margot asked, "Do you think that maybe... Do you know *anything* about what happened to my father after he left my mom? This would've been in the late eighties."

"We met in Chicago in 1990 or 1991," Mrs. Kim said, voice scratchy and weak. "He was at that time working at his cousin's import and export business, and he had bought a small supermarket there eventually. He never really talked about what his life had been like in LA. I figured it was because back in the day, when he was in his twenties, he had a wife who died."

"Another wife?"

"Yes, that must have been in the early eighties so—before you, before your mom." She coughed away from the receiver. "He didn't have his papers. After we married, he got his green card. But he had never told me about your mom or what had happened between the two of them." She paused. "I'm sorry. I'm afraid I'm not much help."

"How did you both end up back in LA?" Margot asked.

"My family is in Orange County."

"I see." Margot sighed. "Maybe you might be able to... tell me more about him? At least how you met? What he was like? I just want to know."

"Sure...okay." Mrs. Kim paused. "Do you want to meet somewhere in Koreatown? I haven't been there in years. I'm trying to learn how to drive again, so maybe after I take my lessons. Or I can hire a car."

"What happened to your driver?" The push at the doorstep. The smell of fresh-cut grass with that undercurrent of something foul—manure or compost. The taste of metal in her mouth.

"I had to get rid of him."

"Really?"

"Yes, it's all very unfortunate." She breathed into the phone. "He was...stealing from me. You can never trust a man who looks like that, I guess." She coughed again. "He was trying to get all these ideas into my head. I found him snooping around my computer, looking through bank accounts and stuff. It's been... I've had a really hard time lately." Her voice broke. "I guess we all have, right? Nothing seems right these days. It's hard to even get out of bed."

"Yes. Yes, I understand," Margot said.

"Maybe you could call the investigator?" Mrs. Kim asked. "I don't know what you've found at your mother's house. But I bet he could share what he already knows. Maybe that could help you fill in some of what you're missing. Have you tried asking him? Your father gave him a lot of business. He was very good at his work."

The next day, Margot called David and asked if he could contact the investigator, who most likely only spoke Korean. The investigator revealed that her mother had been married in her twenties and had a daughter in Korea, who was killed with her father by a car speeding in the road. They had been walking to the grocery store. Her mother had been at home.

Her half sister had only been eight years old. Her mother had only been four when she had lost her parents. These children had been lost to their parents through recklessness and war.

Perhaps, despite the distances between them, the differences in their experiences as a mother and a daughter, as individuals, as women of a certain time and place, what had made them a family was not simply blood but never fully giving up on each other. Forgiveness was always a possibility. One day, you could dive into the dark water and float because of a lightness in your life now that you had taken off your clothes, abandoned all those stones. You were free from every net. You relaxed like you had never been able to before.

She had so much information now. She had so much to create. What would her grandmother want to know? She would be the only audience who mattered at this point.

And now Margot inched the car down the pier, nervous about hitting one of the pedestrians in the crowd that funneled down to the end. The Ferris wheel flashed hot—red and white. She cracked open her windows to the cacophony of voices, of different languages and laughter. The wind seemed to attack her as she climbed out of the car, shivering, zipping her jacket closed.

Through the smell of carnival foods—cheeseburgers, nachos, funnel cake, hot chocolate—and the bodies, jostling, walking, and lingering, hands outstretched for selfies, she walked on the wooden boards of the pier, carrying her mother's ashes and a plastic grocery bag with a single Honeycrisp apple and a bottle of soju like an old Korean man—all sadness and yearning, dark humor fermented inside.

At the very end, she sat on a bench with her mother beside her. Maybe one day she would spread her ashes here. It was probably illegal, but who cared? For now, she inhaled the salt air, stared into the most distant water, with the moon waxing ripe and bright, and bit into the apple.

She picked up her phone, and within one ring, a woman answered, voice gravelly and worn: "여보세요?"

Tears streamed down Margot's face as she wondered: *How much weight can I bear?* She was not her mother. She was weak, spoiled, American. The whistle of a bomb dropping, an explosion blasted in her head. She clung to that rope—now inside of her, too—the braid they had made was the apple that she squeezed in her hand.

"여보세요?" the woman repeated.

Margot could hear the woman's breath on the other end, its warmth like the sun on her face, a bed full of seeds.

"I'm Mina's daughter. 미나. 딸," Margot said, but the shaking of her voice implored, *Please, please understand.*

* * * * *

Acknowledgments

My editor, Natalie Hallak, supported this novel with her keen intellect, imagination, and warmth. She has been an exceptional partner and it has been a dream to work with Park Row Books. My agent, Amy Elizabeth Bishop, is not only incisive but hilarious and kind in every way. She has been a tremendous advocate, and by believing in my words, she changed my life.

Teachers and mentors David Wong Louie, who passed away in 2018, Russell Leong, King-Kok Cheung, Maya Sonenberg, Colleen J. McElroy, Shawn Wong, Alexander Chee, and Randa Jarrar created pathways for my work through their generosity and dedication to storytelling and craft. The UCLA Asian American Studies Center provided me with a sense of place and history; *Amerasia Journal* published the first short story I wrote.

Editors and literary journals sustained me by sharing my

words: *Los Angeles Review of Books*, *Guernica*, Asian American Writers' Workshop's *The Margins*, *Apogee Journal*, *The Rumpus*, *Electric Literature* and *The Offing*.

Family and friends nourished me through the years of writing this book: in particular, Eva Larrauri de Leon, Talia Shalev, the Lee and Kim families, the Goodman and Robin families, Corinne Manning, Ever Jones, Keiko and Naomi Namekata, Gabrielle Bellot, Anca Szilágyi, and Paula Shields. My writing group shared wisdom and magic: Ingrid Rojas Contreras, Yalitza Ferreras, Meron Hadero, Amber Butts, Angie Chau, Tanya Rey, and Melissa Valentine.

I am indebted to my mother as a model for how infinitely complex and wondrous a single life can be. She taught me to define success through how I feel about myself and the world. I would have been lost without her and her courage, her storytelling, and the exceptional meals that she makes.

My husband, Paul, stood by me through every draft and lived with me and my characters, which required endless faith, resilience, and a sense of humor, for years under one roof. Each time I experienced a setback, he reminded me of where I was and how far I'd gone. This novel wouldn't have been without him (and our dogs).

Thank you all for making this possible.

THE LAST STORY OF MINA LEE

NANCY JOOYOUN KIM

Reader's Guide

PARK
ROW
BOOKS

1. Margot has spent most of her life trying to be different from her mother, whom she views as a perpetual foreigner, both in the United States and in Margot's life. Yet they both feel like outsiders, searching for what it means to truly belong. Discuss the similarities and differences between Margot and Mina. How would Mina and Margot each define home? What does home mean to you?

2. *The Last Story of Mina Lee* explores issues of immigration, the realities of the American dream and the limitations placed upon women and their roles in society. Did the novel affect your opinions about these topics? How so?

3. The perspective shifts between Margot and Mina, alternating between the present and the past. Why do you think the author chose to structure the novel this way? How did this affect your understanding of Margot and Mina's relationship and their difficulty communicating with one another? How does Mina's past inform the kind of mother she is for Margot? What do you wish you could ask your parents in order to better understand them?

4. Mina and Margot can only partially speak to each other because they have limited knowledge of each other's respective languages, Korean and English. Do you have similar gaps in language within your families, as well? How can we understand other people regardless of language?

5. Discuss Mina and Mr. Kim's relationship. How did the traumas of their pasts shape their trajectory as immigrants in America? Do you think their relationship would have worked out if Mr. Kim had decided to stay in LA instead of fleeing from Mr. Park? What did you think about Mina's decision to not tell Mr. Kim about Margot?

6. "[Margot] hated to draw her own face—a face she couldn't quite recognize in her mother or anywhere else on TV or in the movies—the face of a stranger, a foreigner, anonymous and plain." Art plays an important yet inaccessible role in Margot's life. What does this say about the role of art in society? What did you learn about Margot through the art that she yearned to create?

7. In *The Last Story of Mina Lee*, unpunished cruelties are inflicted upon the most vulnerable characters by privileged people abusing their power, such as Mr. Park. Were you surprised by the reveal of who killed Mina? How does the book question traditional notions of justice? Do you think right versus wrong is always black-and-white, or are there areas of gray? Why?

8. The grocery store, the restaurant and the kitchen are important locations in the book. What is the role of food and eating in this novel for Margot, Mina and Mrs. Baek? What role has food played in your family's story?

9. How did you feel about Mina, Margot and Mrs. Baek by the end of the book? Did your opinions about them change

over the course of the story? Were you satisfied by the ending?

10. What do you think the meaning is behind the title *The Last Story of Mina Lee*?